Malfus

Necromancer Unchained

Casey Sutton

Casey Sutton Writes

This is a work of fiction. All the characters, organizations, and events portrayed herein are either products of the author's imaginations, delusions, or hallucinations and are used fictitiously. You have the author's explicit permission to make a necromancer named Malfus in your next RPG campaign.

Copyright © 2023 by Casey Sutton

All rights reserved.

No portion of this book may be reproduced in any form without written permission from the publisher or author, except as permitted by U.S. copyright law.

Thank you Viktoria for supporting my dreams from hospital bed to book page.

Thank **YOU** for reading, you're giving an indie author a chance to make his dreams come true.

Contents

Map of Ossoria, left	VIII
Map of Ossoria, right	IX
In Chains	1
1. The Prisoner	3
2. Time to Run	12
3. The Fort in the Middle of Nowhere	16
The Command Room	22
4. Colonel Peshka	23
5. Perspectives	32
6. Just a Stone's Throw Away	42
7. We're Under Attack	50
8. To the Gates!	60
9. All is Lost	70
10. The Lone Tower	82
The Stone Giant	90
11. Urgo'Etrudzke	91
12. The Bargain	102
13. Now, Where Are My Things?	110
14. A Little Necromancy Never Hurt Anyone	118
15. As the Crow Flies	130
16. Bolstering the Defenses	140

17. A Giant Problem	154
18. One Last Drink	166
19. Springing the Trap	176
Arise!	184
20. Plugging the Leak	185
21. The Last Stand	192
22. The Fall	204
23. Eternal Emperor of the Sand Sea	214
Rammani	225
24. Giant Problem Solver	226
25. Siege Breaker	237
Peshka's Charge	253
The Final Fight - Malfus	254
The Final Fight - Deza	255
26. The Next Day	256
27. Epilogue	269
Malfus the Necromancer	276
To Be Continued…	277
Also by… Greedy as a Ghoul	278
Thanks for reading!	279
About Author	280
Acknowledgments	281
Social Links	282

May Yesenia's light guide you through this cursed land

MALFUS - IN CHAINS — ART BY DEJAN DELIC

Chapter 1
The Prisoner

"The world is dying. It is better to know this now, child. Though you live and breathe, love and hate, beneath your feet the world suffers a mortal wound—the Scar. We are but maggots writhing atop a corpse."
— 'Mother' Magrid, Orphan-Minder, DeGaullis

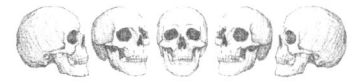

Malfus shouted in despair as the Inquisitor dragged him behind his mount, but the cloth gag reduced the sound to a muffled cough.

Neither horse nor rider paid Malfus any mind. The black horse pranced up the rocks of the canyon, pulling the rope taut. Before Malfus could protest further, the rope yanked his wrists, pulling his blistered feet free from the ground. He attempted to aim his fall, but the mud puddle beneath him offered few options.

He prayed for a hidden rock. One sharp rock was all it would take. He turned his head sideways. *Come on—right to the temple.*

Kill me now, before I take one more step with this sanctimonious bastard.

His face hit wet mud. A rock stabbed him, but not where he'd hoped. Instead, a fire erupted across his ribcage, making his lungs seize. Malfus gasped for air through the gag. But before he could breathe, the rope pulled taut again, dragging him by his metal cuffs.

The black-clothed Inquisitor turned in his saddle. His long-brimmed hat did little to hide his perpetual sneer.

"Come, necromancer," he said in his Castillean accent. "We have much ground to cover today." The Inquisitor gathered his reins, urging his steed down the narrow path. "I have no need to be slowed further by your theatrics."

Theatrics! Malfus gritted his teeth. *I'll give you theatrics, you boot-licking toad!*

He glared up at the Inquisitor, defiance burning in his eyes. But the pain of the rope extinguished it as his manacles dug into the sores lining his wrists. He pulled his knees up, then clambered to his feet, groaning.

His long black hair, wet with mud, plastered his back. The bags under his eyes made him look far older than his mid-twenties. His scanty rations since he'd been captured had done little to improve his gaunt figure.

He scurried up the rocky incline, managing it with the dignity of a three-legged lizard. The horse pawed at the ground as it waited, watching him slither on his belly. After years of enduring spurs from ungrateful riders, the horseshoe was finally on the other foot.

Malfus wheezed as he crested the incline. He could hardly breathe through the gag. He reached up with his hands to clear away the muck; he might as well have attempted moving an ocean with a bucket.

"Come," said the Inquisitor, amused. "No time for that."

The Inquisitor lifted the brim of his hat and leaned in his saddle, looking westward to the horizon. The Scar stretched in that direction as far as the eye could see: a massive blemish, like a black vein pulsating across the land. The land surrounding the Scar was gray and cracked like necrotic flesh—barren and lifeless. Black tendrils of smoke curled above it, writhing and dissipating. They obscured the sun, curling around it as it neared the horizon.

Malfus had never gotten this close to the Scar before. Only a madman would come here willingly.

The Inquisitor clicked his tongue and moved forward. Malfus ground his teeth and stumbled after him before the rope could bite. Each step sent jolts of pain down his side. The grit from his wet clothes began to chafe his neck and shoulders—the latest additions to his growing collection of discomforts.

With his hands tied, he couldn't check if his rib was cracked. He couldn't adjust his gag, and he certainly couldn't cast any magic. But the gag and his bonds had less to do with that than the red-hued metal of his manacles—arcanull.

Only the Vesenian Inquisition knew the techniques to forge arcanull. It clouded the wearer's mind, making concentration painful. But if that mind dared consider *magic*, the pain became absolute torture. Merely thinking about his bonds and restrictions made him blink his eyes; the throbbing behind them threatened to set his mind ablaze.

Malfus could have fallen asleep, standing. *What I'd give for just five minutes to lean against a tree.* The rope bit into his wrists as it jerked taut.

Had he stopped walking? He hadn't even noticed.

"Come!" The Inquisitor yanked on the rope. "Don't make me tell you again."

Malfus howled, falling to his knees. Tears welled in his eyes, and he imagined all the things he would do to the Inquisitor if his chains were removed. The best he could manage was a growl.

"Now, now," said the Inquisitor. "Hold your temper." A smile crossed his thin lips as he pulled out a waterskin. The Inquisitor guzzled from it, a trickle of water spilling down his waxed goatee. Malfus instinctively licked his lips, but tasted mud.

The Inquisitor smirked as he strapped the waterskin back to the saddle. "Don't worry," he said. "We will stop for your turn soon."

His turn? Malfus snarled. *Bones take you and your damn water. Just let me go. Give back what you've taken from me.*

Do that, and I might not parade your bloated corpse around as a warning for other Inquisitors.

He plodded forward, staving off the urge to collapse. He wasn't sure how much further spite would carry him. What was the Inquisitor going to do? March Malfus all the way back to Castillea? That would take weeks, months. He glanced down at his boots, wondering how much longer they had left together. The boots had been brand new, a few weeks prior; now, they were little more than flapping strips of leather tied to his feet.

He sighed. At least boots were replaceable. After making a breakthrough in his research, Malfus had been captured, and his entire laboratory burned to the ground. Priceless necromantic scrolls from the Shal-Umbra Empire, gone forever. He glared at the Inquisitor.

This goon of the church, with his black cloak—black hat—black horse, even. Not even I wear that much black, and I'm the damn necromancer.

At least the Inquisitor wasn't the type to preach. Self-righteous, certainly, but his jailor kept his sermons to himself; Malfus was grateful for that. His previous captor had been the opposite: lecturing him with Vesenian sermons so often that Malfus could still recite them.

He'd been able to escape his previous captor after a few days. But there had been no arcanull. This time around, escape wouldn't be so easy. No, this captor was an actual bloody Inquisitor. The bastard never seemed to sleep. Hardly even blinked. Malfus would need to be patient. Wait for the right opportunity.

His feet counted each step, like grains of sand in an hourglass. Those steps added up to minutes, and the minutes to hours. The rocky path made each step taken in his ragged boots a painful reminder of the blisters he'd have to tend later. *Bones take these damn blisters.*

Malfus was so absorbed by his vast reserves of self-pity that he nearly collided with the horse, not realizing it had stopped. He would have taken a kick from it if he'd taken another step. He took a few measured steps back.

The Inquisitor looked around warily before dismounting. "We'll stop here," he said.

They were in a copse of cypress trees. A hill to their left blocked their view of the Scar. The trees here were bent, like old men leaning on their canes. It was the most vegetation Malfus seen in this dusty canyon, which usually offered no protection from the sun.

The Inquisitor grabbed the leather waterskin from his saddlebags and approached Malfus.

Malfus sagged. *Water, finally. Give me a drink. End one of my sorrows—or drown me, and end them all.*

His tongue quivered in anticipation; his mouth felt full of sawdust. The Inquisitor pulled the muddy gag down Malfus's neck.

Malfus took a few ragged breaths, relieved. "That's much bet—"

He sputtered as water poured down his throat. He struggled at first, then welcomed the stream as it drenched the desert his mouth had become. Malfus coughed as the Inquisitor lowered the waterskin. "More?" asked the Inquisitor.

Malfus gave something closer to a gurgle than an affirmation, but the Inquisitor got the gist. A few more precious gulps of warm water. It ran down his dry, cracked lips.

"That is enough," snapped the Inquisitor. He stoppered the skin.

The water rekindled Malfus's mind. He turned to the Inquisitor and smiled, ignoring a cut in his bottom lip. "Come, Inquisitor," he said. "Why such animosity between us, hmm? We both have such matching sunny dispositions and penchants for dark clothing." He'd expected a slap by this point, but none came, so he continued. "For me, it's the way black makes me slimmer. Complementing, wouldn't you agree? With so much in common, we should be friends. Our only *real* difference of opinion is which side of the ground corpses should occupy."

The Inquisitor snorted. "Must you continue this? In the face of your coming trial, this sarcasm is—what is that word you Akkadians use…"

"Brave?"

"…puerile," said the Inquisitor, turning his back to Malfus.

As the Inquisitor walked back to the horse, a high-pitched whine sounded, followed by a wet *thwop*. The waterskin in the Inquisitor's hand burst, spraying droplets that glimmered in the sun. The Inquisitor yelled something, and his horse reared up, kicking its hooves.

A second whistling. Air brushed against Malfus's cheek, and something plucked at a strand of his black hair. Dirt peppered his face.

A thin length of wood sprouted out from the ground next to him, still quivering. The Inquisitor shouted again.

Realization finally broke through the arcanull-induced haze—they were being ambushed.

"Get down!" yelled the Inquisitor, his words finally registering.

Get down? Where? I'm tied to your horse, you idiot. What do you want me to do, get behind it? Let it kick my teeth in? Malfus ducked as another arrow shot overhead, sticking into a nearby cypress tree and cutting a bald spot in the bark.

Strange sounds echoed from the surrounding hills. A shrill, high-pitched cacophony—one part howl, one part laughter. A drunken cackle. The type of sound Malfus imagined he might hear in some demonic inn on the edge of hell.

But as he listened, he recognized the noise.

Gnolls.

Half-human, half-hyena monsters. Malfus had never seen any before, but he'd read about them at his academy in Akkadia. When he was still an aspiring apprentice. *Before my life went to shit.* He tried to remember more, but failed. Malfus shook his throbbing head, trying to clear the arcanull fog creeping back into his mind.

Another arrow hit the dirt just a few strides away, looking like a small plant, growing feathers instead of leaves. Malfus laughed. He wasn't sure why. Perhaps it was how silly the arrow looked; perhaps it was the look on the Inquisitor's face, or the realization that his doom had drawn closer. Laughter wasn't an appropriate response, but Malfus couldn't help himself.

Another arrow snapped against a rock nearby, closer than the last. The horse reared up again. Malfus could see the fear in its eyes and swallowed, feeling the same himself.

"Arms out!" said the Inquisitor.

Malfus glanced at him, puzzled. The Inquisitor loomed over him. The razor edge of his rapier glinted crimson in the dusk.

"Arms out! Now, dammit!"

Malfus tightened his jaw and held out his arms. The blade came down in a silver flash.

There was a ripping sound. Then the severed rope fell from his hands. The black horse bolted away as another arrow flew by, its hooves throwing up dust. The rope trailed behind it like a long tail, twisting madly against the rocks. Malfus imagined his body still attached, the stones dashing his skull to pieces.

The Inquisitor's voice snapped Malfus back to the present. "Stay here! And stay *low*." He shoved Malfus to the ground. "Run, and I'll chop off a foot. I'm sure you can stand trial with just one."

The arcanull chains rattled as Malfus clapped. "Most clever, Inquisitor. Don't you have some fighting to do?" He gestured at the nearby hillside as several hulking figures ran down it.

The first gnoll was covered in mottled tan fur, its armor a patchwork collection of strapped plate. Its canine snout curled into a snarl, baring long fangs. It howled as it ran down the hill, brandishing a fat sword overhead. The weapon looked large enough to chop a man in two.

It looked silly, waving an ungainly sword like that while running down the hill. Silly—and dangerous. *I guess dangerous is the whole point, after all.*

Malfus squirmed backward, realizing he had ducked behind a tree. As ever, he masked his cowardice with a healthy coat of sarcasm.

"Best of luck, Inquisitor," he said. "Kill one for me? I'd hate to travel to Castillea for my trial all alone. Try to stay alive."

"Count on it," said the Inquisitor. He darted away, his long cloak in one hand, Castillean steel in the other. He ducked close to the ground as he ran, like a fox sprinting across a farmer's field at midnight—with hunger in his eyes to match.

Malfus did not have an appetite for armed combat. He'd never developed a taste for it. Especially against a gnoll two feet taller than him. It always amazed Malfus how eagerly people would throw themselves into armed combat, with as little care as a drunken bet in a tavern.

I suppose it's an effective form of population control. Two enter, but only one leaves. Even the winner seldom comes out unscathed—and death is so permanent.

At least, without a little necromancy.

No, Malfus decided. Leave combat to those of a baser nature. His was a more noble calling: to further the science of necromancy. Comforted, he crouched even lower behind his tree, contorting his narrow body to remain hidden. He watched the Inquisitor fight while keeping an eye out for more arrows.

He doubted he'd be spotted. At least, he hoped he wouldn't be. His blistered feet were far too sore for him to run.

The Inquisitor moved from tree to tree until he reached the bottom of the hill, right as the first gnoll did. It swung its giant blade in a downward arc. Malfus winced at the shriek of steel clashing. Then he balked in surprise. So did the gnoll. The Inquisitor effortlessly parried its hefty cleaver with his slender blade. The size disparity between the two made it even more shocking. The gnoll stood at least two feet over the Inquisitor, its cleaver as wide as a man's head.

The gnoll lashed out again. The Inquisitor sidestepped, then retaliated with a riposte. He stabbed into the gnoll's thigh, then ripped the blade outward in a spray of blood. The gnoll yelped, leaping backward, slicing wildly as it lost balance.

The Inquisitor dodged, launching two more stabs of his own. The first sent the gnoll reeling backward on its injured leg; the second, the gnoll barely managed to bat away with its heavy sword.

But as skilled as the Inquisitor might have been in a solo duel, Malfus doubted the other two gnolls running down the hill would improve his odds.

Then a glint of light caught Malfus's attention. The steel tip of an arrow danced in the sunlight as it reached the apex of its flight, then dropped downward in a lazy arc. It angled to fall right where the Inquisitor stood.

Time slowed as the arrow dropped. Malfus could have called out a warning. Instead, he focused on the arrow, pleading with it. *Please, by all that is unholy, hit him right between the eyes—right between the shoulders—right between something, dammit!*

He wasn't excited about becoming a captive of the gnolls. But being a potential meal—or haggling for his freedom with these brutes—gave him better odds of escape than remaining with the Inquisitor. *You can reason with an idiot, but not with a zealot.*

Malfus licked his cracked lips in anticipation. The gnoll barked as it unleashed a flurry of savage blows, demanding the Inquisitor's full attention to parry each strike.

But right before the arrow reached its target, the Inquisitor dropped low and spun in a tight circle. His cloak snapped out behind him like a banner, catching the arrow harmlessly in its folds. Malfus cursed and spat. *Nice trick, Inquisitor—but you can only get it wrong once.*

In a fluid movement, the Inquisitor snapped his cloak outward, covering his opponent's face, then jabbed his sword forward in a measured strike.

The gnoll tottered backward as blood gushed from its throat, then collapsed.

The Inquisitor didn't spare a moment as the remaining two gnolls closed in. One carried a spiked flail the size of a skull; the other bore two wicked battle axes it wielded like hatchets. The gnolls chittered at each other in their language, then the axe gnoll circled to flank the Inquisitor.

The flail gnoll growled and closed in, its weapon swinging wildly. The Inquisitor dodged left and right, timing the flail's rotations. Its chain swung fast enough to whistle. But its song stopped on a flat note as the gnoll lashed out at the Inquisitor's ribs. The Inquisitor ducked into a roll beneath it, landing beside the gnoll. He continued into a spin behind his opponent, twisting his blade into its side before kicking it in the rear. The gnoll yelped as its unwieldy weapon threw it off balance.

The axe gnoll sprang in, hacking at the Inquisitor. It forced him to parry backward, taking his attention away from its injured companion. The Inquisitor thrust at the axe gnoll, turning his back to the flail gnoll as it regained its feet.

The flail gnoll swung its weapon in an overhead windup, then brought it down in a diagonal arc to stop the nimble Inquisitor from ducking. The Inquisitor spun to dodge, but his cloak tangled around the head of the flail, jerking him off his feet. He landed hard on his shoulder, losing his hat as he rolled. The Inquisitor struggled to right himself, but the axe gnoll jumped on him, kicking at his ribs.

The Inquisitor rolled away, flicking his wrist. The gnoll's head snapped back. Then it dropped an axe. It stumbled around for a few seconds before collapsing, a dagger protruding from its eye.

As much as Malfus might have hoped the Inquisitor would fail, the man was a sight to behold. Two dead gnolls lay at his feet, and he was close to having a third. His sword was crimson to the hilt, moving in a blur of feints, parries, and thrusts.

Malfus felt laughter bubbling up again. He giggled uncontrollably.

He plays judge, jury, and executioner for a handful of gnolls, but I have to be carted across the entire Empire to a trial where death is certain. Why not save us both the trouble? Kill me, and be done with it? He could even blame it on the gnolls.

Another gnoll snuck through the woods toward the Inquisitor, hefting a spear, while the flail gnoll kept him busy. Malfus crouched lower and looked around. *Where has their archer gone?* Malfus decided he wasn't going to stick around and find out.

Behind him, on the other side of the path, the ground sloped downward into a grove of thicker, sturdier trees. They offered both the perfect hiding spot and cover from falling arrows. Malfus turned from the violence and sauntered away, keeping as close to the ground as he could manage. If the Inquisitor managed to win—he'd face those consequences later.

Then a twig snapped behind him.

He froze like the dead. He dared not move at all, waiting instead for another noise. All he could hear was his heart pounding in his throat. He could run, yell for the Inquisitor, or simply turn around—but the fear was too strong to do anything.

Another twig snapped behind him. This time it was unmistakable. Another crunch followed, accompanied by an eruption of pain in his side.

The unseen blow threw him forward. Malfus landed hard in a puddle of mud for the second time that day. He bit his tongue, ignoring the throbbing pain, and tasted salt. He spat blood and look up with tears in his eyes—but was kicked again, this time in his injured rib.

He rolled over on his back to curse, but instead howled out in the universal language of pain. The silhouette of a gnoll towered over him, blocking out the sun. Malfus would have pled for mercy, but all he managed was a painful moan.

The gnoll grabbed him by the throat and hoisted him into the air.

Chapter 2

Time to Run

"They came like the wind. One moment, nothing. Then the hills were covered with them. The worst part was that damnable laughter. All around us, all night long. None of the others made it." — Cormyn Gebberd, Monrovian wool merchant

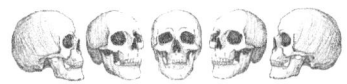

Malfus hadn't known how much taller gnolls were than humans, until he was face to face with one, his feet dangling in the air. This close, he could see the notches cut into its rounded ears and patches of mange on its neck. As he looked down its snout, it stared back with yellow eyes that displayed fury and intelligence in equal measure.

As well as *hunger*. He didn't want to think about that.

Malfus instinctually reached for magic. But as soon he had the thought, icy fingers of pain lanced into his mind.

Thrice damn this arcanull! He might have screamed in agony. He wasn't sure. When his vision returned, the gnoll had a knife drawn, its gleaming point inches from his eye.

The gnoll shook him and barked in its guttural language, pulling him closer. Yellow fangs foamed with spit at the corners of its mouth. The gnoll's breath smelled hot and sour, and its musky odor was acidic, like urine.

Malfus looked down. No, that urine smell was him. The gnoll sneered, then snapped its teeth in his face, less than an inch from his nose.

He realized how little he knew about the dietary habits of gnolls. *Will it eat me right here? Bite my face off before devouring the rest?*

Perhaps pissing myself was a good idea, after all.

Malfus had welcomed the prospect of death many times over while imprisoned by the insufferable Inquisitor. Now that death stared him in the face with a set of sharp, snapping teeth, he felt a change of heart. He'd walk back the way they'd traveled and start this journey all over again—without boots, without complaining, even without sarcasm.

Anything, if he survived this.

He gasped as the gnoll's claw tightened around his windpipe. It pushed its knife against his neck until it bit into his flesh. At least the knife was sharp. He was more grateful that the gnoll didn't seem interested in devouring him.

Malfus closed his eyes as he felt the knife press harder.

No! Open your damn eyes, you coward. Face your fears, for once in your life! Face them in your death, at least.

He forced his eyes open. The gnoll stood there, as if waiting for him to do something. Maybe it wanted him to beg, or scream more, or soil himself again. Unsure of what to do in this most intimate of moments, Malfus spat a mouthful of blood in the gnoll's face.

It snarled like it was reconsidering not biting his face off. Before it could, the gnoll hesitated, making a confused expression.

Then a silver blade erupted from its snout.

The gnoll gave a disappointed hiss as it crumpled to the ground. Malfus fell with it, but for once, he managed to land on his feet—next to the Inquisitor.

Blood covered the Inquisitor. Malfus wasn't sure it all belonged to the gnolls. The Inquisitor's hat was crumpled, and its red feather was missing; his cloak was tattered, his black leather armor torn. He breathed heavily, and favored one leg. It was the weakest and most vulnerable Malfus had ever seen the Inquisitor—perhaps the only time he had ever the Inquisitor with the word 'vulnerable.'

Overpower him! Strangle him with these damn chains. Take your freedom.

But the Inquisitor met his eyes without saying a word. His gaze cut right through. *Try me, you pathetic worm,* it said. *I won't kill you. I'll just injure you enough to make your journey that much more miserable.*

Malfus cleared his throat. "Guess you'll need a new rope," he offered, holding his arms out. The frayed scrap of rope dangled a few inches from his wrists.

A distant howl sounded behind them. Another gnoll appeared atop the hill. Malfus wondered why it howled. Did it mourn the death of its comrades? Or was it cursing them?

He didn't need to wait long. A second howl matched the first, then another from a different direction. Several more followed, too distant and too numerous to count, blending into a single mournful note of impending doom.

Malfus gritted his teeth, then wiped the sweat from his face with his filthy sleeve. He glared at the Inquisitor. *Now you've done it, you idiot. Led us right into a bloody clan of gnolls with a single horse. You could have just left me in Monrovia instead of leading us on a suicide mission.*

The Inquisitor grabbed Malfus's collar. Malfus jumped, but his reflexes were an afterthought compared to the Inquisitor. He pulled Malfus as close as the gnoll had. Malfus hoped the Inquisitor couldn't smell his urine-soaked robes through all the blood. If he could, he made no sign.

The Inquisitor lifted two fingers to his mouth and let out a shrill whistle next to Malfus's ear. Malfus reeled, trying to pull away, but the Inquisitor held tight.

"What are you—"

The question lurched in his throat and the sky flashed overhead as he was lifted off his feet by his collar. The pain in his bruised ribs stole his breath as he landed on the horse, perched between its neck and the Inquisitor.

"Hold on!" cried the Inquisitor, and the horse took off in a gallop.

Malfus wanted to call out, scream in pain, curse Vesenia, or say something dripping with sarcasm—but all he could do was hiss through clenched teeth. He would have cushioned his ribs from the bouncing, but holding on to the saddle occupied both of his bound hands.

He attempted to focus instead, to remember some scraps of training from the academy. Anything to shut out the pain. It didn't help. In his mind, all he could see was a dark cell in the inquisitorial dungeons, a red-hot poker being jammed into his side.

The more he wrestled with his thoughts, the more focused the pain became.

This won't work. Something else. Think of something else.

Malfus looked up at the sky instead. It was getting darker. How quickly darkness came, once the sun began to crest the horizon. Minutes ago, it had been a fiery orange; now it was a maroon bruise, with stars glimmering under a shy moon. Wind whipped at his hair as they raced past long, thin trees. He pulled his head and feet closer to the horse, sending pain shooting down the side of his body.

He winced. *Better than dashing my head against a tree.*

The whistle of an arrow—a sound he was increasingly familiar with—shot overhead, followed by chittering laughter.

"Hyah!" The Inquisitor kicked his horse into a harder gallop.

Several more arrows flit around them. Malfus squeezed his exposed sides closer to the horse. He wasn't sure if being shot by an arrow he couldn't see was worse than being shot by one that he could.

Taunting hyena laughter filled the air, echoing through the trees. The maddening noise was made worse by the night's darkness and the uncountable numbers it suggested. Malfus might have soiled himself again, if his bladder had anything left.

Where are we going? What's the plan here? He wanted to ask, but his side hurt; all he could muster was a cough. He wasn't aware of his ribs anymore—just their pain. It came in nauseating waves, each threatening a tide of vomit. Would some sort of confession get tortured out of him whenever they reached the Inquisitor's destination? The Inquisition's methods couldn't be much worse than this.

His head spun. He might have blacked out for a few seconds. Golden lights swirled far ahead of them. Malfus blinked, shaking his head, but the lights remained, forming a steady line.

It looked like a city.

Not a hallucination. Salvation.

His head reeled, and he felt the darkness coming back. The Inquisitor's voice called, as if from far away.

"Hold on!"

Chapter 3
The Fort in the Middle of Nowhere

"Henceforth, the dead shall be shackled in chains before burial—and thus shall any who practices necromancy be chained as well." — Attributed to Vesenia

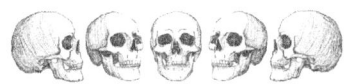

The whistle of arrows jolted Malfus back to the present—a throbbing, painful nightmare. The horse plunged through the trees. Branches snapped around Malfus, tearing at his robes and whipping his face.

Inhuman laughter echoed from the dark woods, sending chills down his spine. The maddening noise grew louder as they approached the golden lights.

What if it's a gnoll city? Do they have *cities?* Malfus grinned, thinking about how the Inquisitor would react if it was a gnoll stronghold. *Let's see his goddess save him then.*

The horse's canter jostled his injured ribs, and his smile faded. His side was on fire. He glanced down at the ground, considering jumping, then clung to the saddle even tighter.

The laughter, no longer an echo, surrounded them. He couldn't trust his throbbing head or blurred vision, but thought he saw shadows darting between the trees. Another arrow whistling overhead confirmed his suspicions. Yelps of alarm joined the chorus of laughter.

Malfus cowered. "We're riding right through them!"

"You think I don't know?" said the Inquisitor. "Shut up and hold on!"

The Inquisitor slapped the horse's flank with the flat of his sword. Over his own rasping, Malfus could hear the horse's labored breathing begin to wane.

His head buzzed like wasps nesting between his ears, but he ignored the pain, craning his neck to look up at the lights. It wasn't a city, but a *fortress*. They were close enough now to make out silhouettes atop its walls carrying torches and long poles, the metal tips glinting in the darkness. Scattered shouts of alarm were followed by the peal of a bell. In the middle of the wall stood a massive, iron-shod gate, barring all entry.

"Open the gate! By Vesenia, open the gate!" The Inquisitor's voice rang out like a bugle sounding a cavalry charge.

Malfus's neck felt too strained to keep looking up, but shouts along the wall grew in number as they got closer. But he did not hear the gate opening.

A distant voice echoed from the wall. A warning? A challenge? Malfus couldn't tell, but the voice was human. A welcome relief from the gods-awful howling of the gnolls, even if the human voice carried a threatening tone.

"Open the gate, damn you!" responded the Inquisitor. "I am an agent of the Holy Inquisition!"

Idiot. The Inquisition? Do you want them to open the bloody gate, or shoot at us?

A brass horn answered. Then, at last, came the lumbering creak of the gate opening.

The sound of our salvation.

"Gnolls!" the Inquisitor yelled to the men atop the wall.

Their crossbows replied, punctuating the air with hissing bolts and rattling strings. A gnoll yelped just feet from Malfus. A dozen pairs of yellow eyes leered back at them from the darkness, reflecting light like hungry mirrors.

Too damn close. No need for arrows at this range. The gnolls were close enough to reach out and grab him.

Before any could, the Inquisitor's horse burst through the last of the trees into an open field. The gnolls barked, brandishing their weapons, but did not follow. Their yellow eyes stared at them from the trees.

Malfus licked his lips at the sight of the gates, cracked open just wide enough for them to fit through. A few strides remained.

Air whisked at his hair as they passed through the gap. Relief flooded through Malfus. His aches melted away, his injured rib a distant memory. *Or maybe this is what shock feels like.*

From inside the walls, Malfus could see precious little, but he heard a great deal: the rumble of the gate closing, the snap of crossbows firing, and the hiss of freshly drawn steel.

Soldiers shouted over one another, giving too many commands to make anything out. Feelings of relief faded as Malfus realized that, though they'd escaped bloodthirsty gnolls, they could be skewered by their own kind.

Before any could, the Inquisitor asserted himself. "I am Inquisitor Damian Deza! On behalf of the Vesenian Orthodoxy, I am guarding a dangerous prisoner! Under the full authority of His Holiness, and the Three Crowns—take me to your commanding officer immediately!"

The group of soldiers lost their bluster like a wave rushing back to sea. Some whispered admonishment for challenging an Inquisitor. A loud, authoritative voice silenced the rest.

Malfus shook his head. *Only someone incredibly brave or stupid would willingly address the Inquisition.* Everyone *has something to hide from them.*

"Make way! Make way!" shouted a gravelly voice.

The soldiers parted, revealing the largest woman Malfus had ever seen. She towered over the other soldiers. From greaves to gorget, she wore full-plate armor, save for a helmet. The plating rattled like an entire battalion of soldiers marching as she approached the Inquisitor.

She was older than the other soldiers, her charcoal hair streaked with silver, tied into a tight bun. Malfus doubted anyone had ever called her beautiful; the scars marring her cheek and eyebrow did little to help.

"You know the drill!" she said. "Check for wounded, then back to your posts. The last soldier here will pull double shifts tonight!"

The soldiers scrambled to be the first to carry out her orders, falling over themselves to get away. Once they dispersed, the woman turned to face Malfus and the Inquisitor. Her gray eyes, cold as the Inquisitor's, passed over Malfus—but her face betrayed neither sympathy nor curiosity before turning to the Inquisitor. "I'm First Sergeant Goren," she said. "The Colonel is this way. I apologize for my soldiers. A bit jumpy, with all the attacks."

"My mission is urgent," said the Inquisitor. "I don't have words for anyone who isn't in charge. Lead on."

The First Sergeant nodded, but Malfus noticed shame hidden under her mask of stoicism. She disappeared from his line of sight, but her plate armor clattered as she led the horse across the grounds.

Malfus calmed his breathing. His heart fell from his throat back into his chest. Now would be a great time to get his hands to stop shaking. They complied, but the relief was short-lived. With his adrenaline gone, fatigue and pain rushed back in, fighting for his attention. His injured rib demanded relief, but his fatigue demanded a bed. He could appease neither, so he ignored them both.

Instead, he surveyed his new surroundings.

A fifty-foot stone wall separated them from the gnolls, with towers jutting out like tombstones at regular intervals. Perhaps a dozen other buildings huddled within, most built of stone, some only wooden. All of them bristled with arrows and were pocked with burn marks.

Malfus got strange looks from guards as he passed by, splayed across the Inquisitor's horse like a dead goat. A few female soldiers stood among them. He'd heard about Galasan warrior culture, and their use of women as guards and soldiers—something he hadn't seen in Akkadia. But almost every one of these wore an injury—weeping bandages over a head or an eye, arms in a makeshift slings, or a soldier limping about, using a spear for a crutch.

I'm the one charged for necromancy—but this camp is full of the walking dead.

All were as silent as the grave, save for chirping crickets and moans from the wounded. The crickets didn't seem to mind the interruption. Any relief Malfus might have felt now leeched out of him by the defeat on every face. One soldier, meeting his stare, was little more than a child—perhaps a handful of winters into his teens. A desperation hid behind those eyes, belying his age. Malfus looked away.

He found, instead, a line of neat rows of fresh earth, adorned with sticks tied in the shape of a diamond—the Eye of Vesenia. A pair of soldiers ignored them as they passed by the graves. Each held one end of a body over a hole, its wrists bound in chains, just like Malfus. They dropped it with a dull *thud*.

Malfus grimaced. *If life is so sacred to the bloody church—why not send Inquisition forces to help these? Sentenced to death and obscurity on this piece of rock, for no crime other than paying the Tithe, imposed by the church in the first place.*

The First Sergeant drew to a stop, motioning to a pair of doors. "He's just through here, Inquisitor. I'd make the introductions, but I have to see to my soldiers."

The Inquisitor nodded curtly, dismounting.

The First Sergeant turned to the two soldiers at the grave. "What are you doing, digging holes? Time for that later. Take your place up on that wall—on the double now." She marched off, shouting orders to any other soldier in her path.

The Inquisitor turned, his brimmed hat brushing against Malfus's forehead. Malfus twisted to look up at him. *Yes, I'm still here, you horse's ass.*

The Inquisitor jerked on Malfus' manacles. He tottered for a second, then rolled off the horse. He managed to land on his feet and remain upright for two seconds, before his soles erupted in needles and numbness. Then he collapsed like an idiotic sack of potatoes.

The perfect way to end this shitstain of a day, as far as he was concerned. He didn't even try to stand—just sat there, rubbing feeling back into his feet.

He ignored the soldiers' leering faces. He found he cared far less for the opinions of others after being put in chains.

The Inquisitor looked down at him. "Come. We must meet the Colonel. Assess our situation."

Malfus stopped rubbing his feet and looked up. "You're taking me with you?" *At last, respect for my intellect. At last, some damn recognition.*

"Don't take it as a badge of pride," said the Inquisitor. "I'm not leaving you unattended while in my custody." The Inquisitor paused, bringing a black-gloved hand to his beard. "Also, having a prisoner in chains establishes a proper respect for authority in my dealings." The Inquisitor narrowed his eyes at Malfus. "Never forget your place."

Malfus glowered. *I'll show you your damn place after turning you into my personal undead boot polisher!* He wanted to spit the threat into the Inquisitor's smug face—but as with all of his best sarcasm, he kept it to himself.

"Come," said the Inquisitor. "Let's go."

The oak door let out a cavernous *creak* as it opened, revealing a corridor lined with torches. Angry shouts echoed down the hallway. A wooden door hung open at the other end—the source of the yelling.

Malfus shuffled behind the Inquisitor, his shackles clinking as he limped. The Inquisitor entered the room. Malfus had no choice but to follow.

MALFUS - THE COMMAND ROOM — ART BY DEJAN DELIC

Chapter 4

Colonel Peshka

"'Strategic decision?' 'Tactical advantage?' Words thrown about by people furthest from the fighting. Discipline wins battles, logistics wins wars; everything else is an excuse to hide behind maps. Your map, no matter how pretty it is, won't fight for you." — General Owen Murmillo, 'A Treatise on Good Soldiering,' excerpt from the Galasan Officer's Academy manual

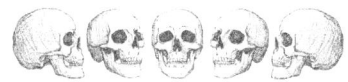

Torches burned low in their sconces, painting the room in long shadows. A portly man paced at the head of a table. One of his hands held a sloshing goblet; the other twisted the tip of a thick, orange mustache. His eyes were so fixed on the table that he didn't notice them enter the room.

Malfus watched the man, amused. The Colonel stomped like a child—a drunken one. His breastplate might have fit him at one point, but now it looked more like a metal bib than a piece of armor, covering only the top half of his belly and bouncing with every step. The Colonel had thick eyebrows to rival his mustache, and a receding crop of orange hair, sprinkled with white, probably more than was fair for his age. One tip of his mustache was a bit shorter than the other—the one he was still twisting. But he maintained an air of authority about him.

Or, at least, the air of sour wine and drunken aggression.

The table between could have served a banquet. Instead, its surface was covered in maps, toppled goblets, and dozens of small pieces of wood painted black or white. Blocks were strewn across the map, as if a spoiled child had grown tired of their toys.

Malfus swallowed. The growing pile of white blocks, cast to one side, made the implications of these 'toys' far more dire than any child's game.

He peered at a map sprawled across the table as he followed the Inquisitor into the room. A giant line of black ink marred one half. *I'm no cartographer, but that is the Scar.*

A small circle had been drawn a handsbreadth away from the dark line. *And this must be our lovely refuge—a fort on the very edge of the Ossory Empire.*

His stomach growled as he walked by a neglected platter decked with leftover pieces of meat and cheese. It had a pungent odor, and some flies buzzed around it. Even so, it made his mouth water. Malfus wondered if anyone would notice if he pocketed a few slices for later.

But as he reached for the platter, the Colonel kicked the leg of the table. "Blast it all!"

Painted pieces scattered across the map; several clattered to the floor. One white piece rolled across the room, stopping at the Inquisitor's boot. He reached down and picked it up.

"You should be more careful with your toys, sir." The Inquisitor set the piece back on the table.

The Colonel looked up at them, blinking. He glanced at his goblet, then back at the newcomers, as if deciding only to address them if they remained after closer inspection.

The man spread his arms out, then spoke in a voice more befitting a street performer than a military commander. "*In your darkest hour, a black-cloaked rider will ask you questions three. If your answers are not true, not even the gods will pity thee.*" He gave a mirthless chuckle. "Isn't that the rhyme they tell children about the Inquisition? Yet here you stand. A black-cloaked Inquisitor, in the flesh, and in my darkest hour. Let's hope I'm not found wanting, eh?" The Colonel raised his cup in a salute, then took a long sip, followed by another.

The man's gaze lingered on Malfus's manacles as he swallowed.

Yes. Hope you aren't found wanting, like me. It is no fun, I assure you.

The Inquisitor stepped forward. "I am Inquisitor Damian Deza. I'm on the holy business of the Vesenian Orthodoxy... and I find myself in need of your aid."

"Ah, yes," said the other. "Let me not forget my manners—quite unbefitting an officer." His speech slurred as he spoke. "I'm Colonel Gregor Peshka." He bent forward in a bow, nearly hitting his head on the table. "I am the local commander of His Majesty's army, and you have come at a dark hour indeed." He took another drink from his goblet. "Though, a member of the Inquisition is the last thing I'd have expected to show up on my doorstep. Don't tell me you came here to inspect our soldiers. We've already had our Purity inspections. No half-elves among our ranks—no worship of any pagan gods. Doesn't matter the god; they've all abandoned us out here." Peshka paused. "No offense, Inquisitor."

The Inquisitor cleared his throat. "No, Colonel. I'm not here for the Law of Purity."

"I don't imagine you bear news of reinforcements? Or better yet, have some with you?" Peshka resumed his pacing, bobbing around like a fisherman's lure.

"No. It's just the two of us." Malfus could hear the Inquisitor's gloves tighten as he clenched his fists.

"Well, how in the hells did you make it through the gnolls?" The Colonel took a drink. "Or do the bloody gnolls cower before the Inquisition?"

"The first group we encountered was small and easily dispatched," said the Inquisitor. "But then they came in number. I was forced to retreat, only making it here by the grace of Vesenia." He took a step forward. "My mission is most urgent, Colonel. I do not make use of this rite of office often—not unless there is no other course. I must call upon the Law of Aid. I must resupply before taking this prisoner to Vesper for justice."

The Colonel coughed. "I'll respect your law, Inquisitor, but the gnolls may bring your prisoner to justice much faster than you realize."

The Inquisitor crossed his arms and looked at the Colonel. "What *is* the situation here, Colonel?"

Peshka paused, looking at his glass. "Wine, Inquisitor?"

"Thank you, but no, Colonel."

Malfus licked his lips. *I wouldn't mind a glass, but no one ever cares about what* I *want.* Peshka's gaze lingered over Malfus for a moment.

"And none for my prisoner, either," the Inquisitor snapped.

"Suit yourself," said Peshka with a shrug. "Perhaps you'll change your mind after you've properly assessed our *situation.*" He waved his goblet toward the maps, wine sloshing and spilling on one. The drops glimmered like tiny beads before absorbing, staining the vellum like blood on a bandage.

The Inquisitor waited for Peshka to continue, his impatience growing palpable. If the Colonel noticed, he gave no sign. He resumed his pacing.

Peshka sighed. "Gnolls have been a pest out here for years, ever since I was first posted here. A constant menace—but never a *real* problem. They're usually content to remain between here and the Scar, with an occasional ambush on one of our scouting parties." He stared into his wine cup. "But some rogue albino has managed to unite enough of the gnolls to become a formidable threat. The soldiers call him Ghostface."

He waved his hand absently over the map. "I sent some troops to deal with him, but they walked right into a trap. They're a lot more cunning than you might give them credit."

Whom? The gnolls, or your soldiers?

Peshka frowned into his goblet. "I lost a lot of good soldiers that night. Lost a lot more since. Now the savages outnumber us three-to-one. Probably more. Hard to tell; they only attack at night." He looked at the smoldering logs in his fireplace. "They've been picking away at us like crows on a corpse for the last month. And by Vesenia, it's been a long one. I lack the soldiers to send out scouting parties. Too many dead, too many injured. But one soldier returned from the last I sent out—covered in blood. Lucky the lad made it back at all. But his days of standing watch are over."

The Inquisitor bowed his head. "Those who fall serving Vesenia are held in her immortal glory." He caressed the holy symbol hanging from his chest.

"Oh, the boy wasn't injured, not *physically*," said Peshka. "Too rattled after whatever he saw out there. I've seen soldiers after battles, but not like this. Had to lock him up. He claimed he'd seen a giant, or some such nonsense. He was a danger to morale, and trust me—morale is bad enough already. The soldiers I have left would desert if they could, but they know how far they'd make it."

"Is there anyone else coming?" the Inquisitor asked—impatience, not compassion, seeping into his voice. "Have you not sent for reinforcements?"

"Of course I bloody have!" said Peshka. "I sent a rider for reinforcements to DeGaullis a month ago when this first started, and then a week later when I didn't hear anything. Then another, a week after that. Not a word. That's three less bodies I have for standing watch, shooting crossbows, or digging graves. You two are the first without fur or fangs to show up at our gates."

Peshka lifted his cup, frowned when he saw it was empty, then grabbed a decanter sitting on a shelf. "It's safe to assume we are alone. Our fates in our own hands."

The cup rattled against the pitcher as he refilled it, his hands shaking. Malfus couldn't tell if it was the shake of an alcoholic or the nerves of a man staring at death for too long. For all his bluster, the fear in Peshka's eyes was evident. It was the same hollowed-out look his men had. *The look of a man before the gallows. One I'm intimately acquainted with.*

"A third of my garrison is dead. Only half of the survivors are fit for combat..." He stared into the fireplace. "One more organized attack could—"

The Inquisitor held up a gloved hand and cleared his throat. "I feel for your plight, Commander," he said, sympathetic as a stone, "but we all have our duties. Mine take me and my prisoner back to Vesper, the Holy Capital. I fail to see how your garrison is *my* problem."

Peshka turned back to him, mouth open. "Then perhaps you have not been listening to me, Inquisitor. We're surrounded by a damn army of infernal gnolls! If you haven't noticed!" Peshka smashed his hand down on the table, toppling the few wooden pieces still standing. "I don't know how you got past them the first time, but you have condemned yourself, and your prisoner, to share our fate. You won't outrun them on a horse with two riders, not out here. And even with all that black you're wearing, I doubt you'll have any better luck sneaking past them."

"Doubt is a weakness that the faithful can ill afford, Colonel," said the Inquisitor.

But Peshka smiled. "Perhaps your goddess protected you from the gnolls so that she could deliver you to us in our time of greatest need."

The Inquisitor paused, frowning.

Malfus nodded. *Well played, commander. The Inquisitor really is a sucker for piety. Pile it on. The thicker and stickier, the better.* He wasn't too invested in either staying or leaving, but Malfus thought his odds were decidedly better facing gnolls behind a wall of stone than alone in the wild with this demented zealot. *And this siege could give me opportunities...*

The Inquisitor straightened. "My mission remains of utmost importance... But your words give me pause. I will pray to Vesenia for guidance. We will remain for the night."

Colonel Peshka saw the Inquisitor was still reeling from his last hit, and pressed his point. "If you do decide to leave, at least lead my men in a prayer, Inquisitor. One final prayer to Vesenia to ease their troubled souls, should you depart tomorrow."

Damn, he's good. Malfus smiled. *In another life, he could have been one of the best wine merchants of Akkadia. Peshka might be a drunk, but he can size people up.* Malfus looked down at his soiled robes, wondering what impression Peshka gleaned from his pitiable appearance.

"Yes, Colonel Peshka," said the Inquisitor, sighing. "Regardless of my decision, I can lead your men in a prayer."

"Well, I shan't press any further," said Peshka.

And there's no need. The seed has been planted. The blow has been struck.

"I daresay," said Peshka. "The prospect of seeing an Inquisitor in battle stirs some excitement in this old warrior's bones. We've all heard how deadly Inquisitors are with blade and chain."

The Inquisitor's hand dropped to his sword hilt. "Do not put too much faith in my abilities. I am but one man, a humble servant of Vesenia. Not a worker of miracles."

"Having you on our side may not turn the tide of battle," mused Peshka, "but it will certainly help the men's morale. Sometimes it's morale that secures victory, not numbers."

Peshka looked over at Malfus. "But sometimes it *is* just the numbers. What about your prisoner? Is he any good with a blade?"

Malfus stopped himself from laughing. *A sword strapped to a scarecrow would pose a greater threat. He must have a fantastic imagination... Or he's more desperate than he looks.* Malfus knew he couldn't look the part. He was already scrawny before being chained, half-starved, beaten, and covered in mud. Though perhaps he wasn't much worse off than the rest of Peshka's soldiers.

The Inquisitor looked down his nose at Malfus. "He is too cowardly for honest combat."

He's not wrong.

"He has probably never held a sword in his life."

Just once—but it's not like I knew what to do with it.

"He is a foul sorcerer. A necromancer."

Malfus bowed low, his chains scraping against the stone.

"A sorcerer, you say?" Peshka's eyes burned bright. "Now *that* could change things."

"Not just a sorcerer. A vile *necromancer*." The Inquisitor's Castillean accent cut out each syllable of the word like a knife. "A spellcaster of the most wretched order, creating unholy perversions of life. Violating divine law."

Peshka pounded the table. "I know what a bloody necromancer is, dammit! I'm not asking for an army of the undead. I just want to know if he can drop a fireball on top of some bloody gnolls or not."

Malfus sniffed. "Nothing quite so crude, I'm afraid, but I can—"

"Absolutely not!" roared the Inquisitor. "He is a prisoner of the Orthodoxy. He will stand before the High Theologian to be tried for his heretical crimes. They will not be replicated under my watch!" He glanced at Malfus. "He is far too dangerous and untrustworthy. As likely to turn on us as the monsters at your gates."

The Inquisitor and the Colonel locked eyes for several seconds before either spoke.

"We all want to live, Inquisitor. Even a necromancer, I suppose." Peshka looked at Malfus.

"No!" The Inquisitor slammed his palm onto the table.

Malfus spoke again, his voice a whine. "Inquisitor, please, if it's so bad, then let me—"

"No!" The Inquisitor backhanded him in an instant, and Malfus's ears rang in pain. "Silence! I curse myself for leaving you ungagged."

Malfus spat blood. "Yes, Inquisitor," he said, his voice dripping with venom.

The Inquisitor turned back to Peshka with the same speed. "Colonel Peshka, I demand a room for myself, a stall for my horse, and a cell for the prisoner. You are keeping one of your soldiers under lock and key, correct?" The Inquisitor continued before Peshka could respond. "I will store my prisoner in your jail. I will need time to pray and prepare. Then we will discuss *strategy*, Colonel. Freeing the necromancer is out of the question. He is far too dangerous."

Peshka sighed. "Very well, Inquisitor. We will trust your wisdom." He took a deep breath, then yelled, "Corporal Higgins! Private Morten!"

A side door opened, and two young soldiers entered the room, snapping to attention and saluting. *By the gods, why are they all so young?*

"Men, this is Inquisitor Deza and... his prisoner," said Peshka. The two soldiers looked at him and the Inquisitor, warily. "Corporal Higgins, escort the Inquisitor to an empty room in the officer quarters. Private Morten, take his prisoner to the stockades. Secure him in an empty cell."

My own cell? How wonderful! The darker the better—so long as it's far away from this bastard.

The soldiers saluted again, then approached the Inquisitor. But he raised a black-gloved hand, stopping them cold. "Thank you, Colonel Peshka," he said. "I appreciate you sparing two soldiers. One can take my horse, but I will escort my prisoner with your other man myself." The Inquisitor looked at Malfus, narrowing his cold gray eyes. "I must assure the *suitability* of his prison cell. He cannot be trusted."

Peshka waved his hand. "Yes, Inquisitor. I believe you've established that. As you wish. Corporal Higgins, stable his horse. Private Morten, escort the Inquisitor and prisoner to the tower where Giles is locked up."

"Yes, sir!" The soldiers walked to the door.

The Inquisitor turned to Peshka a final time. "Once I am assured the prisoner is secured, and I have seen to my own needs, I will return to get a better appraisal of your tactical situation. We can discuss what changes need to be made. Faith favors the unfaltering."

"I will joyously await your return." Peshka poured himself another drink.

Chapter 5

PERSPECTIVES

"How many times must I tell you, Brother Rizzo? If you let them die, if you let them pass out, then they are in control. Not you. You must always remain in control." — Master Interrogator Groznik, of the Vesenian Inquisition

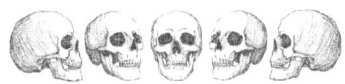

"This way, Inquisitor, sir," Morten said, his voice cracking, betraying his age. He swallowed, unsure why his mouth had gone so dry. He tried to clear his throat, but the damn prickling wouldn't go away. Neither would the Inquisitor.

Why had he gotten stuck escorting the Inquisitor? Higgins outranked him. Shouldn't *he* be the one to escort an official agent from the Inquisition?

Morten sighed. He hadn't been in the army long, but it had been long enough to know that the worst jobs always went to the lowest ranks. Every soldier there would have opted to muck out stables for a week before escorting an Inquisitor for one minute.

Every child, in any of the three nations of the Ossory Empire, had heard tales and rhymes of black-cloaked Inquisitors taking misbehaving children from their parents in the dark of night. He'd never seen an Inquisitor before, but the man clad in black standing before him, leading his chained prisoner, did little to dispel the stories.

The Inquisitor's stovepipe hat—one of the dreaded signs of the Inquisition's agents—had a dent in the side of it, bending at the top at a funny angle. Though Morten doubted anyone would laugh at an Inquisitor, bent hat or not. The Inquisitor wore a dueling sword strapped to his hip, the kind Castilleans were so fond of—so much thinner than Morten's own. He wondered how it would fare against gnolls—but if this Inquisitor had made it through them with no more than a bent hat and torn cloak, he must have been damn good with that slender blade. His black armor glistened in the moonlight. When Morten dared look closer, the armor was wet with blood.

Aside from his penchant for black clothing, the Inquisitor looked little different from any other man—except he looked like he had forgotten how to smile long ago. And his eyes were strange, like two pieces of ice-cold flint staring at Morten from under the brim of that hat, weighing him, penetrating into Morten's soul like shards of glass, uncovering his every thought before he had the chance to think it.

Morten couldn't meet the Inquisitor's gaze any longer. Instead, he looked at the miserable man in chains limping behind him. A pitiful shell, the prisoner had long black hair covering a pale face, with high cheekbones and hollow eyes. Dark bags hung beneath those eyes, either from lack of sleep, or perhaps regular beatings.

It was hard to tell who the prisoner might have been, or what his clothes would have looked like underneath all that dirt. Morten had some trouble pinning down the prisoner's age, but he couldn't have been too much older than himself. Certainly younger than the Inquisitor and Colonel Peshka. What crime could he have committed that warranted the attention of the Vesenian Inquisition itself? The prisoner didn't look evil—a bit weak, and untrustworthy—but not dangerous.

Things had been grim for the last month, but even still, he wouldn't want to swap places with the prisoner. Judgment from the Inquisition was a fate Morten wouldn't wish on anyone.

"What are you waiting for?" said the Inquisitor. "Lead on, soldier."

"Yes, Inquisitor, sir. It's this way."

Morten swallowed, and led them toward the tower on the west wall. His helmet, a bit too large, bounced on his head with every step. He dared not to say a word unless addressed first, which he hoped he wouldn't be.

All day on the wall. Now I'm stuck escorting this cold bastard. Just finish this, then get some shuteye.

Morten could *feel* the Inquisitor's gaze burrowing into the back of his skull. His oversized helmet did little to protect against it. He quickened his pace, his helmet bouncing faster.

The moon hung low, like a swollen peach. The excitement of new arrivals had died down; the camp had become as quiet as an undertaker's parlor. The silence was interrupted only by occasional moans from the infirmary, or by Goren's voice echoing somewhere along the battlements.

"Are there many other prisoners kept here?" The Inquisitor's voice made Morten's stomach knot.

"Uhhh... No, sir. Just the one." Morten's hands were sweating.

"Ah yes, the Colonel mentioned him. The one who survived the *giant.*"

"*Alleged* giant, sir. Giles has always been a bit prone to tall tales."

Morten chose his words carefully, afraid of saying too much; he wished saying nothing at all were an option. Morten maintained a brisk pace without looking back, avoiding eye contact with the Inquisitor out of fear, or the prisoner out of pity.

Whatever crime the prisoner had committed, it made no sense to lock up anyone at a time like this—not when they needed every available fighting man. If the man was condemned to death, why not put a sword in his hand and make him fight with the rest of them? Put him on the front lines, even. Soldiers shouldn't have to give their lives to protect someone already sentenced to death. If they died and the fort fell, he'd be killed by the gnolls anyway.

None of it made any sense, but things seldom had since joining the army.

Morten sighed, his thoughts drifting back to his home. They often had, this last month. Something in his life had gone terribly wrong; he had made a wrong choice somewhere. Why had he wanted to leave the farm so badly? His father drank as much as Colonel Peshka, and his mother could be overbearing, but at least they loved him. His younger siblings may have annoyed the piss out of him, but they looked up to him.

Their farm, in a little town outside Víadalla. He doubted he would see any of them again. Never again taste one of his mother's homemade meat pies, or see his sister's sweet smile. He even missed his younger brother's voice, always begging to play swords. He should have been kinder. He regretted being so mean to his brother. Instead, he'd tried to toughen him up. Teach him to be man of the house after Morten left to pay the Tithe.

But his brother hadn't shown up when he left with the others from the village. Probably thought he was a bully. He'd never get the chance to apologize.

Home seemed so far away now—like a box of someone else's memories he got to glimpse on guard shifts, or when he lay awake at night. The more he viewed his memories, the hazier they got. He hardly remembered his own mother's voice over the gnoll's chittering laughter. That scared him more than the gnolls did. Almost.

What was wrong with being a farmer, anyway? He'd been in such a hurry to see the world, only to be sent to the Farlands—the armpit of the Ossory Empire. For what? To do his duty for Galasa and pay the Tithe? Protect the Ossory Empire from the Scar? What a joke.

The hairs on his neck crawled again. He could feel the Inquisitor's gaze worming inside him, digging the truth out of him—make him admit he was terrified, that he regretted ever leaving the farm. That he wished he had run when his name had been called for the Tithe.

Was it all just his imagination? Surely the Inquisitor couldn't *really* read his mind.

"Is this it, soldier?"

The Inquisitor's voice snapped the box of memories shut. Morten looked up. He hadn't realized they'd already made it to the western tower.

"Huh? Oh yes. Sorry, Inquisitor, sir."

The door creaked open, and Morten led the Inquisitor and his prisoner inside.

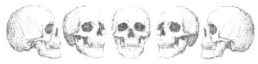

The Inquisitor ran a gloved hand along the wall as he paced the cell's perimeter. He paused to rub at a seam of mortar between two bricks. A piece of it crumbled between his fingers. He hummed in dissatisfaction before examining the iron bars. He grasped them firmly and tried to shake them, nodding when they didn't rattle.

While the Inquisitor inspected the cell, Malfus took stock of his surroundings. One other cell occupied the tower. A man sat on a wooden chair in its middle, staring out a window too high to reach. Half a small loaf of bread lay on a table beside him. The prisoner showed no interest in it or the newcomers.

Malfus's mouth watered. He should have grabbed some meat and cheese from the Colonel's room.

The young soldier called out to the prisoner. "Giles. How are you holding up?"

The man in the other cell didn't answer.

"We brought you someone to keep you company," said the soldier. "Want to greet your new roommate?"

Again, no answer.

Malfus's feelings weren't hurt by the other prisoner's lack of interest. He was too entranced by the lump of uneaten bread in that cell to care.

The Inquisitor stepped out of the cell. "This will do, I suppose. Nothing to rival the Inquisition's holding chambers. Normally, we don't allow prisoners windows or company." He turned to Malfus. "Enjoy the luxury while you can."

Then the Inquisitor shoved him into the cell. Malfus sprawled on the cold stone floor. He rolled over, glowering at the Inquisitor with as the iron door slammed shut. The crash snuffed out the fire in his glare.

"This should hold you for tonight," said the Inquisitor. "Don't do anything foolish, or I shall cut the regret from you later."

Malfus pushed himself to his knees and dusted himself off. "I wouldn't dream of it. You wound my pride to think me capable of such mendacity. I shall be here, eager to continue our journey in the morning."

Ignoring Malfus, the Inquisitor pulled at the iron bars one more time. He nodded, satisfied, then turned to Private Morten. "Where is the key for this cell?"

The soldier blanked for a moment, then looked around. "Oh. Here, Inquisitor." Private Morten grabbed a two-pronged iron key from the wall and handed it to the Inquisitor.

The Inquisitor tested the key, unlocking and relocking the cell, then hung it around his neck, next to his key to the arcanull cuffs.

"This will suffice. Come, soldier. You may escort me to my quarters now."

"Yes, Inquisitor, sir." Private Morten opened the tower door. "This way."

The Inquisitor followed Morten, shutting the door with the finality of a coffin lid.

Malfus sighed in relief. *At last.* His body might have throbbed in pain and exhaustion, and his wrists still bound together with accursed arcanull, but it felt like a weight had been lifted from his shoulders now that his damn shadow had departed. For the first time in nearly a month, those dead fish eyes weren't watching his every move.

Sweet solitude, even if for one night.

He yawned, stretched, then got to his feet. Time to get a better measure of his temporary accommodations.

They were dark. There were no torches inside the tower—only a small window, too high to reach even with a jump; his blistered feet were too sore to jump anyway. Malfus brushed his fingers along the walls as he paced the cell's perimeter, feeling the grooves of mortar beneath his fingertips. The room's only furnishings were an empty wooden bucket, whose purpose was easy to ascertain, and a lump of hay piled in one corner.

As he got closer to it, mildew assailed his nostrils, forcing him to hold back a sneeze. He continued his tour unabated. It would take more than a little mildew to dampen his spirits. A rotting pile of hay was the best deal his back had gotten in weeks.

He sighed, ready to retire on his probably lice-infested pile of straw to get some rest, but a growl in his stomach reminded him of his hunger. He patted his angry stomach. *Behave yourself. We all want things we can't have. Let's compromise and get a little sleep.* His mouth watered, unwilling to accept defeat. The extra nudge made him remember the other prisoner's bread.

He slinked back to the front of his cell, on the side facing the other prisoner.

"Psst. Hey!"

Nothing.

Malfus crept as close to the cell's corner as he could. Gaps in the bars were too narrow for him to stick his head through.

"Hey. I know you're over there. Are you awake?"

Still nothing.

Better pour on the charm.

"Come on. Don't you want to get to know your new celly? Why don't you tell me what you're in for? I consider myself a *gifted* listener." He added the most convincing sincerity to his voice he could manage.

Still nothing. Malfus sighed and walked back to the pile of hay. *I still have blisters to work on, anyway.*

"I was locked up for telling the truth!" cried a voice.

Malfus walked back to the bars.

The man in the other cell carried on in the same voice, disturbed. "They're coming. They're coming! Why won't the others listen? We should all retreat! But it doesn't even matter. They've got a bloody giant with them. A *giant!* You hear me? It pulled Korlick apart right in front of me. Why? Oh, why won't anyone listen? No matter what I said. Don't they know they're coming? It's too late now..." The man's voice trailed off into a sob.

Eesh. A dramatist. "There, there," said Malfus. "It'll be all right."

Definitely crazy. He'd seen men like that in the markets of Akkadia, muttering to themselves while rummaging through trash, or standing in the street and shouting at the sun. *No use mincing words with these types; best get straight to the heart of the matter.*

"Are you going to eat your bread?" he asked.

The man stopped ranting. There were several seconds of silence, followed by a clatter on the stone floor outside his cell. Malfus's chains clinked against the bars as he snatched the bread from its plate.

"Enjoy it," said the other. "Might be the last thing you ever eat."

Malfus only half-heard him as he crawled on the cell floor, cradling the bread in his arms like a newborn, moving into the light from his window to get a closer look at his prize. The prisoner began ranting again, but Malfus ignored the words; he was too focused on the bread.

As he brought it into the moonlight, he saw several green blotches of mold on its bottom. But that wouldn't stop him. Not on this blessed night, free from the Inquisitor. *A feast fit for the occasion.* He picked away the mold as best he could, then stuffed some bread into his mouth.

The stale bread tasted like sawdust. It turned into a lumpy putty that absorbed what little moisture remained in his mouth. Malfus didn't care. The Inquisitor had only fed him at night when making camp, and he hadn't eaten since yesterday.

The other prisoner droned on, but it was like the cry of a child at the market—someone else's problem to deal with. Thoughts of escape hounded Malfus, but he knew he wouldn't last a day in the wild with these arcanull chains on.

What good is escape, anyway? Not without my spellbook.

Not without what's left of Kiara.

He stared out the window at stars impossibly far from his reach.

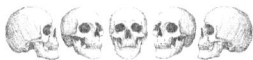

"Here it is, Inquisitor."

Morten opened the door to a room not unlike the cell they had just taken the prisoner to, except it had a wooden door instead of iron bars, and it was better furnished. There was a bed that rivaled the quality of an average inn, and a desk that had a mirror. A pair of boots lay under the bed, with a crisp uniform still spread on top.

"This used to be Lieutenant Erikson's room," said Morten. "Guess no one's packed his belongings yet. I doubt he will mind you sleeping in his bed."

"Thank you, soldier," said the Inquisitor curtly, his back to Morten. "This will be suitable for my needs."

Finally free, Morten turned to leave. He grabbed the door handle, excited to salvage what little sleep he could from the night.

"Wait," said the Inquisitor.

Morten froze, one foot still in the room, the other a step toward sleep.

"Yes?" Morten asked, shielding as much of himself behind the door as he could.

"Tell Colonel Peshka I will be with him soon. I must seek guidance first," said the Inquisitor, still not facing Morten.

"Yes. Of course, Inquisitor." Morten closed the door before breathing in relief. Then he paced down the hall quickly, his helmet bouncing.

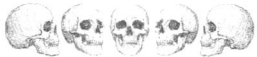

Deza folded the dead officer's uniform, then placed it behind the boots under the bed. He removed his hat, revealing a head of shortly cropped raven hair, peppered with age, and with faint curls, like most other Castilleans. He unstrapped his sword belt, laying it on the bed beside his hat. He unsheathed his rapier, wrinkled his nose at the dried blood that tarnished his blade, and set it aside to clean later. Then he took off his black gloves and placed them on the bed next to his belt, one on top of the other, fingers folded together as if in prayer.

From a small leather pouch at his side, he took out two sticks of incense, then lit them with the room's torch. They streamed a bluish-white cloud of smoke, filling the room with a sweet smell and a haze that hung like a ghost. Deza pushed the chair away from the desk and placed his incense in front of the mirror.

He reached into his collar, pulled out the leather cord with the keys to the prisoner's cell and cuffs, and placed it on the bed. Then he pulled a second cord from around his neck. Tied to it were two barbed links forged from brass, overlapping to form an eye—the all-seeing eye of Vesenia. The barbs signified an agent of the Inquisition.

He laid the holy symbol on the wooden desk, next to the burning incense. Then he unfastened his tunic, revealing a muscled back covered in pink scar tissue. He folded his tunic and laid it on the bed next to the rest of his articles. After straightening the items on the bed, he reached for a folded piece of leather the length of his forearm.

Deza closed his eyes and took a deep breath. His breathing quickened as he unrolled the leather across the desk. Inside shone a dozen metal tools. Someone might mistake them for a woodworker's kit; a closer inspection revealed a more insidious purpose. Barbed and hooked metal glittered in the torchlight. There were several pairs of shears, lengths of chain with razor edges, and a few others that required a generous imagination to understand. The varied tools were devoted to a singular purpose—pain.

Tools of confession. Tools of the Inquisition.

Deza's eyes gleamed as he brushed the cold metal with his fingertips. He rested them on a length of neatly folded chain. Each link had been hammered flat, their edges filed to keen points. He picked it up, letting its length drop to the ground. It resembled the spiked chain whips Inquisitors used in battle, albeit much smaller.

From another pocket, he took out a small vial of holy oil, blessed by priests of Vesenia and infused with Ranneara's Mercy—an herb that slowed the healing process and inflicted pain in open wounds. The Inquisition used it to extract confessions from prisoners, as well as in other sacred rites. Deza mouthed a prayer, then trickled golden oil down the chain. Its sharpened edges glinted amber in the torchlight. He steadied his breathing, calming himself, but his hands still trembled as he poured.

Finished, he dropped to his knees and closed his eyes, folding his hands in prayer. The chain, glistening with oil, dangled between his outstretched hands like a metal snake. It swayed as if alive. Even hungry.

"Blessed Vesenia, hallowed be thy name," Deza prayed. "Watch over the lost, but be stern when setting them on the path of the righteous. Blessed are those who walk already in your grace. Yet spare not your rod. May your hand be most severe to those who walk in your wisdom, lest they stray from your path. Teach them well the price of their folly."

He flicked his wrists. The chain blurred as it arced over his shoulder.

Crack!

The metal sang as links bounced against the stone floor. It glistened crimson in the torchlight. Veins on Deza's neck bulged, but he stifled his cries of pain.

"Vesenia, grant me grace to walk always in your light."

Crack!

The chain bit deeper into his flesh, cutting a new crease into the scars crisscrossing his back. Rivulets of blood ran down the ridges of scar tissue. Deza's breathing came in ragged gasps; beads of sweat covered his forehead. He took a few more breaths to steady himself.

"Vesenia, grant me forgiveness for my failures." A slight strain in his voice bled through its normal frigidity.

Crack!

He hissed through clenched teeth. Fresh cuts joined the countless scars. Blood ran freely, soaking the hem of his pants. Blood splattered across the flagstone floor behind him in a broad X. The chain's links rattled in his shaking hands.

"Vesenia, grant me strength to walk in your light. Guide my hand. Make me an extension of your divine will." His voice stifled a sob.

Crack!

Deza shuddered as he let out a muffled cry, but any seasoned prostitute, from the merchant-city of Pomanća to the dice-pits of Monrovia, would recognize the ecstasy mixed in with his pain. The oil was doing its job now, his burning from the alchemical mixture. His salty musk mingled with the coppery scent of blood and the wafting incense.

"Show me the path, Chained Mother. *Show me* what I must do." His voice was a shallow gasp.

Thwap!

The chain made a wet slapping sound as it met his lacerated back. Deza collapsed in front of the desk. A few moments later, his bloodied hand reached out to the wooden table, pulling him up. His face, reflected in the mirror, was unrecognizable from the one he wore earlier. It had transformed into a carnival mask of pain and ecstasy. His teeth clenched together in a rictus grin, his eyes wild with fervor. A single tear rolled down his cheek and joined his maniacal smile.

"Yes. I see," he gasped. "I am... your humble servant."

Chapter 6

Just a Stone's Throw Away

"Never allow your enemy to catch you by surprise—and if they do, never allow them to know it." — General Owen Murmillo, 'A Treatise on Good Soldiering,' excerpt from the Galasan Officer's Academy manual

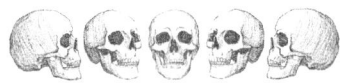

Colonel Peshka fumed. "Where is that bloody Inquisitor, eh?"

His voice echoed in the empty room. He slurped from his goblet; wine dripped from the tips of his mustache. He continued his pacing around the table. The gait made his breastplate bounce, wine sloshing from his cup.

He wasn't about to let this Inquisitor Deza usurp his authority, backing of the Church and Three Crowns or otherwise. Peshka finished his cup, then refilled it from a dented pitcher on the shelf.

His anger faded to regret. How long had it been since he'd had any decent wine to drink? All the way out here in the Farlands, the bloody armpit of the Ossory Empire, for something that wasn't even his damnable fault. An illustrious military career—with high marks for bravery!—brought to a tragic end through a simple misunderstanding. *You're only as good as the last five minutes of your service, no matter how shiny your medals are.*

He'd been forced to serve his remaining years at this border-fort along the Scar. More a prison sentence than a command post. But as the months went by, it had started to resemble an execution more than an exile.

Now this Inquisitor would take away the only thing left to him—his command. But no. Peshka couldn't let down his soldiers by letting Deza challenge his authority. So many of his men had been killed by those savages; there weren't many remaining to let down as it was. Their constant fear of the gnolls was bad enough, but they'd be downright terrified if they learned an Inquisitor had assumed command.

That butcher wouldn't give two shits for their lives. He wouldn't hesitate to send them to Vesenia for questioning.

No, Peshka couldn't let Deza take command. No matter the cost.

He poured himself another cup and knocked it back, emptying half of it in one swallow. He couldn't be empty-handed when Deza returned. He had to think of something. He twisted his mustache, looking at the map for the hundredth time. The terrain, the fortress walls, the wooden pieces—he desperately wished something would magically save them. He studied the map, as if a self-evident answer stared back at him, waiting for him to find it, yearning to be discovered. Yet, as usual, nothing came. No matter how many long nights he spent staring at the map, no matter what decisions he made—the survivors continued to dwindle away.

His gaze lingered on the pile of fallen pieces. How many days remained? How many more could fall before they were all overtaken by the gnolls?

Would it be tomorrow? Tonight?

Peshka sighed, raising his cup to his lips, then paused. What if his requests for reinforcements *had* been getting through to Duke Tyebald—but he'd been ignored? All because of that one little incident.

He pushed the thought away. He'd had a little too much to drink, was all. He hadn't even touched the girl. Not that he hadn't wanted to—but he *hadn't*, and that was the important thing. Never touched her. Just told the duke's daughter how beautiful she was. He hadn't meant it for himself. Hadn't he said that? He had meant for a future husband—again, not himself. Surely she knew what he meant. A simple misunderstanding. That, and perhaps too much to drink. He swished another mouthful of wine as he mulled it over. Even if he'd been sentenced to rot here, there was no bloody reason to punish his men for it.

He shook his head. *No. It was just gnolls killing messengers before they could make it out of these bloody Farlands.* Peshka peered into his cup and scratched at his chin. The riders could just be deserting, damning him and the rest of the garrison to their fate. Couldn't say he'd blame them. He wasn't too sure what he'd do in that situation. He sighed, twisting his mustache.

Several spindly orange hairs came off between his fingers. "Fuck!" Peshka threw the hairs to the floor and took another drink—but his glass was already empty. He growled as he stumbled back to the pitcher.

By the gods. How he wished for something stronger than this shit that passed for wine. Some of that Baskavian brandy he got to sample, back on that night when he was promoted to captain following the Siege of DeGaullis.

He had saved the entire city, dammit. It had been *his* idea to use the sewers to sneak under the enemy at the gates. *His* idea to use their own horses against them—and he'd led the bloody charge himself. Even got to see the King of Galasa at his promotion ceremony. *The bloody king himself, dammit!*

A smile crossed his worried face. What a grand night that had been. Promoted straight to captain. They had even thrown a ball in his honor. Oh, how he missed those rich noblemen's daughters wearing their fancy dresses—each dress likely cost more than his annual wages. But the way they had watched him in his dress uniform... He'd cut the impressive figure back in his prime. Back when his name was passed around the circles of nobility. Lauded for his strategic mind, his bravery, his horsemanship. They spoke only of his bright future, of the possibility of generalship, perhaps even marriage into royalty...

"Now *there* was a fine young soldier," he said, pacing. "Saved the whole bloody city... A *real* war hero." He looked down at his cup. "What happened to him?"

He'd give anything, for another dance at that ball—anything, to be that young soldier in that captain's uniform. A chance to do things right.

Though, in truth, he'd be happy for one more glass of that Baskavian brandy.

It would be his last request, if anyone gave a shit enough to give him one. He wasn't overly picky. Just give him something *strong*. Something that burned on the way down, reminding you that you were still alive.

Funny, how good those reminders felt. How sparse they were these days. Days when the end just stared at you—as close as your own reflection in a cup of wine.

Pity there were no more of those dwarven spirits they'd gotten. *Now those would curl your mustache hairs, all right—and just about anything else that wasn't nailed down. Probably for the best, though, with that bloody Inquisitor around.*

He wasn't sure how Inquisitor Deza would react if he discovered they'd exchanged goods with 'sub-humans'—or, even worse, risked human lives to save a dwarven mining party. He doubted the Inquisition would look very kindly upon either decision. Might even put *him* in cuffs. He knew, surer than the Nine Hells, that Deza would have some choice questions if he found the gift those dwarves had given them. Luckily, it was stored in...

Sweat beaded on Peshka's forehead. By the fates. He'd forgotten the bloody contraption was housed in the same tower he'd sent the prisoner to. Peshka began pacing faster. His shaking hands nearly spilled the remaining wine from his cup.

"No reason to go up there." Peshka swallowed, then took a deep breath. "*No reason* to go up there," he muttered again, with a little more resolve.

Peshka took another swallow, then went to top off his cup before that damn cold-blooded Inquisitor got back. He picked up the pitcher, then paused and growled. "What's taking that damn Inquisitor so long?" he said, the words slurring. "He's waiting me out, dammit! Trying to rattle my nerves."

He tipped the pitcher over his goblet, but nothing came out. He shook it, then looked inside before finally accepting it was empty. "Blast it all!" he bellowed, and threw the pitcher across the room. A particularly *glorious* throw.

But right as the pitcher reached its apex, the door cracked open.

"Sir," began First Sergeant Goren. "One of the soldiers on watch—"

The pitcher smashed against the wooden door. Luckily, Goren had the reflexes and good sense to use the door as a shield.

Flustered, Goren stepped into the room. She was only a few inches shorter than the door and nearly as broad, dressed in her full plate. She looked down at the metal pitcher, then narrowed her eyes at Peshka. Whether it was because she'd nearly been hit, or because she related to the metal object and took offense at its abuse, Peshka wasn't sure.

"And how many bottles of wine have you helped yourself to *tonight*, Colonel?"

"It isn't my bloody fault," said Peshka. "The damn Inquisitor's got my nerves ragged." But she didn't know that most his drinking tonight had happened before Deza showed up. He looked down at his feet like a scolded child. "Couldn't help myself…"

Goren said nothing; she only raised an eyebrow, which said infinitely more. *You've been helping yourself just fine, you fat liar. This is no different from any other night.*

Peshka blushed. "Ahem. I think you had something to say, First Sergeant?"

"Yes, one of soldiers on watch saw—"

An earsplitting crash rocked the entire building. The room shook. One of the remaining wine bottles on his shelf fell to the ground and shattered, but Peshka hardly even noticed. His stomach sank as he recognized the noise. He hadn't heard anything like that since the Siege of DeGaullis. It sounded like it had come from the western tower.

He looked up at Goren. "What the bloody devil was that!?"

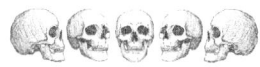

The soldier in the other cell continued to babble. "It's coming now. It's coming. It'll all be over soon…" His voice had calmed after two hours of feverish rambling. A few more muffled sobs echoed through the wall—then, at last, blessed silence.

I thought he'd never shut up. Time for some shuteye.

Malfus sank into the hay, waiting for exhaustion to claim him. He did his best to ignore the curious lice crawling on his skin. He didn't despise them—they had to eat, too. His time on the road had acclimated him to sleeping among small, creeping things.

The pain shooting through his body quieted to a whisper. If he didn't lie on his horse-bruised side, it was manageable. But try as he might, he couldn't keep his eyes shut. They kept wandering over to the barred window high above him. It allowed only a sliver of moonlight to shine on him. Mocking him. Making him envy the lice. They could scurry up the wall and right out that window if they chose.

How many more nights did he have left to see starlight—even if only through a barred window? He doubted he'd be afforded that luxury in the Inquisitorial prison. Rumors about it said prisoners were kept deep underground—though rumors were hard to come by from a prison that no one left alive.

The more Malfus thought about it, the more the pit of dread gnawed at his stomach. Perhaps that was just the moldy bread. Regardless, he found sleep as elusive as his freedom. He was finally alone. Finally, in silence. The conditions were ripe and fertile for sleep—like a field piled with fresh cow shit—and yet, his mind crawled with as many thoughts as there were things crawling on him.

Damn that dreadful Inquisitor.

He balked at the unfairness of it. A small fortune in silver had gotten him a laboratory suitable for his purposes. It had taken him months to locate that ancient necromantic rod the swamp-hag Yagyii told him about. He'd faced ghouls, a haunted mansion full of ghosts, an entire thieves guild, and even a werebat posing as a vampire. All while in that swampy shithole Monrovia—a dreary waste only marginally better than the Farlands. It wasn't even a part of the Ossory Empire, or under the Inquisition's jurisdiction.

Had he been doing anything so wrong? He hadn't hurt anyone. Did that Inquisitor have any idea how hard it was to find fresh corpses without resorting to murder? How would anyone ever achieve a greater understanding of necromantic arts if all its practitioners were burned at the stake? Not every necromancer was hellbent on lichdom and world domination. Not every necromancer created cataclysms like the Scar. *All it takes is a few rotten apples to give us all a bad name.*

Then his thoughts drifted back to her, as they did every night—Kiara. Her raven curls. Her piercing blue eyes. The way she had walked. The way she had *smelled*. Her magnificent mind. He could remember every sharp angle and soft curve of her face. It stared at him from the darkness of his mind. And now, all that remained of her was her middle finger.

Chains rattled as Malfus punched at the air above him. By all the gods, he hoped the finger wasn't rotting. He'd done everything he could to slow its decay. He'd worked so hard to preserve her. *For years now. Years!* Now it withered away at the bottom of the Inquisitor's bags, without him there to prevent its gradual necrosis.

He hoped there was enough magic lingering in the finger to prevent it from decaying completely. If it rotted away to a husk, Malfus didn't know what he would do. Didn't know what he would do *to* the Inquisitor. He had to find a way to save her, to bring her back...

How long had it been since he'd last cast the incantation? It had been so long. Could he even remember the spell? He scoffed. Surely he could. It was the first necromantic spell he'd learned. The first he'd been able to cast without struggling every step of the way, unlike all the other schools of magic. He could almost remember the first—

"Gahk!" Electric knives stabbed at his brain. The arcanull around his wrists throbbed.

"Damn things!" Malfus ripped his hands apart. The chains chimed, but only rewarded him with even more pain as the cuffs dug into the chafed skin around his wrists.

Malfus sighed. His anger melted away as reality set in. There was no escape. Not without the key to these damn cuffs, and getting his possessions back from the Inquisitor. He would have to see how things played out. If they managed to survive this latest debacle, he might have another chance to escape on the long road between here and Castillea. Though, the closer they got to Vesper—the sprawling Holy Capital, seat of Vesenian Orthodoxy and beating heart of the Inquisition—the less likely his chances became.

Why couldn't that zealot just let me be?

Perhaps it was the hopelessness of his situation finally catching up to him—perhaps it was his lack of sleep—but Malfus decided to do something he'd never done before. He crawled toward the lone beam of moonlight, got on his knees, and prayed.

"Not sure exactly how this is supposed to go," he muttered. "I know it's pretty weird getting a prayer from a necromancer, but—Vesenia. If you are real. Please. I know I've made mistakes. I know I'm far from perfect. But please, let me escape." He looked up at the moonlight. "Give me a chance to make things right."

He waited for a sign. Waited for anything.

But nothing happened.

Malfus sighed. "That's what I thought."

He turned away from the window and crawled back to the hay, then closed his eyes. His thoughts finally died down long enough for sleep to claim him. Even the lice seemed to be satiated. Currents of sleep flowed around him, lifting him up and away in their embrace. A small reprieve from the nightmare his waking life had become. The Inquisitor, the army of gnolls, the prison cell—they were tomorrow's problems.

BOOM!

A deafening crash ripped Malfus awake. The very world was being torn asunder. Shards of brick pelted his face. He rolled instinctively; the wall next to him collapsed, its bricks slamming into the pile of hay. He scrambled to the far side of his cell, coughing uncontrollably as dust filled the tower. His ears rang. He couldn't see. He waved his hand in a futile attempt to clear the dust, to see what happened.

What the fuck—

Chapter 7

We're Under Attack

"Do not seek to understand heresy. Just destroy it, in all its forms. Do you allow rot to spread across your fields, seeking deeper understanding? No. You start burning, and you don't stop until the rot is gone. Now, throw that torch on the roof." – Inquisitor Horace Vygrath

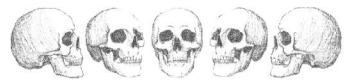

Morten opened bleary, bloodshot eyes. What was that? Had he heard something? He groaned. It couldn't be morning already. His head was still full of fragments of some bizarre, half-remembered dream. Something about a crowded tavern, dancing with dwarven women, spinning him about violently.

"What the fuck was that?" said a thin voice from the darkness of the barracks.

Finn, that weaselly ginger from the slums of Pomanća. Morten's mother had always said never to trust anyone from the city, especially so close to Monrovia. Now—with his luck—he'd gotten stuck bunking next to a slippery urchin who'd been peeled out of the gutter and thrown in armor. Finn had so many freckles, it looked like mud from a gutter had been spattered across his face. He was only a year Morten's senior, but made damn sure to let everyone know. Finn had dodged being the youngest on the squad, leaving Morten with that bullseye on his back.

"You heard that, too, right?" Finn asked again. Morten didn't bother wasting his breath on him.

"Heard it?" said Big Duncan. "It shook the whole fort." Big Duncan's bunk groaned as he sat up. When the calls to pay the Tithe had been sent, Duncan been the son of a butcher in a small town close to Morten's village. He looked big enough to heft a dead cow onto the butcher's block by himself.

A bright spark flashed in the darkness. Morten squinted, covering his eyes. Then the room grew brighter under the orange glow of a torch flickering to life. The flames revealed Sergeant Donovan's impassive face. Sergeant Donovan, or *Sarge*, was the leader of what few remained of their squad. Sarge was older than the rest of them, but not by much. Morten didn't know where Sarge came from; he'd been too afraid to ask. He didn't know what Sarge had done before joining the army, either; he couldn't imagine Sarge being anything other than a soldier.

"Come on, lads, get your kit on," barked Sarge. "Sounds like those furry fuckers are up to their usual shit. We'd best get up to ours." As ever, Sarge's voice was steady. He already wore his armor, somehow.

Maybe he slept in the damn stuff.

"Again? Damn those dogmen." Corporal Heimrich sighed, blinking as she put on her dwarven-made spectacles and tied her mousy hair back. "The lowest rung of sentient life. They create nothing—only destroy."

Heimrich rarely said much; when she did, it was with words Morten had never heard before. He wasn't sure what she was doing here. She had the mind of a scholar, not a soldier. She should have been a clerk copying legal papers behind some desk in DeGaullis, or studying wizardry in far off Akkadia. *But the Tithe isn't too picky when it calls.*

"Come on! Get ready!" screamed Corporal Higgins. "You heard Sarge!"

Morten rolled his eyes. They called Higgins *Little Echo* to his face, but plenty of other things behind his back. He'd been the fourth- or fifth-born son of some horse breeder in Cavílla, always going on about how rich his family was. It hadn't kept him from being sent out here to the middle of the Farlands with the rest of them.

Morten yawned, looking wistfully at his pillow. But on cue, the familiar toll of the alarm bell shattered any hope of going back to bed. He sighed, throwing on his too-large chainmail coat, then grabbed his crossbow and quiver beside his bed.

"It's not fair!" said Finn. "Can't night shift handle this? It's probably nothing—"

An ear-splitting crash cut Finn's protest short. The foundations of the barracks shook, and a stream of dust fell from the rafters. Morten had to grab his bedpost to steady himself.

"On the double, lads!" yelled Sarge. "Grab your crossbows and get to the battlements!"

"Come on! You heard Sergeant Donovan! Get to the battlements!" Corporal Higgins echoed Sarge's commands in his raspy voice, hoarse from always yelling.

Morten gripped his crossbow tight to his chest. The smooth wood felt heavier in his hands than usual. He didn't know what that crash was, but he had a bad feeling. He took a deep breath and followed his squad out the door.

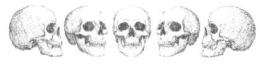

Coughing on dust, Malfus struggled to breathe. He rubbed his ears, trying to rid himself of that deafening ringing. He peered through the settling debris. Bricks fell from the crumbling wall that had once separated the two cells. In its place sat a massive granite boulder.

"Hey?" Malfus coughed again. "Gillfrey? Gilly? Uhh... Giles. That was your name, right? Are you over there?"

No response. Malfus looked closer at the pile of bricks and spotted Giles. His head and one arm stuck out from beneath the boulder. But the rest...

"Alas, poor Giles." Malfus bowed his head. "I hardly knew you."

The boulder was gigantic, even for a catapult—or so Malfus supposed. He doubted the gnolls had the collective brainpower to build a catapult, much less aim one, but that reasoning did little to comfort him or remove the boulder from the room. He took a few steps back as blood spread from beneath.

A draft of cold air blew in from his cell's newly remodeled window. A few bricks fell from its top, disappearing over the side. Malfus shifted from one foot to the other as he glanced at the hole across from him, then back at the farthest corner in his cell, away from it.

You goblin-livered coward! This might be your only chance at escape, and you'd rather sit and hide? You'd rather wait for the Inquisitor to come get you?

Malfus groaned as the chance for freedom won out against his safety. He slunk toward the opening. *Curiosity killed the kobold*, the voice in his head mewled, but he ignored it, hugging close to the floor as he crept to the exposed edge.

His hands shook as he reached for a brick at the edge of the hole. He pulled himself up with it, pressing his back against the wall, and leaned over the edge—then felt immediate regret.

His stomach dropped, his head reeling with vertigo. Wind howled in his ears and whipped his long hair back into his face. A sheer cliff stared up at him, dropping into a rocky valley far below. Malfus grasped the brick to steady himself, but as he did so, it fell free from the mortar. It plummeted, bouncing off the cliff just once before dropping into the abyss.

Malfus stumbled backward, sprawling. His breathing became choppy. The safety of the darkness of his cell beckoned to him.

Come on. Don't piss yourself. Get it together, you coward. Go take a proper look. With some effort, Malfus regained control of his breathing, then got onto his belly like a snake and slithered back to the hole. He ignored sharp rocks digging into his ribs. Reaching the edge, he swallowed, gripping the broken wall so tightly his knuckles turned white. Slowly, he stuck his head out over the ledge.

Wind buffeted his face as he peered down the cliff. A full moon lit a clear sky—dark, but with enough light to cast everything in dappled shades of gray. This side of the fort straddled the edge of a rocky cliffside, dropping over two hundred feet into a rock-strewn valley.

The ground at the foot of the cliff churned with shapes that blurred as they moved. His ears had stopped ringing now, but he wished they hadn't. The chittering laughter of the gnolls sounded twice as maddening as it echoed from so far below. Malfus couldn't begin to imagine the sheer numbers swarming below him.

There were no torches—no fires—just the occasional glint of sharpened steel or flicker of yellow eyes in the moonlight. Then, spotting a dark silhouette against the sky, Malfus gasped and blinked, rubbing his eyes, not wanting to believe them.

It seems Giles wasn't one for tall tales, after all.

The giant didn't look anything like he expected.

Yes, *giant*—as the name suggested—but so lean for its height, and with such long limbs. The one illustration he could recall from his studies at the academy was a far cry from what towered over the gnolls. The number of artists that had managed to return and draw pictures of giants from firsthand experience must have been in short supply. But no amount of artistic accuracy could have prepared Malfus for the sheer magnitude of it, even from this distance. The loose bricks next to him shifted each time it took a step. It moved with an unnatural fluidity that belied its massive size, which made Malfus uneasy—for a reason he couldn't quite grasp.

The giant abruptly stopped. The wave of gnolls ignored it, skittering past its legs like a swarm of ants. Dread clawed at Malfus as he watched the giant turn its bald head toward the tower, as if looking right at him with its dark, beady eyes. It reached down and hefted another boulder, shouldering it with ease.

A voice in the back of Malfus's mind yelled at him to run, but he stared on, too transfixed by the giant's lithe movements to move a muscle himself. Mixing with his insomnia, it looked so unreal, like a distant dream.

The chime of an alarm bell broke through the air like a thunderclap, snapping Malfus back to his senses. The implications of the giant readying another boulder pierced through his arcanull-addled mind.

"Oh shit." Malfus scrambled to the far side of his cell.

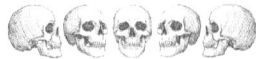

Outside was chaos. Arms of flame leapt angrily from the building across from Morten. Thick, black smoke billowed into the night sky. Soldiers ran past him in disarray, some armed with crossbows, others with buckets of water. The smoky air was filled with frantic orders, cries of pain, ceaseless pealing of the alarm bell, and the staccato snap of crossbows. In the distance barked the harrying laughter of the gnolls.

Flaming arrows hissed through the air like angry serpents, leaving amber trails in the night sky. Beautiful—almost enough to forget how deadly they were. Morten looked up. Finn and the rest of the squad were already two buildings ahead. He gritted his teeth as he ran after them.

It's the little things you noticed, when life was on the line. Death's finger tapped at his shoulder, and all Morten could think about was his little toe and the hole in his sock. Every step he took, that little toe improvised a new way to fish itself out of the hole, smashing against the inside of his boot. It didn't matter how many times he scrunched his toes up, working his disobedient toe back in; it proved quite the escape artist. Morten did his best to ignore it as he ran, but it slid around in there, slippery as an eel.

He yelped as a flaming arrow whizzed by, landing in front of his boot. If he'd been two paces faster, he'd be as dead as their old lieutenant. Better a hole in the sock than in the foot. He'd have to worry about new socks later. He was almost there.

"Come on, Private Morten!" Sergeant Donovan stood by the ladder, torch in hand.

Morten reached up with one hand to stop his oversized helmet from bouncing and clutched his crossbow with the other. Then he ran, cursing his toe the entire way. How much easier would his soldiering be if he were a bit bigger? He doubted Big Duncan's helmet was too big for him. *Why is it some men get all the size and others get none of it?* Between holed socks and bouncing helmets, soldiering was damn uncomfortable business.

"Up the ladder, Morten, quick time now," ordered Sarge. "We've got a battle to win." He gave Morten a reassuring clap on the back, then braced the ladder.

"Yes, Sarge," said Morten, panting.

The rungs of the ladder slipped in his sweaty hands as he climbed. As much as Morten wanted to believe Sarge's enthusiasm, he wasn't sure how favorable the odds looked tonight. Burning arrows flew overhead in droves. It wasn't the first night he'd woken up to flaming arrows lighting the sky, but he'd never seen this many before, and with that horrible crash from earlier... He tried not to think about it.

The closer he got to the top of the wall, the louder the gibbering laughter grew. Morten threw an arm over the ledge, nearly dropping his quiver as he did, but a large hand grabbed him, pulling him up on top with the others.

"C'mon, Sarge!" bellowed Big Duncan as he crouched by the ladder, nearly as tall hunched over as Morten was when standing.

Morten pressed himself against the parapets next to the others, close enough to smell their sweat. Arrows snapped hungrily against the wall next to them; the rest passed by overhead, close enough to reach out and grab. He ducked, ensuring his helmet didn't stick above the wall.

Big Duncan pulled Sarge onto the wall top.

"Well? What are you lads waiting for?" Sarge yelled. "Start firing back at these fu—"

Another crash shook the wall, with so much fury Morten dropped to his knees. From the corner of his eye, an explosion of bodies and bricks flew from the wall at the opposite end of the fort. Soldiers screamed as they sailed through the air like dolls. Morten shuddered as their screaming abruptly stopped. A boulder three times the size of a man thudded into the courtyard, bouncing once before rolling to a lazy stop.

"Where are those fucking rocks coming from?" demanded Finn, his eyes wide. "Do they have a bloody catapult or a, or a... t-trey-bucket?"

"It's *trebuchet,* you dolt," Corporal Heimrich said.

Finn made a sour face at her. "Well... do they have any of those, then?"

"Unlikely. Those savages aren't capable of creating anything. More specifically, they aren't capable of *not* destroying." Heimrich slid her dwarven spectacles onto the bridge of her nose. "Even if they managed to steal one and not burn it, they don't have the mathematical acumen to fire it with that level of accuracy." Finn just looked at Heimrich as if waiting for her to finish. "It means *no*, Private Finn. It's not a catapult or a *trey-bucket*."

"Then what is it?" Finn stuck his ratty teeth out.

"Come on!" Sarge yelled. "What are you sitting around talking for? Return fire, or we'll be dead by daybreak!"

The chittering laughter grew steadily louder. By Vesenia, how Morten hated that damn noise. He poked his head over the wall, unsure he wanted to see what waited out there. He swallowed as a horde of gnolls spilled out from the trees. More than he had ever seen. Certainly more than he had crossbow bolts for. The ones on the front lines shook their weapons in the air or pounded them on shields, dancing in a frenzy to some silent song of violence. Flickering orange dots among the trees betrayed the positions of their archers. Morten took careful note of those before ducking back behind the wall. He cranked the windlass of his crossbow, joining the ratcheting chorus of his squad as they did the same.

"Where's the fucking Colonel and first sergeant at?" Corporal Higgins yelled, still crouched behind the wall.

"Why? Do you need a personal invitation to return fire, Corporal?" Sergeant Donovan hefted his crossbow over the battlements. "Consider yourself cordially fucking invited!"

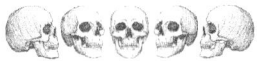

The alarm bell's shrill cry rang into the night. Unfortunately for Colonel Peshka, it hung directly over his chamber. He lifted a hand to his throbbing head as it hammered away to the same cadence as the bell's endless racket.

We already know we're under attack, dammit. Do we really need that bloody thing ringing the entire damn time? That was one fewer soldier with a crossbow in their hands.

Hazy orange lines streaked through the night sky above him. A bit blurry to his inebriated vision, but he knew what they were. The smell of smoke already hung in the air. *Third bloody night this week. Couldn't those gnolls give it a damn rest?*

"Are you sure?" Peshka asked, clutching his stomach.

"Yes, sir," First Sergeant Goren said. "I saw it with my own eyes. Private Giles was telling the truth after all."

"Of bloody course he was." Peshka looked across the courtyard at the damaged section of wall, a massive boulder lying among the bricks. He belched, filling the room with the stench of stomach acid.

"Well, what do you want to do, Colonel? What are your orders?"

Peshka absently lifted a hand to his mouth, wishing it held a glass of wine—but settled on twisting at his frayed mustache instead. "Make sure every bloody body that can hold a crossbow is up on that wall and firing! I don't care if they're in the infirmary! I don't care if someone has to bloody carry them up there on a stretcher so they can start shooting. We can't spare a single soldier, Goren. You hear me? Not a single bloody soldier to spare!"

She nodded. "I'll see to it, sir, but—"

"What? Out with it!"

"Can a crossbow bolt kill a giant?"

"I don't bloody know! Maybe... Maybe enough of them will."

If looking unconvinced was an art form, then Goren had mastered it.

Peshka scratched at his chin, then looked over at the western tower. A second later, a fire of his own lit behind his glossy eyes. "Wait. Find Corporal Heimrich. She'll know what to do."

Goren paused, looking even less convinced now. She glanced over her pauldron and dropped her voice to a whisper. "Are you sure that's a good idea, Sir? With the Inquis—"

"Don't you worry about that. Leave him to me. Just get it done, dammit!"

"Yes, sir." First Sergeant Goren's armor clattered like a banquet table during an earthquake as the big woman trundled toward the fortress wall.

"And get that damn bell ringer off the tower and on the wall with a crossbow!" Peshka yelled after her. He burped again, clutching his stomach. "Damn bloody gnolls," he muttered, then continued walking.

He didn't want to admit how much that boulder's crash reminded him of the Siege of DeGaullis. Though they had won, and though *he* had been the one to save the city, it had still been the worst three weeks of his life.

His stomach had no trouble recalling that fact as it twisted itself into knots over the memory. He burped again, this time tasting bile. "Bloody indigestion."

He groaned. Some days, he considered drinking less. But perhaps he needed to drink. He only felt this vile after he *stopped* drinking, not during. And he couldn't imagine leading a siege defense while sober.

Especially against a bloody giant.

He stifled another acidic burp, then surveyed the wreckage by the western wall. "Damn giant. Hope this works," he muttered.

"Colonel Peshka." A prickling, monotone voice called out from behind.

Peshka turned and saw the Inquisitor.

"Inquisitor Deza, why are you so *sweaty?*" asked Peshka. "You look like you saw a ghost." Deza's face betrayed slight surprise as he lifted a hand to wipe at his forehead.

Peshka didn't wait for him to answer. Turning on Deza, he pointed at the Inquisitor's face as close as he dared. "Well? Still need a sign from Vesenia on whether to let your prisoner aid us? Does a bloody giant work?" Peshka motioned at the boulder near the smashed section of wall. "*They* have a giant. *We* need magic."

"Absolutely not," Deza snapped. "I am going now to ensure that my prisoner remains secure."

Peshka rubbed his eyes. "Let me get this straight. During the middle of an attack with a sodding giant, instead of letting your prisoner use magic to help us, you're going to make sure he's still bloody locked up?"

"Yes."

Peshka could feel his face turning a deeper shade of red. "Even though he'll be tortured to death by your Inquisition if he survives the night… You're going to ensure his *safety*?"

"No, Colonel." Deza turned to walk away. "I am ensuring *our* safety."

"Our safety? *Our* safety?!"

Peshka yelled after Deza, but the Inquisitor kept walking. He didn't so much as flinch as two flaming arrows landed a few paces in front of him; he strode undeterred toward the western tower. His black cloak trailed behind him like a funeral veil.

Peshka growled, wanting to shout something with a good deal more profanity at the Inquisitor, but a painful series of burps kept him from saying anything he would regret.

"Damn lunatic," he grunted as Deza vanished. If the Inquisitor wasn't going to help, Peshka would have to take matters into his own hands.

Chapter 8

To the Gates!

"Bravery and courage? Ha! Lies, written in storybooks for children, so there'll always be more soldiers. Fear. She's the real constant in battle. But that doesn't mean you can't learn to fight by her side." — General Owen Murmillo, 'A Treatise on Good Soldiering,' excerpt from the Galasan Officer's Academy manual

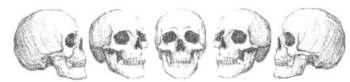

"I'm out of fucking bolts!" Finn yelped from nearby.

Morten reached into his quiver to check his own supply—less than half remained. He fished around with his free hand, grabbed as many as he could, then tossed his quiver to Finn. It landed short, skidding across the stones. Morten hated to admit it, but Finn *was* the better shot. Morten didn't give the street urchin much credit, but at least the other soldier knew his damn way around a crossbow.

Finn nodded at him, his ratty teeth sticking out in a crooked smile.

Morten nodded back, then gritted his teeth as he fought with his crossbow's windlass. Each crank made the muscles in his arm burn like fire. It finally locked into place and he grabbed a bolt. It slipped from his fingers. "Shit." His hand shook so much he dropped it *twice* before he got it loaded.

He clutched his loaded crossbow to his chest. Jaw clenched, he rose from the protection of the stone battlements—slow as the rising sun—with the gleaming point of his crossbow leading. He looked down its sights, searching for a target and waiting for the right moment. Damn, but the gnolls were close now. Every time he looked over the wall, there were more and more of them—close enough to count, but too many of them to do so.

Their eyes occasionally caught the moonlight, glinting yellow like beasts. It reminded Morten of the wolves that would prey on their chickens back home. Yellow eyes in the darkness, followed by chicken blood on the snow the next morning. Feathers everywhere.

He remembered the anger he'd felt. Finding Buckler lying there, the dog's throat torn out. Killed for barking, warning them about the slaughter. Killed for doing his job.

No time for that now. Not many bolts left. He had to make each shot count. *Always pick a target, even in a crowd.* The words of his crossbow master, Sergeant Clark, echoed in his head. Morten picked out a pair of those yellow eyes and focused on them. He thought about Buckler one more time, then took a deep breath, his finger inching down the trigger.

There was a *crack* like a whip and hot pain knifed into his cheek. His hand clenched as he lurched backward. His bolt flew wild into the night sky. "Dammit!" he hissed, reaching up to touch his stinging face. His fingers came away damp with blood—luckily, not with much. Just a few splinters, not an entire arrow. Morten hissed through clenched teeth and shook his trigger arm out. Nothing worse than going through all of that, only to miss.

His arm started burning again the moment he began cranking. He glanced around at the rest of the squad to take his mind off the pain. Finn, Big Duncan, Heimrich, Higgins, Sarge—all were busy cranking their crossbows, reloading, and firing. None of them showed weak nerves, not even Higgins. He wondered if all of them were a bunch of churning worries, like he was. Wearing stern faces to hide the terror stewing in their guts. Or maybe only he was scared. But being scared didn't do any of them a lick of good. The barking of their crossbows offered a small measure of comfort.

Morten finished reloading his crossbow and brought it up again. At least his hands weren't shaking anymore. He wanted to throw the damn thing over the wall and run away from this awful place. Leave this foolish business of soldiering to the others.

Why couldn't he have been content with farming?

He took his frustrations out on the gnoll sighted through his crossbow. His steady finger pulled the trigger, and it barked in response. He watched with satisfaction as his bolt struck the gnoll as it ran across the field, catching it in the throat. It dropped its axe, crumpling into a ball mid-stride, its legs folding underneath it like paper.

Morten smiled. He couldn't follow every shot. But he had to make sure he was hitting some of these bastards, dammit. Otherwise, what was the point? It didn't seem to matter; a dozen more had already taken the fallen gnoll's place. There were far more of them than he had bolts, and that was a fact. He shook out his arm, stretching. Nothing to do but get back to cranking.

The pain of cranking was easier to ignore, now that the burning in his arm had faded into numbness. It wasn't long before he finished cranking again. He slid another bolt onto his crossbow, then lifted its wooden stock to his cheek, squinting with one eye as he picked another target.

There was a loud crash, and the entire wall shook. Morten fell back, firing a stray bolt for the second time that night. He looked behind him and saw a boulder and a shower of bricks flying from the western wall. At least the boulders were coming from the other side, but now there was a gaping hole in the wall. If this kept up, the gnolls would bring down an entire section of it soon. But where were the boulders coming from?

"There you are," a voice called out.

He turned and saw First Sergeant Goren cresting the top of the wall. The wooden ladder creaked, struggling under the weight of her heavy armor.

"First Sergeant," Sergeant Donovan said, hurrying over to the ladder to give her a hand.

Goren refused the help, taking the last few rungs and making it atop the wall on her own. No small feat for someone up in their years and decked in full plate.

"Gather around!" Goren stood at her full height on the battlements. A flaming arrow passed right over her head, but she ignored it. "Sergeant Donovan, I need you and your soldiers to listen closely. A giant is attacking the western wall from the valley below." She paused a moment as her words landed, hitting them with the weight of an anvil.

"A giant," Finn echoed meekly.

"It's a giant?" wailed Higgins. "Giles wasn't lying? What can we do against a bloody giant? We're all doomed!"

"Get yourself together, Corporal!" Sarge grabbed Higgins by his mail, shaking him.

"A giant," sputtered Higgins, slumping against the wall like a wet sack.

A moment of silence passed. A weight hung in the air as they each realized that no matter how many gnolls they killed, their efforts wouldn't make a difference against a giant.

Morten hung his shoulders. "Our crossbows are just toys."

"That's right, Private Morten," said Goren. "That's why I'm here. To give your squad orders to ready the ballista. It's our only hope for launching a counter-offensive." First Sergeant Goren turned to Corporal Heimrich. "And I know you're the only one here who can read those runes."

There was more silence as they considered the First Sergeant's orders. That is, if you counted the constant alarm bell, screams of the wounded, and cackling gnolls as silence.

Corporal Heimrich looked to the western wall. The top half of an entire section had already crumbled into a pile of rubble. "A few more boulders in the right spot, and the gnolls could climb over," Heimrich muttered.

"It's your big day, Heimrich," Big Duncan said.

"Lucky me."

"Guess we better get to old trusty, rusty Gertrude," said Finn.

"Don't call her that, you peasant," said Heimrich. "Use her dwarven name, Urgo'Etrudzke, or no name at all."

Goren nodded to them. "You have your orders, Sergeant Donovan. I need to see to the rest of the defenses." She was already getting back onto the ladder.

"You heard the First Sergeant," Sarge said, standing and brushing himself off. He glanced over at Higgins, still squirming against the wall. "You, too, Corporal. On your feet."

Higgins covered his face with his hands, muttering to himself, just like Giles had when he returned from his patrol alone, covered in blood. Higgins had been the most vocal in denouncing Giles as a madman and a threat to morale. Morten shook his head.

"Luckily, the ballista is already in the tower over there," Heimrich said.

"And it's still standing. For now," Big Duncan added.

Sarge clapped. "Let's go! The rest of the garrison is depending on us!"

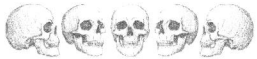

Malfus grabbed another brick from the pile, then heaved it through the hole. As it sailed into the abyss, he hoped it brained one of the bastards below—but he didn't wait to find out. *Only about a hundred more bricks to go, but perhaps...* He checked the partly collapsed wall that had separated the cells. Then he wiggled another brick free from the side next to the cell doors.

Outside the tower, the alarm bell kept ringing. Distantly, he heard shouting soldiers, but he couldn't tell if they were soldiers readying for battle or already *in* battle. Thankfully, the sounds came from other areas of the fort—with the exception of those flying boulders.

He threw his brick out the hole.

A painful sting dug into his scalp. "Ow! Dammit!" Malfus growled, scratching at it. Some of his bedmates had apparently clung to him for protection. He dug in his greasy hair until he found the offending parasite and plucked it free. It wriggled between two fingers as he squeezed harder. But he stopped as it was about to burst. Sighing, he flicked it out the hole in his cell instead.

He loosed another brick, raising it joylessly above his head. But before he could toss it, a familiar voice spoke behind him. He jumped.

"Ah, good," said the Inquisitor. "I see you've managed to survive."

Malfus dropped his brick like a child caught stealing a pie from a windowsill. *How does the bastard move so damn quietly?* He turned to the Inquisitor and grinned. "Wouldn't want to miss my own trial," he said, masking the surprise in his voice.

Inquisitor Deza sheathed his sword, then whistled as he surveyed the damage. "Seems your cellmate did not fare as well. I hope you didn't waste time getting acquainted." He shook the bars of Malfus's cell. "You have a new window, but your cell is still secure. Nowhere to go but down."

Malfus shook his head. "Aren't there more pressing matters than my security? Even if I got out, it's not as if I could do anything." He shook his shackles. "You do realize that there is an army of gnolls out there, with an actual *giant*?"

"So I've seen," said the Inquisitor, leaning against the bars of the cell, unconcerned.

So you've seen?! This smug prick. "What's the plan? You do have a plan, don't you? To get us out of here alive?" Frustration crept into his voice.

The Inquisitor yawned. "My goddess has little need for plans—only faith. I wouldn't expect a necromancer to understand. No, Vesenia has given me a vision of what will come." He turned to Malfus, with a light in his eyes that wasn't there before. "And it is *glorious.*"

Malfus would have scoffed, but his bone-dry mouth lacked the spit for it. He made a gagging sound instead. *What a time to run out of saliva.* This was it, though—his moment. He doubted he'd get another. *It's now or never, baby.*

He rested against the bars of the cell, just a few paces from the Inquisitor. He leaned over casually, as if to whisper a secret to a friend; he didn't let his utter inexperience with friends stop him.

"You know," he said, "I can help us. Why not let me raise a few dead to bolster the fort? They already have plenty to spare. It's not like we have to *kill* anyone." He waited for the

Inquisitor's response; none came. He didn't even bother looking at Malfus as he checked the security of the cell door.

Malfus had no choice but to continue, nervous as a merchant selling a dwarf a shaving kit. "Think of the lives we could save with just a little bit of undeath. If not for the fort, then for us. To ensure I make it safely to my trial, of course. You could add it to my long list of crimes! With a few eyewitnesses to bolster your case." His voice skipped past nonchalance and landed on wheedling.

The Inquisitor said nothing for a few moments. Then he turned to face Malfus, the steel in his eyes making Malfus step back. "You think I would simply watch as you commit heresy against my goddess? Vesenia, who offered her life to end the reign of the Eternal Emperor? For the sake of my own life?"

Malfus swallowed. He searched for something—anything—to get through to this zealot. "You know, had I been in the other cell, I would have been crushed to death. Then there'd be no need for a trial."

A faint smile crossed the Inquisitor's lips. The smile of a patient parent. "But even the clouded eyes of the faithless can see that you were not. Clearly, it is in Vesenia's divine plan that you face proper justice."

Malfus ground his teeth together. "Well, what about the *gnolls'* plans? What about when they storm the fort and chop us up for meat? What do they care about your goddess, or her justice? Why not just kill me and be done with it?"

"Kill you?" The Inquisitor looked genuinely surprised. "Necromancer. You are not going to be merely executed for your crimes. No, there will be questions. We are the *Inquisition*. Our priests will cut away your falsehoods so that only naked truth remains. They will catalog the true nature of your heresy as they excise each sin from your broken body. You will be begging for death by the end. Death is Holy Vesenia's final mercy. A gift." The Inquisitor looked at the hole in the wall. "You are welcome to jump out of the tower now, if you wish. I wouldn't be able to stop you before unlocking this door."

The Inquisitor's response hit Malfus as hard as the boulder had hit Giles. The calm way he said it made it worse. No malice. Just a man stating facts.

He gave Malfus an icy glare before turning away. Malfus watched as the Inquisitor strode away, wondering if he had enough spit to wet the back of his head. But before he could check, something at the foot of the door caught his eye—glistening in the moonlight.

"Most peculiar," whispered Malfus.

The Inquisitor turned around, impatience lining his face.

"You're bleeding, Inquisitor," said Malfus, pointing at the dark splotch in front of his cell where the Inquisitor had stood, and the spattered drops leading away.

The Inquisitor checked his arm. A thin trickle of blood dripped from his sleeve. He wiped it with his other hand, then left without another word.

Malfus mused. "Peculiar indeed."

Once he was sure the Inquisitor was gone, he scurried to the pile of hay, grabbed a handful, then returned to the bars of his cell. He smashed his face against them, reaching out with shackled hands. With his long, lanky arms, he could barely reach the blood. He dipped the straw in it, soaking up as much as he could. Then he settled back in his cell and began to weave the bloodied straw together.

I guess it's up to me to escape from this nightmare.

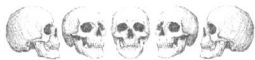

"We're almost there!" Sergeant Donovan yelled. "Just need to push past the front gate!"

The fighting was thickest there. A dozen other soldiers atop the gate rained crossbow bolts on a cluster of gnolls, which were using a fallen tree as a battering ram. The gnolls held shields overhead, but those did little against crossbows firing from such close range. For every gnoll they picked off, another took its place.

The battering ram hit the gate with a splintering *crunch*. There was no way to see the damage from up here, but it didn't sound good. Neither did the panicked shouting from the soldiers bracing the gate below.

The air stank of burning pitch, the smell rising from a steaming cauldron near the edge of the wall. Several soldiers struggled with it, heaving it closer to the parapets overlooking the gate. Morten grinned. *Pour some of that on those bastards. Send them back to the woods with tails tucked between their legs.*

He looked back at the squad, then cursed at himself for falling behind. Big Duncan's head towered on the other side of the crowded platform. The three soldiers next to Morten grunted as they hefted their cauldron. It squealed on rusted tracks as it lurched forward. Morten covered his nose as the acrid smell neared.

He paused. Something caught his eye, below the gates.

A gnoll with shock-white fur.

"Ghostface," Morten whispered. The gnoll was far larger than its comrades, wearing bone armor, and wielding a curved sword broad enough to cleave a man in half. Ghostface leered at Morten with blood-red eyes. Then it barked something in its growling language, pointing up at the wall where the cauldron was.

Morten ducked behind the battlements as he heard the snapping of bowstrings. The three soldiers pushing the cauldron didn't. One slumped against the burning cauldron, dead—which was good, since his skin began bubbling against the hot metal. Another vomited blood, pulling at the arrow sticking through his neck, red spurting between his fingers. The third screamed as he tumbled over the wall onto the gnolls below. Morten couldn't tell if he screamed after he landed, or if the fall killed him. The gnolls didn't wait to find out; they hacked the body to pieces.

Morten wiped spatters of blood from his face, his hands shaking as he ducked behind the parapet. Another *crunch* sounded as the battering ram smashed into the gate. Wood splintered and the soldiers holding the gate shouted in panic.

Where was everyone else? Morten looked around frantically. His squad called to him from across the gate. They sounded so far away. The soldier with the arrow in his neck stared through him.

"No," whispered Morten. It felt like someone else's voice. He didn't know why he was so angry; he hadn't known this soldier, but it reminded him of Buckler, lying in the snow. The next thing he knew, he was running toward the cauldron.

He smashed his shoulder into it, but it barely budged. Where was Big Duncan? He would have made short work of this thing. Perhaps his small frame was to his advantage for once. Though he struggled against the cauldron, the lack of holes shot through him meant the gnolls couldn't spot him behind it.

He yelped as hot metal burned his hands. *This won't work. I need to find something else. Quick, before they shoot me.* He looked around, trying to find something, anything, to help.

Then his helmet slumped over his eyes. *That's it!* He tore off his oversized helmet and put his hands inside it, using it to push against the cauldron.

The wheels of the cauldron made a crunching sound as they rolled over an obstruction—the dead soldier's hand. Morten tripped as the cauldron slid forward on its metal tracks, squealing like a pig. It neared the end of its tracks in silence and leaned toward the edge, tottering for several seconds, like someone finding courage before diving into an icy lake.

The cauldron groaned, then slammed forward.

Then its bubbling contents rained down over the wall.

Steam hung in the air. Then the screaming began. The battering ram thudded to the ground as its gnolls howled, tearing off their burning armor, melted flesh pulling off with it. Even from here, that stink of burning pitch, mixed with seared flesh and fur, was horrendous. Morten knew those screams would haunt him for nights to come. If he survived this one.

He peeked over the wall. A dozen smoldering gnoll corpses were strewn around the gate, motionless. Several more screaming gnolls were running away, or writhing on the ground as their flesh burned.

Morten could feel the hairs on his neck rise as the albino gnoll glared directly at him. It raised a ram horn to its mouth and blew a single note, wailing into the night. Ghostface glowered up at Morten one last time, then stalked away into the trees. The other gnolls fled into the woods, leaving their dead and injured behind.

"They're falling back! They're falling back!" someone yelled, snapping Morten out of his trance.

"He stopped the battering ram! The gate is saved!" Morten heard more shouting and cheering behind him, but now wasn't the time to celebrate. He needed to get back to his squad.

But before he could take a step, that blaring horn sounded a second time. It hung in the air like a curse.

The ground rumbled and shook. Trees in the distance rustled as something moved through them. They creaked, snapping apart, toppling over to make a path for something.

Something big.

"Another fucking giant!? Two fucking giants!?" someone yelled. Morten could barely make sense of the words; he was transfixed by the figure emerging, its head and shoulders towering over the tall pine trees.

Its smooth gray skin, like polished stone, stretched over lean cords of rippling muscle. Lanky, like a colossal scarecrow brought to life. As tall as the wall, if not taller. It carried a huge boulder, as big as the gate's massive doors. The giant continued its approach, the entire wall shaking with every step. It paused for a second before lunging forward and tossing its boulder into a bouncing roll.

Morten watched as the boulder hurtled toward the gate, right at him. He needed to move, but he couldn't help thinking how silly the boulder looked. Bouncing on the ground like a toy. Morten and the gate were part of some game the giant was playing. It was about to be his turn.

He closed his eyes. There was a violent explosion of stone and timber. Morten tumbled through the air, feeling weightless for a sickening second, his hands clutching at nothing.

And then—darkness.

Chapter 9

All is Lost

"Don't grasp your hilt unless you're drawing your blade." – Galasan saying

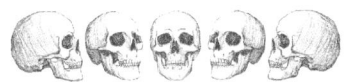

The gates exploded in a rain of bricks and timber. Private Vincent stood frozen less than a dozen paces away as debris flew past him. He thought he saw a soldier sailing through the air above him, but he couldn't tell. There was too much chaos—too much noise—too many things happening at once.

The soldiers that had been bracing the gate were standing there, one second. The next, they were gone. No screams, no bodies. Only a colossal boulder and a pile of bricks in their place. It was like they'd never existed. One of the gate's massive doors was little more than a pile of firewood; the other held on desperately by one hinge.

A deafening crash, then silence. Vincent wasn't sure which was worse. He swallowed, feeling exposed as he realized he was the closest to the open gate. His sword was in his hand, though he didn't remember drawing it. What good it would do with his hand shaking so badly?

Then he heard the gnoll. Its damn chittering laughter. One at first, calling out almost curiously, and then—dozens. A chorus of laughter, like a screeching swarm of locusts. The remaining door fell in a heaving crash, kicking up a cloud of dust. Vincent coughed, holding his shield in front of him. When he lowered it, he saw them—a pair of yellow eyes glinting in the dust. The haze cleared, and then there were more gnolls than he could count. All looking right at him. He swallowed and turned to run.

"Fire!"

Vincent ducked as a volley of crossbow bolts whistled above his head. Yelps cried out behind him.

"Form ranks! Form ranks now, dammit!" called First Sergeant Goren, her distant voice a beacon of order in the chaos.

Vincent was suddenly swept into a mass of moving bodies. Soldiers to his left and right formed lines around him, shields raised and swords at the ready. Vincent did the same, relieved his sword arm wasn't trembling quite so badly anymore.

He'd been the best swordsmen in his small village. Practicing with sticks, as all young boys did, then with wooden blades in the ring as a young man. He didn't mind when his name was called for the Tithe; the army felt like the only logical choice. But this was his first real fight against the gnolls—his first fight against anyone outside the ring, for that matter.

"Don't worry, lad, we can do this," said the mustached soldier next to him. "Let them fill those bastards full of bolts first. Soften them up."

Vincent nodded, gripping his sword tighter. He tried to remember everything Goren had taught him in the sparring ring. He didn't always win, but he did pretty damn well against the other soldiers his age. They'd always used swords blunted and heavier than the real thing. The one he held felt light as a feather and, by Vesenia, it was sharp. He'd made damn sure of that. How different could this be from the sparring ring?

"Fire!" the voice shouted again, followed by the reassuring snap of more crossbows.

Vincent ducked reflexively, even though the bolts were more than a foot above him. The gnolls pushing through the gap yelped and fell in a bloody pile. There were still crossbowmen on top of the walls firing down at them. Vincent allowed himself a nervous smile. Maybe they'd show these bastards the right end of a sword tonight after all.

Then the mournful cry of that damn horn sounded from somewhere outside the gates. That got his hands shaking again, back the way they were. The mocking laughter of the gnolls increased to a feverish pitch, and they pressed in, swarming over their dead and into the keep.

"Forward!" someone yelled.

Vincent didn't want to charge forward. The soldiers to his sides and behind him were, though, so he was given little choice. He was lifted and carried with the others like a leaf on a stream. He had thought he'd be one of the brave ones, but now that he was in the front ranks, all he wanted to do was turn and run. But there was nowhere to go. Trapped, like salted herring in a barrel. He couldn't breathe. He wanted to tug at the chainmail around his neck, loosen it so he could get some air, but he lacked a free hand with this stupid shield and sword.

The gnolls were getting closer. He'd seen them before, but not this close. So big. Snarling, with yellow teeth. Like they didn't have a care. They looked excited. *Bloody excited for this shit? Murdering one another?*

"Stop!" yelled Vincent. But who would listen, even if they could hear him? No, there was no stopping; the gnolls rushed forward in a tide of steel and fangs. No stopping the soldiers pushing him forward, either.

"Hold steady!" yelled the mustached man.

Vincent looked up. A gnoll an arm length away locked eyes with him and raised its sword. Vincent raised his shield and closed his eyes. Then there was a clash of metal that rattled his jaw. The gnoll in front of him howled inches from his face. Vincent wanted to smash his sword in its teeth, but there was no room. No room at all. He couldn't breathe again. He managed to raise his sword arm above his head, but he couldn't do much with it. So he pushed his shield against the gnoll's and cursed the best he could. Seemed like everyone else did the same.

Something hot and wet sprayed against his face. Blood. His? It didn't feel like his. Vincent glanced to the side, not daring to take his eyes off the gnoll completely. The mustached man clutched at his face, blood gushing between his fingers. By Vesenia, by all the gods, Vincent wanted to drop his sword and shield right there and run. But where was there to go?

"Close the ranks! Close the ranks, dammit!" First Sergeant Goren bellowed behind him.

He saw it. A glint of steel flashing in the moonlight. It was the only warning he got before a sword tip came right for his face. His sword rang as it whipped in front of him, parrying the other blade away. His entire arm rattled from the force of it—but damn, was he fast with this real blade. Blind Goddess, he was happy that training swords were so heavy. It all made sense now. Perhaps a real fight wouldn't be so bad after all.

The gnoll in front of him wasn't done. It barked, then swung from a different angle. Vincent parried again—fast as a viper—then smashed his shield into the bastard. It reeled into the one behind it.

Vincent saw his opening and lunged forward, catching the gnoll in its ribs, running it through nearly to the hilt. Blood gushed from its wound, making his hilt slippery. A look of surprise hit the gnoll's face. Then the light left its eyes. It fell forward, flopping onto him.

"No! Get off me, you bastard!" He pushed the dead gnoll away with his shield, but it was too heavy. He pulled on his sword, but its hilt slipped from his fingers.

This wasn't how it was supposed to go. Not how his first fight was supposed to go at all. He'd never had to pull his sword free from ribs in the sparring ring. Never had slippery blood all over his hand. Why was it so slippery? Why hadn't anyone trained him for this?

"Stop! Get off! Get off!" he yelled, but it didn't do any good.

The dead gnoll couldn't speak his language, couldn't speak at all, and the next gnoll was coming, its axe held high.

Vincent squirmed. He pushed at the corpse. Tried to twist free his sword. Nothing worked. The other gnoll was coming, and all he could do was stare up at its axe like a lamb. All he could do was turn his head and close his eyes, as if that would make it go away.

There was a *crunch*, followed by a wet, popping sound. He found himself lying on his back in the dust, the dead gnoll's face next to his. A terrible pain burned his cheek. He couldn't see out of one eye. Couldn't see! He wanted to touch his face, feel how bad it was, but his arms were trapped. All he could see from his other eye was a forest of angry legs stomping the ground around him and kicking dust in his face. One of the boots stepped on his hand. It hurt so bad he wanted to scream. Couldn't they see him down here? Why wasn't anyone helping him?

"Help!" cried Vincent. But all that came out of his mouth was a groan. The gnoll on top of him didn't feel so heavy. The fighting didn't seem so loud, either. His eyelids felt heavy.

Just needed a little rest. Then he'd be ready for the next round.

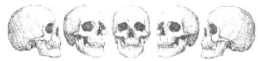

Being stuck in the second rank was like waiting for a turn in the chow line, except you were waiting for something worse than army food—if that were possible. There wasn't much Private Erich could do for the mustached man in front of him. He just held his shield up for him in case the other got knocked back, trying his best not to crowd him, though Erich kept getting shoved from behind. *Just look out for the soldier next to you.* That's the most important part of being a soldier, Private Erich reckoned.

He ducked as the sword in front of him nearly knocked him in the head on its backswing.

"Careful, you dolt!" Erich yelled, shoving the mustached soldier with his shield.

But who could hear anyone in this madness? The soldier in front yelled something unintelligible, probably even to him, then swung his sword.

Erich gripped his sword tighter, trying to find some small reassurance in the sharpened steel. He'd been the son of a blacksmith. He'd always played around with unfinished work in his father's forge. Pretended scythe blades were swords, shovels were pikes, and plows were giant shields. Then he'd run off and vanquish imaginary kobolds and goblins, or even an orc or two if he was feeling brave.

He looked down at the blade in his hand. For all a sword's glory, paired with the imagination of a scrawny twelve-year-old, its magnificence was lost on him now. It felt as dangerous as a cheese knife in his sweating hand as he looked at the horde in front of him.

"Hey! What are you doing?" shouted Erich as the mustached man's sword whipped back again, nearly clipping him in the shoulder.

But then the sword dropped from the other man's hand. He fell backward onto Erich's shield, nearly knocking him over. Erich saw his face. The mustached man looked up at him like he was asking for answers as he clutched at it. Erich wanted to help him, but there was nothing he could do with his hands full—not with the countless bodies pushing him forward, or the gnolls bearing down on him. And he didn't have any answers for this madness. He shook his shield until the dying man slid off and disappeared.

Now, all of a sudden, it was Erich's turn. He was in the front lines, and, by Vesenia, he wasn't ready for this. How could anyone be? He'd never *really* wanted to join the army. His name hadn't even been called by the Tithe. He wanted to stay, to become a blacksmith—but no; he had to escape.

The gnoll swung a hook-beaked sword at him, its blade still covered in blood from the last poor bastard it carved open. Erich managed to block it in time, but the impact knocked him backward. A shield shove him hard in the back, reeling him forward. The gnoll waited for him, popping its shield up and smashing it into Erich's jaw.

His teeth crunched together; he tasted blood. It hurt so bad it made him flush hot all over. Reminded him of the heat of the forge. Reminded him of his father's heavy hands. Metal wasn't the only thing his father hammered away on. Especially after a few drinks and a few bad hands of cards.

Erich spat out blood. The warm feeling inside him only got hotter, like flames of a furnace. That was fucking it. He'd bloody had enough. Had enough of being pushed around, hit, and beaten. It had gone on his whole life, and he wasn't going to take it anymore.

The gnoll wasn't there anymore. It was his father was now. He could see his blotchy, broken hammer of a nose, his cauliflower ears, his leathery skin. He could smell the alcohol on his breath. Could hear his mocking laugh.

"Fuck you! You bastard!" he tried to yell, but instead he growled, savage enough to rival the gnolls.

Erich grunted as he swung his broadsword in a perfect arc at his father's head.

Clang! He felt the reverberations jolt up his arm, his fingers numb from the force of it. The skull of his opponent gave out under the force of his blow, like soft, orange steel. The mostly headless corpse of his father tottered for a second, then fell backward. But there was his father again, standing right behind his fallen corpse. His father looked just as surprised as Erich was to see him for a second time tonight. But it didn't matter. No time for introductions—only time for steel. Time for his father to pay.

"Come on! Let's go! You bastards!" someone yelled nearby.

Orders echoed behind him, but Erich could hardly hear them. It sounded like *stop, come back,* and *hold the line.* But those were commands for someone else, not him.

Rage swallowed everything else. He ignored the forest of metal gleaming in the air in front of him. He stepped forward, his jaw clenched, his heart pounding, blood pumping so hard its beating was all he could hear—pounding in his head like a hammer on an anvil. His lungs took deep breaths, like bellows on coal, fanning the molten rage pumping through his iron veins.

"Let's go! Let's go!" someone yelled. Was it him?

It *was* him. He was the one yelling—roaring now, like a dragon. He might not have been the most graceful of swordsmen, but he swung his sword like a blacksmith's hammer.

Clang.

His father snarled, spraying spit in his face as Erich's sword cleaved into his shoulder. His father's lifeless body fell to the ground like a sack of coal.

Clang.

His sword smashed a wooden shield to pieces.

Clang.

His father dropped his broken shield to clutch at his open throat, falling to the ground.

His father, standing behind that one, stumbled forward now, scared, holding his weapons.

Clang.

His father's skull dented like iron straight from the fire.

Erich took another heaving breath, refilling his massive bellows, fanning that coal again—but it was going out. He looked up. His father was gone now, and a gnoll looked at him instead, as surprised as Erich was. One stood behind him, too.

What had happened? Gnolls were suddenly all around him. He'd pushed to the gates. Where were the others?

Something hit Erich in the back of the head, hard. Dropped him to his knees. He felt dizzy, almost drunk. He looked up; his father stood over him. He'd messed up bad this time. Knew his father was right mad, was going to beat him good.

Crank, reload, shoot.

That was the mantra that had gotten Sergeant Clark through every other battle, and it'd be what got him through this one. He'd tried to drill it into these young pups.

Clark cranked his well-oiled crossbow, reloading it in half the time it took the other soldiers. Hadn't he told them to use swine fat on the gears? But these youngsters never listened. That was just the way with them.

He picked a target from the crowd, looked it right in the eyes, then fired. Didn't bother to see if he hit his target—just went straight back to reloading. He knew he'd hit it. Besides, what would it matter if he missed? That was none of his business; not for any crossbowman worth their salt. His job was putting more bolts downrange than there were enemies. Time spent watching your bolt flying through the air wasn't time spent reloading another. Didn't matter if they were orcs, goblins, elves, or gnolls; the more bolts you put in those bastards, the quicker it would be over.

Clark had been issued a crossbow over a decade ago, when he'd first enlisted. He knew it better than he'd known any woman. Better than he knew himself. He'd shot crossbow bolts at every major battle in recent history. At orcs in the battle for Baskavia, on the goblin scourge Zyl-Tan in the battle for Dagger Pass, and even against the Monrovians in the Siege of DeGaullis. Though Colonel Peshka had only been a young lieutenant then, and he himself only a private, fresh from training like these young pups.

"Hold the line!" shouted First Sergeant Goren somewhere behind him.

The line of soldiers had begun to crumble in front of him. Hardly a line anymore—just a mass of churning bodies, screaming and trying to kill one another. Not at all like the Siege of DeGaullis. The troops had more discipline back then, unlike these young excuses for soldiers. Several gnolls had already slipped through the line's crumbling flanks. Those would be the bastards he'd pick off next.

Crank, reload, shoot.

As Clark fired his next bolt, something caught his eye before he could reload. A black-clothed figure appeared on the left flank, dark cloak whipping behind him as he darted from gnoll to gnoll, cutting down anything that made it past the soldiers. Clark had heard other soldiers say that an Inquisitor had shown up in the night. He thought someone had made it up.

Crank, reload, shoot.

He cranked his windlass, but couldn't keep himself from watching the Inquisitor fight. Weaving that sword like a needle, threading it through every gnoll that got past. The man swung some spiked metal chain or whip with his other hand, whistling through the air faster than Clark could track. The chain lashed out behind him, catching a gnoll that ran past by its leg and taking it off below the knee. The Inquisitor dodged another gnoll charging him, stabbed the one flailing on the ground, twisted into a pirouette, then skewered the one in front of him through the throat.

Two gnolls dead before Clark could finish reloading. He knew he had to get back to reloading, but he couldn't take his eyes away. He'd never seen anyone fight like that, not in any of the battles he'd fought in. Not with weapons like that, sure—but it was the Inquisitor's unnatural grace and disregard for his own life that made him so deadly. He didn't care about the danger he put his life in; didn't even have proper armor on. But his movements were so decisive, so certain, with not a second of hesitation. No anger on his face; just cold mechanical precision, like Clark's crossbow.

Clark heard whistling, then wind brushed against his face. He lifted his hand up lazily as if to swat at a fly, but it did little to stop the arrow that pierced him through the throat.

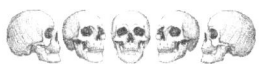

Corporal Nykah ran.

Past the gnolls at the gate. Past the soldiers fighting them. Past the crossbowmen, shooting their bolts into the fray. One of those unlucky bastards got shot right through the throat with an arrow, but she couldn't stop for him. There was no crossbow in her hands, and no sword either—just two buckets of water.

She was in charge of the stables. There were more pressing matters than the gate. She panted as she ran. Her full buckets threw her wildly off balance. Other soldiers ran past her in the opposite direction, weapons drawn and shouting. Some yelled at her, pointing toward the gate, but she didn't have time to stop.

Nykah felt like she'd been running her whole life. From her village, into the army. Running from the truth. From who she really was. But hey—at least she got to care for horses. If she could get to them in time.

A flaming arrow sailed past her, close enough for her to feel its heat against her cheek. She lurched sideways, almost tripping from the weight of her buckets. Why did the fucking dogmen have to light those damn arrows before shooting them?

She rounded the corner and saw the stables. Damn. This was bad. Flames licked at the night in anger, spreading fast across the stable's thatched roof. She dropped the buckets. Their water spilled—they were as useless as horseshoes on a hog now. She could hear the horses. Their panicked screams made her heart skip a beat.

"I'm coming!" she yelled, unsure why.

Her heart pounded in her throat as she ran into the doorway, ignoring the black smoke pouring out. Her eyes burned, filling with tears. She could barely breathe or see, and had to rely on muscle memory to find the first stall, fumbling blindly for its latch. The metal burned her hands, but she yanked on it anyway. The gate opened. The horse inside stared at her for a moment, then bolted. Nykah sighed in relief as the animals' instincts kicked in. She didn't have time to see them out one by one.

She moved on to the next stall, then the next. She made it to the end of the stable, freeing all the horses on one side. Halfway done. One more side to go. She would free them on her way out. But she stumbled, almost collapsing. Air scorched her throat. She coughed on the smoke. Everything began to fade to black. She had to get outside, fill her lungs with air again. Then she could save the others.

Everything went black.

Nykah thought of the night before she left for the army. Sneaking into the baron's stables. Taking his fastest horse. How she wished she could have stuck around to see his fat face. She could feel the horse coursing under her. It must have had a devil in it—by the all the gods, it was fast. She was going to meet Renya. Meet her at their secret place, and then...

No! Get up! A voice screamed inside her. She heard horses screaming. She coughed. She spat blood on the hay. Then she got up and ran outside.

She made it into the open air as her shaking legs felt near to collapsing. She took sobbing breaths. It felt like breathing in ice water, but her head began to clear.

The horses cried out again. She'd never heard a horse make noises like that. "I'm coming!" she said, wheezing as she pushed on the door. Before she made it in, something bit her on her back. A shiny bit of metal sprouted from her chest. Like a tiny metal acorn.

Nykah turned around. A gnoll stood a dozen paces away from her, clutching a bow. "You bastard!" she cried as she stumbled into the stable. For gods sakes. Couldn't the gnoll see she was already headed into a burning building? Why waste an arrow? Breathing through this smoke was hard enough already.

She fell inside the burning stable. Breathing felt harder now; her lungs refused to cooperate, making wet sounds. Everything tasted like copper and smoke. Horses screamed in terror as a wooden beam split in half and fell from the roof, wreathed in flames.

She had to hurry. No time for self-pity.

She lumbered to the first latch; her blistered fingers ignored the pain from the hot metal. The smoke didn't burn her throat anymore. She felt lightheaded. Tired. She had to hurry. A few horses left.

Rushing, Nykah reached the next stall, and then the next one. One more left. She stumbled and fell forward, hitting her head. She felt like she would pass out again. The arrow didn't hurt. Everything was so damn hot. Needed some water. Where had she put those buckets? So thirsty now. Some water and a little rest, and it would be better. Her throat was so parched.

She collapsed.

She was in her own personal hell. All over again. Like the night before she'd run. Her mother was crying, clutching her prayer beads after finding out. Her father wouldn't even look at her. But what hurt most of all was her younger brother. The things he had said to her. How had he even learned those words?

What was she doing in here?

The horse cried out, snapping her back to the horror of the present. Nykah lunged for the latch on the final stall. Opened it. The horse inside thundered past her. Its brown eyes wide with fear, and maybe—gratitude.

Nykah turned to flee, but no. She was lying on her back for some reason. So tired now. It didn't hurt. She just wanted a drink of damn water. Maybe Renya would bring some.

Sunflowers surrounded her. She watched them swaying in the breeze. Renya would come this time. It would be different; they'd meet in their special place. Who cared if Renya was the baron's daughter? If she'd given her word, then Nykah knew she would keep it. Renya would be here, and Nykah wouldn't have to join the army. They could run off together. This time Renya would be with her. She wouldn't have to run alone anymore.

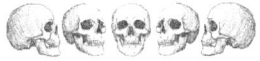

Morten opened his eyes, staring up at the stars in the sky. Orange lines streaked overhead. That was the second time tonight he'd dreamed of dwarven women throwing him. He felt peaceful. Something soft held him in a warm embrace. He wanted to close his eyes and sleep right here.

Then the pain slammed into him like a hammer. He groaned and grabbed his head. His ears rang, and his ankle throbbed. Pain was good. It meant he was still alive.

He fumbled around for his dented helmet and put it back on his head. Hay fell from it, into his face and hair. He hardly noticed. He was lucky to be alive. Grateful, even.

Morten pushed himself up from the wreckage of the broken haycart. He'd landed to the side of the gates, or what was left of them. Men fought there now, holding back the gnolls, but they had started to slip through. Morten reached for his crossbow, but he'd lost it somewhere in his fall. His squad was nowhere in sight. He looked up; the western tower stood in the distance. Had the others made it? He had to get to them.

Shaking his head, he began making his way there. His ankle was tender, but he pushed through the pain with a limping jog. He turned a corner, cutting past burning stables.

Then he froze. "Oh fuck—"

His voice caught in his throat. A gnoll stood over him, its bow and arrow pointed right at his chest. There was nothing he could do. Nowhere he could go. Morten closed his eyes and sucked in his breath. Why he decided to die with a lungful of air, he didn't know—but it seemed like the right thing to do.

Then a riderless horse thundered from the burning stables, smashing into the gnoll. It yelped and flew through the air like a rag doll. Morten swallowed, looking into the deep brown eyes of the horse as it sped past.

"Morten!" a familiar voice called out. "Over here!"

Finn waved for him. He and the rest of the squad were making their way across the courtyard to the tower. Morten did a quick headcount—everyone was there except Corporal Higgins. Morten allowed himself a sigh of relief, then ignored the pain in his ankle as he hobbled after them.

Chapter 10

The Lone Tower

"A soldier's worth is derived from their ability to endure suffering, not their capacity to inflict it." — General Owen Murmillo, 'A Treatise on Good Soldiering,' excerpt from the Galasan Officer's Academy manual

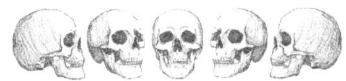

Morten licked his dry lips. He stumbled after the other four, favoring his left ankle. The fortress was a ghost town over here. Eerily silent. Shouts of soldiers and ringing steel echoed behind them like a horrible dream. Smoke rose from the buildings around them. But their orders took them in a different direction.

A twisted arm stuck from a pile of bricks next to a giant boulder. A crumbling section of wall next to it threatened to collapse entirely.

The western tower was just ahead. Still standing, for now.

Morten's heart pounded, and his hands were sweating, but he was reassured by the rest of the squad being here. All of them making it past the front gates had been no mean feat. All except Corporal Higgins. No telling if Higgins was dead, or if he'd run off to hide. At least Morten didn't have to hear his constant yelling.

The wall next to them exploded. Morten lunged forward, landing on his stomach and knocking the wind from his lungs. Another giant boulder smashed onto the ground behind them with a crash that Morten felt more than heard. Bricks cascaded from the wall. A section of wall larger than he was toppled into the courtyard. The wall was little more than a pile of bricks and rubble, half its original height.

"By Vesenia, hurry! Before it takes the tower down, too!" yelled Sarge. Then he stepped forward, kicking the tower door in.

Morten swallowed, trying not to think how close that boulder had been to the tower. Then he pushed himself up and followed the squad inside.

Something was off. Wind blew through the tower and out the door behind them. Blood was thick in the air.

"Well, that's new," Finn said.

Morten wasn't sure if he meant the gaping hole that opened into the night sky, or the giant boulder nestled between the two cells.

"Ugh, what's that smell?" Big Duncan pinched his nose.

"Giles?" Morten ran to the cell, grabbing the iron bars and peered inside.

Black ichor spread in a glistening pool from under the boulder. A strange shape masked in shadows stuck out from one side of the pile of rocks. Morten leaned forward to take a closer look. It was Giles. Or what was left of him. His one arm was bent at too many angles, splayed out in front of him like he had attempted to crawl away in his last moments. Flies already buzzed around what remained of his face. It looked more like a swollen plum fallen from a tree.

Morten didn't want to remember Giles like that. But he couldn't look away. It was seared into his mind now, branded behind his eyelids, sharper than his memory of his own mother.

"Oh, hello!"

He jumped as the Inquisitor's prisoner emerged from the shadows. The thin man strutted over and leaned nonchalantly against the iron bars of his cell. Covered head to toe in brick dust, he looked like a ridiculous ghost.

"This the prisoner you were talking about?" Finn asked. "Doesn't look so scary to me."

"Yeah. What should we do with him?" Morten asked. He had nearly forgotten about him.

"Nothing," said Sergeant Donovan. "We've no time to babysit."

Heimrich looked at the stone ceiling. "The structural integrity of the tower is intact for now. We'll need to move the ballista before it collapses." She glanced at the prisoner. "If it does... Honestly, it's a better fate than whatever the Inquisition has in store for him in Castillea."

The prisoner smiled. "Trust me, I've considered diving out that hole a few times already. Haven't quite worked up the courage yet, but—the night is still young."

The prisoner's grin unnerved Morten. How could he smile at a time like this? And with Giles's corpse right next to him.

"Let's go," said Sergeant Donovan. He marched up the stairs, and the others shuffled behind him.

Morten started after them, but paused. He looked back at the pitiful prisoner, thinking of something to say.

The prisoner let out a hollow laugh. "Oh, don't worry about me," said the prisoner, as if reading Morten's mind. "I'm probably safer in here than you are." His fingertips brushed one of the iron bars. "Might be nice having these bars between me and the gnolls, once they make it in. They'll save me for dessert."

Before Morten could think about that, another crash swayed the foundations of the tower. Morten grabbed the bars of the cell, stopping himself from falling face-first into them. Bricks crumbled from the hole in the wall. It was several terrifying seconds before the entire tower stopped shaking.

Sarge's voice echoed down the stairs. "Let's go, Private Morten! That's an order!"

"Shoo, off with you." The prisoner waved him away, chains rattling.

Morten turned and left. He ignored the pain in his ankle as he took the stairs two at a time.

"Hey, watch it!" Big Duncan lumbered past, hefting two wooden crates stacked on each other.

"Sorry," said Morten. He stepped down the stairs to make room before climbing up.

It was dark and cramped up there, lit only by moonlight trickling in through a single window and Sarge's guttering torch; both cast long shadows around the room. The air smelled like rotting wood and old leather.

"Give me a hand with this, will you?" said Finn, grunting as he struggled with a crate. It was the same size as the crates Duncan had carried two of. It took both of them to lift one.

"Where the fuck is Corporal Higgins?" Sarge smashed his fist on a crate. "I've had it with that coward! If he's alive after this, I'm going to lock him up in there with Giles!"

Heimrich, smaller than the others, squeezed through stacks of boxes. "Hold that torch steady for me! I'll start getting her ready." She made her way toward a large shape in the corner, obscured by a brown tarp. She pulled off the tarp, filling the room with dust. It made Morten's nose itch, but he didn't have a free hand for scratching.

When the dust cleared, Morten stared at a marvel of engineering. The ballista was as beautiful as it was deadly, its craftsmanship far beyond anything made by human hands. The entire thing shone with a green metallic tinge, even its most intricate gears. It had been forged from a dwarven alloy Heimrich called mythril. Its slender curved bow arms contrasted with its angular frame. Besides its two horizontal arms on the sides, a third, vertical one provided extra power. The three arms intersected at the front, its prow adorned with a dwarf's bearded face hammered from solid mythril. Bolts were loaded through the dwarf's mouth, and all shots fired under the scrutiny of its gaze.

The entirety of the machine was scrawled with ornate runes. Most were embossed in silver, but some by the cranks and levers were painted bright red or yellow—command runes that explained the device's operation.

Only Heimrich knew how to read any of those. She'd explained some to Morten once, but it'd been the closest he'd ever gotten to a girl that wasn't his mother. He desperately wished he'd paid more attention then. *Just a bigger crossbow...* Morten almost laughed at the absurdity of that thought. This was nowhere near as simple as pointing and pulling a trigger. He wasn't even sure where its trigger was.

He couldn't believe the dwarves had given away something so priceless. Heimrich said one of the dwarves they'd rescued was the son of a prince—or merchant, or merchant-prince; Morten couldn't remember which. He wasn't sure how Heimrich knew dwarven in the first place. Never thought to ask. He'd have to find out, if they survived the night. He'd do better to know everyone from his squad. Even Finn.

"Hey! Come on dummy!" piped Finn. "What are you waiting for?" Morten hadn't realized he'd stopped moving.

"Sorry," said Morten, then resumed hefting the heavy crate, walking backward. He couldn't help it—the greater the danger, the more his mind sought an escape from the present.

They stepped onto the outer wall, into the chill air. Several crates had been stacked on the edge of the wall by Duncan. Morten walked over as quickly as he could.

Fires had spread around camp. Smoke obscured his view of the front gates, but he could hear the clash of steel, the screams of soldiers, and the howling laughter of the gnolls. At least he wasn't at the gates, though a stray boulder could crush him at any moment. But it seemed those had stopped, for now.

He smiled at the twist of fate. They'd saved a group of dwarves from gnolls, and now the dwarves would save them. He wondered what the Inquisitor would say if he knew their only hope for salvation tonight came from dwarves.

Morten had never been particularly devout, but he'd attended services to Vesenia growing up. He hadn't questioned his religious beliefs deeply—and probably wouldn't have at all, had an Inquisitor not shown up the same night they needed to deploy a dwarven ballista. How could dwarves and other sub-humans be as bad as the Inquisition taught, if they created things as intricate and beautiful as this? The Inquisition proclaimed dwarves were nothing but greedy miners, focused only on worldly riches. Yet they had given them this weapon freely.

Finn yelped at him. "Watch out behind you!"

Morten cried out as his injured ankle smacked something hard, wrenching him sideways. The heavy crate shifted, smashing him against the wall before toppled over the parapet. A wave of vertigo pulsed through him as the crate dashed into pieces against the cliff wall in an explosion of horseshoes. They looked surreal, glinting in the moonlight as they rained on the gnolls at the foot of the canyon. Finn's hand on his shoulder was the only thing that had kept him from tumbling over the edge and joining the horseshoes far below.

"Are you okay?" said Finn.

"Y-yeah. I think so. Thanks," said Morten, sheepish.

"That was close. Come on, let's go."

Morten followed Finn back into the tower. Strange. He'd only had a second to look, but he hadn't seen the giant down there among the gnolls. Inside the tower, they'd cleared a path for the ballista, no doubt thanks to Big Duncan, who leaned against the wall, drenched in sweat. Sarge stood over the ballista, holding a torch for Heimrich, who labored over the machine with the patience of a midwife.

"Almost ready," Heimrich said. She poured oil on ballista gears, then checked the cables running to the bow arms. Satisfied, she nodded, then pulled a side lever.

"Get pushing, lads!" Sarge said, holding his torch aloft.

Morten grunted as he pushed the front of the ballista with Finn. It wasn't until Big Duncan lent his aid that the contraption creaked and budged. Heimrich steered it from the back, while the rest of them hauled on it from the front. Sarge led their little parade, torch first.

There was a dull rumble, and the entire tower trembled.

"What was that?" asked Morten.

"You felt it, too?" said Big Duncan.

"There it is again!" yelled Finn.

The foundations of the tower shook a second time. Thin streams of dust fell from above, leaving silver threads through the beam of moonlight. Then the shaking came again, a few seconds later. Now the entire tower shook. It was different from the boulders—not as severe, more constant. It came every few seconds, in a steady, thumping cadence, like a marching drum.

"Get that fucking thing outside now! On the double!" yelled Sarge.

"Whatever that is, it doesn't sound good," said Morten.

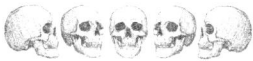

That doesn't sound good.

Malfus braced himself against the cell bars. A few bricks tumbled from the nearby hole. The boulder beside him trembled with each shake, making wet noises as it ground the corpse beneath it into paste. The entire tower swayed, like a twig in the breeze. Malfus could hear something else, a rhythmic sound from below—like two rocks cracking together.

Go on. Look outside. Take a tiny peep.

He ignored the voice in his head and pressed himself further against the bars. A growing pit of dread was sawing his stomach in half. Every passing second, that cracking noise got nearer. The seconds between shakes stretched into an eternity. A terrible thought occurred to him—he would be in the direct view of whatever appeared through that hole.

Malfus darted forward, slid across the stones, and pressed against the wall beside the hole. Right as he did, something huge moved outside it. Malfus held his breath; his throat was paralyzed with fear as the thing rose into view.

At first, it looked like another rocky section of wall cresting the edge of the hole. But it kept rising, timed with the tremors shaking the tower. All he could hear was the crunch of stone—aside from his pounding heart. The rocky surface covered the hole now, blocking the moonlight. A glistening sphere, black as onyx, emerged—close enough for Malfus to reach out and touch. He squinted at it from the shadows.

Then the dark sphere *blinked.*

That's no rock.

More of the giant's terrifying visage came into view. A second black eye, a craggy outcrop of a nose, and finally a mouth, twisted into a sneer. Its head was taller than the hole in the wall, and nearly as wide. *Big enough to swallow me whole. He wouldn't have to chew very much.*

Its black eye squinted through the hole, inspecting its handiwork.

Then the tower shook as it leaned back. Bricks tumbled from the side of the tower as a gray finger—wide as a tree trunk—pushed through the hole. Malfus pressed himself so hard against the bricks, he could feel their jagged edges digging into his spine.

The giant rolled the boulder forward. There was a faint popping sound as Giles's head burst like a ripe melon. The giant laughed. It began as a dull rumble, and grew into a roaring landslide. Malfus covered his ears as the laughter shook the walls of the tower and reverberated in his ribcage. He coughed.

The laughter stopped.

Malfus uncovered his ears, clasping his mouth instead as an itch pricked his throat. He pressed backward, thinking very small thoughts. He was a tiny insect. Too small to be seen.

Go on. Jump out, wave your arms. Show him you're here. Give him something to laugh about. He can smash you like the cockroach you are. End your time with the Inquisitor. No more Inquisition. No more torture. A tiny squish, and it's all over.

Malfus shook the thoughts away. *Shut up! Shut up!*

The giant stuck its nose through the hole. It sniffed, then sniffed again. Air rushed past Malfus, pulling at his long hair and tattered rags. Then—silence.

He didn't dare move. Didn't dare breathe, though his lungs burned. He closed his eyes and pressed against the wall, the bricks grinding against his cheek. He wished he could turn incorporeal, like a wraith. He'd slip through the wall and fly into the night. *There must be a spell for that.*

The giant exhaled, a foul gust of wind filling the tower with a smell of sour milk and wet earth. It muttered something to itself that sounded like boulders grinding together. Then the tower resumed shaking.

Malfus's lungs were about to burst. He finally allowed himself a few gasps of air. His legs shook uncontrollably. It was several more seconds before he gathered the courage to look at the hole. The giant's face was no longer there. Instead, he saw a wall of gray flesh, as dark and hard as the stone brick around it. The torso slowly ascended as the giant climbed the tower.

Ugh. I hope I don't have to see its massive—

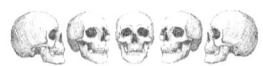

Morten looked up. "What is that?"

"I don't know! But it's getting worse!" said Finn. The entire tower swayed.

"Hurry up, lads!" said Sarge. "Get this damn thing outside! Now!" He motioned at the doors behind them, waving his torch so hard its flame sputtered and went out.

But Morten and the others had stopped pushing. Instead, they stared up, in unison. Bricks in the wall pressed inward, like a potter pushing their thumbs into wet clay. Dust fell from the ceiling as wooden rafters creaked. Then the room darkened as something blocked the window.

Heimrich clutched the ballista as she examined the crumbling mortar. "Get away from the walls!" she yelled.

But it was too late.

A crash split the air like thunder. As Morten's world exploded in loose bricks and debris, a huge blur of gray ripped past him.

The force of its fury threw him into the air, tossing him into a pile of crates. Rock shards pelted him. The wooden boxes splintered apart. He heard a strange, hollow *pop*, followed by a wet *slap*. Something warm sprayed his face. He wiped blood from it for the second time that night, then looked through the settling dust. He wished he hadn't.

A pair of legs stood where Sergeant Donovan had been, but the rest of him was gone. All that remained was a pink smear of meat and chainmail splattered across the far wall. Blood spurted from the legs. Then they toppled over, falling to the floor and kicking like headless chickens.

The giant pulled its arm back, its horrible face leering down at them through the new hole in the tower.

MALFUS - Stone Giant Attack   Art by Dejan Delic

Chapter 11

Urgo'Etrudzke

"A well-made anvil fears no hammer." – Dwarven saying

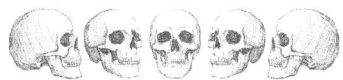

The giant clung to the outside of the tower, glaring down at them with coal-black eyes. It was an even more terrible sight than it had been at the gate. It peered down at the bloody stump of Sarge's remains, then gave a heaving laugh, as loud as a mountain collapsing.

Morten flung his helmet off. He had to cover his ears before the sound ruptured his eardrums. Even with his ears covered, the noise vibrated in his bones.

Heimrich stood in front of him, pointing at something while her mouth moved. Morten's ears still rang from the giant's laughter. Was Heimrich yelling at him? Dammit. Where was his crossbow? How could he lose it at a time like this? His brain was a bowl of day-old porridge. Where was Sarge at? He would know what to do. He always knew what to do.

Heimrich grabbed Morten by the shoulders, pulling him back to the present. She looked him right in the eyes and yelled, "Crank!" She pointed her sword at the ballista. Morten hadn't seen her draw it.

"Duncan! Grab a bolt and get it over here!"

"Aren't we supposed to load it first?" asked Finn. "Isn't this unsafe?"

"Unsafe!? That ship has sailed, Finn!" yelled Heimrich. "Now crank!"

Crank? What could the ballista do against this monster? Morten felt nauseous at the sight of the splattered remains of Sarge dripping from the bricks. But he didn't argue—he gritted his teeth and cranked for all he was worth. Finn cranked on the other side. Big Duncan ran for the stack of bolts on the far wall. Heimrich worked on the ballista's gears and levers.

The machine roared to life with an angry, mechanical growl. Its gears ratcheted together, pulling back the thick steel cables of the bow arms. A drop of sweat rolled down Morten's forehead and got stuck in his eyebrow. He didn't dare stop cranking to wipe it, no matter how badly it itched. If cranking a crossbow was bad, this was ten times worse. His arms were on fire, and he'd only begun.

"No, no, not the one with the rope!" Heimrich yelled at Duncan. "Never mind. Just hurry! Hurry!"

The bolts were bigger than a halberd and forged from solid steel. A wicked barbed tip glinted at one end and a line of rope trailed from the other. Duncan ran back, cradling the giant bolt. Even he strained from its weight. They used to joke about Big Duncan being half-giant. It didn't seem so funny now.

Where *was* the giant? Why hadn't it smashed them all to a bloody pulp? Morten dared to glance out the hole in the wall, expecting a massive hand to reach through it and crush him at any moment. But the giant just watched them, amusement on its horrible face. Stones above him groaned as the tower swayed in the giant's direction.

"Duncan!" Heimrich screamed.

He scrambled forward. Only a few steps to go.

"Look out!" Finn shrieked.

The giant reached into the hole and backhanded Big Duncan, as if swatting away a pesky fly. Duncan flew across the room and hit the wall with a sickening noise. The giant roared in pain; the ballista bolt stuck out from the bottom of its palm. It shook its hand, and the bolt thudded to the floor, a dozen paces away. Its barbed tip glistened with dark blood as thick as tar.

"Duncan!" yelled Morten.

But Duncan just lay against the wall, whimpering as he nursed his shattered arm. He tried to push himself up, slipped in a pool of blood around him, then slumped over, motionless.

"Finn, grab that bolt!" shouted Heimrich, her knuckles bone-white around her sword hilt. "Morten, keep cranking!"

"Cranking? We should be running!" yelped Finn.

"Grab it now, dammit!" Heimrich pointed her sword at Finn's throat, a crazed look in her eyes that her glasses did little to hide.

Finn swallowed, then ran for the bolt. Morten kept cranking. Heimrich gave him another look, then set her sword against a wooden box and pulled levers covered in red runes.

Morten gritted his teeth, fighting the windlass on every rotation without assistance. Finn struggled, too, the tip of the bolt scraping on stone as he dragged it. Morten fell backward as the ballista arm locked into place with a satisfying *click*.

It was ready to fire.

"Morten, help Finn!" Heimrich twisted a small dial that angled the ballista upward, toward the gaping hole where the giant howled in pain.

Morten hefted the trailing end of the bolt and carried it the last few steps. He and Finn grunted, lifting it to the stern-faced dwarf's mouth. The heavy bolt slid into the grooved track of the ballista. There was a mechanical *click* as it locked into place. It was ready.

Morten breathed a sigh of relief—but then he heard a hair-raising growl. A shadow passed over them. Looking up, the giant's hand was poised above the ballista, ready to smash them, like a spoiled child tired of its new toys.

He heard Heimrich yell. She jumped on top of the ballista, brandishing her sword. "Don't you lay a fucking finger on Urgo'Etrudzke, you cur!"

Time slowed to a crawl as she leapt from the ballista, thrusting her sword into the giant's hand. It howled. Her sword stuck from its palm like a tiny nail, with Heimrich holding on for dear life.

The giant growled, shaking its hand until the sword pulled free. Heimrich fell with it, landing hard on her back against the ballista. The giant pressed its middle finger and thumb together, then *flicked* its tree-sized finger. It ripped Heimrich's sword arm clean off at the shoulder. Her spectacles glinted in the moonlight as they flew across the room. She fell onto the ballista in a heap, pinned between its frame and its taut cables.

The giant lurched its horrible face into the gaping hole, letting out a roar that shook the entire tower. Morten covered his ears, fumbling backward into against a stack of boxes. He was going to vomit.

"*Kelak ni'bodan, Urgo'etrudzke!*" Heimrich yelled—something in dwarven. Then she grabbed the lever with her remaining arm and pulled it back with a grinding *clank*.

Several things happened at once.

The ballista's cable snapped forward with a hiss, slicing through Heimrich.

The top half of her body fell to the stone floor.

And the bolt launched, lancing the giant straight through one of its eyes and disappearing. Only the trailing length of rope remained.

The giant batted at the air in front of its face. Its remaining eye bulged wide, darting frantically from side to side. Then it toppled backward, a choking sound in its throat turning into a bloodcurdling roar as it fell from the tower. The scream seemed to last forever. But then it cut off abruptly. It was followed by an even longer silence.

Morten shuddered. He would never be free from that horrible noise—not for the rest of his life.

Dazed, he looked around. "Heimrich." Morten ran to her side.

Blood smeared her round face. Her chest rose slowly. She reached up to him.

"My—where did my glasses go? Can't see a damn thing. Did we—did we..." Her hand dropped.

"*You* did, Helga. You did." Morten gently closed her eyelids. He wasn't sure why he used her first name—he'd only heard it once or twice—but that's what friends called each other, wasn't it?

A metallic groan beside him tensed every muscle in his body. The ballista lurched forward, pulled by the bolt's rope, its frame squealing as it scraped against the stone. He rolled out of its way right as the ballista crashed past him and flew out the hole in the wall.

He breathed a sigh of relief, but it was cut short. His foot jerked from under him, smashing his jaw against stone. Time froze. Then he was yanked across the floor.

He managed to roll over. The rope had coiled around his ankle. He kicked at it with his other boot, but it was no use. He flailed his arms around, grabbing at anything, but the ledge was approaching fast. Finn watched him with wide eyes. Heimrich's top half also stared back at him from the stone floor, her one arm outstretched, as if trying to save him.

He managed to kick the rope free from his ankle, but he was rolling too fast to stop. He felt his feet clip over the edge.

"Morten!"

Finn leapt after him as the ground fell out from under him.

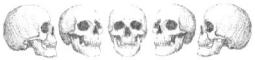

It was bad now. Really bad. A bloody slaughter down by the gate. Private Pyke was glad she was up on the wall instead.

There wasn't even a front line now. Not one she could see, anyway. Only a chaotic press of bodies, screaming in rage and pain. There was scarcely any room to swing a weapon in the melee. Both sides spent more time snarling, shouting threats, and bashing each other with shields than swinging their weapons. A pocket of space would open up long enough for a lucky soldier to smash a weapon into the packed bodies, to brutal effect. Their helpless targets had nowhere to move, no way to raise their shields. That was all there was to it. No glory in it. It was no great contest of strength—the fight went to whoever got lucky enough to find space to swing.

Pyke cranked her crossbow while watching in helpless horror. A gnoll lifted its spear above the crowded front ranks, sliding it above a soldier's shield. The spear tip pressed against chainmail. The gnoll didn't have room to thrust, but it didn't have to. The press of bodies behind it would do its grisly work for him.

"No! No! No!"

She could hear the soldier, even all the way up here. Quite the set of lungs. But it didn't do him any good. No matter how he shouted, it wouldn't stop the soldiers behind him—there was a battle to fight, after all. His shouts of protest turned into a long scream, ending in a wet gurgle.

The gnoll grinned as the man wriggled on the end of its spear, flopping like a fish. Pyke felt her windlass lock into place, then pulled her trigger. The gnoll dropped its spear and stopped laughing, instead choking like something had caught in its throat. That was her most satisfying shot of the night. *Smug prick.*

Her admiration of her kill was cut short by a whistle, followed by whipcrack. An arrow splintered against the battlements beside her.

"Bastard!" Pyke hissed, ducking. It was safer up here than in the mess below, but the arrows kept coming. She thought it'd been a blessing when the gnolls stopped lighting them. Then she realized she couldn't dodge them anymore. Instead, she had to stay low and pray to the Blind Goddess she wouldn't be hit. She doubted Vesenia gave a flying shit about any of them.

Pyke started cranking again. No time to think about how bad things were—only loading the next bolt. That's what Sergeant Clark had taught, and he'd survived the Siege of DeGaullis. Pyke had lost count of how many times she'd heard that story. The number of bolts Clark claimed to have fired increased by at least a dozen with each telling.

She wished, for the hundredth time, that she had a real bow in her hands. A longbow, like her da had taught her on. Let them count how many of these bastards she would put down with a proper bow. Her scarred cheek creased in a smile as she remembered her first kill. It had been a big boar for that late in the season, and she'd been all on her own.

Pyke looked around. Most other crossbowmen up here had been picked off, but she was reassured by the cranking of another crossbow down the wall. New kid—Garrett, or Gareth. From Vascay. Not far from her home, actually. That all felt a lifetime ago. Someone else's life.

She finished cranking, loaded a bolt, and peered over the parapet. Droves of gnolls pressed against the wall outside, ready to replace their fallen numbers. So much cranking, just to kill one of them. She shrugged, then lifted her crossbow. Before she fired, she checked over the wall again, nervous.

The giant lounged in the shadows of the tree line. It had smashed their gate like a bloody toy; now it sat under the trees, watching, as if bored of the entire affair. It didn't make sense to Pyke, but she didn't question it. The giant was so large it looked closer than it really was, making it difficult to tell its distance. But as she studied it, she bet she could hit it. She'd picked off gnolls out there by the trees before. One bolt wouldn't do much besides piss it off—unless she could nail that big bastard right in the eye. That would be one hell of a shot. But if she made it, Sergeant Clark might finally shut up. Damn, she wished she had a bow.

Sparks flew from the tip of an arrow as it hit the wall below her face. Pyke fell back, squeezing her trigger instinctively and firing her shot into the sky.

"Dammit!" She threw herself behind the battlements, taking a few breaths before peeking over again. She could pick out the one which had shot at her. A hooded bastard with a longbow—and he knew how to bloody use it.

Pyke began cranking again. She'd show that mongrel.

She turned to the new guy. "Hey! Garrett! That was your name, right?" she called out.

No response.

Pyke looked over. He was lying on his side, an arrow sticking from his eye socket.

"Fuck."

She ground her teeth. If she could do one thing tonight before the gnolls sucked marrow from her bones, it would be putting a bolt between the eyes of that son of a bitch. Her windlass locked into place, and she loaded another bolt. She gripped her crossbow tightly to her chest and took two sharp breaths. Over the battlements, find your target, take the shot, then back down.

And take out that fucking archer.

Before she could look over the wall, a terrible scream echoed in the distance. Too loud and monstrous to be human, but an unmistakable cry of pain. It came from behind, by the western tower. She glanced that way, unable to see much through the smoke hanging over the camp. The noise came again—a horrible, agonized roar. It muffled into a cry before fading away.

Everything froze. Even the fighting below paused for a few moments as both sides tried to make sense of that dreadful sound. But their silence was broken by another ear-splitting roar—this one from much closer.

Near the tree line, the lounging giant cried. The noise was haunting, demanding silence.

It waited a painfully long time.

Then it wailed. Its cry of anguish ended in fury. It stamped the ground, thrashing its arms in a fit of rage. Tall pines splintered apart like kindling.

Then a horn cut through the air. Pyke looked down.

Ghostface. Standing there, in the open, blowing its horn. As the horn faded, the gnoll laughter turned into frantic yelps and howls. The surviving gnolls scrambled over one another below, each trying to be the first through the gate.

"They're retreating!" Soldiers below her cheered as the gnolls fled.

"Push them back!" shouted First Sergeant Goren. "Make them pay!"

Pyke couldn't believe it. The gnolls had so many more warriors. She didn't know why they retreated, but she was grateful.

The wall shook, and her newfound elation guttered. The giant at the tree line stamped its feet, like a boar getting ready to charge. The entire fortress shook as it stamped.

Then it charged. Right at her.

"Dammit!" Pyke swallowed as her hands fumbled with her crossbow. She thanked Vesenia, finding her weapon loaded somehow.

Her hands trembled as she looked down the sights. She had one shot. She'd take the giant right in the eye, or she'd be mashed into paste. Pyke rested her crossbow on the battlements, getting ready to take the impossible shot.

Then Ghostface stepped in front of the charging titan's path, blowing its horn.

The giant kept running. The white gnoll didn't budge. The giant roared in defiance, but stopped charging just short of the gnoll chief.

Sweat poured from Pyke's forehead as she stared down her crossbow. Her finger trembled; her vision blurred as she focused on her target. It would be a hell of a shot—but if Sergeant Clark could make it, she could, too. She could end it all right now. Ghostface's white fur made him an easy target. She closed her other eye, exhaled, then pulled the trigger—

Her head snapped back. Everything went black. She opened her other eye; a long stick with a feathered end stuck from her face. How silly. Why feathers? That didn't make any sense. She found herself staring at the ground below the wall. She didn't remember looking that way. First feathers, and now a tickle in her stomach.

Why was she falling? How very silly.

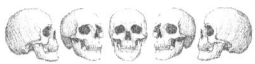

Morten's legs dangled over the abyss. He clung to the tower ledge as if his life depended on it—because it did. His hands were slipping fast.

"Morten, hold on!" Finn ran toward him, eyes wide as silver coins. He was still too far.

He felt himself slip further. Stupid, heavy chainmail weighed him down.

Now that he was about to die, he wasn't scared anymore. Not angry, not sad. Just disappointed. He hadn't really expected to survive the night, but he'd thought his death would be more heroic than falling from a cliff. At least it would be over quickly.

He closed his eyes. Tried to remember his mother's face again. Only Giles's bloated face waited in the darkness. He gave a hollow laugh.

His hand slipped.

But then something grabbed his legs.

"Don't worry," said the Inquisitor's prisoner from below. "I've got you."

Morten couldn't look down. He would have offered the prisoner thanks, but couldn't do much other than grunt. Finn slid forward in a cloud of dust and grabbed Morten's hand. Slowly, Finn pulled him up on the ledge.

Morten collapsed beside Finn, both of them gasping. Before they could catch their breath, the wooden ceiling creaked overhead as the top of the tower began to lean ominously.

"Come on! We have to get out of here!" yelled Finn.

"No," said Morten. "Wait a moment."

"Wait!?" Finn had already taken a few steps down the stairs.

"I need to save the prisoner." A few bricks fell from the hole in the wall behind Morten.

"What? Why?"

"He just saved me! I can't leave him."

"Well, how?" said Finn. "We don't have time! Or the key!"

The tower was shaking. Morten looked around. "Here!" He grabbed a length of rope and ran back to the ledge. Finn groaned as he looked up at the tower, as it leaned further and further, but followed Morten anyway. They threw the rope over the ledge.

"Grab on!"

At first, there was nothing but the sound of the tower groaning.

Then Morten felt the rope pull taut.

"Pull!" he yelled.

They pulled. After a few strained steps, the weight came easier. Fortunately, the prisoner had the build of a scarecrow. His dust-covered face and long black hair appeared over the ledge. Morten pulled him the rest of the way up by his manacles.

"Thanks," wheezed the prisoner as he stood up. His eyes widened at the carnage from their battle with the giant—some of it still dripping from the walls.

"Come on!" said Finn, running for the stairs.

They ran. The wooden beams above them snapped, bricks falling from the ceiling. Something metallic glinted on the stone floor. Morten reached down to grab it before chasing the prisoner down the steps. He nearly fell on top of the prisoner as they ran past the cells. Finn was the first out the door, and the prisoner and Morten were right behind him.

The tower collapsed. It seemed to happen in slow motion. The top of the tower leaned further away from them. Then a rumble of bricks grew into a hollow roar. The tower fell over the cliff like a wave crashing against the shore. They covered their ears, taking a few steps back, but there wasn't much they could do except watch in silence.

A cloud of dust filled the air. Morten couldn't see his hand in front of his face. It was almost a full minute before it cleared.

After the prisoner finished coughing, he spoke. "Thank you for the rescue. Though I can't say there is much value in saving someone already condemned to death. I suppose it's the thought that counts."

Morten wasn't sure if the prisoner was being sarcastic, or had no concern whether he lived or died. Knowing what lay ahead for the prisoner, he couldn't say he blamed him.

"You saved me, too," said Morten.

The prisoner made an elaborate bow. "Don't mention it. My name is Malfus. Though it seems names don't last very long around here." He smiled and extended his chained hands.

"Private Morten." The prisoner's chains rattled as Malfus shook his hand.

Morten had several questions. Malfus had the hint of an Akkadian accent, but something else was in there, too. And what had he done to become a prisoner of the Vesenian Inquisition? He had a strange demeanor; it was difficult to read much from his disregard for the horror surrounding them.

Finn hunched over. His breath came in rapid gasps. "How did we... A giant? I can't believe we're alive." Then he stood up, looking around in panic. "The gnolls!"

Morten also glanced up, fearing what he might see—but the courtyard wasn't overrun with gnolls like he had expected. Soldiers were yelling from the other side of the fort, but this was different from their earlier cries of combat. Were they cheering? Had they actually pushed back the gnolls?

Morten held out his hand. Heimrich's dwarven spectacles lay in his palm, the moon reflected in their broken lenses. Everything that had just transpired crashed into him, as hard as the tower falling from the cliff.

It had been less than ten minutes since the five of them had entered the tower. Now, one dead giant later, only two of them remained. Not counting the prisoner. Morten had known his squad for less than a year, but they had become his friends—no, his family—in this forsaken place. A lot could happen in a few minutes.

Finn cleared his throat, gave Malfus a look of suspicion, then turned to Morten. "Come on. We should go find—"

Finn's voice cut off as a dark-cloaked man approached them, silent as a specter, his robes whipping behind him. One hand held a bloodied sword; the other clutched a coil of chain, bits of gore stuck to its spikes.

Morten swallowed. Finn and Malfus did the same.

"I believe you have something of mine," said the Inquisitor.

Chapter 12

The Bargain

"The word of a Monrovian." — Galasan saying for someone who can't be trusted

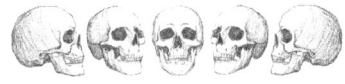

Malfus regarded the Inquisitor with as much joy as a merchant opening their door to a tax collector. The crazed look in those fish eyes was magnified by the blood covering him.

Ugh. Of course he's still alive. I survive a damn giant attack, only to end up back in the black-gloved hands of the Inquisition. I've got as much luck as a dwarf at an orc family reunion.

He sighed. "Hello, Inquisitor! I can't begin to tell you what a relief it is to see your face again—and alive, to boot. I must admit that I feared for the worst."

"Save your sarcasm for another time. I am not in the mood," said the Inquisitor. "I told you Vesenia would keep you alive for your trial."

"No," said Malfus. "I'm alive thanks to these soldiers. We all are. They just killed a giant. Stopped it from turning the rest of the fort into a pile of rubble, like this tower. It would have collapsed on me if he hadn't thrown me a rope and pulled me up."

The Inquisitor raised an eyebrow as he turned to Morten. "You escorted me earlier," said the Inquisitor, then looked him and the other soldier up and down. "Two of you killed a giant?"

"Yes, Inquisitor, sir. Well, not just us," said Morten. He glanced back at the pile of bricks that would serve as a grave marker for the others.

The Inquisitor gave the pile of rubble one more look, then turned to the two soldiers. "For ensuring the safety of my prisoner, I thank you, the Inquisition honors you, and the Blind Goddess blesses you. Both of you. And all those who gave their lives in her service."

Your hollow thanks won't bring their friends back. Only I can do that.

"Thanks," said Morten, looking wistfully back at the tower.

"How did you manage this task?" the Inquisitor asked, staring at the rubble.

The younger soldier piped up. "We had a ballista that we got from the dwarv—"

Morten elbowed the other in the side as he stepped forward. "A ballista, Inquisitor," said Morten. "Sent from the Duke of Almarada himself. The finest engineering Galasa has to offer. At such close range, not even a giant could withstand it."

The Inquisitor nodded, then turned back to Malfus. "Come, necromancer. We must find Colonel Peshka. I must find another place to sequester you until this is all over."

"Oh joy! Can I request a bigger room? One a bit less drafty, perhaps?"

"Silence! The sooner we get through this, the sooner we can return to Castillea."

"Of course, Inquisitor," said Malfus. "Anything you say."

Malfus raised his shackled hands to his mouth, and mimed locking his lips with an invisible key before tossing it over his shoulder. The Inquisitor glowered at him.

"We were on our way to the front gate ourselves—or, what's left of it," said Morten. "I'm sure Colonel Peshka will be there."

The Inquisitor nodded. "Lead on, soldier."

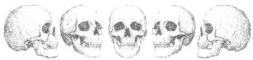

All that remained of the scattered fires were wisps of black smoke rising high in the air, the smell of embers rising with them. It reminded Malfus of the smell of the academy's cooking; he never thought he'd miss such barely passable food.

What I would give to be back there. A chance to start this all over. I'd study twice as hard in Magistrex Dis'elauxe's classes. I wouldn't be arrested as an illusionist. I never should have picked up that black book. Should have left it well-enough alone.

But Malfus knew the truth. He had failed miserably at the academy. None of the seven *legal* schools of magic had come naturally to him at all. He had worked twice as hard as his peers to make half their progress. No, the only speck of talent he'd been given was in the one school of magic punishable by death.

A horse thundered past, breaking Malfus out of his reverie. Several other horses galloped around the camp as soldiers chased them down. He envied the freedom of the horses, even if it was short-lived.

The cries of the wounded and not-quite-dead got louder as they approached the front gate. A soldier screamed as two others carried him past. Blood spurted from the stump of his leg, missing from the knee down. The uninjured, or the survivors able to walk on their own, were busy separating the wounded from the dead.

Corpses were strewn everywhere.

Some soldiers had been killed with swords, or hacked apart by axes, or shot full of arrows. Others were too disfigured to tell what had befallen them. Corpses of men and women were laid out in neat rows off to the side, while the gnolls were heaped into a pile by the gates. Any gnoll that showed signs of life met a quick end before being thrown on the pile. The troops' rage had burned out. They killed surviving gnolls as a matter of business.

Malfus surveyed the wreckage of the front gate. He swallowed. Crumbling sections of the wall remained standing at its sides, but the gate itself was a pile of rubble now, like the western tower. The massive doors that had opened for them earlier that night were no more than kindling. A gigantic boulder rested triumphantly atop it all. Malfus was no military expert, but he knew a fort without a gate wouldn't last long.

Nearby, Colonel Peshka stood beside First Sergeant Goren, overlooking the ruin. Goren had to bellow for her orders to be heard over the cries of the wounded.

"Well, this is a fine fucking mess," muttered Peshka. Soldiers gathered around the massive boulder, arguing over how to move something so heavy.

"Ahem." The Inquisitor cleared his throat.

"Ah. Just what I needed to deal with," said Peshka, loud enough for Malfus to hear. "I see you survived the attack—and your prisoner, too." There was a glimmer in his eyes when he looked at Malfus. Malfus wasn't sure if that was excitement, or the glassy-eyed look of a drunk. "I saw that the tower had collapsed and assumed the worst."

"Of course we survived, Colonel," said the Inquisitor. "I told you I had a sacred duty to Vesenia. She protects her faithful subjects"—the Inquisitor looked over at Malfus—"and those awaiting divine justice."

Malfus rolled his eyes. *Yes. Unfortunately. I do wonder if I should have jumped out the hole in the tower—if only to prove this smug bastard wrong.*

"Yes, well..." Peshka looked at the rows of dead soldiers. "Pity that she didn't tend to her entire flock."

"Sacrifices must be made for the greater good, Commander." The Inquisitor waved his hand toward the pile of gnoll corpses. "The gnolls certainly fared worse than your soldiers."

A soldier stood next to the pile of gnoll corpses. It was stacked higher than he was. He doused them in lamp oil, and now fumbled with a flint and steel. Sparks flashed as he scraped his steel against the flint.

"Give it a wait on that, will you?" Peshka called out.

The soldier gave him a look. "But, Colonel. They'll start smelling."

"Dammit, man! Just wait on that, I said!" Peshka growled, then clutched at his stomach.

"Yes, sir!" The soldier shrugged, then walked off to help the others with the fallen.

Peshka turned back to the Inquisitor. "Soldiers these days... no respect for authority."

"I find I seldom have that problem, Colonel," the Inquisitor said, coldly. "A tighter fist will instill greater discipline."

"Yes." Peshka's voice trailed off, then he raised a bushy eyebrow. "Private Morten, didn't see you there, lad." Peshka turned to Morten, then looked around. "Where is Sergeant Donovan? And the others?"

"Dead, sir. Sergeant Donovan, Corporal Heimrich, and Big—Private Duncan." Morten hung his head. "Private Finn and I were the only survivors. But one of the giants is dead, sir." He looked down at his feet, blinking.

Peshka raised both eyebrows. "Was that all that ruckus over there? You boys are damn heroes! Both of you deserve bloody medals after this is over."

"It was Corporal Heimrich, sir. If anyone deserves a medal, it's her."

"I'll get a detail together later to search the rubble for their bodies," said First Sergeant Goren, mostly to herself.

The Inquisitor stepped forward. "Yes. And with the western tower gone, I'll need a new place to secure my prisoner."

Goren frowned. "The western tower had the only—"

Peshka cut her off, waving his arms in the air. "No, don't worry! I know just the place. Follow me, Inquisitor. Goren, come with me."

Goren glanced back at the bodies lying in neat rows. "I should finish getting a count of the wounded, see who can still pull guard—"

"Nonsense. Plenty of time for that later. Come along. Morten, Finn, you as well."

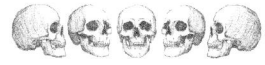

"Here we are, Inquisitor."

Peshka opened the door with a loud creak. Malfus's eyes adjusted to the gloom as he stepped inside.

Hello darkness, my old friend. At least it'll be easier to get some shuteye in here.

Peshka lit two torches, handing them to Morten and Finn. Dusty boxes and barrels filled most of the room. Wooden racks lined the walls. Most of them were empty, but there was the occasional polearm, sword, mace, or crossbow scattered throughout.

Goren shut the door behind them with a resounding slam.

"This was the old armory," said Peshka. "Now it's a graveyard for everything forgotten."

I wonder if it will become my graveyard. I suppose it's as good as any other.

"This will hardly suffice as a holding cell." The Inquisitor looked disapprovingly at the weapons.

It's not like I can swing any of those brutish weapons. Certainly not with my hands chained together.

Peshka smiled. "No, not here. The room is over there."

The Colonel sucked in his gut as he squeezed between the boxes, until he made it to a reinforced door. He grabbed a key on a leather cord around his neck and unlocked it.

The door creaked open, revealing a dark stone stairway leading downwards. Peshka grabbed Finn's torch. "My personal wine cellar. Well, it used to be. Almost bone dry now," said Peshka, a tinge of sadness in his voice. "It's not as secure as the cell doors in the tower, but it does have a lock, and there is nowhere else to go. Those are the two basic requirements for a holding cell. It should be suitable for your prisoner—but you are, of course, welcome to examine it yourself..." Peshka gestured toward the stairs.

"Of course I'll need to inspect it," snapped the Inquisitor.

"Be my guest." Peshka handed the Inquisitor the torch and stepped aside.

The Inquisitor paused in the doorway briefly before descending into the dark. Peshka followed. Malfus came next, sandwiched between Peshka and the large, armored First Sergeant, who clattered behind him. *You big brute. Do you have to walk so damn close?*

The room below was much smaller than upstairs, and quite crowded after the two soldiers joined them. It was cool and damp. An odor somewhere between mildew and sour grapes permeated the room. A few wooden kegs had been inset into one wall, while racks for wine bottles lined the others. They were mostly empty; less than half a dozen bottles remained on a lonely shelf. A much larger pile of empty glass bottles glistened in another corner.

"I suppose this will suffice, if we have no other options." The Inquisitor's eyes lingered on the few bottles lining the shelves. "But first, I will have to remove whatever alcohol remains." He wrinkled his nose.

Like a wet fart in a new pair of trousers—you sure know how to ruin anything.

"That won't be a problem, Inquisitor," said Peshka. "I'll be taking the rest of my wine with me. Pretty sure I'll need a drink after this..." Peshka grabbed one of the bottles.

"After what, Colonel?" asked the Inquisitor.

Peshka ignored him. He looked past the Inquisitor and gave a nod.

A metal fist slammed the Inquisitor in the back of the head. The Inquisitor's hat fell off, and he stumbled forward, grabbing at his head with one hand. He started to turn around, but First Sergeant Goren clobbered him again, harder.

The Inquisitor tottered, then collapsed.

Goren caught him in her big arms, gentle as a mother ogress. "Don't worry, I've got you." She laid him on the stone floor.

Malfus, Finn, and Morten all watched the unfolding scene with equal shock.

Well, now. Looks like my luck might be changing after all!

"What have you done?" Finn stammered in disbelief. "Striking an Inquisitor? The Inquisition will execute you. They'll execute all of us!"

Peshka sneered. "I'd rather survive to deal with those consequences than have the entire garrison dead because of this zealot. Now, let's go upstairs." He turned to Malfus. "We have *much* to discuss, necromancer."

"Wait. His key!" Malfus held up his manacles and shook them.

"Where is it?" Goren asked.

"Around his neck."

"Best confiscate that sword of his, too," said Peshka.

Goren reached down and unclasped the Inquisitor's sword from his belt. She grabbed the spiked chain coiled on his belt as well, then pulled on the leather cord around his neck.

"Unhhh. What's..." The Inquisitor groaned, reaching for Goren's gauntleted wrist.

"Shhh. Sleep now, Inquisitor." Goren struck him again, this time with the pommel of his sword. The Inquisitor's head hit the floor, and his black-gloved hand fell limp. Goren cut the leather cord free with the sword, then pulled the keys free.

She scoffed. "Such a tiny blade. And who fights with a chain?"

Peshka, for his part, looked nervous. "We'd best clear out of here before he wakes up. He'll be as cordial as hornet nest when he does." He turned to leave the room.

Malfus followed Goren and the others upstairs. Peshka closed the door behind them, turning the key until a hollow *click* echoed in the storeroom.

"I hope you're making the right choice here, sir," Goren said, tossing the Inquisitor's key to the Colonel before looking Malfus up and down. "I must return to the soldiers and get a proper count of our wounded." She set the chain on one of the empty weapon racks. She paused to set the rapier down, but then took it with her as she headed outside to the courtyard.

Malfus watched Peshka. The Colonel held the red-tinged arcanull key in his open palm, feeling its weight.

"Am I mad for freeing a necromancer?" said Peshka. "Trading one evil to fight another?"

Malfus grinned. "We're each but a finger's breadth away from madness, Colonel—but I'm sure we just locked up the crazy one." Malfus nodded at the door, then turned to Peshka. "Is wanting to survive madness?"

"Never thought I'd get a lecture on the value of life from a necromancer," said Peshka.

Malfus shrugged, impatient. "We're well past the point for having second thoughts."

"I hope you're up to the task, necromancer. You're right. We're *committed* now." Peshka reached over and unlocked Malfus's manacles. Malfus could smell the alcohol on the Colonel's breath.

The manacles fell from his wrists, hitting the stone floor with a resounding *clang*.

Malfus rubbed at the sores covering his wrists as he looked down at the chains. *Is this really happening? Am I dreaming?*

Peshka twisted a tip of his mustache. "Do we have a deal, then? You know what needs to be done. I don't need to spell out the details, do I?"

Malfus rolled his shoulders back. His joints clicked and popped as he stretched his long, lean arms out to his sides, like a scarecrow. "Do you know *how long* I've been waiting to do that?"

"Well, necromancer?" Peshka asked again, impatience growing in his voice.

"Weeks!" cried Malfus, popping his neck from side to side. "Yes. We have a deal. Though, if I were you, I'd think about what you're going to tell the rest of your soldiers. Not all of them will be so excited to see their fallen comrades fighting again. Even to save their lives."

Morten and Finn looked at each other uneasily.

Peshka spat. "Gods dammit, I need a drink already. Damn fool for leaving those bottles in there." Peshka fidgeted with the cork of the bottle he'd taken.

"Oh, it won't be so bad," said Malfus. "All your dead have already given their lives to protect the fort. Just tell your troops that I'm giving their comrades the opportunity to do it again."

Peshka's red skin turned a few shades paler; he grabbed at his stomach as it churned audibly.

Malfus sighed, tapping his chin. "I'll need my effects before I can begin. Where was the Inquisitor keeping his equipment?"

"I took the Inquisitor to Lieutenant Erickson's old room. I can take you," said Morten.

"All right," said Peshka, stroking his long mustache. "Private Morten, take the necromancer to his room. Private Finn, you guard this door. Make sure our guest doesn't try anything *fishy*."

"Me? Why me?"

"Would you rather escort a necromancer?" asked Peshka, already walking away.

Sullen, Finn crossed his arms and leaned against the door.

"This way," said Morten, leaving the room.

As Malfus followed Morten, a grin spread across his face for the first time in weeks. A real taste of freedom. Freed from arcanull, his mind raced to catch up with the changes to his situation. He began to formulate a plan.

Chapter 13

Now, Where Are My Things?

"They're just gnolls. How good with a bow can they be?" — Lieutenant Erickson

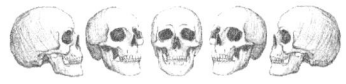

Malfus followed Private Morten, escorted for the second time that night by the same soldier—once with chains, once without. *It's amazing how quickly luck can change in a few hours.* As they walked past the front gate, he rubbed at his wrists for the dozenth time since the cuffs had been removed.

Not much had changed out here. Some soldiers toiled with the fallen. Others struggled with massive bricks from the destroyed wall, using spars of wood as levers to form a makeshift barricade. The boulder sat there, unmoved.

Cries from the wounded were more distant. They'd been isolated to the infirmary. Smoke curled around a few piles of charred wood, but the all the fires from the battle had been extinguished.

The surviving soldiers worked their tasks, oblivious to the transition of power. No one noticed that the Inquisitor was missing, or that Malfus walked around unchained. No one even bothered to glance up from their assigned tasks. Their fates were now in his hands.

If he decided to help, that is. It looked like a better chance for escape with every passing moment. As long as Malfus could find his possessions—as long as he could find *her* finger.

"So, you said you were from Akkadia?" said Morten.

Malfus nodded. "Where else would a wizard come from? It's the last sanctioned magic academy." Before he'd fled the academy, he'd heard rumors that the Inquisition had agents there, posing as students. *The Vesenian Orthodoxy, keeping mages under their thumb for the last five hundred years.* He spat on the ground.

"And the Inquisitor arrested you because you're a wizard?"

Malfus rolled his eyes. "Not because I'm a wizard—but the *kind* of wizard I am." *Gods, his questions never end. He should have joined the Inquisition; he'd make a great interrogator.*

Morten continued. "A traveling entertainer would come to our village. He'd tell stories with illusion magic. But I think he was a bard. Not a real wizard." Morten shrugged his shoulders. "I don't think I've seen any real magic before."

"Then you're in for a treat," said Malfus, looking at the neat rows of fresh corpses.

Morten swallowed, then grew silent, turning a few shades paler. "I've never seen the dead—the undead, I mean." He whispered the words, as if the corpses might be listening. "It's funny. We've been Tithed here to guard the Scar in case the undead rise up—but none of us have seen any. Only the monsters they chase from the Scar. I guess part of me assumed they were just scary tales invented by the Inquisition."

"If that were true, there'd be no reason to keep me shackled, would there?"

Morten paused, then opened the door to one of the few buildings left intact from the fire. Malfus followed him inside, down a torch-lined corridor.

"How do you know the undead won't hurt us?"

"Oh, not to worry. I wouldn't be a very good necromancer if I were devoured by my own creations." He winked at Morten. "I can control them." *Though I've never controlled anywhere near as many as this will require. Hope I'm up to the task.*

"Can they really save us from the gnolls?"

Malfus paused. "That, I can't answer. But I suspect we will discover that together." *If I'm not already twelve leagues away from this place before the sun comes up.*

"Here it is," said Morten, reaching a door at the end of the hall. "This is where I took the Inquisitor after I put you in the tower." He opened the door for Malfus.

Malfus entered. "Thank you. I can take it from here. Can you ensure that I'm not disturbed? I'll need time to prepare."

"I'll do my best." Morten stood outside the door.

"Perhaps a bit further down the hall," Malfus said. "I can't promise you'll like the things you hear."

Morten swallowed, nodded, then strode away.

Malfus slumped against the door as it shut, breathing a long sigh. *Finally. Free from the Inquisitor, unchained, and—most important of all—alone.*

He took a deep breath and closed his eyes. This was the first total solitude he'd enjoyed since his capture. He'd forgotten how much he missed it. After keeping company of only yourself and the silent dead for so long, you became accustomed to it.

As much as Malfus wanted to appreciate it and organize his thoughts in silence, time was of the essence. And there was only one thought on his mind.

"All right, you bastard," he growled. "Where are they? Where are my things?"

The room didn't answer. A spare set of Inquisitor robes and effects had been meticulously arranged on the bed, as if awaiting a military inspection. Malfus looked over the room, searching for a clue—a sign—anything at all, to suggest where his possessions might be.

What's going on here?

Only one thing stood out from the rest of the room—the dried blood splattered across the stone in the rough shape of an X. A bloody handprint had caked to the edge of the desk; more had been smeared across its surface.

There were few things Malfus could claim expertise in, but the amount of blood in a body was one of them. This appeared to be a quite a lot of it. *I guess this explains why he was bleeding earlier. But just—why? How could he do this to himself?*

If the Inquisitor inflicted this kind of torture against himself, the thought of what lay in store for Malfus in the Inquisition's dungeons sent chills down his spine. *Death by torture if the Inquisition takes me. Death by gnolls if I stay here. I need to find my damn things so I can escape. Kiara's finger, my spell book, and the rod. I don't care about the rest, but I'm not leaving without those three.*

He tore sheets from the bed, scattering the Inquisitor's neatly arranged clothes. He rifled through drawers in the bloody desk, ripping them from their tracks and dumping their contents—pieces of paper, small trinkets, an ivory comb. Malfus pocketed the comb, but none of the drawers had what he was looking for.

Where is he keeping everything? He couldn't have thrown them away. He'd need them for evidence, or something. They must still be here—they must.

He couldn't face the possibility of not finding them. He'd be dead without them—dead on the road if he escaped, and useless as a corpse if he remained here.

Sweat beaded on his forehead. He was running out of room to search. His hands shook as he tore through a footlocker at the end of the bed, throwing its contents on the floor. Folded uniforms, a few pairs of boots, rolled up socks—but no book, no rod, and no finger.

Malfus growled in frustration. He grabbed the wooden desk and toppled it over. The mirror exploded across the stone floor. *Here's to thirteen more years of bad luck. After a lifetime of it—what's a few more?*

Then he spotted them. The Inquisitor's saddlebags, sitting in the corner so plainly that his eyes had passed over them. *They must be in there.* Malfus grabbed the bags and rifled through them.

Two sets of spare clothing—road-worn, neatly folded, all black. *Good to have some variety.* A few glass vials filled with clear liquid, most likely holy water. *A waste of perfectly good vials. A few healing potions would have been much more useful.* Handwritten papers and legal documents, their swooping signatures and wax seals identifying him as an Inquisitor. Affording him unilateral power throughout the Ossory Empire. *I wonder how much trouble he'd be in if I tore these up.*

Malfus set them aside and kept looking. A devotional book for the Blind Goddess, Vesenia, bound in leather and brass. Malfus was always one to appreciate a well-made book. He paused his search and rubbed his fingers over its cured leather cover and brass adornments. *I'm a bit jealous. The brass is a nice touch. But where's* my *book?*

Something jingled in his hands. *What's this?*

He removed a folded case of black leather as long as his forearm. The muffled chime of metal shifted inside. He untied its string, and the leather unrolled. Metal clattered as a dozen tools scattered across the floor.

He held back bile from his churning stomach. The instruments could have been mistaken for carpentry tools—but a closer inspection revealed hooked edges, pincers, saw-teeth, or other insidious mechanisms, designed to flay skin—or for other purposes Malfus could only begin to imagine. *This is only the start of what waits for me if we make it to Castillea.*

He grabbed a straight-bladed scalpel from the torturer's kit. *A sharp knife has countless uses, for both the dead and the living.*

The rest of the saddlebag was empty. *One more.* Malfus swallowed. What if the Inquisitor hadn't kept them? What if he had cast Kiara's finger aside and left it there? It was just a finger. He could have sworn he'd seen the Inquisitor take it, but everything had happened so fast that night. It was all a blur.

Malfus clenched his fists. These weren't just his things. They were irreplaceable. The culmination of his life's work. They were his purpose.

He licked chapped lips. His hands shook, sweating. He reached for the bag.

Another set of black clothes, a coil of rope, and a pouch of the Inquisitor's food—a few strips of dried meat and hardtack bread. *The Inquisitor can keep these.* Hungry as Malfus was, the thought of taking another bite of those rations nauseated him. He'd need to steal food from the fort's larders before he left, as he had no hunting skills of his own.

His desperation tightened like a noose. He lifted the saddle bag to upend it, but something at its bottom caught his eye. His heart skipped a beat. A tied leather bag. Malfus felt an immediate sense of familiarity from the shapes of objects within.

His heart fluttered with anticipation as his shaking fingers fumbled with its knots. "Come on! Come on, dammit!" He cursed, then grabbed the scalpel sitting next to him, slicing through the cord. He flung it across the room, opening the bag with bated breath.

He reached into the bag, pulling out a thick black book. He held his breath as he ran his fingers reverently over its leather cover. They had memorized this lacquered, dimpled surface. He sighed as relief flooded over him.

Every wizard treasured their spellbook. It was a physical embodiment of their lifelong devotion to the arcane arts. Each page held occult rituals that peeled back the veil of creation itself, manipulating the secret energies of the universe.

Priests have prayer books; wizards have spellbooks. Each holds the same weight to their souls.

Every spell within had been earned, painstakingly transcribed into its pages from another source—a copy of a copy. Then came the real work: memorizing the hand movements, words, and mental visualizations necessary to cast the spell. Each spell required hours for a wizard to learn, and many more spent mastering its nuances.

And for necromancers, each spell was even more sacred. Most books on necromancy had been burned when the Vesenian Church rose to power five centuries ago. *As well as anyone who owned them.*

The Church had outlawed any study on life after death, in any form. Every surviving copy of a necromancy spell was either five centuries old, or had been copied from one that was—and they were much harder to come by than scrolls from the other seven schools of magic.

Malfus thumbed through the pages, making sure they were all still there. They were scrawled with arcane runes and symbols. Nothing had been torn out, and no water damage; its pages had been coated in a special wax that protected them from everything but complete immersion.

He swallowed as fear wormed back into his mind. Even if he decided to help the Colonel, he doubted he'd have sufficient time to prepare before the gnolls attacked. Even if he began immediately and worked through the night, he could raise perhaps a dozen corpses, maybe a score. *All the more reason to get out of here.*

He set his book on the bed, then continued digging into the bag. Malfus pulled out the Rod of Manni-Ra.

The rod was roughly the length of his forearm, forged from a dark gray metal with flecks of black in it—like bits of charred flesh sticking to smooth bone. Its top ended in a bony hand clutching a star ruby. Though a ruby, the gem looked closer to a lusterless gray than red, its surface almost greasy.

Yagyii, the swamp-hag, had told him where to find it. Advised him that it might be the only way to bring Kiara back. She'd warned him about the rod, but hadn't told him how to use it. He'd only managed to get his hands on it before his capture. All those months of preparations, and the small lab he had cobbled together—destroyed. Razed to the ground by this zealot, who had tracked him all the way to the swamps of Monrovia. *Not even in the bastard's jurisdiction.*

How long the Inquisitor been on his trail? How had he found Malfus in the first place? All pieces of a puzzle, just like this rod. Malfus had always enjoyed a good puzzle, but now he wished the answers were more forthcoming. Whatever aid this artifact could render would certainly make his escape easier.

He could detect a strong aura of magic emanating from it, even without a detection spell, but it was as inert and lifeless now as it had been when he'd found it. *Fine. Keep your secrets.* Malfus sighed, rolling the rod away; it made a hollow sound as it clattered to a stop.

He kept scrounging through the bag. He needed one more thing before he could even consider an escape.

His breath caught in his throat. There it was. Wrapped in its black silk, just as he'd left it. It had been at least a month since he'd cast the spell. A month since he held *her* finger. He feared it had withered to the bone. His hand trembled as he unwrapped the cloth.

No!

Some bluish signs of necrosis curled around the fingertip and its severed end. But not as much as he had feared. There must have been plenty of residual necromantic energy remaining from his past efforts. The finger felt cold, like a lump of wax. He thought of the life that once flowed through it. *I will find a way to save you. To bring you back. I haven't given up.*

He closed his eyes and took several deep breaths, seeking the mental focus to cast the spell. He cradled Kiara's finger in one hand, holding his other hand over it. Such a simple spell—more of a mental exercise. No verbal components, no gestures or reagents. All he needed was the right frame of mind and a lack of those arcanull manacles.

Clearing his mind, Malfus visualized energy traveling through the pathways in his body. He focused that energy into the palm of his hands, and then—

Nothing. He snapped his fingers and shook his wrists, then tried again. More nothing. He grunted as he strained. He heard a faint *pop,* but couldn't tell if that was magic or a blood vessel.

Not now, not now. There's no time for this. Get your shit together. He stood up, stretching like a cat. He cracked his neck, popped every willing joint in his fingers, then clapped his hands together.

This spell was child's play. It was the first necromancy spell he had learned, back at the academy. He'd found that tome in the restricted section of the library. Stayed up after hours, studying from the black book until the sun came up. From that night onward, he attended two different schools of magic. One by day, where he failed constantly—and one at night, where he flourished.

Malfus concentrated, shutting out the external world. He focused on the energy pathways coursing through his body. Concentrated on nothingness. Other schools of magic taught their students to focus on specific thoughts, mantras, or feelings. But necromancy demanded nothing—and *only* nothing. The void. The thoughts skittering in his mind broke into words, which turned into whispers, and then those whispers shredded into fragments of nothing. His worries floated further and further away, until they became tiny bubbles and burst apart.

Only the void remained.

He felt it. Slowly, at first. A scratching, like bony fingers clawing at the lid of a coffin, trying to escape. A cool mist roiled in his veins, flowing up his forearms. It pushed through the blockage in his wrists, and out of his palms like a billowing fog.

Ah. Hello again, old friend.

His heart rate slowed, and something within him *pulled.*

The energy trickled into Kiara's finger.

He exhaled; drops of perspiration beaded on his forehead. Slowly, he opened his palm, unsure of what he'd find. A smile pulled at the corners of his mouth. The bluish signs of necrosis had faded, returning the finger to its natural color—white, as if carved from marble. Relief flooded into Malfus as his greatest fear vanished.

Something buzzed nearby, like a bumblebee beside him. The gem atop the rod glowed a faint red. Its light pulsated weakly, like an irregular heartbeat. It lay next to the dried stains of blood. Malfus picked it up, and held it closer to the patch of blood; it shone even brighter.

Blood? Had it really been that simple, this whole time?

He picked up the scalpel and held out his hand, then cut a small incision into his fingertip. A bead of blood welled up before dripping onto the gem. The ruby grew a bright, hungry red. Malfus felt void energy flow through the rod like a conduit—a blood battery.

"You like that, do you?"

The rod pulsed as if in response.

Malfus gathered his things and stood up. "Come on, then. I'm sure we can find more of that around here somewhere."

CHAPTER 14

A Little Necromancy Never Hurt Anyone

"Zombies are a peculiar species of undead. They're usually enthralled by necromancers, but that's not always the case. They can also be found in graveyards, wandering as if looking for something. Unlike ghouls, they are not driven by hunger—yet an untethered zombie will kill the living on sight. No, there is more there than shambling bones and rotting meat." — Dietrich Kynebold, author of 'A Treatise on the Dead That Yet Live'

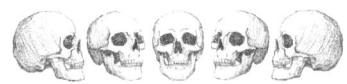

Shards of mirror crunched under Malfus's shoes as he stepped past the overturned desk. The room had surrendered his possessions, but not without a fight. Clothes and bedsheets were strewn across the floor, draped over broken furniture. Snowy feathers from a torn pillow dusted the room like giant dandelion seeds. Papers littered the remaining space—some belonging to the Inquisitor, others to the dead lieutenant.

Malfus set the glowing rod on the bed beside his spellbook and Kiara's finger, which he'd wrapped in its gossamer veil. These might not look like much to most, but Malfus's entire life—his past, his future, his crimes, his purpose, his very identity—sat in front of him.

Now he could finally get out of here. Away from the Inquisitor, this siege, all of this madness. The rod's flickering ruby caught his eye. He picked up the rod; it was surprisingly warm. *Maybe I can escape after a little experimentation. No telling when I'll have access to so many spare corpses. Stay or go—I'll need to animate a few either way.*

"One more thing." Malfus looked at the overturned footlocker at the end of the bed, and its precious exposed cargo—fresh, clean clothing.

Then he examined his own attire. Torn, threadbare, covered in dried mud, blood, and horse sweat, along with unidentifiable grime from his month on the road. It was impossible to tell what color they'd been. He wasn't sure if he could remember.

He peeled his old clothes off like a snakeskin. He had to admit that his stench rivaled some of the corpses he'd animated. He'd strangle someone for a bath and a shave, but now wasn't the time—not that either were available. A fresh set of clothes would have to do.

His wardrobe options were limited. He could take the Inquisitor's clothing and bulky gambeson, or the officer's dress uniform. An easy decision. He grabbed the officer's pair of navy blue trousers, a gold seam sewn down its legs. He held them to his bony hips to check the fit. *Not bad; same height, at least. I'll need a belt, though. I've lost a bit of weight on this little misadventure.* His stomach growled in agreement. He hooked a leather belt around his waist.

Then he took a gray shirt, long-sleeved with buttons. He took his time fastening them. *How long has it been?* It had been quite a while since Malfus could afford clothes with proper buttons. He took pleasure fastening each one. He had been the son of a tailor-merchant, after all.

He looked down at the pile of clothes once more. Something was still missing. He picked up a navy blue overcoat, the officer's dress uniform. Ostentatious, the coat featured golden embroidery wrapping its sleeves, epaulets with braided cords, and a smattering of polished gold buttons. Malfus pressed his scalpel against a button; it gave, slightly. *Real gold. I could sell them for a decent amount on the road. But these will have to go.*

He cut away the epaulet shoulder-boards and rope braiding. His slender fingers moved as delicately as a surgeon, cutting away stitching without damaging the jacket. He didn't know how long it would need to last him. Finishing his alterations, he put it on. Like everything else, it was a bit baggy on his slender frame. At least the height was a match.

Malfus looked down at his feet, and his toes stared back at him. Taking the scalpel, he sliced off what remained of his ragged footwear. His socks had dissolved after his first two weeks of marching. He unrolled two wool socks, testing their softness between his thumb and forefinger. *These will do nicely.* He stretched his dirty, blistered feet out and pulled the fresh wool over them. These socks were the best thing to happen to his feet in over a month.

He grabbed the officer's pair of polished black boots from under the bed and compared them with his feet. He'd worried that they would be too big, like everything else. But he smiled as they pulled on with a pleasantly snug fit. *This is a delightful turn of luck.*

He considered the various shards of mirror on the ground. Finding the biggest piece, he carefully picked it up and set it against the wall. He took a few steps back.

The new clothes, though slightly baggy, were a significant improvement over his previous garments. He'd always been slender, but a month of barely eating had only made it worse. *Beggars can't be choosers. At least I no longer look like one.*

His gaze rose until the sunken eyes of a stranger stared back at him. So pale and gaunt. He scarcely recognized himself. A man in his mid-twenties, old enough to have made enough bad decisions to ruin his life, but with nothing to show for it except a fabulous set of cheekbones. His long, greasy, black hair hung past his shoulders. Assorted wispy patches on his cheeks couldn't decide whether to form a beard or retain their independence. He usually shaved them, but there was no time for that now. He sighed, turning away from his reflection. His new clothes couldn't hide the wretch hiding beneath them. He felt like a worm sticking from a shiny new apple.

He grabbed the leather pouch the Inquisitor had kept his possessions in and tied it to his belt. He wrapped the scalpel in a bit of cloth and stuck it inside, then gingerly placed Kiara's wrapped finger within, along with the effigy he'd woven from the straw he'd stained with the Inquisitor's blood.

He grabbed the two glass vials of holy water, holding them close as he inspected them. He emptied one, then put both the full and empty vials in his pouch. It was starting to get full. He surveyed the room one last time. *Ah, yes. If the road has taught me anything, it's that these are worth their weight in gold.* He grabbed two extra pairs of socks.

He hefted his spellbook, then glanced at the Inquisitor's prayer book. *Hmm. That is a nice touch.* He unfastened a pair of leather straps from the prayer book. Tossing it to the floor, he fastened the straps around his spellbook, clipping it to his belt.

The rod throbbed on the bed, the time between its pulses stretching. "Fine," said Malfus. "No more delays." He grabbed the rod, then threw open the door and stalked out into the hall.

Morten waited at the end of the hallway. He raised an eyebrow when he saw Malfus in uniform. "It's a good look on you." Morten looked Malfus up and down. "I'm sure Lieutenant Erickson wouldn't have minded. Did you find everything?" His gaze followed the glowing rod.

Malfus nodded.

"Where to now? The bod—"

"The bodies," said Malfus.

Morten swallowed. "This way."

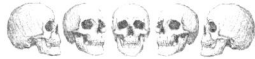

Outside, the sky had turned a melancholy shade of mauve and gray—like a swollen bruise. Malfus could hear birds waking in the distance. He followed Morten, enjoying the pleasant fit of the new boots, and the caress of the wool socks against his tender feet.

A soldier next to them grunted as his shovel bit into the earth. It was the start of a new grave, next to several others.

"I wouldn't worry about that anymore," Malfus said, giving the soldier a pat on the back as they walked by.

The soldier gave him a look, but didn't say anything. He shrugged his shoulders and dropped his shovel. He either didn't notice the missing embroidery on the jacket, thinking Malfus was an officer, or he was too tired to care where the change in orders came from.

Malfus silently weighed his options. One part of him wanted to follow Morten. He'd never get access so many fresh corpses again—or so much blood. He gripped the rod more tightly. *And this could be the key to bringing Kiara back.*

On the other hand, every fiber of his chickenish instincts told him to run as far as he could from this place. Though he wasn't sure how far he'd make it. *With my luck, I'll be shot in the back by a crossbow bolt before I make it to the trees. Right where the gnolls are waiting.*

His curiosity won. He wasn't in the mood for running, anyway. The mere thought of it was exhausting.

They passed the remains of the front gate. Fewer soldiers guarded it; more stood guard at the gaping hole in the wall. Their earlier attempt to form a barricade from the leftover bricks had been abandoned.

"Well, here they are," said Morten.

The human corpses had white sheets thrown over them, arranged in neat little rows. A mound of gnoll corpses sat between them and the gate.

"I'd best get started." Malfus rolled his shoulders back, then cracked his knuckles. He bent down to lift the corner of the first sheet, but a voice over his shoulder stopped him cold.

"Oi! Who's he? What's he doing, touching the dead?"

He looked up. Three soldiers approached. Blood covered their chainmail, and they rested their hands on hilts.

The closest spoke up. "I said, who are you? A bloody graverobber?"

"Why's he dressed like an officer?" asked another.

"First I've seen a grave-robbing lieutenant," said the third.

"No, no, it's okay," said Morten, his voice cracking. "Colonel Peshka knows about it. He's the, umm…"

"Corpse inspector," Malfus said, matter-of-factly.

Everyone paused to look at him, including Morten.

"What's going on here?" a gravelly voice called out behind them.

First Sergeant Goren strode toward them like an armored ox. The soldiers grew silent as the corpses. Goren gave the soldiers a stern look as she drew close.

She pointed. "You three, you're relieved from grave watch. Get cleaned up and rest. There's no telling when the gnolls will be back."

"Yes, First Sergeant!" they shouted in unison. Their ringleader gave Malfus a sour look before trotting off. The other two followed.

Goren turned to Morten. "Private Morten, stay here and keep an eye on our new *friend*. Make sure he isn't disturbed. Let me, or Colonel Peshka know if he needs anything." She gave Malfus an icy glare, then turned back to Morten. "More importantly—if he does anything suspicious or tries to run, you put a crossbow bolt in his back. *Then* come find me."

"And you," she said, turning to Malfus. She towered over him, and her voice grew quiet. "I'm going to have a talk with Colonel Peshka about those soldiers. I'll make sure he says something to them before they wake up and see—whatever it is you're about to do." She paused, looking down the rows of dead soldiers. "I may not agree with his decision, letting you do this. But I swear to Vesenia, and all the gods, that if I don't see *something* over here by the time I'm done talking with him, I'm going to lock you up with the Inquisitor. Do you understand me?"

Malfus swallowed, nodding.

She looked Malfus up and down. "While you're wearing that—completely out of regulation—uniform, you work for me. Got it?"

"Yes, ma'am," he managed.

"Not 'ma'am'. I work for a living. That's 'First Sergeant' to you."

Malfus sprung to a salute. "Yes, First Sergeant!"

She grumbled as walked away, like a box of angry nails.

Malfus sighed in relief, then kneeled by the first covered body. He could feel the rod buzzing in his hand, more eager than he was. He closed his eyes, preparing himself for the task.

"So, what do you need to do first?" asked Morten. "Need me to do anything?"

Malfus opened his eyes, pressed his hand to his temple, then stood up. "Listen, Morten." He put his hand on Morten's shoulder. "I'm going to need some space. Besides concentration, necromancy takes a bit of *privacy*."

I can't do this with you breathing down my neck.

Morten looked hurt for a moment, then smiled sheepishly. He yawned. "That's fine. I could use a bit of shuteye. Been a long night." He sauntered away, sat against a nearby building, and started nodding off.

Malfus turned back to the rows of bodies. Their white sheets were stained in various colors—bright red, rust, or muddy brown—depending on the quantity and quality of blood. Eight square sheets arranged in a row, with three rows of sheets, all told. Red mud squished beneath his new boots as he walked around the rows of corpses, concentrating.

Then he circled the mound of gnoll corpses. These were stacked higher than his head. He looked closely at the face of a gnoll corpse. Its tongue lolled out of its upside-down mouth, almost silly, but it didn't make its fangs any less deadly. There were so many gnolls that a rivulet of blood oozed downhill from the pile. The coppery smell in the air was so strong that he could taste it in his mouth, along with the faint scent of the lamp oil poured over them.

The rod pulsed in his hand. "Yes," said Malfus. "I think we'd best get started." He had no desire to be locked up with the Inquisitor; Goren would make good on her promise.

He walked back to the sheets, bent down, and lifted an edge. Here lied a glassy-eyed young soldier, perhaps a few years older than Morten. The corpse stared back at him, its mouth agape, as if surprised to see Malfus. Perhaps he hadn't thought his life would end with him staring face-up underneath a sheet, next to so many others. It looked like this young man had just shaved.

He shook off the thought. *I can't think about who they were—just what I* need *them to be.*

He inspected the corpse further. *A single wound. Deep, cutting almost all the way through. A spear pierced him straight through the chainmail, with a twist that broke and spread his ribs.* This corpse would be suitable. The limbs were still intact, which was the most important part. Zombies were slow enough already; a missing leg would make one useless. A zombie with a broken leg would lack the balance needed to carry anything, and couldn't keep up when traveling. The time and energy required to reanimate it wasn't worth it.

Even with such limitations, the undead certainly had their advantages. A soldier with a broken leg couldn't walk on it at all, or do much of anything, while an animated corpse with a severed leg wouldn't mind standing watch. Not a whine or complaint. No need for food or water; no breaks to relieve itself. Not even the need for sleep.

Malfus unclasped his spellbook from his belt and flipped through it.

A few utilitarian cantrips were scrawled across its first pages. These were the first he had learned back in Akkadia, when he had first arrived at the academy as a teen—hoping to become a trained wizard, with a bright future ahead. Such cantrips were spells that all first-years had to learn, weeding out students with no aptitude at all, before they could specialize in one of the seven high schools: evocation, illusion, transmutation, divination, abjuration, conjuration, and enchantment.

The eighth school, necromancy, was outlawed by the Church. Malfus looked through those first few pages, remembering how he'd struggled to learn them. His peers had surpassed him so quickly, including Kiara.

Those first rudimentary spells were all he'd recorded before his necromantic notes began. *Before I found my true calling. It's not my fault I struggled with the other schools. It's not my fault it's against the law. Why shouldn't I learn it? It's what I was* meant *to do.*

Thin handwriting and intricate diagrams filled each page, crammed into the corners and margins. Malfus had taken copious notes, but never had been talented at organization. He couldn't be faulted too much for it, as he'd had to scribble most of his notes under dim candlelight, in the rafters of the library.

His first necromantic spell was on the preservation of decaying flesh. He'd cast it nearly every night since fleeing the academy. Somewhere, much deeper in these pages, was a more difficult version of this spell. It did the opposite, causing rot and decay to spread into still-living flesh. He continued through the pages of his spellbook, passing a spell that allowed its caster to take on the appearance of a corpse—even stopping the heart for a short period.

The spells for dealing with undead came next. The first few were rudimentary, such as detecting the presence of undead, creating wards against them, or communing with spirits. Then came a spell for projecting the will of the caster onto existing undead, controlling them. This could be used on anything from an untethered zombie to a vampire, but it would be a battle of willpower between the caster and anything sentient.

His spells for animating the dead were much later, toward the very end of his transcribed pages. These were some of the final spells he'd learned, and for good reason. They were much more complicated, with many more steps in the process—and many more ways to mess up. Before casting such a spell, he had to prepare the corpse. Then he'd create a connection to the plane of death, calling for an echo of a soul to animate the body. Finally, he would bind the will of the echo to his own mind, so the arisen creature didn't turn into a mindless ravening undead—untethered, as much a danger to its creator as it was to anyone else.

With the arcanull cuffs gone, he could sense his mental connection to the plane of death returning—but it felt so tenuous, fragile as a silk thread. He took a deep breath as he pored over the pages, paying careful attention to words, runes, and hand symbols.

His eyes focused and unfocused as he studied. *Was it 'xi venis' tal' or 'xi venis' tol'?* Dried blood had smudged some of the ink. Might have been some of his own, from the night he was captured. He cleaned off the smudge, then read through the ritual again, using his finger to guide his concentration. It didn't help; the words swam on the page. He sighed, pinching his fingers into the bridge of his nose.

His concentration was as frayed as an old rope. The days he hadn't slept were too numerous to track. It had been a month since he'd had the opportunity to practice any magic at all. He needed more energy first, and he had to be able to concentrate enough to use it.

The rod began throbbing impatiently. He hefted it. "All right, then. Let's see what you can do. But do it quickly, before that armored brute comes back."

He held the rod out, next to the gaping chest wound of the first corpse. The ruby in the rod began glowing a brighter crimson as it neared the wound.

"You want blood? Here it is."

At first, the rod did nothing. But then, as it got closer to the wound, its gem pulsed faster, like a heart fluttering with the excitement of rejoining a long-lost love. Then it stopped pulsing, instead glowing a solid red while emitting a thin humming noise, barely audible.

Tendrils of blood rose from the open wound, crawling from the body like tiny worms. They climbed into the air, spiraling in a helix toward the star ruby. Malfus couldn't believe his eyes as the tendrils rose, as if through invisible veins.

The rod grew warm as the blood drew closer, until the heat became uncomfortable. Malfus tried to pull his hand away.

"Ow!"

Pricks of pain rippled across his palm, as if a hundred ants had bitten him. He tried to pull his hand away again, but it held fast. His fingers felt prickly, even numb, like they had fallen asleep.

As the blood reached upward, its tendrils merged together into a single strand, thick as a rope, pouring into the gem. His eyes widened as the blood disappeared. The ruby shone brighter, a light shining from depths that belied the gem's small size. He could sense its *hunger*.

Blood flowed into the rod for a few minutes before trickling to a stop. It never ceased to amaze Malfus how much blood a single corpse could hold. When the corpse finished draining, feeling flooded back into his hand and forearm—along with something else.

His pulse quickened, and his heart started beating harder. All he could hear was the blood rushing in his head, pounding behind his eyes. He clutched at his chest. *My heart. What's happening?* The surge was overwhelming.

Just when he thought he couldn't take it anymore, the rush stopped. A wave of ecstasy flushed through him as his heartbeat returned to normal.

Something was different now. His mind felt sharp. Like jagged glass. He wasn't tired at all. He no longer felt his aching rib, either. No, his body felt rejuvenated. No longer hungry. *Did I just eat blood?* He tried not to think about that. Instead, he felt grateful. He wouldn't need to spend countless hours meditating and studying his spells—it felt like he already had. His connection to the plane of death had changed from a tenuous thread to a constant stream.

Raising a few corpses would be child's play.

Something else echoed through the rod—and not the entropic void of the plane of death. This new sensation carried a silent promise.

A promise of power. *So* much power.

The corpse under the sheet was left a dry, withered husk. Its skin had turned grayish-brown, looking like the tattered leather shoes he'd cut from his feet. Its mouth hung open, lips peeled back to reveal white teeth, jawbones visible under the drawn skin. Its eyes had sunk into their sockets, dried like raisins. Its chain armor looked oversized, and its spear wound was a dark hole in gray meat. The young man under the sheet had disappeared, as if he'd never existed. Malfus shook the corpse's earlier appearance from his mind.

This is it. His hands shook with excitement. He glanced over the words and hand gestures in his spell book, committing them to memory. Closed his eyes, Malfus focused on the void, on the darkness in his mind. He held up the rod and, with his other hand, contorted his fingers into complex patterns, evoking ancient runes of power.

He chanted words in the dead tongue of the ancient Shal-Umbra Empire. Sharp syllabic words, with harsh consonants. He thought he heard another voice repeating the arcane words in the recesses of his mind. A chorus of scratching whispers, like gnawing rats. The memory of rats made him shudder. He shook them from his mind, focusing on the key symbols. They appeared in his mind more clearly than ever before. The void energy flowed through him so effortlessly. In his mind, he wove that energy into a strand, like a spider spinning a web.

There was a *pop*. Black and green motes sparked from his palm, flitting around the corpse like flies before entering its open mouth.

The corpse trembled as the void energy flowed into it. It opened its hand, slowly. Then its arm rose, pulling the sheet from its body. Bones and sinews creaked as the corpse pushed itself from the ground. It stumbled about awkwardly, in boots now comically large. Finding its balance, it swiveled to face Malfus, its jaw hanging slack.

Malfus projected his will at the zombie. He spliced a tiny strand from the great cord connecting him to the plane of death, and visualized that tiny filament running to the zombie and back, tethering it to him, ensuring its obedience. The strand pulled from his cord of energy, fraying it ever so slightly.

Now, to test it out.

He closed his eyes, focusing his awareness into the energy strand. He crawled through it to the corpse, as if squeezing through a narrow tunnel. His consciousness faded, flowing from him into the corpse. He only sensed a vague awareness of his body; it was a distant memory, in a faraway room.

Suddenly, he could see what the corpse saw. It was a bit unnerving seeing himself through its raisin eyes. He didn't want to consider how it saw anything with its eyes so shriveled; his experiments on how skeletons could see at all had only spawned more questions.

Remnants of the corpse's final moments bled through his mind: fear, the press of bodies, sweat, a spear against the chest; a slow, agonizing death. Those emotions faded, swallowed by a lasting hatred for the gnolls—and, more faintly, an envy for the living.

Malfus gave the zombie rules to adhere to. Other humans were not to be injured, but gnolls should be killed—*after* alerting him. Satisfied, he released his hold on its thread, snapping him back into his own body. The world swam.

After taking a moment to regain equilibrium, Malfus visualized clearing the rubble by the gate, arranging it into a makeshift barricade. A moment later, his zombie shambled away, as eager to do his bidding as a corpse could be. It wouldn't be able to move larger stones on its own—but it would soon have help.

Either the thin strand stemming from his connection to the plane of death was smaller than normal, or there was far more there for him to pull from. *More energy means more connections.* He turned to the other bodies. *I'd better start on the next one. I've got much to do.* He moved to the next corpse and raised its white sheet. This woman was older, with scars on her cheek and half an arrow sticking from her eye.

Malfus breathed in, focusing on the black pool of energy in the back of his mind. The rod pulsed with hunger. Tempting him. He still felt vigorous from the last corpse. That initial rush had been overwhelming, but had felt so *good*.

Perhaps a little more blood before moving on to the rest.

The rod pulsed in agreement.

Chapter 15

As the Crow Flies

"What do you mean, they're coming from behind us?" — Fenwick Derth, Monrovian Captain, on the last day of the Siege of DeGaullis

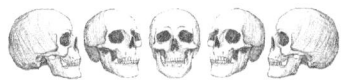

Colonel Peshka stared at his blotchy-faced reflection. His orange combover looked thinner and less convincing by the day. The uneven tips of his frazzled mustache drooped beneath bloodshot eyes.

He'd been up all night. As a commander, he never really slept. It was something he'd gotten accustomed to in his years of command, but it had taken a gradual toll. Constantly alert to the needs of his soldiers, as they fought or fucked in the barracks, or decisions about spoiled food—all at the most obscene hours.

He glared at his reflection, as if it were a stranger that had wronged him. Long gone was the young military officer. Brave, clever, perhaps a bit reckless, but he'd had a bright future at one point. And this stranger had robbed him of that. Now, he was the commander of nothing, in the middle of nowhere. He lifted his bottle of wine and took a long drink, sucking from it like water. He wondered if he could get drunk enough to bury his self-contempt; he wondered if he could even get drunk anymore.

"This is a fine mess you've gotten us into," Peshka said to his reflection. "A half-demolished fort, defending against an army of gnolls and a bloody giant. Barely any soldiers left. An Inquisitor locked up in my wine cellar. And the only help I can get to salvage this clustershit of a situation is a bloody necromancer!" He slammed his fist on his desk.

"Is it the right bloody choice?" He sighed. "Have I made any good choices in the last two decades?"

He looked at his bottle. A full-bodied Baskavian red, year 513. "Good year. The year I became a major. Not too many of these left." The bottle was already half gone; none of the wine he had left would be this nice. He wished he'd taken a few more bottles before locking the cellar, but everything down there had happened so damn fast. They should have done a better job stripping the Inquisitor; at least they'd confiscated his sword, and that chain whip. He could wake up angry, but couldn't do much else, locked away in there and disarmed. *Except help himself to some of my wine.*

Peshka took another swig of wine, then returned to his mirror. There was a good chance that freeing the necromancer would be his last real decision as a commander. This might be his last day as one. These fortress walls would take weeks to repair, maybe months. No, whatever happened today would be a glorious battle, the likes of which got written about in military histories—like he'd studied at the officer's academy. Maybe he'd end up in those pages. Force entire classrooms full of arrogant cadets—like he had been—to study his decisions that saved this fort. Even though they were greatly outnumbered.

They could just gloss over all the parts about the necromancy…

Peshka sighed. He knew the truth. He wouldn't be in any books. No one would remember his name. No one gave a shit about him, or any of them, out here in the middle of bloody nowhere. Offered for the Tithe, then forgotten. Left in the dust. If the Duke sent reinforcements, he'd find a tomb here—or, more likely, a bloody gnoll warlord with his own fortress.

"That bloody necromancer better keep his bargain. He has skin in this, too." Peshka wasn't sure what the necromancer was capable of, but doubted it could do more than delay the inevitable.

He took another swig from his bottle. He tried to think of what he'd tell the soldiers, once they realized their deceased comrades were up and walking. Nothing came except a sharp pang in his stomach. It growled, threatening another painful bout of indigestion. "Not now," he pleaded, then groaned, clutching his stomach.

He'd told most of the troops to get some rest. Only a few were assigned to guard duty, though the gnolls could attack at any moment. Goren was speaking with the few guards on duty so they wouldn't sound an alarm about the necromancy—but it was up to him to officially address the situation when the others woke up in a few hours. He hoped they'd understand. There weren't many left to disagree with him, anyway.

Peshka had faced death before. He'd seen its ghastly face throughout his military career, but it never seemed closer than it did now. It didn't matter how many gnolls they killed; their numbers seemed endless, while his soldiers dwindled away like sand in an hourglass. With the fort's defenses destroyed, he wasn't sure they would survive another direct assault—especially if they returned with that damn giant.

That white gnoll, Ghostface. It had proven quite the tactician, a much cleverer opponent than Peshka had faced before. The wily bastard was difficult to predict, but he knew Ghostface wouldn't squander this opportunity. The gnoll would wait until nightfall—perhaps not even that long—then press the offensive.

"That's what I'd do," Peshka said, sighing. "If this is my last day in command, I may as well stand on decorum. Look the part." He opened the wooden armoire beside his desk, pushing through his clothes until he found his dress uniform.

The navy blue uniform had been tailored several times over his career, but still fit—albeit a bit tightly. He donned his overcoat, covering his breastplate. Smoothing the golden rope hanging from his epaulets, Peshka brushed his fingers over each medal and ribbon pinned to his breast, remembering each battle. His silk sash of command wrapped over his belly, its teal length embroidered with his name and the date he took over this miserable fort. Still, he beamed with pride when he put it on. Last, he grabbed his cavalry saber from the wall, coughing as a cloud of dust came with it. He strapped the saber to his belt, then stood before the mirror.

"Tight in the back, but still rather dashing, I must say. Good wine gets better with age."

Peshka smoothed his mustache, but the short side frazzled even more, refusing to cooperate. He sighed and reached for the bottle on his desk. Right as he pressed it to his lips, a pounding on his door made him jump. The wine spilled all over his silk sash.

"Gods dammit!"

Peshka set the bottle down, gaping at the spreading stain on his teal silk. He turned, searching for something to wipe the stain with, and the hilt of his sword hit the bottle of Baskavian red. It fell to the floor and shattered.

"Dammit, Goren! Do you have to knock like a damn battering ram?!" Peshka growled. "Come in. It's unlocked."

Goren entered the room and closed the door behind her. She alternated looking at Peshka in his dress uniform and the shards of green glass on the floor. She didn't say anything—just fixed him with that look of hers.

A part of Peshka knew she should have been in charge of this garrison. Every so often, he caught her looking at him like she knew it, too. She was the perfect soldier. She'd risen through the ranks. Loud, brash. But disciplined. Always by the book, but doing right by the soldiers, too. Though she towered over the men, Peshka knew that her not being one was why she wasn't in charge of this garrison, or even a general.

If he survived all this, it was time to pass on his mantle. His glory days were over.

"Well? What bloody is it? Can't you see I'm busy?" Peshka bent over, using a dirty sock to pick up shards of broken glass.

"I finished my rounds," said Goren. "Checked back on the necromancer... He's done it, sir. There's no going back now." She looked at him levelly. "I hope you know what you're doing. This can't be another inebriated decision. This isn't some drunken bet in a card game. These are my—our soldiers' lives."

"I know! You think I don't know that?" Peshka threw the sock against the wall.

"You're going to need to say something to them. Before we have a mutiny on our hands. Have you thought about what you're going to say?"

"I'm working on it, dammit," Peshka snapped, then clutched at his stomach.

"I released most of them to get some rest, but the sun is coming up. They'll be up again before long." She sighed. "Respectfully, sir"—she looked him up and down—"get your shit together. We're counting on you." She turned to leave.

Peshka's stomach growled again, and he let out an acidic belch. Several more aggressive burps followed, doubling him over. Goren stepped forward to help him, but Peshka held out a hand as he righted himself.

"I'll work on what to say." He stifled another burp. "In the meantime, have the cooks whip up something special. Get some of that bacon from the reserves. Double portions. Seeing as how we won't have to be as strict with our rationing..."

"Yes, sir." Goren turned to leave.

"And, Goren..."

"Sir?"

"Keep an eye on that bloody necromancer. And the Inquisitor. Both of them, dammit. I'm not sure who I trust less."

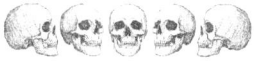

It was morning now. A murder of crows had gathered to protest Malfus's performance. They perched on the wall and rooftops, cawing angrily, cheated from their meal. A brave few swooped close enough to perch atop the pile of gnoll corpses, pecking for morsels.

He uttered the last few words of power. They dripped from his lips, thick as lantern oil. The arcane words tasted rotten, like spoiled milk, but at least they didn't make him retch anymore. He'd gotten used to the flavor.

The next cadaver rose from beneath its bloodied white sheet. This soldier had a cloven wound atop its skull, large enough for Malfus to stick his hand inside, but it didn't bother the zombie at all. It shuffled off to the gate, joining the others.

"Wait," Malfus commanded.

The zombie stopped. Malfus walked over to it and reached into his belt pouch, then pulled out his empty glass vial and scalpel. He made a small cut on its wrist and held the vial up. It slowly filled with blood.

"That should do," Malfus said, waving his hand dismissively. The zombie hobbled to the gate, where the others were already working. Its legs moved in jerking, erratic strides. *Like the awkward son of a rich cloth merchant, heading to their first ball. Oh, how we've all been there.*

He wasn't sure why zombies were afflicted with such poor movement. Even without broken limbs, they all suffered from spasmodic muscles. The less flesh remaining on them, the less of a problem it was. Completely skeletal remains were much more coordinated—agile even—lacking rotting meat to slow them down. But skeletons were significantly more fragile. One good blow from a mace could ruin hours of preparation.

He looked at his score of undead. They'd nearly finished assembling a barricade from the leftover rubble, near the giant boulder. *It's amazing what the combined force of a bunch of bodies can do when working in unison, instead of independently.*

Like ants. Big undead ants.

Malfus smiled, feeling a swell of pride from this small family he'd created. *Let's see that big metal ox say something now.*

His expanding ego pressed against the confines of his skull, looking for more room to stretch and grow. He closed his eyes, embracing his newfound power. He'd only raised this many dead once before; his connection to the plane of death had never felt so strong. In the past, the strain of each new animated corpse taxed the durability of his connections. Now he hardly noticed it when he added another.

Those connections radiated outward to each zombie, tiny pinpricks of awareness. Each was a strand in his growing web. He was the spider in the middle, sensing the minute vibrations of wind against the strands. Tiny pieces of him were in several places at once, stretched across a vast ocean of awareness.

He couldn't *see* what the undead were seeing—not unless he closed his eyes and took a moment to focus on one of the individual threads. But he was constantly fed bits of sensory information. His subconscious worked overtime, presenting only the most relevant scraps. Malfus rubbed a temple with his free hand. This hyper-awareness was a bit overwhelming.

The star ruby no longer flickered, but glowed a steady crimson. Its red light was brighter, and its magic aura, stronger. He'd caught himself staring into the gem as if hypnotized. It was the size of his fist, but it contained a depth that belied its physical dimensions. He felt as if he could climb inside of it, wading into a vast red sea. A thread to it gnawed at the back of his mind—a connection very different from the kind he shared with the undead. Something else emanated from it as well: a sense of something about to awaken, like an egg.

It seemed satiated for now, but it didn't protest when Malfus drained blood from corpses to replenish his focus. Whenever his fatigue started to catch up to him, or his concentration ebbed, he drained another corpse. Perhaps with every fifth or sixth corpse he raised; he had lost count. He was getting more accustomed to that surge of energy. It wasn't as overwhelming, but it still invigorated him each time. Even now, his heart pounded harder, stronger, faster. *Perhaps I'll reward both of us with a bit more blood on the next one.*

He closed his eyes, then reached out to his central entropic connection. He pulled away another strand, then focused on the corpse. *Like threading a needle in the dark, using only your mind.*

"Caw! Caw! Caw!"

He lost his grip on the thread. His eyes snapped open, and he glared at the offending crow. It perched on the top of the corpses, proud-as-you-please. Malfus threw a stone at it.

But draining blood only improved his mental acuity; he was cursed with the same lack of coordination he'd endured since childhood. His rock smacked the bottom of the gnoll pile. The murder of crows got the message. Their black wings fluttered in unison as they took off.

"Caw! Caw! Caw!"

All except for one. The lone bastard still perched on top of the corpses. It glared at him with its beady eyes. Malfus sneered at it, then looked for another rock.

"Caw! Key! Caw! Yar! Caw! Ra!"

"What did you say?" said Malfus, whipping around. The crow cocked its head, unflinching. Its eyes pierced his soul. "How could you know that name?" *I must be imagining things. Am I really talking to a crow?*

Malfus shook his head. *I'm just tired. Letting a bird get in my head. I still have so much to do.* He closed his eyes, trying to focus.

"*Kiaraaaa!*" screamed the crow.

His eyes snapped open; his arm lashed out instinctively, and the crow cut off.

Malfus looked up, eyes wide, as he saw a gnoll claw strangling the crow. After a moment, the gnoll's arm dropped limp, but still clutched the bird. It no longer moved.

At least it's no longer accusing me. Or saying her *name. It wasn't my fault!*

He'd never spontaneously animated a corpse like that. No preparation, no arcane words, just sheer force of will—if only for an instant. He'd only *read* about that kind of power before, from necromancers of old.

He looked back at the clump of black feathers. *I'll have a use for you yet, you diseased vermin.* The clawed hand held the feathered body like a treasure. Malfus gripped the rod in one hand, then carefully climbed the slippery pile of bodies. After an embarrassing display, he managed to scramble to the top.

He pulled the dead crow from the gnoll's grasp, examining its corpse. He concentrated, unwinding a thread from the back of his mind, then focused on the pile of feathers, still warm with fading life. He spoke the arcane words needed to complete the ritual, then tied the thread back to his primary cord to the plane of death, anchoring the bird to him.

A few long seconds passed. Then the crow fluttered, its left wing stretching, then its right, as it reanimated in his hands. Its beak snapped open and shut, but no sound came out. It thrashed for a moment, then grew very still, looking up at Malfus with those same piercing eyes.

Waiting.

Malfus threw it upward, visualizing the crow flying around the camp. It launched high into the air, much more impressive than his rock throw earlier. It soared higher and higher, reaching an apex, then dropped back to the earth. It hit the ground, then bounced in a pitiful, flapping display. After a flutter of feathers, it flapped its wings furiously, taking off again. It hovered clumsily at first, fighting against gravity, but then it found its rhythm.

He visualized the sky above the fort, and the crow flapped harder in response, flying upward, until it was high above him. He could feel the thread tethering it to him stretching, like letting a kite drift until it pulled taut—the end of his aura of control.

He stretched his awareness, through the thread and into the crow. He'd never attempted this on something so far away—much less anything flying—but, in theory, there was no real difference in transference between an undead crow and an undead human.

His consciousness slipped from his body. There was a split second of jarring darkness and rushing wind. Then he found himself very high up, and moving very fast. It was disorienting, being this far off the ground, but the feeling passed after a few moments of flight.

The fort looked so insignificant from up here. He could see its broken walls and the tiny toy soldiers manning them. *Is this how we look to birds? Like insects?* Their struggle against the gnolls seemed so trivial. The collapsed tower where he'd been kept prisoner was just a tiny pile of stone. Even the giant's broken corpse, strewn at the bottom of the cliffs, looked as small as a normal man. Malfus brought the crow closer to the fort while maintaining his remote viewing.

Below, on the opposite side of the courtyard, soldiers assembled in formation. Colonel Peshka stood in front of them. The crow continued its flight over the camp, wheeling back toward Malfus. As it got closer, he spotted Morten standing up and stretching his arms, approaching him. Malfus released his grip on the crow and had it continue to circle over the camp, keeping an eye out for any threats.

Malfus turned to Morten as he neared, still yawning.

"Is that them?" Morten asked, glancing uneasily at the zombies working at the crumbled gates, completely oblivious to both of them.

"Don't worry. I'm in control," said Malfus, doing his best to sound ominous.

Morten recoiled from him. "Your eyes, they're—"

"What?"

"The white parts are all red now. And the veins on your neck..."

Malfus pulled up his sleeve and inspected his forearms. His veins were swollen, distinctly purple beneath his pale skin, and pulsing.

"A side effect of mass production, I guess." *More than acceptable.* Even his voice sounded slightly different. Not quite his own—like a quiet whisper spoke at the same time. Malfus cleared his throat, ignoring it.

"What's going on over there?" Malfus gestured to the other side of the camp, where the soldiers had formed up.

"Something big for morning formation," said Morten. "Guess I'd better go, too."

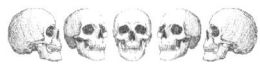

Inquisitor Deza groaned and clutched his aching head. It throbbed in response. He gritted his teeth and pushed himself to his knees.

The room was dark and damp, smelling like sour wine, moldy books, and onions. Deza felt at his neck. It wasn't there. His cord was gone.

He reached into the darkness, frantically searching the stone floor. "Where is it?" he hissed.

There was a grating sound as metal slid across stone. Deza sighed in relief as he felt the familiar object through his gloved hand. Four links of brass chain, fused into a diamond—the all-seeing Eye of Vesenia. Its edges had been sharpened with small barbs at their ends: a reminder of the suffering required to remain true to the path of the righteous. He removed his glove, feeling the sharp edges of the links against his fingers. He closed his hand around it, tightening his grip until its burrs dug into his palm. He gripped the symbol even tighter, and the pain faded into a burning warmth. Blood trickled from his clenched fist.

He closed his eyes and clasped his hands. "Blind Mother. I, too, am blind. I beseech you—illuminate the path of your servant with your wisdom."

The brass amulet bloomed with a golden light, growing warm to the touch, until a gentle amber light filled the room, softening the darkness. Deza searched his surroundings, but didn't see his keys anywhere.

"Where are they? Those fools don't know what they've done."

He absently reached down to his belt for his sword. It was gone, too. He clenched his bleeding hand into a fist. They would pay for aiding a heretic. The Colonel, the First Sergeant—the entire battalion would be condemned to the penal colony of Bleakmont, mining arcanull for the rest of their lives. But he would need to escape first.

Deza retrieved his crumpled hat from the floor and placed it back on his head. The room was small, filled with barrels and debris, none of which appeared useful. Its only exit was a narrow set of stairs leading up to a thick wooden door. Getting sufficient strength to kick down the door—or enough momentum to charge at it—would be impossible with those stairs.

Deza felt at a pouch on his belt, relieved that it was still there. He reached inside, his fingers searching its contents. He smiled as they clasped a small glass vial.

Chapter 16

Bolstering the Defenses

"Sure, I've seen them. Walking around the graves at night. Lumbering, with missing limbs. Like they're looking for something. Don't ask me what they're looking for. Don't ask me what I'm looking for either." — Sylas Horton, 'alleged' graverobber

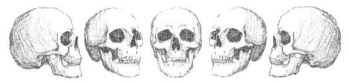

Peshka stepped onto the raised wooden platform in front of the soldiers. This wasn't where he normally held formation, but he'd chosen this spot next to the infirmary so that those who couldn't stand could still hear him.

It was also far enough from the front gate that the troops wouldn't see what the necromancer was up to—though Peshka knew that word was already spreading among his soldiers, faster than crotch-rot. The appetizing aroma of bacon wafted from the mess hall, pleasant but out of place in the gloom.

Is this really all of them? He surveyed the ranks. A few wounded hobbled out from the infirmary, some on crutches, others assisted by soldiers. Roughly sixty men and women stood before him. Perhaps two or three dozen huddled in the infirmary, too injured for formation—or for fighting. Many of the wounded would be dead by nightfall. Most the troops assembled in front of him sported fresh bandages.

Peshka shook his head. More than a score had been killed last night. The worst single attack so far. And now the gnolls had a bloody giant.

He looked into each haggard face. Most were so damn young. He knew every man and woman in his regiment by name—who was skilled, who was a lazy shite, and who he'd want fighting next to him. Knew each loss, knew each death. They all looked distraught. Haunted. They reminded Peshka of his soldiers at the Siege of DeGaullis, right before the battle. He wondered how many of those faces never made it back after the Siege. He'd still rather face that all over again than this mess. Even those odds had been better than what they faced now.

The soldiers looked scared and tired, but they still had a glimmer in their eyes as they watched him. Hoping he had the answers. Peshka's stomach rumbled. His mouth felt slick with spit, nauseous. He cleared his throat, swallowed, and held back his vomit. He tried to remember what he'd told his men before the Siege of DeGaullis—tried to find some of that fire—but nothing came. If only he'd gotten one more mouthful of wine before he had to make this address.

Best get this show on the road.

Peshka swallowed, then cleared his throat.

"Soldiers. At ease. I thought I'd have something prepared, but... I don't. Instead, I'll tell you what's on my mind."

He started pacing atop the platform. "We've endured many nights of struggle. Watching our foe kill our comrades, our friends, our brothers, our sisters—our family! Taking them away, one by one.

"Last night was the worst of it. And now, with our gate destroyed, they will come tonight to finish the job. We still have before us a most grievous ordeal. We will not survive on our own. Not without help."

Peshka stopped pacing and twisted at his mustache, debating how to continue.

"And I've asked for help! I've done everything I can to change our plight. I've sent to the Duke for reinforcements more than a dozen times. I've told him the direness of our situation. I've told him how ill-equipped we are. I've sent messengers requesting aid until I could no longer spare any men. I've heard nothing. Nothing! I have done everything I could. Could you imagine what I'd do, if I could? If I were given the chance?"

Peshka paused to scan the crowd. Most watched with undivided attention. A good sign.

"Through a twist of fate, arranged by the gods—no, arranged by Vesenia herself—I've been given a chance. Should I ignore it? Decline her aid? When no one else has lifted a bloody finger to help us? I have stood here before you, many a night before, with nothing to offer you but my blood, sweat, and a few words. But now I have something else to offer you. *Victory.*"

Now he had their full attention. Their expressions changed from resignation to bewilderment as they listened in silence.

"I promise victory, though the road will be long and hard. Without absolute victory, there will be no survival. For any of us. But our victory comes at a price. There can be no flinching, no thought of surrender. Are you willing to pay it?"

The soldiers murmured among one another, but no one spoke up.

"Damnation is our only road to salvation..." Peshka muttered to himself. *No beating around this bush.*

He cleared his throat and spoke loud and clear.

"A necromancer was delivered to our doorstep last night, before the attack." He winced as the words came out, but felt better for saying them, as if at confession.

The murmurs grew louder as the implications set in. But Peshka didn't give the troops a chance to speak up or for his speech to lose momentum.

"We have honored the memory of our fallen. And now they will honor us—by fighting at our side once more, so that we may live. They will bear the burden of combat for a second time. But let not our honored dead have given their lives in vain. Allow them to offer us a chance to make it home. To see our families again. I'd give my life to protect each of you. And if it comes down to it, I'll give my *unlife* to protect you as well.

"We've been forgotten. Left to fend against a foe that has given us no quarter. They know only butchery, with no respect for life, understanding only death. Let us answer in kind!

"Grim though our task may be, tonight the tide will turn! With our fallen comrades fighting at our side! We! Can! Win!" He punctuated his final words with a stab of his finger.

Peshka held his breath, unsure of the response he'd get. A standing ovation, or a lynch mob.

It was neither. The men remained silent as the grave. No one spoke for several excruciating seconds.

"It's not right!" someone yelled.

"Would you rather fight on the front lines instead?" another voice snapped back.

"What would the gods think?" yelled another. "What about Vesenia?"

The soldiers started shouting and arguing.

"Enough!" Peshka yelled over them. "I've made my decision. And it will be my guilt to bear." He turned to First Sergeant Goren as he left. "Make sure everyone gets their share of bacon."

"Where are you going?" she called after him.

"To talk to that bloody necromancer."

Malfus scratched a stick in the dirt, drawing a thin line. Counting twenty paces from the rubble of the ruined gate, he stopped.

"You there!" He pointed his stick at a zombie carrying a skull-sized stone in its hands. "Come here." The zombie ambled toward him. "Yes, yes. As quickly as you please." He tapped his foot as he waited for it to lumber over.

"Right here will do." He pointed his stick at the end of the line. The zombie dropped the stone, and it landed with a dull *thud*. Malfus rolled it a few inches with his foot, then waved his hand away. "That will be all."

The zombie made a raspy groan as it turned around, then walked back to where the other zombies excavated stones for the makeshift barricade.

"Wait," he commanded. He walked to its side, grabbed it by the wrist, and turned its hand over. Tips of bone stuck out from bloody fingers where the flesh had worn down from digging. Malfus shook his head. "This won't do. Not at all." Without a living mind in place to keep it from injuring itself, zombies would literally work themselves to the bone.

Footsteps approached from behind; he let go of the zombie's bloody fingers. "Go on, shoo. Back to work." He slapped it on the buttocks, and it ambled back to the others.

"You there! Malfry, was it?" called out a gruff voice.

"It's *Malfus*."

He turned to see Peshka approaching. The Colonel wore a polished breastplate, adorned with a ridiculous number of ribbons and medals. It rang like a dull wind chime with each step. His polished boots squelched, sinking into the bloody mud. The certainty of his gait faltered as saw the undead working at the ruined gate.

"That was quite the speech earlier. Bravo." Malfus held the rod and stick in the crook of his arm, clapping dramatically. "And I see neither torch nor pitchfork following you, so it must have had the desired effect."

Peshka stared at the walking dead, as if forcing himself to accept they weren't a drunken hallucination. "Yes, well—I see you've kept your end of the bargain, too."

"Of course." Malfus feigned a look of hurt as he touched his fingers to his chest. "What? Because I'm a necromancer, you didn't expect me to keep my word?"

"Not exactly. I figured you would have turned and run at your first opportunity." Peshka paused. "I would have."

"Trust me. It crossed my mind more than once."

"Still, I'm glad you're doing the honorable thing. These undead may not turn the tide, but every little bit helps."

"Don't flatter yourself, Colonel. Honor isn't keeping me here. If I could have run, I would have. I'm just not much of a horseman, you see." Malfus glanced at the dozen horses tethered to the side of the burnt stables. "Where would I run to, with the fort surrounded? As for risking my neck—as a necromancer, I'm a firm believer in safety in numbers. As you can see." He motioned to the undead. "So the only logical decision was to hold my ground here."

Convincing enough. Don't want him to suspect I'm still considering it.

"I guess you've got a point."

"Well, now that you're here—" Malfus cleared his throat. "I need a few things. Tools for my workers. Some shovels and a few pickaxes should do."

Peshka scoffed at the undead. "Why do they need them? They're doing just fine."

Malfus sighed. "Can't you see how busy they are, rebuilding the fort's defenses? Tools will make it go much faster. Besides, I can't have them scraping their fingers to the bone. None of them will be able to hold weapons when the time comes. And we still need to do something about that boulder."

Peshka nodded, holding up his hands. "All right, all right. That can be arranged. I'll have Goren see to it."

"Another thing that metal bucket can do. Earlier, some of your soldiers were throwing rocks at my zombies."

Peshka coughed and raised a hand to his mouth, stifling a laugh.

Malfus frowned. "This is no laughing matter. I don't want to see my hard work wasted for the amusement of some soldiers. Those were *their* previous comrades. They should show some respect for the dead, dammit." *And some for me, too.*

At that moment, a zombie carrying a stone passed by and let out a horrid noise, followed by a foul smell.

"Ugh. Is that normal?" Peshka pinched his nose and took a step back.

"Most men shit themselves when they die. Sometimes, it just happens... after the fact."

"All right. I'll see to it that the soldiers don't harass them anymore. Now, was that all?"

"One more thing." Malfus looked him level in the eyes. "I need assurances, Colonel. That once all of this is over, I'll go free. I need to know that you won't turn me over to the Inquisitor once I've served my purpose." Malfus paused. "Or, at the very least, give me a few days of a head start. He'll be too busy chasing me to report what you've done. You don't want him bringing the Inquisition's wrath down on you and your men, do you?"

Malfus paused again, letting Peshka squirm. He put a hand conspiratorially around the Colonel's shoulder. "Or—you could always just kill him. Accidents happen in the heat of battle. Besides… dead men tell no tales." Malfus grinned, eyeing a nearby zombie.

Peshka wiggled away from Malfus, uneasy. "I guess we'll have to cross that bridge when we get there." Then he walked off, lacking his usual bluster.

Malfus called after him. "Another thing. Some of that bacon I've been smelling would be just lovely!"

Peshka grumbled as he stormed off. Malfus smiled, then grabbed his stick, extending the line in the sand.

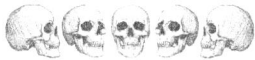

Inquisitor Deza held the glass vial up to his glowing amulet. Its amber light shone against the vial, the delicate glass housed in a metal cage fashioned after the Inquisition's gibbets. Its stopper had been carved to resemble a grinning gargoyle head. Deza held the vial closer to the light, leaning the glass until a viscous yellow liquid neared its lip.

Satisfied, he replaced the stopper and put the vial back in his belt pouch. Then he held his amulet aloft. The holy symbol's light cast long shadows against the walls. Rats and roaches scurried away.

Deza paced the perimeter of the room, inspecting the debris, looking for anything useful. He found an assortment of cracked wine barrels, a few pieces of broken furniture, eleven empty glass bottles, and a pile of flat wineskins. The Inquisitor counted the leather wineskins. Twenty-seven. He picked one up, took its stopper off, and held it upside down. Empty. He looked closer at the leather; it was still in good condition. Pulling a small knife from his boot, Deza began cutting the wineskin into strips, laying them in neatly organized rows.

When he finished, there were one hundred and twenty-eight strips of leather in total. He picked them up, one at a time, measuring them against each other. He tossed away several that were too short, and trimmed a few that were too long, until he was satisfied with their uniformity.

He tied one strip around his holy symbol, hanging it from his neck, freeing his other hand to work. Then he collected the rest of the strips, wrapped pairs of them together, and tied them end-to-end. His movements were meticulous and mechanical, like a dwarven-built machine.

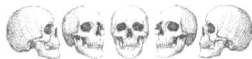

Malfus leaned against the stone wall, chewing his salty bacon as a shovel crunched the dirt nearby. A dozen zombies dug with the shovels Goren had brought over. They possessed only the bare amount of coordination needed to get the job done, flinging dirt wildly over their shoulders; only some of it made it out of the hole. But digging holes was a war of attrition. After a few hours, they had excavated the entire section knee deep, ten feet by twenty.

Another pair of zombies worked together, carrying a huge spar of burnt timber on their shoulders. They dropped it on a pile next to several others, then walked back to the camp.

Yet another zombie wavered on top of the giant boulder by the gate, raising its pickaxe. The tip gleamed in the sunlight, before dropping on the boulder with a piercing metal *chirp*, sending pieces of rock flying. More zombies dug at the boulder from the bottom, while others grabbed chunks of rock from the ground and stacked them on the growing barricade.

Malfus jumped as a dead gnoll sidled up behind him. He wasn't used to the undead gnolls yet; his instincts told him to run every time he did. The creature still reeked of lantern oil. This close, he was reminded how much larger they were, compared to humans. Cords of muscles bulged under its mangy fur. It carried a rock so large Malfus couldn't have rolled it by himself if he tried.

The pile of dead gnolls behind Malfus remained stacked as high as his shoulders. He'd raised a dozen of them, but even with the aid of the rod, he needed a break.

A crowd had gathered to watch, coming as close as they dared. None approached closer than thirty feet, and most were further back than that. The troops were interested, amused, and abhorred in equal measure; most were likely grateful it wasn't them doing this backbreaking labor.

Malfus stuck the last few bits of bacon in his mouth, then licked his salty fingertips. It was certainly much better watching the labor happen rather than doing it himself. One of the most underappreciated perks of necromancy was its endless reservoir of unskilled manual labor.

Once this madness was over, he would take advantage of that—if he survived. Perhaps he'd start a farm somewhere, far away from the Ossory Empire, where the Inquisition would never find him. All he needed was some fertile soil and fresh corpses. *That would be the life. All the time in the world to study necromancy—away from the uneducated, away from the Church and the Inquisition. Then I'll solve the mystery of this rod and bring Kiara back. I know I can.*

He could even raise a few undead oxen, or other beasts of burden, working them through the night, plowing fields. No complaints from farmhands. Not even a hungry mouth to feed.

No wonder necromancy is illegal. If nothing else, it would completely overthrow the economy.

If he learned more about farming and construction, there was nothing he couldn't accomplish. All he needed was an adequate supply of bodies. Especially now that he could raise so many. First a farm. Eventually, an entire village.

Why shouldn't I? Then, once I bring her back, she could rule over the village with me. She'd like that. Malfus smiled at the thought of his undead paradise.

A loud *crack* brought an abrupt end to his daydream. The boulder split in half. A chunk as large as a man crashed down, smashing a zombie below with a dull *slam* that reverberated through the earth.

Uh-oh. Workplace injury—better go see how bad it is.

Malfus waved a hand. All the zombies near the boulder immediately stopped working and took a step back. He hopped down into the hole and meandered over to the accident.

Only the top half of the zombie was visible; its bottom half was pinned under the slab of rock. Malfus inspected it, watching as the zombie clawed at the dirt in front of it, struggling to get free. It made no sign of any pain—no sign of anger or loss. It merely clawed at the dirt, trying to extricate itself. To get back to work.

Malfus wondered if the zombie knew he intended to sever the connection and cast it aside like a broken toy, now that it had outlived its usefulness. Was the zombie trying so hard to escape because it desired undeath? Did it enjoy having a purpose again? Or did it feel robbed of the cold, quiet peace of death? Did it even care?

Malfus shook his head and laughed. *They're an extension of my will. Nothing more. Not until the connection is severed, and they become 'mindless', wandering on their own.*

Though he wasn't sure how mindless the untethered actually were. Necromantic tomes weren't too clear on that point, either. They offered mysticism and theory: *"an echo from the soul is summoned from the plane of death, granting unlife, to serve the necromancer's bidding."* But that didn't explain how the mechanics of necromancy actually worked. It ignored the role of consciousness, the role of the soul. *If you believe in that sort of thing.* Not to mention how zombies could see with rotting eyes, or how eyeless skeletons saw anything at all. But that was another matter; he wasn't prepared to tackle that, just yet.

He raised his hand to sever the connection, making room for a corpse with a functional lower half. But he paused, watching his zombie claw in the dirt, oblivious.

A part of him empathized with it, as it clung to its purpose. He sighed, lowering his hand. "We'll find a use for you. If nothing else, we'll put you on guard duty." He snapped his fingers, then beckoned at a couple of zombies nearest to him. "You two. Pull him out."

Malfus climbed out of the pit, then closed his eyes, transferring his awareness back to the crow. The sudden transition of height and speed was less disconcerting each time he made the swap. Now it felt exhilarating. The height made everything insignificant, while the speed made him feel alive. The irony of feeling alive while inhabiting a corpse wasn't lost on him.

He circled the pit, watching the two zombies pull the torso from under the boulder. The rest continued their digging. He glided over them, over the field of tall grass facing the gate, and then as close to the line of trees as he could manage. The thread connecting him to the crow pulled taut, then began to fade as he reached the tree line, just a few hundred feet away. *I guess this close will have to do.*

Even if it was a short leash, the freedom of flight was intoxicating after being a prisoner for so long. He wished he could fly away without turning back. Life as an undead bird wouldn't be so bad. *If only it worked like that.* But once he flew too far, the connection would sever. He'd be stuck here, while the bird would became untethered, wreaking some small amount of terror on its own.

He willed the crow lower until it flew right over the tall pines, peering through them. He didn't see any signs of life. *No gnolls yet. I guess that's something. We'd best make good use of our time.* He performed one more pass, then flew back to the front wall.

Below, a group of soldiers approached, carrying long objects with shiny metal tips. *Uh-oh. Looks like the welcoming committee has arrived.* He released his grasp on the crow, returning to his own body, as a jeering voice called out from behind.

"Well, well, well—if it isn't Lieutenant Graverobber."

Malfus turned around to face the sneering soldier from earlier. His two friends were with him, along with several more, perhaps a dozen in all. It was hard for Malfus to count them as they towered over him. The lead soldier held a shovel, and the others behind him hefted shovels, axes, hammers, or other tools to use as makeshift weapons.

Malfus swallowed, the taste of bacon still coating his mouth. He mentally reached for a few of the nearest undead, drawing them closer. He clenched his fist to keep it from shaking before he spoke. "I see you've brought some friends with you. I've got some of my own as well. I'll warn you—if you're here to cause trouble, they won't hesitate to protect me." Then he raised the glowing rod in a manner he thought befitted a dangerous sorcerer.

The soldier slapped his belly, laughing heartily. "Nothing like that. Look, we got off on the wrong foot." The soldier extended his hand. "Name's Kaye."

"Malfus." He cautiously extended his hand.

Kaye shook it in a bone-crunching grip, smiling broadly before releasing it. Malfus flexed his sore fingers and popped his knuckles.

Kaye leaned closer. "Listen. Not all the troops feel the same way about seeing their dead mates again." He gestured behind him. "Me and my lads wanted to lend a hand."

Malfus hid his surprise. "Are you sure? That won't be necessary. There are more than enough of—"

"Nonsense. We're in this together. Can't sit around waiting for the damn bastards to show up. It's driving us mad. Idle hands, and all that."

"Well, I certainly won't protest. Go right ahead." Malfus stepped out of the way.

The soldiers watched him, wary, but nodded to him as they filed past. Jumping into the hole, they looked at their undead comrades uneasily, still coming no closer than arm's length.

"Don't worry," Malfus called out. "They won't bite."

Morten was the last soldier in line. Malfus hadn't spotted him until now. He just looked at Malfus with a big, beaming smile, fit for a dragon counting its hoard.

"What are you smiling about? Was this you?"

"I might have put a few words in with some of the guys."

Malfus was taken aback. "Well—knowing that not everyone wants to stab me in the back when the battle begins makes me feel a bit better. Thank you, Morten." *Nice to know I have at least one friend out here.*

"Don't mention it," said Morten. "Besides, they were curious. Wanted to have a closer look. There were already a few bets going around."

Malfus was about to ask Morten what that meant, but the soldier had already jumped down into the hole with the others, digging alongside the zombies.

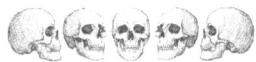

Inquisitor Deza dabbed sweat from his forehead, then stepped back to admire his handiwork. It had taken a few hours to finish. A cord of braided leather rope, three times the length of a man, lay on the ground before him. Deza wrapped the cord around his hands and snapped it taut a few times. Satisfied, he coiled it around his shoulder.

He took off his hat, then placed his holy amulet inside it, muffling its radiating light. He climbed the stairs, taking them one step at a time, listening. Reaching the top, he pressed an ear to the thick wooden door. Snoring came from the other side. He raised his hat to the side of the doorframe, letting a beam of light trickle through the crack.

Three steel pin-hinges fastened the inside of the door. This wouldn't have measured up to the Inquisition's standards for a holding cell. Luckily for him, the wine cellar was not built with that in mind. On the other side of the door, a metal panel protected the locking mechanism, with a small metal loop for a door handle jutting above it.

He examined the keyhole. Narrow, but just wide enough to work with.

Cutting a narrow strip of cloth from his cloak, Deza pushed a loop of it through the keyhole, wrapping it around the bottom of the metal loop. He lifted it, then dropped it. It thudded softly against the metal panel. Then he tied his leather cord in a knot around the handle, slowly unwinding it as he retreated down the stairs, counting out sixteen steps.

At the bottom, he wrapped the cord around his arms and behind his back, pulling it taut. The knot tied to the handle held fast. He released his grip, then jerked it taut once more, testing the knot.

Deza grabbed the other end of his makeshift rope and secured it to the handle of his small knife. He swung the bladed rope with a few practice swings at the bottom of the stairs. It wasn't as effective as his chain, but it would do. He tightened the knot, then coiled his rope, tucking the excess atop the last step. Everything was in place.

Like a coiled viper, he only had to wait for the right moment to strike.

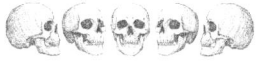

Less than an hour had passed, but their progress had doubled with the help of the living. Malfus walked through the hole in the wall, watching the zombies and soldiers work. They'd broken down the boulder, stacking its fragments into a barricade with bricks from the ruined gate. It was only half as high as the adjoining walls, but it completely filled the gap. A pile of twenty sharpened stakes lay nearby, each one twice as long as he was tall. They had dug the hole all the way out to his markers. It was nearly waist deep now.

Halfway there. Just a little deeper.

He stopped next to one of the soldiers. The man stared intently at a zombie while it toiled away with its shovel.

Malfus patted him on the shoulder. "What's wrong? Worried he'll attack you? I assure you he won't."

The soldier jumped slightly, then turned to face him. "Oh, nothing like that, necromagicker. It's just that Jerond has been staring at me the whole time he's been working."

Malfus glanced at the zombie, who was indeed staring back at them with a craned neck as it dug.

"Yes, well. I don't see how that's a problem. He's not going to—"

The soldier's voice dropped to a whisper. "Do you think he remembers that I owe him money?"

Malfus laughed, then stepped in front of the zombie and met its gaze. "I highly doubt it. Only a few fragmented memories remain. They don't even know their names anymore." Malfus hooked the rod to his belt, then grabbed the zombie by the head. "He's just got a broken neck." There was a crack as Malfus twisted its head, snapping it into place. "There. That's better."

The head of the zombie now flopped in the opposite direction. Malfus turned back to the soldier, but he'd dropped his shovel, covering his mouth. Then he turned and ran.

The other soldiers let out a chorus of laughter. Malfus smiled, then joined them. It'd been the first time he'd truly laughed, for longer than he could remember.

He smiled as he walked away, leaving the soldiers and undead to their work. He had some work of his own. He walked to the far side of the pile of gnoll corpses.

He closed his eyes, probing his connection to the plane of death. It had never been this strong before, and it felt like it was still growing in power. He'd never dreamed of raising so many undead at once. Thirty-one now: two dozen humans, six gnolls, and a crow. He could feel their invisible strands of negative energy connecting him to each one.

Malfus looked down at the rod. Would his connection to the plane of death still be so powerful if he lost it? Or would he need a constant supply of blood to maintain this? *Problems for another time.* He held the rod closer, not wanting to look away or put it down. It tugged at him, pulling at him.

Motes of light flickered within its star ruby, swirling together, then breaking apart. He watched as the patterns shifted hypnotically.

"Just a little bit longer. Just a little bit *more.*"

Malfus shook his head. Had he just said that? Or had someone else? He wasn't sure. He pressed his fingers to his temple. *I'm just tired. Need a bit more blood to keep going.* He turned to the pile of gnoll corpses and held out the rod.

Chapter 17

A Giant Problem

"Those buried in sin will seek death and not find it. They will rise with insatiable hunger and unquenchable thirst. They will chase death, but it will flee from them. This is our punishment for the cardinal sin of tampering with the cycle of death—the sin of necromancy." – Attributed to Vesenia

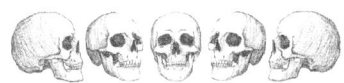

The sun dipped lower in the afternoon sky, setting the clouds aflame. Malfus chuckled, realizing it had been this hour yesterday that he and the Inquisitor were first ambushed by the gnolls, forced to flee here. In a bizarre twist of fate, he now oversaw the fort's defenses, working as a free man. *With my personal army of zombies.*

The only downside, of course, was the coming battle, where there was a good chance he'd join the ranks of the dead himself. *Luck is a capricious mistress.*

More soldiers had begun to show up. Judging by most of their faces, it was their first time seeing the undead. They had dressed for battle, most in chainmail hauberks, but many wore no more than thick tunics. Soldiers too wounded for the thick of combat bore crossbows, and were already stationed on the walls. A few with missing legs had needed help getting up there. Still, they held their crossbows, and were ready to do their part, wounded or not.

Though there'd been no sign of the gnolls, the atmosphere had changed to an air of inevitability. The undead weren't helping the mood, either. Seeing your dead companions fighting was one thing; knowing it could happen to you, if you fell in combat, was quite another.

The troops looked grim and alert. With the defenses mostly taken care of, they fussily tightened the buckles of their armor, sharpened weapons, filled quivers with bolts, or checked their crossbow strings. A few whispered to each other, but most were as talkative as the undead. Malfus felt a growing dread gnawing at his stomach. He did his best to ignore it, focusing instead on the pit in front of him.

Two zombies near its edge stood to either side of a long wooden stake, thick as a tree, and twisted it into the ground. Their jaws hung open, their cheeks drooping like melted wax. Singularly focused, they continued to work, oblivious to the effect they had on the living. *They certainly don't seem bothered by the impending battle. Facing death is a lot easier the second time around.*

The pit was finished. It had been dug deeper than a man at full height, its walls smoothed. They'd lined its edges with wooden stakes, every few feet along its perimeter, angled inward over the pit. The stakes had nails hammered into their ends—a reward for anything attempting to climb out. Shorter wooden stakes jutted from the pit's walls and bottom. Jagged rocks too small for the barricade were stacked in piles as ammunition for later.

A single gnoll corpse remained, waiting to be animated. Its left arm had been hacked off above the elbow. Having been at the bottom of the pile, it was covered in blood. Malfus held out the rod, closed his eyes, and drained some of the excess blood. His pulse quickened, but the feeling was a far cry from what it had felt like the first time. Gnoll blood also left an unpleasant, oily taste in the back of his mouth. He still shivered as the energy surged through him. Then he began to harness void energies to grant the gnoll undeath. *Last one.*

The corpse started to get up, but Malfus waved his hand, and it stopped. He closed his eyes, focusing on the multitude of strands connecting him to the other gnoll zombies. He willed them to come to him, leaving the human zombies to finish installing spikes around the pit.

The living soldiers kept their distance, but Malfus noticed how they looked on in horror and anger as the gnolls walked past. A few soldiers grabbed their weapons as they watched the macabre parade.

The zombie gnolls formed up as if awaiting an inspection—forty-five in total. Malfus walked in front of them, hands clasping the glowing rod behind his back. The brutes towered over him, each gnoll a head taller or more, and double his width at its shoulders. They stared past him, their slack jaws baring canine teeth. Seeing them standing at attention made Malfus feel powerful. It was more than he'd ever raised before. An entire army, ready to do his bidding.

Let's see that Inquisitor imprison me now.

He raised his arms, then spread them; the gnolls split into two groups. Half of them climbed into the pit and lied down. He lowered his palm, and the remaining gnolls collapsed where they stood.

Malfus looked over his shoulder and whistled. Morten approached from the crowd of soldiers. He paused as he got to the line of gnoll corpses on the ground. He scanned them, his curiosity tempered with fear.

"One more coat of lantern oil, and they're ready to go," said Malfus.

Morten nodded. "I'll let Kaye and the others know." He glanced at a nearby building. "I found some lantern oil. But I'll need someone to help carry it over."

Malfus grinned. "I can help with that." Two of his gnolls stood up. "Just point them at the barrel. They'll take care of the rest."

Morten looked at the two gnolls as they walked up next to him. He wrung his hands together. "Do I need to say anything, or…"

"No. Just point"—Malfus pointed at Morten's chest—"like this." The two zombie-gnolls looked at Morten as he did.

Morten swallowed. "Got it." Then he walked away, trying not to look over his shoulder.

It wasn't long before Morten returned. The two zombie gnolls lumbered behind him, carrying a large wooden barrel. When they got to the line of gnolls, Malfus nodded to Morten. The soldier drew his sword and pierced the barrel. A gout of viscous black liquid spurted from it.

Malfus waved the zombies along. They walked along the line of gnoll corpses, carrying the barrel at an angle so oil sloshed over the gnolls as they walked past. At the end of the line, the two gnolls doused themselves in oil and lied down with the others.

"Fetch Kaye and the gang, would you?"

Morten nodded.

Most of the soldiers still refused to approach the undead, or Malfus—all except for Morten, Kaye, and their companions. They returned a few moments later, staring at the oiled gnolls with bewilderment.

"All right," said Malfus. He motioned at the gnolls. "They're ready."

"Can't they walk out on their own?" Kaye peered at the motionless corpses.

"No." Malfus shook his head emphatically. "There's no sign of the gnolls, but they could be watching from afar." He looked over his shoulder. "They can't see these moving, or none of this will work. They have to think they're dead."

Kaye nodded, then turned to his friends. "All right, lads. You heard him. Let's start moving these slippery bastards."

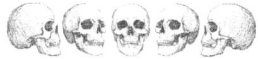

The crow soared high above the fort. Malfus watched through its eyes. Below him, the pit looked like a gaping maw in the ground, surrounded by long wooden teeth. Soldiers placed limp gnoll corpses in the open field, outside the wall. It took two soldiers to carry each. The heavy gnoll bodies were difficult to grip after being doused in lantern oil. The soldiers trekked halfway between the wall and the trees, then spread out, dumping the corpses unceremoniously in the knee-high grass.

I've never had undead play dead before.

He sent the crow back to the edge of the trees, then brought it low. *Still nothing.* Malfus took one more pass over the forest canopy. Satisfied with the lack of signs of the gnoll invaders, he relinquished his mental grasp on the crow. It resumed its circuit over the fort's perimeter.

He leaned against the wall and closed his eyes, taking a moment to appreciate the vastness of the web growing in the back of his mind. At the end of each tiny strand shambled one of the corpses he'd animated. He could sense each of them, knowing what they knew.

The two dozen human zombies stood near the pit, each hefting a weapon of some kind—spears, axes, a few with shovels. Better weapons were reserved for the living. Some stood still, while others shuddered with minor convulsions as magic energies coursed through them.

He also felt his connections to the forty-five gnolls. Half lurked at the bottom of the pit, motionless. He'd scattered another two dozen around the fields facing the gate. Tall grass swayed in the wind above them. The crow flew above them all. Gliding unceasingly, untiring.

Malfus felt tethered to every one of them. Seventy in total, with the crow. His mind felt full; it was difficult, keeping it from overwhelming him. He could flit through each of his connections, focusing on their individual perspectives, but he also had a vague idea of their collective awareness. It was disorienting at first, but he sensed a general aerial perspective of the camp, even as he stood below.

He'd never been able to channel so much void energy before. Never with enough concentration to command so many undead at once.

All arcane magic posed danger to the spellcaster. While plenty of evokers had exploded by channeling too much power from elemental planes, and any number of illusionists had driven themselves insane, necromancy posed greater risks to its caster than any other school of magic. The necromancer literally channeled through their body the energies of death.

The Scar—a blemish on the face of the world—had been created by the necromancers of the destroyed Shal-Umbra Empire. A permanent reminder of their hubris and the dangers of necromancy.

Many simpler and better-known necromantic spells had magical wards and barriers built in, protecting the caster from their energies. Malfus had gotten several tattoos that directed void energies, preventing them from accumulating in his body—something else he'd learned from the Swamp-Hag Yagyii.

He already knew that his expanded connection to the plane of death had grown beyond the power of his tattoos. The winds of negative energy passing through him slowly ate at his lifeforce—but, thanks to the rod, he could channel more energy now than ever, could control more dead, and he knew he could raise even more, if needed.

He'd raised all the corpses available to him. Now that he'd run out... he wanted *more*.

He squeezed the rod. This was more than being able to control so many undead at once. No, his connection to the plane of death *was changing*. In his mind, he had sensed the row of dead soldiers that had been buried when he'd first arrived. He could *feel* them now. They remained in their shallow graves, buried not far from where he stood.

If a living soul was a burning candle, then corpses trailed dwindling threads of smoke, stretching into the plane of death. Threads of void energy. Entropy. Negative energies, interwoven into the fabric of the universe. Death resided in every living thing, building in their bodies—dancing with the energies of life. Occasionally, it manifested in the form of a disease or malady, when too much had built up.

The more Malfus focused on the buried bodies, the stronger he felt a pale echo emanating from them. Those vessels had once carried life, but the light inside was darkness now. He could peel back their layers and see their last sights before dying. Digging further, he sensed, beyond his fingertips, some of their final memories prior to death. *Like plucking petals from a flower*. He could taste who each of them had been. Fragments of memories—a scent, a feeling, a knowing.

But the six dead men were too insignificant to be worth his attention. It would take too much time unburying them and removing the chains they'd been buried with. *Another silly tradition to thank the Orthodoxy for.*

His mind drifted further. Beyond the row of corpses, a charred body huddled beneath the burnt remains of the stables. For some reason, it carried a faint recollection of sunflowers. Inside the infirmary, negative energy oozed from the plane of death like pus from a wound. The energy pulsed as a soldier, grasping for life, finally lost the will to hold on. *So many in there, so close to death—and of no use to anyone, lying around, waiting to die. But it would be highly frowned upon if I hastened their journey to scrounge up a few more zombies.*

His mind drifted even further. Corpses hid, crushed under the rubble of the fallen tower, where he'd been kept prisoner. Beyond the debris, the broken giant sprawled at the bottom of the canyon.

"Any sign of them yet?" a voice called out, snapping Malfus from his trance. Peshka.

Malfus gripped the rod until his knuckles turned white. *This drunken oaf.* "No. I said I'd tell you if I saw anything."

Peshka nodded, then inspected the pit, raising an eyebrow at the gnolls lying at its bottom. "And your defenses? The pit and barricade are finished?"

"Yes," Malfus snapped. "Can't you see it yourself?" *No thanks to your soldiers. Only a handful of them helped, or dared approach the undead at all.*

"Will it work? What happens when they return with that damn giant?"

"I don't suppose you have any more ballistas? 'Ballistae'? Whatever it is."

"Fresh out of stock, I'm afraid."

"I guess I'll solve all of our problems myself," Malfus muttered.

Peshka squinted at him. "You don't look so good. A bit paler, and sweating like I do after a hangover. Have you rested since the chains came off?"

Malfus scoffed. "Rested? I've been raising an undead army. I'll have time to rest in my grave. Don't worry, I'm fine." *Never been better.* Malfus turned to walk away.

"Where are you going?" Peshka called after him.

"I've got one more thing to take care of."

Malfus wasn't sure why he felt so on edge. It was probably pre-combat stress. Blood would ease his nerves, and he knew where he could find some. A lot of it, actually.

And, at the same time, how he could solve their *giant* problem.

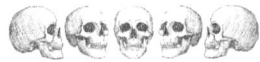

Deza put his leather gloves back on. Then he carefully lifted his glass vial, holding it up to the light. Unscrewing its gargoyle head stopper, he slowly lifted the glass container out of its metal cage.

As he unstoppered the vial, Deza covered his face with his hat, then extended his arm. He held the vial over the door's bottom hinge, then painstakingly tilted the glass, letting a single drop careen over the side. It landed on the pin of the hinge, then hissed. Acrid yellow smoke filled the air. Deza poured another drop on the bottom hinge, then worked upward, quickly and carefully. Two drops on the middle hinge, then two more on the top one. Finally, he angled the vial so its top slipped into the eye of the keyhole. He poured in the rest of the mixture. Smoke poured from the metal keyhole as it melted like wax.

A muffled voice sounded from the other side of the door. Deza tossed the empty vial into the darkness below, then sprang to the bottom of the stairs with the grace of a cat. He grabbed the coil of leather rope in both hands and began counting down from ten.

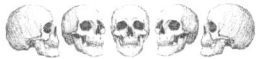

Malfus wiped sweat from his brow, holding tightly to the rod. He struggled as he climbed the pile of rubble that had once imprisoned him. Then he stood at its top, alone, appreciating the silence. This side of the fort had been deserted.

His newfound death-sense—at least, that's what he decided to term it—was still working. He could feel the corpses of Morten's companions entombed in the rubble beneath his feet. They called to him, like tiny beacons of darkness, wisps of smoke seeping from beneath the rocks.

Further below, he sensed a much larger flame, smoldering on the canyon floor. Malfus looked down and saw the giant's corpse. He froze. Part of him expected it to get to its feet and climb after him. It looked like a great monument to some heroic warrior, cast aside and thrown down the cliff. Its massive limbs bent at disturbing angles.

The cliff below was a sheer drop. There was no way down to the canyon floor except by falling or climbing; the trail back up took a winding road, leading through the forested canyon, where the gnolls were waiting.

He reached out to the plane of death, feeling its void energies flow through him. He sorted through the threads in the back of his mind, like a spider fortifying its web. Then he followed the massive beacon of smoke, reaching out to the giant's corpse. He could feel it down there. A great empty void, waiting to be filled. *Waiting to do my bidding.*

He felt nervous about controlling something so powerful. He'd never tried anything like it before. Well, he'd never had the opportunity. He concentrated on his connection to the entropic energy, focusing it. Then he reached out to the giant, so far below, as he'd done with the dead humans and gnolls.

And then—

Nothing. No echo, no response. Only the cold void.

Have I done something wrong? Forgotten a word? Mispronounced something? He reached for his spell book, flipping through its pages. The spell for animating the dead rested at his fingertips. He'd done everything right—pronounced everything correctly. *Is there a different spell for something so large?* Another thought crept into his mind. *Am I just not strong enough, even with the rod?* He didn't want to think about that.

So he tried again. He strained as he pulled on his connection to the plane of death. But it was too much. Like lifting a giant boulder on his own. If the zombies required a small thread of energy, the giant required a rope. Without drawing more energy from the plane of death, he couldn't do it. Not without sacrificing half of his other zombies—maybe more.

Maybe if I was closer—or if I had enough blood. Surely the giant's veins were full. But how would he get down there? And if it didn't work, how would he climb back up?

Malfus gripped the rod tighter in his hand. "Time to wake up. I need your help."

The rod ignored him. Its connection to him hummed in the back of his mind, but it felt distant. He shook the rod angrily. "Hello!" The red light inside bounced and flickered, but made no other sign.

Doubt washed Malfus down a stream of insecurities. A familiar current—but one he hadn't swam in since the magic academy in Akkadia.

His shortcomings at the academy replayed in his mind. Magistrex Dis'elauxe's shrill voice, chiding him for not making the proper hand gestures for the most basic of illusion spells. Telling him he would never become an illusionist—that he would never learn magic at all.

It was true. He lacked talent for every school of magic, other than necromancy. And if he were perfectly honest, he was a necromancer of middling skill, at best. *It's not like I can find a mentor—much less any tomes or scrolls to study from.* But now he realized that without this rod, he was nothing. Just a sniveling worm, pretending to be a magician. And what was he, without his necromancy? *Less* than nothing. No skills of any kind, and an aversion to manual labor. No great physical traits or looks. He was no orator, no leader of men. A forgettable face, with no talents of any kind. Something his arcanull chains had made him painfully aware of.

"Please," he pled. "How do I appease you? More blood?"

Malfus pulled out the vial of blood he'd saved. He opened it, letting a drop fall on the ruby. It rolled off the surface. There was no answer from the stone. The ruby continued to glow with its unearthly light, but it felt distant, impatient.

He emptied the vial, pouring the rest of the blood on the gem. Still nothing.

"What do you want from me!?"

Malfus growled, hurling the vial off the cliff. The power he'd borrowed from the rod was still on lease, but for now, his credit had run out.

As he was about to fall further into despair, he felt something pulling at the back of his mind, tugging at one of his strands, like a fly caught in his web. He followed the vibrating thread back to the crow. He peered through its black eyes. There was movement in the forest below.

The gnolls. They were back. *Dammit. Already?* He had to warn the others. This giant problem would come later. Malfus turned to jog back to the front gate.

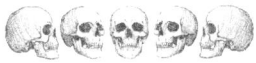

Finn propped himself against the wall, struggling to keep his eyes open.

Earlier, he'd been relieved to get some bacon and a short rest. The bacon was tasty, but he didn't get a wink of sleep. *Who can sleep at a time like this?* Finn couldn't remember the last time he'd gotten a full night's rest.

Now it was back to guard duty. Guarding that creepy Inquisitor. He wondered why they needed to. The Inquisitor hadn't made a sound since he'd gotten locked up. First Sergeant Goren had probably clobbered him to death—the woman had hit him *hard*. And with metal gauntlets, no less. Finn wondered if he'd need to keep guarding him when the gnolls attacked. Neither First Sergeant Goren nor Colonel Peshka had been very clear on what to do once that happened.

Inquisitor or not, guard duty was better than the front lines. Not to mention, it beat watching the undead shuffle around. Just the thought of it made his stomach turn. He didn't want to fight a giant again.

Finn shook his head, remembering how Big Duncan—the biggest man he'd ever seen—whimpered like an infant after the giant hit him. Duncan's size hadn't done him a lick of good. Sergeant Donovan had splattered against the wall. He'd been a living, breathing model of military discipline, and that hadn't helped him. Nothing was left but meat. Heimrich's entire arm, *flicked off* by the giant. Like a toy—like one of his sister's dolls.

Killing the giant had brought him little comfort. That memory came with the sight of its eye getting impaled, followed by the awful noise it made as it fell, screaming, from the tower. That memory was more horrible than watching his companions dying.

Finn looked down. His hand was shaking. He never should have signed up for the Tithe. Life in the slums of DeGaullis wasn't this bad. Stealing bread, conning for some coppers—that was a lot easier than fighting monsters. With the exception of today's bacon, his food and pay was about as bad or worse than life as a beggar. He still wondered about his sister. Worried about what happened after he left. He hoped she had enough to eat.

Maybe he could steal a bit of shuteye to calm his nerves before the battle. The Inquisitor wasn't going anywhere. And he hadn't made so much as a peep. Surely a little sleep wouldn't hurt anyone. Then he could stop thinking about his dead squad. It might be his final chance to take a nap, if the gnolls really were coming tonight.

Finn closed his eyes and leaned against the door. It did no good. The smeared meat of Donovan against the wall—Heimrich's spurting arm—the jelly erupting from the giant's eye. They waited for him behind his eyelids.

A hissing sound in his ear gave him a start.

Finn whipped around. Yellowish smoke poured from the keyhole. There was an acrid smell unlike anything he'd smelled before. He froze. What was he supposed to do? Run and get help? Guard the door? Neither First Sergeant Goren nor Colonel Peshka had been very clear on what to do if the door began *smoking*. Finn took a step back as he considered his options. He reached for his sword hilt.

Then the hissing slowed. It turned to a faint sputter, and the smoke stopped billowing from the keyhole.

Finn drew his sword. His hand shook so badly, he could barely get his blade out of its scabbard. Sword in one hand, Finn reached out to touch the door with the other.

But before he could, there was a loud bang as the door was ripped inward, crashing down the darkened stairs, as if pulled by magic.

Finn stood at the top of the stairs. He couldn't see anything below—just darkness. The metal hinges on the doorframe steamed as if melted. What could do that to metal?

"Hello?" he called. But why? Why wasn't he running? Why had he drawn his sword? He could barely hold it. What could he do with it? He knew how dangerous Inquisitors were. Every child of the Ossory Empire had heard the tales. But he didn't need those stories; he'd seen this Inquisitor himself, covered in blood, as unbothered as if it were rain.

Finn turned to run, his mind finally registering. He should have run as soon as he saw the smoke. But it was too late.

He heard three sounds in quick succession: a whistling, a scraping of metal against stone, and a crack like a tree branch snapping. Pain lanced through his foot, and Finn found himself lying on his back. He looked down; a knife blade stuck from his ankle, a leather rope affixed to its handle. So much blood—his blood—spurted from his foot. His leg was skewed at an odd angle, the rope coiled around it.

The rope swept him off his feet, dragging him across the floor. His ears rang and his face felt hot. He wanted to cry for help, but all he could think about was the pain in his foot. He screamed as the rope jerked taut, then felt the cold floor drop out from under him. For a moment, he was weightless, flailing in the dark. He dropped his sword, clutching at the air. Then he landed on the stone floor with a jaw-rattling crash.

The Inquisitor stood over him, illuminated from below by an amber light. His stern face, all bright angles, looked like a marble statue from a Vesenian cathedral—frowning upon the masses, ready to mete out divine justice. Those eyes knew Finn's every sin. Not just his complicity in locking up the Inquisitor, but everything Finn had done on the streets of DeGaullis to feed himself and his sister. They were all reflected in the Inquisitor's stern gaze.

The Inquisitor held the other end of the leather cord. Finn felt dizzy looking at it, his head throbbing. His helmet had done little to protect him from the stone floor. As his heart slowed, breath rushed back into his lungs. Finn squirmed away, but the Inquisitor loomed over him.

He screamed as the Inquisitor reached down and pulled the knife from his ankle.

"No, please," said Finn, holding his hand up as he sobbed. "I didn't do anything. I had no idea what they—what the Colonel was going to do. They just had me guard the door. That's all." He sat up, ignoring the pain in his leg. "I was raised in a Vesenian orphanage. A chapel in DeGaullis. Please!"

"Mercy for the guilty is cruelty to the innocent." The Inquisitor raised his knife above Finn, its blade gleaming in the amber light.

Chapter 18

One Last Drink

"Vesenia isn't like other, uncaring gods. She understands us. She walked as one of us! Suffered for us. Died for us. She healed the Scar to unite the Ossory Empire! And still you reject her grace." — Priest Rowen Orlanzo, to his congregation at the Church of Her Eternal Flame, in the Holy Capital

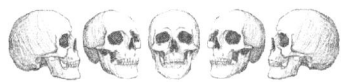

Malfus peered down at the giant one last time. His shortcomings and failures stared back at him from its massive eye socket. A murder of crows cawed mockingly from below, as they claimed the giant as their own, feasting greedily on its remains. The empty eye socket seemed to be the crowd favorite.

The blood-orange sun nestled between two distant hills, filled with the unspoken promise of freedom. Yet that freedom remained as unreachable as the giant far below. Part of him wanted to run; another, to jump off the cliff. Instead, he sighed, turning away from the edge. Hopefully, he wouldn't regret passing up the opportunity later on, however the night turned out.

Before heading back, Malfus switched his consciousness to a distant point of awareness. After a squeezing through a few moments of darkness, he sensed damp earth and tall grass swaying in front of him. He saw only grass, and couldn't hear anything but chirping crickets and, more distantly, the tolling of the fortress bell, raising an alarm.

Not yet. It's too soon!

He swapped his awareness back to the crow. From above, the two dozen bodies placed in the field looked like moth-eaten holes in a tapestry of swaying grass.

Where are they?

At first, he didn't see anything. Then he noticed signs of movement in the trees. The gnolls were amassing in the woods facing the fort. The shadows moving through the trees were small; from up here, it looked like the ground was moving. He swooped with the crow, getting a rough count. Endless rows of yellow eyes and sharpened steel reflected the fading light of the sun. There had to be hundreds of gnolls.

Malfus released his crow, swapping back to his own body—only to be greeted by a wave of nausea and a racing heart.

Calm down, you coward. They aren't here yet.

He hurried toward the front of the fort, the last place he wanted to be.

He unclasped his spell book and flipped through its pages as he walked. Refreshed the arcane rituals in his mind—and gave himself something other than the gnolls to think about. His mind raced, frantically imprinting the arcane words and gestures into his memory, but he couldn't decide which spell to start with. He couldn't focus on anything over the sound of his pounding heart.

But something else was there, too. Not just fear—excitement.

He'd never been in a real battle, nothing like this. He practiced magic for experimentation rather than combat. Most of his spells, he cast on the dead, not the living. Sure, he'd used his magic to defend himself a few times, only killing when his hand was forced, and even then, fewer times than he could count on one hand. *Or has it been more?*

As he neared the front of the camp, soldiers ran past, carrying quivers full of bolts, crossbows, spears, or other equipment. Malfus heard orders shouted by First Sergeant Goren, her voice unmistakable.

He continued his search through his spellbook, scrambling for the few necromantic spells he kept for combat. He'd managed to find a handful in his travels through Monrovia; there were far more with defensive capabilities, rather than offensive. The pages slipped through his fingers as he sought any spell with potential.

The first spell that fit was *fear*. A simple defensive spell, one of the few Malfus had used on living targets. But it was used to prevent combat, rather than ending it. *Wish I could channel some of my own fear. I certainly have more than enough.* He turned the page. It would take more than fear to survive this night. There was no running this time.

The next spell that caught his eye was *contagion*, an offensive spell that spread necrotizing rot through flesh. Unfortunately, its effects took too long to be of much use. *Though the shock is still immediate.* Still, he made a mental note of some of its words and hand gestures.

Now we're talking. A spell that drained the life force of its victims—*enervation*. He smirked as he remembered the first time he'd cast it, in an attempt to save a tavern from robbers. *What a shitshow that was. Look what good being a hero did for me then.*

He was so focused on his spellbook, he didn't notice Peshka standing in front of him. They collided, and Malfus fell backward into the mud. He managed to hold onto the rod, but his spellbook flew from his hands. Cursing, Malfus snatched it from the air, keeping it from falling into a puddle.

He gripped his spellbook until his fingers turned white. "Can't you watch where you're going?" he hissed at Peshka.

"I thought you were going to raise that giant." Peshka stared at him with hands on his hips, like a disapproving father.

"Do you see a giant? I tried—and I couldn't."

"Couldn't? What do you mean, *couldn't*? Don't give me that! I thought you were a bloody necromancer!"

"Yes, well—I never said I was a particularly good one."

Malfus stood up and brushed himself off. *Was that the best you could come up with? You idiot.* He strode off, leaving Peshka stammering as he clutched at his stomach. Malfus, in the meanwhile, tried to cobble together his remaining dignity.

The closer he got to the gate, the more chaotic things grew. First Sergeant Goren stood above the madness like a metal lighthouse—a shining beacon of order. She shouted commands in monotone barks. Soldiers ran past him, carrying equipment or weapons.

"There you are!" she bellowed, as Malfus tried to slip past.

Not again. Malfus looked up at the imposing woman. "Yes? What is it?"

"I've been looking for you. The gnolls could attack at any moment."

"I'm aware. That's why I'm here."

"Well..." Goren hesitated. He could see the wheels turning as she considered. "Do your zombies need anything? Do my soldiers need to *know* anything? Should they keep out of the way once the fighting starts?"

Malfus snarled. "I've already told you." *I swear, the dead listen better than the living.* He sighed, then took a deep breath before continuing. "The undead will fight on their own. They already know to only attack gnolls. Everyone can fight alongside them, but the undead act best as our front line. They are far more *resilient*." *And the living are so fragile.*

Goren waited, as if expecting more. Malfus growled, then continued.

"Listen. Have your troops rain bolts and rocks on the gnolls from above. Then have the ones on the ground take care of any bastards that make it out of the pit. Your soldiers can stand away from the pit; my undead will focus on gnolls that get through—and take care of any *unforeseen* surprises."

Goren nodded, looking galvanized. "I'll let them know."

Malfus snapped his spellbook shut. If only he had more time. He'd read about some of the battle-magi of legend, back at the academy. Powerful names, like Phoros the Living Flame, Kivin Torre the Marked, or Illaria the Mirror-Queen. Incredible wizards, with brilliant minds for strategy, besides their arcane mastery. Jazelle of the Amber Blade had used an ancient elven weapon as the locus for his spells, instead of the traditional staff.

Almost all of them had been evokers. That school of magic channeled primordial forces from the elemental planes, to devastating effect. He remembered his evoker peers back at the academy. Arrogant and headstrong. Physically imposing, at least for mages. Channeling such forces was the most physically demanding magic to study. But it made evokers the bullies of the academy—undoubtedly encouraged by their evoker instructors. He'd hated them, and yet—he'd wanted to be one of them.

Like Kiara was.

Malfus couldn't have felt further from those battle-magi. He was no evoker; he was just a necromancer. Though necromancy was universally feared, necromancy itself begot cowardice, as it relied on directing undead puppets to do your fighting for you. It also required immense foresight. Most other schools of magic were more reactive, adjusting to the rhythm of battle.

Malfus sighed. *I have to use the tools I've been given.*

He walked over to the spiked pit, standing on tiptoe near the edge. The stone barricade was stacked so high, he could barely see over its top. Though he'd seen the gnolls through his crow, he wanted to witness them himself. If he saw them with his own eyes, he could bury his fear of them. At least, that's what he told himself.

He neared his zombies assembled near the pit. They stood still, like statues, save for the occasional convulsion as energies flowed through them. Passing them, he ambled to a ladder leaning against the stone wall. He buckled his spellbook to its holster, tucked the rod into his belt, and began to climb.

On top of the wall, several soldiers leaned against the battlements. They were busy checking their crossbows, making last-minute adjustments to their armor, or wrapping crossbow bolts in strips of oiled cloth. No one paid Malfus any heed.

There was a gap between the soldiers, near the battlements; Malfus took it. Before he could see the gnolls, he heard them. Their chittering laughter in the distance grated on him, burrowing under his nerves like a worm in a coffin.

He swallowed as he approached the balustrade, forcing himself to take each step. It was dusk now. The twilit sky was a stain of bruised charcoal, punctuated by a few shining stars.

As the sun set, the gnolls became easier to see. There were so many, it was hard to pick out one in the underbrush. All Malfus could make out was a writhing wall of fur, fangs, and steel. The gnolls lurked among the trees, outside of crossbow range—chittering, howling, stomping their feet, pounding on shields, and waving their weapons. It was dark enough that their eyes reflected the dusk like yellow lanterns. How many were watching him?

He swallowed as he spotted yet more eyes reflecting from the woods, behind the others. *So many.* He tried to swallow, but his mouth was dry. His pulse felt weak, and his fingers were bone-white as they gripped the stone wall. He wished he had more blood to drain—that he hadn't thrown that vial off the cliff. But, even if he'd kept the blood, using the rod in front of so many soldiers—it wasn't the right time. He looked over the battlements again, taking comfort that he hadn't seen the giant yet.

"Oh, there you are," Morten called out behind him. He jogged over, his helmet bouncing.

"What? You need something too?" Malfus snapped.

Morten looked hurt. "No—er, yes... I just wanted to wish you luck." He turned around.

"No, wait." *So much for being a good friend.* Malfus sighed. "Sorry. My nerves are getting to me, is all."

"That's okay. I get it." Morten gripped his crossbow tighter as he looked across the field. "You said we don't shoot until we see the undead gnolls, right?"

"Shoot as many of the bastards as you damn well please. But wait to use flaming bolts until my zombie-gnolls stand up."

Morten nodded. "Got it. I'll make sure to tell the others."

"They're just standing there. Why not attack? Send the undead after them now!" Kaye leaned against the battlements a few paces down.

Malfus scoffed. "Don't be silly. There aren't nearly enough undead. Besides, we need them to come to *us*."

All three of them looked to the gnolls. The monsters pounded on their shields. Each echo counted down to their attack.

"Why don't they just get it over with?" Malfus hissed. "All this waiting is horrible."

"I know," said Morten. "It's the worst part... Until the fighting begins, at least."

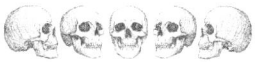

Colonel Peshka twisted his mustache as he kicked at a small rock in his path. "Bloody necromancer. Can't raise a bloody giant. *They* still have one."

Peshka's stomach joined his disgruntled mutterings. He clutched at it as he walked. Two soldiers rounded the corner of a nearby building, carrying a long wooden beam. Peshka ignored the pain in his stomach. He couldn't let it diminish his command presence in front of his troops.

As they approached, he nodded at them. Maybe he'd offer words of encouragement. But something was wrong. One soldier was missing an arm; both moved with the dead-man shuffle. Shaking his head, Peshka gave the two zombies them a wide berth as they stumbled past, dropping the wood next to the gaping pit. Peshka raised an eyebrow as he peered into the pit; its bottom was carpeted with dead gnolls, lying motionless, as if it were their grave.

"Spotty work. He couldn't be bothered to raise them all? And on a night when every bloody body counts. Bet he'll have an excuse for these, too. He's got more excuses than—well, *magic*, that's for certain."

A zombie next to the pit stared back at him. "Private Erich," Peshka breathed. Erich had been a young man in his early twenties from Almarada. A blacksmith's son. Peshka's stomach felt full of rusty nails, his mind full of broken glass. The latter only became an issue when alcohol relinquished its sweet caress.

He looked through the gap in the wall. The gnolls waited in the trees, beating their weapons on their shields. A bunch of heathen savages. Peshka pulled out his spyglass and surveyed the amassing army. There was still no sign of the albino or its pet giant. "Still got time," he muttered, walking away.

He'd drunk most of his remaining wine to calm his nerves before giving his speech. Then he'd had a bit more, to celebrate how well it had gone. Then, after a few more cups to steady his nerves through all this waiting, he ran out. He didn't have enough to steady them again.

"A few more bottles in the cellar." He was certain of it. That liquid courage stood between him and becoming who he'd been at the Siege of DeGaullis. "Just one bottle."

It was a sound plan. His only uncertainty was how he would deal with the Inquisitor. Deza likely wasn't very pleased with the situation. He'd have the soldier on guard duty accompany him. Who had that been? Oh, yes—Private Finn. Surely the two of them could handle an unarmed man. Inquisitor of Vesenia or otherwise.

Peshka turned a corner and passed a soldier struggling with an uncooperative crossbow. "Dammit!" said the soldier, sputtering. He lifted his crossbow overhead as if to smash it on the ground.

"Wouldn't do that," said Peshka, shaking his head. "Not too many left. You'll be stuck with your bare hands if you break it."

The soldier froze, then lowered his crossbow. "It's the damn windlass. Keeps freezing up on me."

"Let me see it, lad."

The soldier handed him the uncooperative crossbow.

"Freezing on you? Best get all the kinks worked out now; can't have it doing that in the middle of a fight. It'll get you killed." Peshka examined the windlass; its gears were a bit rusty, but one of the screws had started unwinding. He took out a small knife and tightened it, then tested the windlass again. Its teeth ratcheted together smoothly.

Peshka handed the crossbow back to the soldier. "There you are."

"Thank you, Colonel, sir." The soldier took the crossbow with shaking hands.

Peshka's brow furrowed in thought. "It's Private Lenny, isn't it?"

"Yes, sir," said Lenny in a small voice.

"You can call me Peshka tonight, Lenny."

"Yes, sir, Peshka, sir, er—Peshka."

"*You* aren't going to freeze up tonight, are you, Lenny? A soldier freezing up in the middle of a fight is as useless as a crossbow that won't fire."

"No, si—Peshka."

Lenny's hands started to shake a bit less.

"What's on your mind, son?" asked Peshka.

"It's these damn undead. They got to my nerves, is all. Seeing my dead friends..."

"Me too, son. Me too." He sighed, putting a hand on Lenny's shoulder, then chuckled. "But if it makes us jumpy, imagine what it'll do to the gnolls, eh?" He slapped Lenny on the back.

Lenny let out a forced chuckle of his own, trying to smile.

"And they'll be our first line of defense. Our tools let us put our smaller numbers to better advantage—like this fine crossbow here, in the hands of a brave soldier such as yourself." Peshka touched a finger to Lenny's chest.

Lenny looked up, smiling.

"There, that's it, lad. Chin up. It'll be fine."

Peshka resumed his walk to the storeroom, clasping his hands together so Lenny couldn't see them shaking. He muttered to himself as soon as he was out of earshot. "The necromancer's bloody plan better bloody work."

The storeroom was just ahead. This side of the fort was a ghost town. Peshka wouldn't have minded a couple zombies stumbling around; the silence was unnerving.

"Better make this quick." He reached for the door handle, but squawked like a chicken as his guts convulsed. He clutched at his stomach with both hands until the pain subsided. "Damn stomach! Can't you work *with* me for once?" He wiped his mouth, and bloody spittle came away on his gloved hand. "Of bloody course." He spat out a mouthful of blood and bile, tasting the copper. "At least I'll be dead before this indigestion can get much worse."

The door creaked open as he pushed on the handle. It was dark inside.

"Awfully dark in here, isn't it, Finn?" he called out. "You taking a nap on us, lad?"

There was no response. He thought he heard a rat scurry off.

"What are you playing at, boy?"

Peshka fumbled in the dark, until he found a lantern hanging from the wall. He grabbed his flint and steel. The scrape of metal against stone echoed in the dark, two or three times before the lantern lit. Peshka lifted the flickering flame up, adjusting it.

Something was wrong. The door to the wine-cellar was missing—completely gone, ripped off its hinges. "What the bloody devil? What could *do* something like that?" His stomach rumbled with a low warning.

A trail of blood led down the steps. There was a metallic hiss, and his cavalry saber leapt into his hand. The polished saber shook along with his lantern, yet Peshka's feet kept plodding forward, like bloody idiots. He reached the top of the stairs and raised the lantern, casting its light down the steps. Finn's pallid face, spattered with freckles and blood, stared up at him from below, lying in a pool of blood a few steps from the bottom. It looked like he had tried to crawl back up.

Peshka swallowed, sweat beading on his face. He whipped his lantern around at the surrounding shadows. The Inquisitor could still be nearby. No, he could be anywhere. Probably had a weapon again. Peshka backed out of the storeroom, his lantern and saber still shaking.

He had to get out and warn Goren. Had to warn the necromancer.

His wine be damned.

Chapter 19

Springing the Trap

"If you're caught in a fair fight, someone higher ranking than you is shit at planning." — General Owen Murmillo, 'A Treatise on Good Soldiering,' excerpt prepared for the Galasan Officer's Academy manual

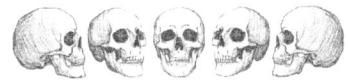

A haunting chorus echoed from the trees—a maddening, gibbering laughter, grating at Malfus's nerves, like a surgeon's rusty saw cutting through a femur. The gnolls pounded on their shields and howled at the moon. They were still out of crossbow range, in the safety of the trees. The laughter hadn't ceased since they'd started. It had been hours now.

Malfus stared at the gnolls from the battlements. *That unceasing racket. Can't they just get it over with?* Either more were coming, or their howling was growing louder.

"A lot of bastards out there." The soldier stationed next to Malfus had given up counting for perhaps the third time.

More than I've ever seen. But that goes without saying.

"Yeah, but at least some of them are fighting for us now." Morten tried to sound hopeful.

"At least they don't have a giant with them this time," the counting soldier chimed in. "Maybe they lost heart after you killed their other giant last night, Morten."

"Morten the giant-slayer!" Kaye clapped Morten on the back.

"It was Heimrich," Morten mumbled, clearly feeling quite the opposite of a hero.

Malfus looked out at the sprawling army. Giant or otherwise, there were more gnolls packed under the trees than he'd seen people in the Akkadian market square on Harvest's Eve. Even with his contributions to their defenses, they were still greatly outnumbered. Perhaps by three-to-one. Maybe more.

A distant horn sounded, a baleful howl from somewhere deeper in the trees. The horde of gnolls roared a united battle cry in response, then charged. They came in a creeping flood, slowly gaining in speed and volume, pouring from the trees. There had been so much build-up, it was almost anticlimactic.

Except that they just kept growing in number.

"Here they come, lads!" Kaye shouted.

As if we needed to be told.

"Make ready!" First Sergeant Goren's voice echoed from below. The soldiers on the ground held sword and spear, standing uneasily behind the ranks of zombies circling the pit. A soldier's trumpet sounded a countercry to the gnoll's horn—a feeble brassy plea, doing little to inspire confidence.

The gnolls spilled across the field, like an upturned vial of ink on fresh parchment. Their shrill howls changed to growls and roars, accentuated by the thundering rhythm of hundreds of feet pounding the earth. Their yellow eyes flashed like flecks of gold in the cloud of dust behind their charging front line.

Morten and Kaye were shouting right next to Malfus, but their voices were muffled whispers, as if his head were underwater. His ears rang, his face hot. His throat was so dry. There was a hollow pit where his stomach should have been.

The gnolls were close enough that Malfus could make out patterns of spots on their mangy fur. Their armor might have been shoddy, but their weapons looked deadly enough—a bizarre collection of bladed, spiked, and blunt implements, ready for murder. Their roars reached a feverish crescendo as they got to the mid-point of the field—where his zombies waited.

This is it. No turning back now.

Malfus swallowed his fear, then gripped the side of the battlements to steady himself as he transferred his awareness. Instead of feeling stones against his fingertips, wind flowed between his feathers as he soared high above the field. Dust churned from the tide of bodies directly below him. The army of gnolls reached his line of zombies, halfway across the field. The last of the stragglers finally left the trees.

A bit further...

Malfus swapped his awareness down to one of the zombie gnolls hiding in the grass. Footsteps thundered around him, like a downpour of deafening rain. A gnoll kicked his zombie in the face, stumbling over it in the dark. The living gnoll yelped in surprise, then reeled, falling forward on top of the corpse. The fallen gnoll squealed as it was trampled to death by its comrades, obstructing Malfus's view.

That one still counts.

He was about to swap to another gnoll, when a nagging sensation pulled at him—a distant voice, near his own body.

"Should we start firing?" Morten asked again.

Malfus looked around. The other soldiers down the wall were looking at him. All waiting on his command. *I'm a necromancer, not a bloody commander.* Though he had to admit—it felt better to issue commands to the living than the dead.

"Yes! Fire as many bolts as you want at the bastards! Just hold off on lighting them!"

"Fire! Fire! You heard him!" Kaye yelled.

As his command echoed down the wall, crossbows barked in response. Gnolls at the front had almost reached the wall. They looked like grains of sand in an hourglass as they wedged into the narrow gap where the gate used to be. They crowded in, scrambling up the rubble barricade, passing them below.

He swapped back to another undead gnoll. The tide of legs had started to ebb, the pounding footsteps subsiding.

A little more...

Finally, the trailing end of the gnoll ranks drew near. One of the last stragglers stabbed a zombie gnoll with its spear as it ran by—a random act of violence to hold it over until it got a chance to stab a living opponent. Malfus swapped back to his body.

"Now! Light!" he yelled.

"Light!" Corporal Kaye echoed.

As the command repeated down the wall, dozens of orange pinpricks lit up in Malfus's peripheral vision.

Now! Arise!

He pulled at the strands of his web, bringing his undead gnolls to life. It was like the marionette puppeteers that performed on the streets of Monrovia. Two dozen zombie gnolls rose from the ground. The living gnolls in front of them marched forward, unaware of the extra soldiers joining their ranks.

Malfus sent them the telepathic command to *charge*, then focused his awareness on one of his zombie gnolls. A moment later, the earth crunched beneath its claws as it scrambled on all fours. The living gnolls were right in front of it. Malfus felt its mindless anger burning like a festering rot; a desire to snuff out all signs of life—except, of course, those deemed off-limits.

It leapt from the ground, crashing into the closest gnoll. They rolled on the ground in a cloud of dust and tangled limbs. Coming to a stop, the living gnoll looked up, shocked and confused. Its questions were left unanswered as its zombie counterpart's claws smashed into its face. They fell again and again, until the gnoll's skull burst like an overripe melon, leaving behind a pool of ichor and bone.

A nearby gnoll watched, shocked, as his zombie perched on top of the gory corpse. The zombie reached out with its bloody claws, grabbing the living gnoll by its head. The other gnoll barely fought back as the zombie grappled with it, too surprised to understand what was happening. Then his zombie leaned forward and bit the gnoll's face off. Warm blood flowed. The victim yelped in pain, and its howls abruptly ended.

Damn. So gnolls can *bite faces off.*

More gnolls were watching now. One stabbed his zombie with its spear, impaling it through the torso. The zombie gnoll ignored the spear and pressed forward, clawing at the air. It pulled itself closer to the gnoll, which could only stare in disbelief. The zombie ripped its throat out with one swipe of its claws. Blood spurted. The living gnoll dropped its spear and clutched its throat instead, choking away its last breaths.

Next to it, another zombie grabbed a gnoll by the shoulder, yanking the gnoll off its feet. Then the zombie gnoll slashed its face open with a bony claw. The living gnoll yelped, then crumpled to the ground like a bag of hammers, clutching at its ruined face.

Malfus pulled his awareness back to himself. He paused briefly as he shuddered from the gore. He didn't want to admit it, but this was *exhilarating*. He could see the appeal of combat now. *At least, as long as I'm not the one in danger.*

Pockets of panic spread through the back ranks, but it wasn't enough. Hundreds of gnolls charged forward, oblivious to the carnage in their rear.

The gnolls below Malfus scrambled up the barricade, loose rocks skittering down the pile as the first of the army crested its top. Then they edged back as they encountered the drop into the spiked pit. Their eager efforts to lead the pack were rewarded by being trampled to death by the ranks behind them, or shot by the soldiers directly above them. A few gnolls, stuck with bolts, rolled limply into the pit.

We need fire now. *What's taking them so long?*

He glanced down the wall. The ratcheting of windlasses, the bark of crossbows, and the whistling of flaming bolts filled the air, lighting the night sky with flickering orange dots.

"Why hasn't anyone shot one of the zombies?" Malfus shouted.

"Which ones are the zombies?" Morten yelled back, cranking his windlass.

"Can't bloody see them! They all look the damn same from up here!" Kaye shouted, as he took another shot.

Through his web, Malfus knew exactly where each of his zombie gnolls were in the crowd, but he sure as sin couldn't shoot a crossbow. His eyes darted along the back ranks of the gnolls as his mind raced, trying to salvage his plan.

"Just keep firing! Aim for the gnolls in back! I'll take care of the rest." He gripped the ramparts to brace himself as he transferred his awareness.

Malfus looked up from the perspective of one of his zombies. A flaming arrow sailed uselessly overhead, landing too far away before going out. He swapped to another zombie.

This one had gotten pushed too far forward. It was in the middle of the crowd—kicking, biting, clawing anything within its reach. *...You just keep doing your thing.*

He swapped to another zombie, but every time he got close to a flaming bolt, its fire had already gone out.

Then he saw his chance. A flaming bolt sailed through the air, then bounced off dirt—still lit. Malfus ran his oiled zombie to the bolt, sliding through the crowd to reach the flickering flame. His glowing trophy lay on the ground, waiting to be claimed. The zombie gnoll reached down and plucked it from the ground like a flower in its bony fingers.

Then it erupted in flame.

The burst of orange light was visible to everyone on the wall. Gnolls fled from the flames as quickly as they could, separating like oil and water. He could hear them screaming and howling in fright, running to get away. *Now who's afraid?*

Like a weaver at his loom, he pulled on the strings in his mind, pulling his other zombies to the one still wreathed in fire, weaving a tapestry of flames in the darkness. Another zombie burst into flames, then another. Those zombies ran to others down the line. Soon, an entire line of bright orange beacons loomed behind the gnoll army.

Not all the zombie gnolls were ignited, but at least twenty had been. Twenty flaming zombies, sowing absolute havoc among the ranks of gnolls. One zombie grabbed a gnoll in a bear hug until it died in its burning embrace. The flaming zombies herded the gnolls better than any shepherding dog could have.

Their flames spread to the dry grass, sparking a curtain of fire. Whoops and war cries wilted into shrieks of terror as the gnolls retreated from the flames, trampling and clawing one another to get away. The rear ranks surged forward to escape the fire, forcing the gnolls in the front through the bottleneck at the gate, dropping them into the pit. Gnolls that couldn't make it through were flattened against the stone wall.

Malfus sensed each death. He could feel gnolls getting crushed underfoot, suffocating. Could feel them smashed against the stone wall, their ribs crushed by their desperate comrades. He smiled as the necrotic energy washed over him, storing it for later use.

By now, the stench of burnt fur and flesh reached them on the wall. One of the burning zombie gnolls was incinerated from the waist up—only its charred skeleton remained. Its legs lurched forward, trailing the gnolls for a few more steps before collapsing in the dirt. Malfus could feel his connection to a few other zombie gnolls fizzle out as the flames consumed them.

He was gaining more information from his zombies. It had been difficult at first, sifting through all the vibrations in his web; he'd never had so many strands before. Now, the fragments of perception began to merge into a vague, collective awareness. Like using your peripheral vision while focusing on something else. But he could feel them all. Out of the two dozen he'd positioned outside the wall, sixteen remained. More than half continued to burn as they tightened their ranks behind the gnolls, corralling them like lambs to the slaughter.

Just a little further. Keep herding them in.

As the gnolls were forced forward, they hurled themselves through the breach, over the broken stones and shattered timber. They were pushed into the pit, quickly filling it to capacity, with more crowding in behind. They screamed in their bestial tongue as they recognized the spikes to the front and sides of the pit. Some tried to turn away, to stop, but the tide of bodies carried them forward, grinding them into the spikes.

Your turn.

He awoke the twenty-one zombie gnolls lying at the bottom of the pit. It was packed so tightly, half of his zombies couldn't even stand up. This didn't pose a problem, however, as Malfus had them rip apart any gnolls they could reach. They grabbed unsuspecting gnolls by the feet, or started chewing through their legs. The zombies that could stand began clawing, biting, punching, and kicking. The trapped gnolls howled in blind terror. The zombies made no noise at all, other than the snapping of bone and tearing of flesh as they bit and clawed.

Panic spread inside the pit. The gnolls at its front and sides tried to push away from the spikes, while the gnolls outside the wall pushed in from behind. The gnolls attacked each other, unsure who was even attacking. It was utter chaos.

Now!

The two dozen human zombies near the edge of the pit made a horrible wailing sound—a mindless, rage-filled roar. A dozen zombies with spears and shovels stabbed down into the fray of gnoll bodies. The rest leapt in on top of the gnolls.

Some of the gnolls tried to escape the pit by climbing over its spikes, but the nails driven into the wood made it difficult to grab hold. The few that managed to make it up were greeted by spear-wielding zombies.

As his undead soldiers attacked the gnolls below, their living comrades fired crossbows from above, each bolt finding a target in the crowded pit. Soldiers fell back to reload their crossbows, as others took their place along the edge. Fire, then fall back. A mechanically efficient engine of death.

As the gnolls were slaughtered, Malfus sensed void energy blooming below him, sending invisible ripples through the air that only he could feel. They gathered like the static pressure before a thunderstorm.

The rod at his side seemed to enjoy it as well. In addition to its steady crimson glow, motes of darkness coalesced inside, pulsing with each new death. They appeared to move in the direction the pulses came from, like eyes following the battle with avid excitement.

Well, look who's awake again.

He didn't have time to get reacquainted with the rod. Some gnolls in the back ranks had overcome their confusion and were fighting back. One group managed to beat a flaming zombie gnoll to the ground and stabbed at it. They were so focused on hacking it apart, they didn't notice an unlit zombie stalking them from behind. It made short work of them.

Elsewhere, another gnoll tried to fight off an unlit zombies by itself. It struggled in horror as its blade got lodged in the zombie's skull. The gnoll pulled at its weapon, but the zombie gnoll shambled forward, and grabbing the gnoll's mouth with both hands. It ripped to both sides until the gnoll's jaw was wrenched from its face with a wet *crunch*.

Yet another flaming zombie gnoll stabbed its hands into the guts of a corpse like a shovel, digging out fistfuls of steaming entrails.

Sounds of battle echoed everywhere: clashing steel, ripping flesh, shouted orders, howls cutting off in yelps of pain. Never silence.

Malfus felt nauseated by the grisly sights flitting in his mind, but it seemed less real when seen through his zombies' eyes. Even though it really was happening right below him. Even though their images were burned into his mind.

Tracking so many zombies, he felt stretched out, like pieces scattered on a game board. *Like playing three games at once.* But he was thoroughly enjoying the challenge.

He walked along the wall, surveying the carnage below. He might not have been a general, but at least he looked the part, striding along the battlements in his borrowed uniform. The fear he'd felt earlier dwindled away. *Maybe some battle-magi don't need to be evokers. Maybe there's room for a necromancer or two in those books.*

As Malfus imagined a dashing illustration of himself in one of those old tomes, he saw Colonel Peshka frantically waving up at him from the ranks of spear-wielding zombies. Malfus struck a pose he thought befitting a legendary battle-necromancer, then waved back.

Peshka cupped his hands, then shouted, "The Inquisitor has escaped!"

But Malfus—due in part to the terribly noisy battle, as well as imagining himself in a book—thought the Colonel said, "The undead are doing great!"

Malfus spread his arms wide. "Isn't it wonderful? Undead gnolls, undead humans, living humans. All united in making more dead gnolls, so I can make more *undead* gnolls!"

Peshka yelled something else, but all Malfus could hear was the shriek of a gnoll as it was eviscerated somewhere below. Then Peshka disappeared in the ranks of soldiers, bellowing commands.

"Yes! The undead are bloody phenomenal. Now, if there isn't anything else, I have an army of undead to manage." Malfus turned away.

MALFUS - ARISE! ART BY DEJAN DELIC

Chapter 20

Plugging the Leak

"If you're stuck in a fair fight because you're shit at planning, then you'd better have at least one more shit plan to fall back on." — General Owen Murmillo, 'A Treatise on Good Soldiering,' excerpt prepared for the Galasan Officer's Academy manual

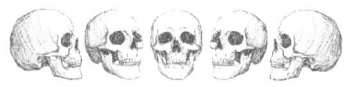

It was a crowded chaos in the pit below. But the initial surprise was wearing off. Most of the gnolls had no idea there were undead among their ranks, but a few pockets of resistance were fighting back. Strands of his web unraveled as several zombie gnolls were hacked apart.

In order for his plan to work, he'd need to replenish his ranks of zombies throughout the battle. *As long as we kill gnolls faster than they destroy my zombies, we might live to see the sunrise.* He shuddered as a wave of void energy flowed through him from one of the many deaths below, energizing him. It might not have been enough energy to raise the giant, but he could certainly raise more gnolls.

On the side of the pit furthest from him, some of the gnolls started to climb out. Enough bodies had piled up that the gnolls could climb over them. After the first few got out, they began to pour from the pit like it had sprung a leak. He moved his undead spearmen around the pit to stop them, but many were busy struggling with gnolls climbing out in other directions.

Goren bellowed commands. The soldiers in the courtyard formed defensive lines, but some gnolls were already slipping past them.

Malfus knew what he had to do.

He could sense the fresh corpses in the pit. Sitting there, waiting to be claimed, like apples on a low branch, or coppers lying in the street. But there was one problem—he needed to get closer to reanimate them. The spell required him to see the corpse and focus on it. Luckily, the breach was on the opposite side of the pit. The area below the ladder was clear. *For now.*

"Cover me! I'm going to raise more dead!" Malfus yelled to Morten and Kaye. He couldn't be sure they heard him. They were too busy reloading and firing. It was so loud; nothing could be heard up here, other than clashing steel, shouted orders, and cries of pain from below.

He took a deep breath, then descended the ladder. He tried to ignore the gnolls churning in the pit, or how sweaty his palms were as he climbed down. He focused on not falling to his death, taking each rung one at a time.

He sighed in relief at the bottom of the ladder, his boots securely on the ground. On the side of the pit across from him, the trickle of escaping gnolls had become a steady stream. A scattered melee was already forming on the far side, as zombie and soldier alike fought to contain the gnolls. His hands shook like a scroll in the wind as he watched a human soldier grab the stump of his wrist before falling into the pit, only a dozen paces away.

I have to hurry.

He froze. Three gnolls had grabbed the side of the pit right next to him, climbing upward. He started breathing again when he realized they were hanging there, motionless. He wasn't sure if they had died from crossbow bolts, zombies in the pit, or if they'd been smashed to death by their comrades.

As good a place as any to start.

He unhooked the rod from his belt, then took a deep breath. He shut out the life-or-death scramble surrounding him, chanting the words for his reanimation spell, drawing a strand from his connection to the plane of death. Then he threaded his invisible needle into the corpse with his mind.

Halfway through his spell, movement caught his eye. Straining his concentration, he looked over his shoulder as he chanted. Four gnolls, free from the pit, stalked toward him—less than a dozen paces away.

He swallowed as the spell's words stuck in his throat; he wouldn't have time to finish it before they got to him. After a quick mental check for nearby undead—like a spider skittering through its web—he sagged. They were too far away: stuck in the pit, or on the other side of it, slowing the gnolls. He looked around for help, but everyone else was busy fighting their own battles. He'd have to fight his.

He cast the quickest spell he had at his disposal, one he'd cast many times before. He was currently feeling its effects: *fear.*

An unholy marriage of necromancy and illusion, the spell flooded the four gnolls with visions of their demise, or images from the plane of death itself, overwhelming them with primordial terror.

One gnoll shrieked, jumping headfirst into the pit. Another froze, dropped its axe, then clawed at its face, trying to stop the visions. The other two paused, then continued forward, unfazed. One held a spear, the other a primitive morning star.

Damn. Malfus backed up a few paces, his mind racing as it searched for options.

The first gnoll crouched low, its spearpoint ready to thrust forward. Mere paces away now. Malfus frantically signed runes in the air as he spat out the words for his next spell.

Sweat beaded on his forehead, and nausea roiled through him. Something was caught in his throat. He coughed until it dislodged, spewing out a gray cloud of miasma. It spread in front of him, hanging in the air like a curtain of greasy mist. The spear gnoll walked through the cloud, ignoring it. It hesitated, coughed, and itched at its shoulder, but kept moving. Malfus cursed. His second spell seemed to have no real effect.

Out of the corner of his eye, the morning star gnoll had circled to flank him. Malfus backed up a few more paces until he pressed against the stone wall. He swallowed and tried to think of something. He was running out of both space and spells.

The morning star gnoll was only paces away. It barked something to its companion in their guttural language. The one with the spear barked back, its response a hacking cough, but it still approached, spear-tip jabbing. A step later, its spear dipped as it scratched furiously at its shoulder.

Malfus saw a narrow window open. He turned toward the morning star gnoll and spat out words for another spell. Focusing a pool of negative energy into his palm, he shaped it into a beam, and then released it.

A spear of black energy erupted from his hand, snaking through the air.

To the gnoll's credit, it displayed incredible reflexes, jumping to the side—but the bolt arced, striking it square in the chest. The gnoll squealed like a pig, dropping its morning star. A second later, its fur turned gray, and its muscles shriveled as it aged decades in mere seconds. Its mummified husk collapsed to the ground, wheezing its last breath.

A glint of a spearhead to his side robbed Malfus of his victory. The spear gnoll jabbed again. Malfus reeled backward, smashing against the wall. The spear lanced forward, shrieking against the wall and flicking orange sparks inches from his face.

The gnoll readied to thrust again. Malfus winced at the coming killing blow. He closed his eyes, but the spear never came. Opening his eyes, Malfus watched the gnoll stab at the ground behind it, a panicked look on its face. Something moved by its feet: the top of a zombified torso clutching the gnoll by its ankles, biting at it. The gnoll yelped as it fell over and kicked at the zombie.

Malfus scrambled back, infinitely grateful for the mercy he'd shown the crippled zombie earlier. But he didn't have time for gratitude; a gnoll that had succumbed to his fear spell was approaching him now, its axe at the ready. Its face featured claw marks, from having gouged its eye out at the spell's visions; the other eye held a murderous glint. The beast pointed at its bloody eye socket, then pointed at Malfus, grunting something in its guttural language. A vicious grin spread across its face.

Malfus didn't speak gnoll, but he got the gist.

He backed away, but something caught his ankle. He squawked as he toppled over, biting his tongue, tasting copper and dust in his mouth. The gnoll on the ground had grasped his ankle with one hand, while kicking at the zombie torso latched to its foot. The axe gnoll strolled toward them, its weapon raised high.

"Let go of me!" Malfus kicked furiously at the gnoll holding his ankle. He was about to kick again, but his eyes and the gnoll's widened at the same time, as his spell finally took effect.

The skin on its hand and forearm blistered and peel back, sloughing off. Greasy, gray meat rotted before his eyes, revealing white bone underneath. Malfus kicked at the bones and steaming flesh clinging to his ankle. The gnoll looked on in horror, too shocked to scream. It stared at Malfus, its jaw hanging open, as if pleading for an escape from the pustulant boils traveling up its neck. The zombie torso behind it bit its legs, ripping out mouthfuls of flesh as the rot ate away his victim's face.

The axe gnoll retched in horror, but gathered courage to close the distance to Malfus. Its axe gleamed wickedly in the flickering torchlight as it swung.

Malfus jerked his leg back as the axe struck, ripping the decaying arm off as he scrambled to his feet. He tried to think of options, but his mind was blank. He'd need a moment to regather his concentration to cast anything. He had to delay. That was all he could do.

Think of something. Anything!

He backed up as the gnoll closed in. It held its axe out, snarling a low growl. Malfus swung the rod in front of him, waving it as he backpedaled, hoping the glowing thing would scare the gnoll off, giving him a moment to figure out something. He couldn't cast anything with the gnoll this close to him. Without the advantage of distance, the odds skewed against most spellcasters.

The gnoll raised its axe again. Something whistled through the air, and the gnoll's arm went limp, its axe dropping to the ground. Blood spurted as a feathered bolt stuck out from its shoulder. The gnoll took another step toward Malfus, then collapsed to its knees. It reached up, grasping futilely at the bolt as blood gushed from its arterial wound.

Malfus brushed the dust from his coat before stepping toward the dying gnoll, holding out the rod. Its star ruby glowed a cherry red, brightening as it got closer to the wound.

The gnoll howled in pain, watching in helpless horror as its blood began to flow through the air, siphoning into the ruby. It reached up with a claw, weak, but Malfus swatted it away as he pressed the rod closer.

Blood ripped from its veins and eye sockets, narrowing into airborne tendrils before flowing into the rod. Feeding the rod. Feeding *him*. The gnoll's cries grew softer, until it silenced and collapsed on the ground, a dried-up husk.

Malfus closed his eyes. His pulse pounded in his temples. Draining blood from a corpse was one thing, but draining blood from someone still alive—that was something else entirely.

Exhilarating.

He looked up. Morten stared at him from the wall, crossbow in hand. Malfus gave him a nervous smile and nodded, thanking him for his help. But Morten's expression was one of horror, tinged with revulsion. He disappeared back over the parapet.

Malfus shrugged his shoulders. Then turned back to the three gnoll corpses. He had work to do.

He raised the gnolls quickly, sparing no delay as the battle raged. One by one, the zombie gnolls clambered to their feet, awaiting his commands. He had them trail him as guards. *No more surprises.*

He turned his attention back to the pit. Only a dozen zombies remained in its depths, and a handful fought above, alongside the soldiers. His defeated zombies were hacked apart into useless pieces, but the fresh cadavers in the pit were a different story. Malfus could sense them, impaled against spikes, smashed and trampled, full of bolts, or savaged by his undead. Several dozen corpses, waiting to be claimed.

He concentrated, then resumed his spell where he'd cut off. He began with the dead gnolls clinging to the side of the pit. It took a few moments of chanting to raise each one, and a few more to weave them into his web. As he finished with each, it dropped from the side of the pit in silence. More surprised yelps sounded from the pit as the new zombies began their bloody work. A gnoll climbing out across from him was dragged back in, screaming.

He pulled from the currents of entropic energy flowing around him, channeling it into a stack of corpses piled at one end of the pit. Several gnolls had climbed partway up the pile, when a claw reached out and grabbed one of them by the neck. Malfus raised another and another, until the entire stack of corpses under the climbing gnolls began to shift. The gnolls yelped as their fallen rose up and attacked.

The soldiers above charged forward, forcing gnolls back into the pit, where a growing number of zombies awaited them. Malfus smiled as the breach in the pit was taken care of. He raised a few more zombie gnolls for good measure, reweaving missing strands in his web. Then he climbed back up the ladder so he could control them from a more secure vantage point. *That's enough excitement for now.*

The soldiers rained crossbow bolts on the gnolls below, taking advantage of the easy targets, and the gnolls in the pit returned to complete disarray. Their advance had faltered; some of them were pushing back against the tide of fresh gnolls, trying to clamber back up the sliding stone barricade. Retreating.

The gnoll's war-horn sounded again, a single mournful cry from deep in the woods.

The back of his neck prickled. One of the strands of his web tugged at him—the crow. He rolled his eyes back, transferring his awareness to it.

Then, flying above the fort, Malfus looked down in terror.

The giant towered over the trees, pushing through the canopy as if walking among toys. An uncountable mass of additional gnolls, fresh for the fight, writhed across the forest floor like ants. At their head marched a massive gnoll, its fur ghost-white. It lifted its great horn to its canine lips, preparing to sound the charge.

Shaking, Malfus returned to his body.

"That's it! They're calling retreat!" A smile spread on Morten's face as the horn erupted.

"I'm afraid we aren't so lucky." Malfus cleared his throat. Words clung to his mouth like cobwebs. He pointed at the forest. "The giant is back."

Chapter 21

The Last Stand

"O brave knight, what good is armor that does nothing to protect the heart? What good is a helmet, protecting the head, but not the mind?"
— Salvatore Cromarbie, philosopher, poet, and playwright of Ashára

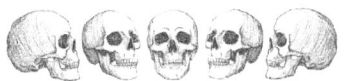

Corporal Higgins inhaled the musk of rotting wood and sour wine with short, panicked breaths. He'd picked a terrible place to hide. He realized that now—too little, too late—as he peeked from the barrel atop the wall, staring at the titan that towered above the trees.

No one was supposed to be over here; all the fighting was supposed happen at the front. This hiding spot had worked last night, when the rest of his squad faced the giant. He'd heard only two survived, the poor bastards. Better them than him, though.

Let the others do the fighting. If they wanted to be heroes, then Vesenia would let them. He'd joined the army for the uniforms, not the glory. He remembered seeing the duke's soldiers in their full-dress uniforms for the first time. It was their victory parade following the Siege of DeGaullis. It wasn't the knights that stood out to him, with their shining armor, but the soldiers marching right behind them, in their navy blue and gold embroidered uniforms—the colors of Galasa. They looked like the wooden toy he'd clutched to his chest that day. He couldn't have been more than four or five, but ever since, he'd wanted to march in one of those parades. Ladies loved men in uniform.

It all seemed silly now, sitting here in this empty barrel, trying not to soil himself. He wanted be brave enough to peek over the edge again—hoping, praying that the giant was just a dream. But no. He knew it was there. He didn't have to check. He could feel it with every shaking step the abomination took.

He forced himself to look. The giant crashed through the tree line, pushing the tall pines over like reeds of grass by a riverbank. The trees crackled like breaking bones as they fell to the ground.

The giant emerged from the trees and towered over the open field between the fort and forest. The gray titan bore a massive skull in one hand—it must have belonged to a great dragon. Its snout dropped below the giant's knee, and the horns went well above its shoulder, like a colossal shield. The twin bone horns jutting from the skull's top were thick as trees, metal caps bolted to their tips. The skull was an off-white, but its razor teeth shone like polished pearl, each long as a sword and just as sharp.

The giant was clad in bone. The massive wyrm's ribs and vertebrae had been chained and lashed to the giant's limbs, sounding like a hellish windchime as it moved. The monster was bad enough on its own, but with its dragonbone armor, it had stepped out from a nightmare.

That horn echoed from the woods again. From here, Higgins could see a carpet of gnolls moving through the forest, waiting within the trees.

The giant answered the horn's cry with a bellow of its own. A challenge, roared in defiance of the gods themselves. It sounded like a thousand madmen howling at the moon. The roar vibrated the wooden barrel; Higgins could feel it in his bones. It felt like an entire minute passed by before the giant emptied its massive lungs. Then it stamped the ground, shaking the fortress.

Higgins didn't know what that titan was about to do, but it didn't look good. He wanted to run, but if he got out of the barrel, the giant would spot him, or worse—First Sergeant Goren would. He considered his options, then froze.

It was too late. The giant surged forward.

Five tons of muscle, flesh, and bone charged straight at him—a living siege engine. It moved with incredible speed for something so large, its massive dragon skull in front, its horns pointed at the wall.

The giant collided into the wall with such force, Higgins thought it would tear the sky asunder. Chunks of stone as large as a man broke from the wall, flying overhead as his barrel toppled and shattered. His face hit the wall, and his teeth crushed together, severing the tip of his tongue. His eyes filled with tears as he spat out fragments of tooth. Uniform or not—what woman would love a man with a mouthful of broken teeth?

Higgins sobbed and tried to pick up the fragments of his teeth. He ignored the fissure in the wall forming next to him; he hardly saw the giant's massive face, leering down at him. Then it opened its mouth in a laugh that rattled him to his core. The giant's breath blew the hair from his face, hot and fetid, deafening him.

Its massive hand appeared overhead. Higgins kneeled, sobbing, not wanting to look up. He should have been content watching parades from afar. Silly business, trying to march in one.

It was the final thought that crossed his mind.

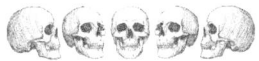

Morten grasped the ramparts to steady himself. In the distance, the eastern wall exploded in a rain of bricks. A massive section of its top broke off, falling into the courtyard.

Corporal Kaye pointed at Morten and the other soldiers near him. "With me! We must protect the wall!" Kaye gave Morten a push forward. "You, too, giant-killer."

Morten swallowed, clutching his loaded crossbow as he followed the others, the shadow of his oversized helmet seeming to grow with each step.

Morten, Kaye, and a dozen others ran down the wall, clutching crossbows to their chests. Morten glanced around at their ashen faces, pushing his own fear into the growing pit in his stomach.

He could see the giant now. Its massive shadow loomed over the wall. It was too far away to see the details, just its horrible size—a full head taller than the parapets. He couldn't see the gnolls from this angle, but he knew they were out there. He could hear them. Hundreds of them. Cheering on the giant's destructive rampage.

He tried not to think about what he was running toward. He looked at his feet so he wouldn't have to see it. His little toe slipped from his sock, and he laughed as he realized he hadn't had a chance to change his damn socks since last night.

The giant rammed into the wall ahead of them with another earth-shaking crash. The shock threw Morten to his knees. His loaded crossbow clattered on the ground, almost firing into the crowd of soldiers. Bricks flew from the wall ahead, raining into the courtyard.

The giant appeared now in all of its horrible glory. Encased in bone armor, and carrying a massive dragon skull, it looked like it had stormed out of the gates of the Nine Hells. It backed up, readying for another charge. Morten's heart was racing, and his breathing—he couldn't be sure he was breathing. In his mind, all he could see was Sergeant Donovan's kicking legs. His meat smeared across the wall. Heimrich staring back at him. His hand felt at her broken glasses.

"Keep it together, lads!" shouted Kaye. "One more giant to kill. We've even got the giant-slayer with us this time."

The soldiers let out a forced cheer. Someone clapped Morten on the back as he stood up. Maybe. He wasn't sure; his entire body felt numb. He felt like he would fall from the wall at any moment.

"Fire!" Kaye yelled.

The soldiers took up their defensive positions against the parapets, at maximum crossbow range from the giant. Shouts from the others melted together into a porridge of echoes, racketing in his helmet. Then the air filled with the familiar ratchet of windlasses, the snapping of strings, and the hissing of bolts.

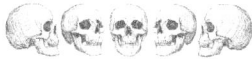

"To the wall!" First Sergeant Goren bellowed at the soldiers waiting by the pit. They hesitated, looking at each other with pale faces. A huge crack was forming in the wall across the courtyard. "Now, dammit! That's an order!"

Their clattering armor and worried whispers soon receded, leaving Malfus to his dark work. He hardly noticed them leave, focusing instead on the next corpse.

A few howls of pain still rose from the pit as his zombies continued their slaughter. A burst of movement caught his eye. Two gnolls pulled themselves halfway over the pit's ledge. Then clawed hands grabbed them, pulling them back. One gnoll managed to grab one of the spikes, while its companion disappeared. The gnoll howled as it held on, its legs flaying into a bloody mess of torn meat, clawed to the bone. Eventually, the zombies pulled it back down. It howled for a surprisingly long time after getting pulled under the mass of bodies.

Two zombies emerged from the pit, dragging a gnoll's limp corpse. They set it on a growing pile of bodies next to Malfus before heading back in.

Malfus concentrated, shutting out extraneous noise. He focused on the corpse, staring up at him with glassy eyes. Arcane words filled his mouth with the taste of vinegar. Then a green light flickered, casting his face in an eerie pallor.

The look of fear frozen on the gnoll's face melted away as its muscles slackened. Then it rose to its feet and ran in the direction of the soldiers, toward the crumbling wall.

Malfus patted the sweat beading on his brow, then turned to the next corpse. He would have loved to drain some blood, but he couldn't stop. His army of zombies had dwindled after holding the pit. *You can rest when you're dead. Get back to it.* Malfus took a deep breath, then started on the next one.

There was so much negative energy here, from all the dying, that it bled into the physical plane. Negative energy often built up around battlefields, graveyards, or hospices—anywhere with death. The energy dissipated on its own, unless enough built up over time, leaving festering sores on the land that took generations to heal. The Scar, a cataclysmic wound left over from the annihilation of Shal-Umbra, might never heal.

In lands like the Scar, plants barely grew, and wounds took longer to heal; the body's natural defenses were prone to contagion, making it easier for disease to spread. One book had mentioned the body aging faster in such places.

Negative energy was invisible to the uninitiated. The unaware might feel a chill, or like someone had 'stepped on their grave', or felt watched, even when no one was around. The most sensitive might hear whispers, bleeding through from the plane of death. But even the most sensitive individual couldn't draw upon such negative energy. At least, not like a trained necromancer could. *Or a self-taught one.*

Malfus pulled from the deadly energy with care, siphoning off only what he needed to raise each corpse. The next zombie gnoll stood up, the bottom half of its jaw barely hanging on. It ran to the wall after the others.

He closed his eyes, readying himself for another zombie. Someone shouted in the distance, followed by another terrible crash, as a section of the wall tumbled into the courtyard. He turned to the next corpse as his zombies hauled more bodies from the pit.

He allowed himself a sliver of a smile. It now took him ten seconds to raise each zombie and send it to the front lines. With each cast, the process became more ingrained in his psyche. He'd cast more spells tonight than in a month of research and practice. He'd never felt such raw power before, so connected to the plane of death. Every strand in his web vibrated in his mind, connecting him to his thralls. It was a small army, now. And every zombie he raised was needed at that growing crack in the wall.

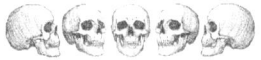

Morten braced himself as the giant charged, its shield's metal-tipped horns dipping toward the crack. The wall shook as the creature ran, each step ripping chunks of earth upward.

It plowed into the wall like an avalanche. The long horn wedged in the crack, breaking off another massive section of stone that crumbled into the fort. A ripple of force ran down the wall, throwing Morten on his back.

"It's going to take the bloody wall down if we don't stop it!" someone next to him shouted.

They sounded miles away. Morten cranked his crossbow, but his arms felt like jelly. The others kept firing at the giant. Most of their bolts skittered harmlessly off its huge dragon skull shield. It wasn't clear if the bolts hitting the giant did anything at all. The titan looked over at them and roared with laughter, like distant thunder.

"We're wasting our bolts!" someone shouted.

"Dammit," Kaye growled, then turned to the others, shouting to be heard. "Start shooting at the bloody gnolls instead! Take out as many of the bastards as you can!"

Morten began to yell a warning, but his voice froze in his throat, his crossbow dropping from his hands. The giant was bounding in their direction, extending its long arm, the dragon skull's gap-toothed grin leering at them.

Kaye pointed at the shadows looming at their feet. Too little, too late.

The skull crashed down on the wall with a crunch, teeth first. Right where Kaye and several others had been standing. Hot blood sprayed on Morten's face, dripping down his cheeks. The dragon's empty eye socket glared down at him. Soldiers screamed on the other side of the skull. He turned to run, but slipped in their blood, sprawling on the stone.

The dragon skull lurched sideways; its horns turned downward until they faced him. Then the giant dragged the skull away from Morten, scraping across the wall top. The soldiers' screams abruptly ended in wet pops. The air filled with a fine mist of blood; its coppery taste was everywhere.

The soldiers next to Morten were no longer there. Only a carpet of meat and blood remained. Some of their faces stared back at him from the wall top, open-mouthed. He could hear the severed heads screaming for him.

No. That was him. *He* was the one screaming.

His feet kicked and slid in the gore as he got to his feet and ran away. Only four others had survived; they were already ahead of him in their retreat. It was like running through a nightmare—his feet shifted, but he wasn't moving fast enough.

He fled from the carnage, not looking back. The panicked screams of the soldiers in front of him were drowned out by the giant's laughter. That grating sound reverberated inside Morten's ribcage. Memories of the tower—of his dead squad—flooded back to him. He could see their faces staring at him, too.

The four other survivors got on a ladder leaning against the wall, climbing down. The soldiers shoved and shouted, each trying to be the first one down.

"That's too many," Morten said as he ran past them. Seconds later, he heard shouts, then a crash, as the ladder collapsed to the courtyard below. Two of the soldiers screamed in pain. The other two would never scream again.

Morten kept running. He didn't give a damn about his ripped sock, oversized helmet, or where his crossbow was. He only slowed when he'd made it back to the ladder by the pit. Morten scrambled down it, almost slipping, his hands and boots still slick with blood.

His boots met solid ground, but before he could resume his retreat, he froze. A gnoll towered over him. Morten raised his empty hands, covering his face, too afraid to scream.

But the gnoll ignored him, running in the other direction. Morten breathed again. It was just a zombie.

Malfus leaned against the wall, panting. Behind him, two other zombies carried another corpse from the pit, laying it next to Malfus. The necromancer was covered in sweat, his eyes sunken, and the air around him *rippled*, distorted.

"The wall—they're all... What do we do?"

"Huh?" Malfus looked up. His eyes were black pools, and he shook as if he were about to collapse. "Sorry, Morten. I'm in two places at once."

"What do we do? The giant—" Morten's voice was drowned out by another stone-splitting crash. Bricks rained into the courtyard. The breach in the wall grew wider.

Malfus snarled. "I'm sending everything into the breach! But there's still more to raise here. And I'll need more bodies. Find them! And bring them here!" Malfus glanced over his shoulder, talking to himself as much as he was to Morten. "I need as much time as I can get."

Morten looked at him blankly, then nodded. He hadn't caught half those words; he'd only made out 'find' and 'bodies.' But there were plenty of those to go around.

He turned and ran.

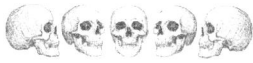

Malfus closed his eyes, then transferred his awareness.

Hunger. Rage.

Those were the only conscious thoughts in the mind of his zombie gnoll; all else was a black void. A row of zombie gnolls, sharing those same two thoughts, assembled behind him. Malfus had raised every gnoll he could. Eighty of them pressed with him against the wall. They stood to both sides of the breach, waiting silently. The living soldiers stood further back, clutching their weapons as they stared up at the growing cracks.

There was another gut-wrenching crash as another massive chunk of brick tumbled off and fell inside the courtyard. The ground shook as it landed, splinters of stone exploding in shrapnel. A fragment sliced into the thigh of the zombie-gnoll, but it didn't even flinch.

The gap in the wall stretched midway down its height now, and a web of cracks ran all the way to the bottom. The giant smashed its triangular skull into the breach, hammering with it again and again. The powerful skull didn't show a single sign of giving way as it ground the stone into dust. Another slab of the wall broke off.

Now!

The gnolls surged forward at his silent command, like a swarm of locusts, crawling over each other. They scrambled up the wall, climbing over the crack, and jumped on the unsuspecting giant.

There was a moment of silence before the giant roared, swatting at the undead gnolls. They jumped on its feet and crawled up its legs like hungry rats, swarming under his singular will, clawing on top of each other to climb higher. The giant howled as it fell back, swatting at his zombies, plucking them off like pests and smashing them in its fists. For each one the giant killed, another took its place. They were halfway up its chest.

The giant stumbled backward, dropping its massive skull to claw away at the undead. Screams of panic filled the air as the giant took an uncertain step backward, landing on several ranks of gnolls, smashing them flat. Some of the zombies it managed to swipe off fell on the gnolls below, then attacked them instead, creating further chaos.

Ghostface blew its war horn, shouting angrily at the gnolls scrambling nearby.

The gnolls gave the giant a wide berth, then rushed in front of it, pushing the zombies back. The zombie gnolls ripped apart a few of their living counterparts, but were quickly overrun by Ghostface's superior numbers.

Enough!

His zombies broke off, retreating back to the wall and climbing through its breach. The living gnolls surged forward, following them. The courtyard inside the wall quickly became a chaotic melee of gnolls, undead, and frightened soldiers, clashing in combat.

Outside the wall, a zombie gnoll had nearly made it to the giant's throat. But the giant plucking it off like an insect, crushing it in its fist before splattering it against the wall.

"Dammit." Malfus put a hand to his throbbing head, groaning as his awareness returned violently to his body. *That should buy them a little time.*

The rod glowed a hungry red. *Almost there.*

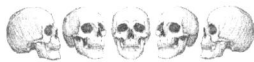

"Shovel! Where the fuck is a bloody shovel?"

Morten ran everywhere, searching high and low. His ragged breath caught in his throat.

Cries of soldiers and the singing of steel filled the air, as well as chittering yips from gnolls as they poured into the fort through the breach.

The area in front of the breach was a churning soup, the battle lines merging into one another. Soldiers and undead clashed with gnolls, and the gnolls fought back. The giant roared, towering over the chaos as it gouged away at the wall, making the crack larger and ignoring the stones it rained down on its comrades.

Something crashed into Morten, almost knocking him over. Morten shouted, fumbling with his sword, but looked up to see a group of zombie gnolls running past him. They ignored him and continued onward to the breach. He breathed in relief, then resumed his search in the opposite direction.

Out of breath, he slowed by the remains of the stables, putting out his hand to steady himself. He couldn't believe he couldn't find a bloody shovel. They're everywhere when you don't need one, but as soon as you *do*...

Catching his breath, Morten raised his helmet off his brow and looked up. His prize stood right in front of him, jutting from a cart of manure. "Finally." Morten set down his sword and sighed with relief as he grabbed the shovel.

He started to run off, but doubled back. He overturned the cart of manure, emptying it, then threw the shovel inside. Then he wheeled the cart off to where he'd first seen Malfus last night, when he had arrived with the Inquisitor.

Where they buried the bodies of their fallen.

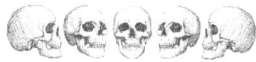

Malfus stood at the edge of the pit, surveying the carnage. All the usable corpses in there had been raised and sent to the fight. Only butchered meat and bits of bone, teeth, and intestine remained. Glistening red ichor covered the ground; even the walls were wet with it. The sides of the pit were gouged with claw marks from unsuccessful escape attempts. A gnoll's severed arm still clung to one of the spikes, dangling like a macabre ornament.

As a necromancer, Malfus had seen plenty of dead bodies before, in various states of decay. He'd dissected them himself, and seen them turned inside out more often than he preferred to recall. He was far from squeamish at the sight of a little blood.

But this was a lot, even for him. This was the most gruesome scene he'd ever witnessed.

He took a deep breath, calming his queasy stomach. Such unease was quite unbecoming of a necromancer—but it was *difficult* when an ear nestled below his foot, and he was pretty sure half a face stared up at him nearby. Just the skin—like a masquerade mask, floating on the surface of a bloody pool.

So much death, concentrated in a single spot. Beyond the visible carnage, the pit was filled with a dense fog of negative energy—raw, entropic force. A thought occurred to him about the balance of life and death. All of this entropic energy had built up, but he wondered how many soldiers' lives had been saved as a result. *The cost of death for life to continue.*

And he could use that negative energy to save even more.

Malfus closed his eyes and grasped the rod. It vibrated, throbbing with excitement, as if it knew what was about to happen.

The gem was lit bright red, like a hungry coal. The star pattern within the ruby moved like the iris of an eye, focusing on the pit. Motes of light floated inside the gem, coalescing into almost identifiable shapes before breaking apart into meaningless blobs. The shapes reminded Malfus of something, but he couldn't quite place his finger on it.

Distant screams of the dying reminded Malfus of what was at stake.

Better hurry. No time to waste.

A gnawing impatience grew within the rod, but he wasn't sure what to do. He didn't know if the rod needed a particular phrase to activate. He shrugged, then pointed it at the pit, hoping it could figure out the rest.

Wind whipped at his feet, flicking the hem of his coat. There was a faint sucking sound, and then the rod drank hungrily, soaking up the oily negative energy. Violet rays warped the air around the rod, making black sparks wink in and out of existence. Waves of force rippled around his hair, enveloping him like a cocoon.

Malfus was amazed at how much energy the rod could store. Before, he had siphoned mere threads of negative energy, taking small sips from the cancerous pool before redirecting it into an empty vessel. He'd only allowed the energy to pass through him, guided by the thin lines of tattoos covering his body—protective wards, his only means of keeping the energy from ravaging his own body.

But this rod drank it in, storing enough void energy to kill someone hundreds of times over. Cold waves shot through him. His tattoos prickled; he felt numb in places where the negative energy was too much for his tattoos to contain. He tried not to think about the side effects as the warping forces careened unrestricted through his body on their way to the rod.

A heaving crash shook the earth. Malfus had to steady himself before nearly tumbling into the pit. He braced himself against one of the spikes, then looked westward, toward the collapsed tower.

And, far below it, the fallen giant.

That's enough. Let's go.

Malfus breathed in through clenched teeth, then ran across the courtyard. The constant crash of battle hounded him. Ringing steel echoed like waves. Occasionally, gaps of silence stuttered the noise of battle, and a single sound would reach his ears with astounding clarity. A lone scream. A solitary cry. Then the tumultuous tide of noise came roaring back in.

The sensations from his zombies painted an imperfect picture of the unfolding battle. His zombies had contained the gnolls in the courtyard, keeping them from overrunning the fort, but just barely. The breach in the wall was narrow, but there were hundreds of gnolls outside, fighting to get in. The giant tore apart the ruined wall, letting in more gnolls every second.

Malfus quickened his pace; he was nearly there. He rounded the corner of a building, then froze in his tracks. Three gnolls surrounded a lone soldier, kicking and stabbing at them. They hadn't spotted him yet.

Malfus hesitated, debating on running in another direction, then gripped the rod. *I don't have time for this.* The rod throbbed in his palm, reassuring him, as he rushed forward. He could feel the power vibrating in his bones.

The gnolls noticed him, turning, but he'd already raised the rod and begun to chant. The gnolls raised their weapons and snarled, but Malfus didn't slow. Before they could take another step toward the approaching necromancer, three bolts of black lightning shot from his hand.

The gnoll's howling shrieks melted together into a mindless wail as they aged and withered before him. Their eyeballs sizzled away, followed by their muscles, organs, and soft tissues. All of it turned to dust, leaving skeletons with mouths open in shock. Tendons and ligaments held the bones up for a moment before collapsing.

Malfus stifled a laugh at the display of power. He'd never felt like this in his entire life.

If only someone could see it. If only some of his old classmates or instructors could see his command over the arcane, even this forbidden school of necromancy. They had told him he'd never amount to anything.

I'd show them now, if they were here. I'd show them all!

A groan caught his attention as he strode past the piles of bones.

The bloodied soldier next to the skeletons tried to move. He was so covered in blood, it was remarkable he'd survived. He held a hand to his side, keeping his guts from spilling on the ground.

The soldier opened his mouth, his lips mouthing a plea for help. But they only sputtered blood. He met Malfus's eyes, as if expecting him to have the answer.

Malfus shook his head. "Sorry. You're already dead."

The soldier glanced at his stomach, then back up at him. Then the man sagged, dying on the spot, horror sculpted onto his face as if etched in marble.

Malfus bent over the four dead and raised them quickly, adding their strands to his web: three gnoll skeletons, and a zombie trailing its intestines. Then he sent them to the wall—he knew they'd need every zombie they could get—before continuing toward the fallen tower.

Chapter 22

The Fall

"An Inquisitor is justice. Without ego, without reward, without remorse. Everything unnecessary chiseled away, until only the need for justice remains." — Inquisitor Horace Vygrath

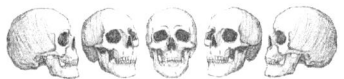

Screams of the dying filled the air. The battle was worsening by the second. Morten looked at his shovel and wondered what good a few more bodies would do if Malfus didn't hurry and do something spectacular. If the necromancer didn't come up with something soon, there would be more than enough dead. Morten ran anyway, gripping his shovel tighter and ignoring his burning lungs.

His mind wanted to be anywhere else; it kept drifting. He couldn't stop thinking of home. But that was so far away. Would he ever see his family or farm again? None of this was worth it. He'd had no idea he'd signed up for any of this. He'd give anything to be a farmer again, to start over. If he could just survive the night—then he'd be done with this soldiering business.

"There they are." Morten spotted the row of makeshift grave markers—a few simple sticks tied together, with the shape of a diamond at the top: the Blinded Eye of Vesenia. He'd crafted them himself only two nights ago.

The mounds of dirt were still fresh. Victims from an earlier raid. He'd buried so many comrades in his time out here. He shook his head. His closest friends still hadn't gotten a proper burial, entombed under the rubble of the fallen tower.

He felt guilty standing over the graves, shovel in hand. These fallen had been buried with their hands bound—as was tradition—and consecrated to Vesenia in their last rites. Promised that the Blind Goddess would keep them from becoming undead.

I guess we'll see if that actually works.

He wasn't sure how he'd feel about being brought back to fight all over again. He pushed the thought from his mind, then kicked over the first grave marker, his shovel biting into the dirt.

It wasn't long before he hit something—the jaw of whoever was buried here. Morten winced. "Sorry," he said.

He gingerly uncovered the body. Luckily, they hadn't buried them very deep—there'd been far too many for that.

He cleared away more dirt, and hesitated. It was Kearns. He remembered when Kearns had helped him fix his crossbow. He was loud, but always had a joke to tell. Now a worm wiggled between his teeth, his bluish-purple face a swollen mockery of Morten's memories.

He tried not to look at that face as he uncovered the rest of the body. How long had he been stationed here? A year? How many friends died in that time? How many more would he see? He finished digging, then moved to the next grave.

One foot stood in the grave, the other on top of the marker to Vesenia, lying in the dirt. Morten was so focused on his task, his ears didn't register the footsteps behind him, silent as shadows, until it was too late.

There was a blur of movement, and Morten felt a stinging pain in his hand. His shovel clattered to the ground.

"Where is he?" hissed a voice behind him, as cold and sharp as the knife's edge now pressed to his throat. The Inquisitor.

Morten swallowed, his cheeks burning as he thought of what to say. He wanted to be brave, but that was a bit difficult with a knife pressed against the throat. He stood in a shallow grave; would it be his own?

"If you kill him, the undead will—"

The knife bit deeper into his throat. "Where—is—he?" Any remaining patience faded from the Inquisitor's voice.

"By the fallen tower."

The Inquisitor growled. "Vesenia thanks you for your honesty."

Morten sighed in relief as the knife was released from his neck.

"I would have spared you, for turning over the heretic," whispered the Inquisitor, "but I can't turn a blind eye to your sacrilege. Vesenia will not turn her Blind Eye from your defilement of her dead."

Steel flashed in the moonlight, and searing pain tore across his throat. Morten couldn't breathe. Then he fell. The stars and night sky reeled above him. He was on his back, writhing in the dirt, clutching at his throat, trying to staunch the blood slipping between his fingers.

It reminded him of the time he'd fallen in the lake as a child. He thought he would drown. The helplessness of that moment—how long it had lasted. Until his father reached into the darkness and saved him.

There was no hand reaching from the darkness this time. All he could taste was blood. A silhouette of darkness blocked out the stars momentarily, then disappeared.

Morten rolled over. Kearns stared back at him, his hooded eyelids covering glassed eyes. The corpse had a strange look of knowing, his dead eyes filled with secret knowledge.

At first, Morten panicked. Then the reassuring weight of inevitability pressed in. The coppery blood was tinged with bitter disappointment. He'd wanted to be so much more, but death also promised a release from the pain. And rest. He hadn't pictured his life ending like this, but he doubted anyone does, in the end.

He let out a wet laugh as his toe wiggled out of his sock. Couldn't even fade into the afterlife with his sock on properly. But he was so very tired. At least he could finally get some sleep.

He closed his eyes. For the first time in months, he could clearly picture his mother's face.

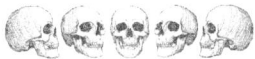

"Hold the bloody lines!"

Colonel Peshka shouted for order, but he knew the truth. There was no more order to be had.

In front of him, a sea of bodies clashed, boots stamping, metal ringing. The shouts of anger, cries of pain, and the howling yips of the gnolls blended together. The giant towered over it all, smashing the dragon skull on the wall in a steady rhythm—a metronome to the madness. Somewhere, Goren shouted her orders. But even her voice couldn't be heard over all of this. In his decades of service, Peshka had never seen a battle so chaotic. He could barely tell the living from the dead.

Gnolls trickled through the breach in the wall like wine spilling from a bottle. It was a matter of minutes, not hours, before they'd be completely overrun. His troops and the necromancer's undead barely held them back. More gnolls slipped into the fort every second. Probably already flanking them, tightening the noose around their necks.

As he walked along the perimeter of the battle, he stared at the giant looming over the wall. How would they stop that monstrosity? It was only a matter of time before it got bored with the wall. It could step over, if it wanted. The giant bellowed, then smashed against the wall again, shaking the earth with its furious rampage.

"Where is that bloody sorcerer?" Peshka looked around the battlefield, but saw no sign of Malfus. He continued grumbling. "He's as useful as he was with chains on. Where the hell is he? Too good to die with the rest of us? Hiding, no doubt."

Peshka clutched his stomach. His forced sobriety was beginning to take its toll. He'd give anything for a bit of liquid courage. Just a swallow. Enough to stop the shakes. His stomach felt as foul now as it did with wine sloshing in it. So what was the point of sobriety, anyway?

A wet *crunch* caught his attention. A soldier in front of him choked as a gnoll's spear exploded through the back of their skull. Crimson gore sprayed all over Peshka's blue sash and the silly ribbons he'd insisted on wearing.

Peshka opened his mouth, but before he could shout, a pair of zombie gnolls rushed in, tackling the offending gnoll. Its tearing flesh and messy yelp were drowned out by the rest of the fighting.

He shook his head as he wiped blood from his face. It was a disgrace, relying on these abominations. It was hard to remember that these monsters were on his side, when his every instinct screamed to flee from them, or strike them down. But they had their advantages.

They fought without faltering after taking mortal wounds. No change in their morale, even against superior numbers. Fearless, disregarding their safety, and merciless. And every gnoll had to overcome its initial shock from seeing the undead. Sometimes that moment of surprise was the deciding factor in combat. Peshka shuddered as the zombies leapt on another gnoll, ripping out its throat. He was just glad they were on his side.

Out of nowhere, a sword swung at Peshka's head, close enough for him to feel the wind from it. He ducked in time to save his receding hairline.

"Watch where you're bloody swinging that thing!" he roared.

He looked up. The ranks of soldiers insulating him from the fighting had been replaced by gnolls—and lots of them.

Before he could think, another swing came in. But his saber was already in his hand.

Peshka parried the blow with speed that surprised even himself. If youthful reflexes youth were his reward for sobriety, perhaps it wasn't so unbearable after all. Though the splitting headache still gave him doubts.

The attacking gnoll's companions pushed it forward. Peshka saw his opening as it stumbled, swinging his saber in an overhead arc. His blade cleaved into its collarbone. The gnoll howled and fell to its knees. Peshka pommel-punched it in the snout—more for his own satisfaction than anything else—and it toppled over.

He saw another gnoll in the corner of his eye. Peshka turned—too slowly, he knew. He swallowed, accepting that this could be the valiant final seconds of his illustrious military career.

A spear lanced in from the ranks. Peshka sidestepped and raised his sword to deflect the blow. The spear batted it away, then caught on his medals. His campaign medal from DeGaullis, his Valiant Fraternal Order of Calvarys, and his medal for heroism in the Battle of Feris, were all ripped from his chest. Then the spear tore a gash in his arm.

"You bastard!" Peshka growled in pain.

The spear disappeared back into the fray of bodies as quickly as it had appeared. Peshka watched as his medals were trampled into the mud. He grunted, taking out his fury on the closest gnoll. Its back was turned toward him, but there was no honor in this bloody melee. Peshka slashed and howled like a madman. His sword cleaved the gnoll's arm to the bone. The gnoll shrieked, but before Peshka could finish the job, a blow to his breastplate folded him in half.

The shiny metal deflected the hammer's blow, but not without sustaining an unsightly dent he knew would never polish out. Peshka fell backward, wheezing, but something kept him from falling to the ground. He turned and found First Sergeant Goren towering over him.

"Look out, sir!" She swung her massive two-handed sword with one hand, cleaving the hammer gnoll from shoulder to sternum.

"Forward! Hold the line!" she bellowed, then stepped in front of Peshka, bashing the flailing gnoll off her blade with her tower shield.

Peshka clutched his sword as a row of soldiers and zombies pushed forward, filling the gap. He wheezed for air as he adjusted his dented breastplate, then cursed as he saw the cut on his arm seeping blood. More soldiers and undead pressed forward, pushing the gnolls back. First Sergeant Goren led the way, cutting a bloody wedge through the gnolls for the soldiers to fill.

Peshka sighed in relief. But it caught in his throat when a section of the wall tumbled from the sky, crashing a dozen paces away. Shouts of surprise ended abruptly as soldiers, undead, and gnolls alike were flattened underneath. Peshka was knocked on his rump from the force of the impact.

"Gods bloody dammit!"

The giant laughed from behind the wall. Peshka had no idea how to deal with that.

But perhaps there was another way. He looked over his shoulder and spotted a few horses tied against the wall in the distance. "It worked in DeGaullis," he muttered to himself.

Malfus stood by the edge of the cliff. The rod thrummed in his hand.

Something was different this time. He could feel it. The rod seemed ready, even excited. The cross of the star within the ruby focused on the massive corpse below, as if anticipating what came next.

The rod wasn't the only thing that had changed. Something had grown within himself as well. He felt more certain, more confident. Energy surged through him, the force rippling in the air around him. He'd never been so capable, nor commanded so many dead.

It was so much quieter out here on this isolated side of the fort. Almost peaceful. Only his connection to the undead gave him nagging reminders of the soldiers dying, spurring him on with blistering urgency.

No rest for the weary.

Grateful for the quiet, he returned his focus to the rotting corpse below. He began chanting the ancient Shal-Umbran words for his spell. The sharp syllables echoed back from the canyon, making the words haunting and powerful.

He closed his eyes and held out the rod. Numbing waves of entropic energy emanated from it, flowing through him and into the giant's corpse. Even the massive amount of negative energy the rod now channeled was a mere fraction of what it had absorbed from the pit. He ignored the damage it was doing to his body. He knew what he had to do.

He concentrated on the web in his mind, rearranging his strands to his other zombies to make room for the massive cord that would connect him to the giant. The thought of controlling that much raw physical power sent a shiver down his spine. The corners of his lips twisted into a grin as he continued casting. *Almost there.*

Sweat beaded on his forehead as he concentrated, focusing on the spell instead of the ecstasy he felt—the sheer power the corpse promised him.

But the final words of the spell froze in his throat.

A knife against your neck will do that.

A gloved hand gripped Malfus by the wrist, pulling the rod back. A body pressed into his, shoving him dangerously close to the edge. His boots kicked, skittering stones over the cliff. He looked down at the long drop to the giant's corpse.

"Looks like your friend was right about being able to find you here," the Inquisitor whispered in his ear.

Malfus swallowed. He briefly wondered what fate had befallen Morten, but the Inquisitor's methods left little room for doubt. *Bastard.*

"Fancy running into you here," he said, teeth clenched. "Come here for the view—?"

The blade bit into his throat. A drop of blood ran down his neck.

"No more sarcasm." The Inquisitor's hand pushed him closer to the cliff's edge. "Unless that's what you want as your final words. My patience has run dry."

Malfus swallowed and said nothing. *Think. I have to stay calm and think.*

He couldn't cast anything like this. Even the simplest of spells required a few words too many, with that knife against his throat. His inability to see his target, and the yawning abyss in front of him, made any plans all the less feasible.

So he kept silent, cycling through the threads at the back of his mind. His undead were so far away, caught up in a growing battle. None of them would make it here in time. The crow? *Perhaps that will have to do. But I need to buy some time.* He tried to think of some way to stall, but the voice behind him continued.

"This isn't what I wanted." The Inquisitor wrenched Malfus's arm behind his back. "I wanted to be there when they tortured the truth from you. When they ripped the confessions from your miserable hide. I wanted to redeem myself with your capture. But I'll have to settle for my own justice. Not Vesenia's."

"What do you want from me? I've done nothing but pursue my studies. I haven't harmed anyone. Yet you've persisted on taking everything from me."

The Inquisitor's knife tightened against his throat. "Haven't harmed anyone? You insolent whelp. You dare to complain about what *I've* taken from *you*? Do you have any idea?"

Malfus swallowed. It was the first he'd ever heard any emotion in that voice.

The Inquisitor took a moment to compose himself. "Do you know how much it has taken for me to refrain from killing you?"

"Why?" demanded Malfus. "Why do you want to kill me? To ruin my life? Who am I to you?"

"You—you were that missing apprentice from Akkadia, weren't you? A failure of a student, washed out of the academy, then fleeing, what—four years ago?" The Inquisitor grimaced. "I've been hunting you for four years now."

Confusion crept across Malfus's features. "Since when does the Vesenian Inquisition hunt down renegade apprentices?"

"You fled," whispered the Inquisitor, as if Malfus wasn't there, "because you murdered my daughter."

Malfus's heart skipped a beat, his breath freezing in his chest.

His memories of that night crashed into his mind. He could picture her face. Her eyes, her raven hair. The similarities were so striking. He cursed himself for not having recognized it.

Damian Deza. Kiara's *father*.

"It wasn't like that. You have it wrong. It was—"

He tried to think of what to say, but the revelation struck Malfus like a blow to the head. It wasn't his fault. But what choice had he been given? He had to run. How could he explain something like that to this man—her father? What could he possibly say to Deza that wouldn't end in death?

He had to think of something. He just needed a little more time.

"Her death—Kiara's death—" Malfus's cheeks burned as the words left his mouth.

"You heathen! You dare to say her *name*?" Deza's grip tightened until Malfus winced. The Inquisitor wrenched his wrist, forcing Malfus closer to the edge.

I need to think of something else. Something to buy time.

"Listen—let me go. Let's talk this through. I'll tell you what happened." He glanced at the edge of the cliff. "If you kill me, it'll release the undead from their tethers. They'll kill everyone. Gnoll and human alike—they won't care."

"Neither do I." Deza pushed him closer to the edge. "That will be their atonement."

Malfus closed his eyes. *Just a little closer.*

The crow swooped low, silent as a whisper, tucking its wings into its sides, then collided into the back of Deza's head. He cried out in surprise, loosening his grip. Malfus's heel clipped the edge of the cliff. He wobbled his arms to balance as he ducked low, slipping out of Deza's grasp.

Then he raised the rod in the air, a spell crackling on his lips.

The rod grew warm in his hand. There was a rush of air against his face, and then a heavy *thud*. He gasped, trying to breathe, but it felt like an anvil sat on top of his chest. The spell fizzled on his lips. He tasted blood.

He looked down to see a dagger sticking from his chest, blood already spilling from the wound. He couldn't make sense of it. It had happened so fast.

And after the horrible realization came the pain. *Real* pain.

He could feel every inch of the blade puncturing his flesh. The cold steel burned like a hot coal. He thought shock would kick in, but all he could feel was blistering agony.

Malfus screamed.

He reached for the dagger, but his vision started to blur, splitting the blade into several. He wasn't sure which to grab. He took a step backward, then felt the ground give out beneath his feet. Wind rushed around him. Was he falling? Cold air ripped at his clothes and hair, roaring in his ears. His limbs flailed uselessly. One hand clutched at empty air, the other to the rod. He tried to scream as the ground raced toward him, but all that came out was a wet croak.

He landed with a sickening crunch in the giant's empty eye socket.

As the dust settled around him, his body seared with pain. Splintering, mindless pain. But as it grew to more than he could bear, it slipped away from him, ebbing in throbbing waves. Receding, like the ocean's tide, replaced with darkness. Malfus tried to hold on to his pain, but there was nothing left. It bled out of him. Abandoning him.

His zombies felt like a distant memory. He wasn't sure what he was doing with so many. His grasp on them faded.

Only darkness remained in his mind. That, and the promise of release. The only thing he could see, other than the void, was a glowing red ember.

It burned like a setting sun.

Chapter 23

Eternal Emperor of the Sand Sea

"Day 27 – Exhausted. Another night without sleep. This week's excavation has yielded little progress. There is no explanation—how such an advanced society collapsed, or what formed the Scar. The remaining ruins should be unearthed soon. I keep hearing whispers at night. No one else seems to hear them, but I know they are leading me right. I feel excited about tomorrow." — Last journal entry of Chief Archivist and Historian Johann Indrics

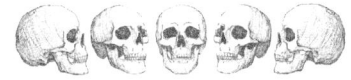

Nothing.

There was nothing.

Only inky, primordial darkness.

He was wrapped in it. It was warm, almost soft.

The faintest sensation of movement. Floating. Like gently drifting downstream, cradled by countless tiny hands. The darkness was wet, soft as syrup.

He felt as insignificant as a bubble of foam on the surf, in an ocean with waves beyond counting. A tiny speck of awareness, insulated from the throbbing horror of existence. Here, he was anointed with an absolution from self.

He didn't have to think. Not if he didn't want to. He didn't have to *do* anything anymore.

Ever.

Thought, feeling, memory—all were overrated abstractions. Ideas that brought only trouble. He tried to stop thinking about his thinking, but that only made the problem worse. What was this feeling, gnawing at him? It itched like a spider bite. A pebble in his shoe. A thorn in his fingertip. A sore on the roof of his mouth. A memory, but only half-remembered.

Something hid in the depths of his mind. A chest on the ocean floor. It opened. Inside it was a thread, like a strand of spider's silk. Why was that so familiar? Curiosity bade him open the chest, pluck at the strand. It was out of place. It didn't belong here.

He pulled at it.

That was a mistake.

Searing light burst into the sanctuary of his dark embryonic nothingness. He recoiled, scurrying back into the darkness like a cockroach, but the blinding light flooded in after him. He couldn't hide. The light made him queasy, vulnerable. He didn't want to know it any longer. He didn't want to remember. He wanted to put the blinding light back, but it was too late now.

Inside the light shone a piece of reflective glass. A mirror.

A somber face stared back at him with sobering clarity. Accompanying it was the alien concept of a *name*.

Did he have one? He hoped not. He didn't want one.

Too late. A single word bubbled to the forefront of his consciousness like a miasma—*Malfus*. The recognition left a bitter taste in his mouth. It slicked over him like oil. The more he tried to wipe himself clean, the more it clung to him. Now it would never come off.

He threw the mirror away, but it was manacled around his wrists, chained to him like an anchor. He didn't float now. He sank instead.

He remembered falling. The pain. The tiny hands that had carried him in the dark covered his mouth now. They smothered him. Pulled him down. He opened his mouth to shout, but couldn't breathe. A roar filled his ears, growing louder and louder.

He coughed, choking for air. The burden of breathing returned to him.

Malfus groaned. Lapping waves caressed his cheek, pulling him back toward the abyss, but the coarse sands of existence rubbed against his face. They refused to let him go.

He pushed himself onto his knees. His palms sank into moist red sand.

Memories trickled back into the cracks of his mind. His eyes opened wide. He tore at his wet clothing, ripping open his shirt. No dagger stuck from his chest. No wound. No pain. He pulled his shirt up and looked again.

His fingers searched the sand, but there was no sign of the rod anywhere. He grabbed a handful of sand, letting it slip through his fingers. Tiny red jewels. Miniscule beads of glass.

Is this a dream, or am I really dead this time?

Malfus stood up.

A sea of blood stretched behind him, vast and eternal. Its hungry waves licked the shore, stretching to the left and right, farther than he could see. Above him, a crimson sky gaped like an open wound.

Malfus turned away from the ocean to face dunes of sand rolling into the distance. Eventually, they rose into mountains and peaks the color of copper, scraping at the sky like knives. Far above him, a massive eight-pointed star dominated the sky.

Was anyone else out here? "Hello!" he called.

His voice echoed across the landscape. The voice that shouted back at him sounded cold and mocking. Hollow.

Alone.

His wet clothing was coarse with sand, clinging to him like lizard scales. He tried brushing off the jeweled sand that encrusted him, but it wasn't going anywhere.

He began walking.

As endless as everything here seemed, it felt claustrophobic. A strange trick of the senses, like holding two mirrors next to one another. Everything felt numb, like the echo of a dream. As isolated as Malfus felt, he still couldn't shake the feeling that something was watching him.

Is this really death? It wasn't at all what he expected death to look like. He figured it would be... darker, blacker; not so red, at least. *Perhaps it's the antechamber of the afterlife.*

Malfus continued hiking toward the distant mountains, not knowing why. It felt like he'd awoken from a long slumber, to find himself surrounded by splinters of his dreams. But when he reached for the fragments, they slipped away.

He remembered his name. He remembered the searing pain of a knife, and falling, but he couldn't remember what led up to it. There was more to this, scratching beneath the surface, but his memories felt tenuous. As unsettled as the sand beneath his feet.

After some time, he slowed. The mountains appeared no closer than they had before. He turned around, and saw the ocean was only a few dunes away. Surely he must have gone further than that? It had felt like so much longer. The white star in the sky followed him as he walked, as if spying on him.

Something appeared in the distance, floating above the ground. A black spot, like a hole torn into this red world. Malfus changed directions and walked toward the darkness. The distant void triggered something inside him—a string of memories. Another name.

"Kiara?"

Images of the mage academy of Akkadia flashed in his mind. He had been a wizard. A necromancer. But who was Kiara? Where had that name come from?

The surface of his mind stilled; a face come into focus. Staring back at him.

Raven hair, waving like the ocean. Green eyes, bright with hope. She'd been a wizard, too. He remembered that. In his mind, she pointed at him, her finger outstretched. Then she faded, until all that remained was her finger pointing at his soul.

His cheeks burned with shame. Guilt weighed down his shoulders. Something was in his mind where the finger had pointed. Something locked in a box he didn't want to see, hidden away. He held the key. It was the bloated corpse of his past, rising to the surface.

Above the black hole, ominous charcoal clouds formed, their undersides lit red. Silent bolts of lightning clawed upward from the clouds on the edge of the sky—as if trying to escape. The wind picked up. Red, glittering dust whipped across the dunes in front of him. Before long, gales howled, shrieking like a lover scorned.

Curtains of sand as tall as the mountains rose in front of him, obscuring the black hole. Walls of sand towered overhead, orange as a funeral pyre. He gritted his teeth and held a hand over his eyes as the sand blew in his face. He pulled his shirt over his mouth and nose so he could still breathe. The unrelenting sands whipped at his face, eroding the walls of his amnesia. He remembered the giant, the gnolls, the fort and its soldiers...

And the Inquisitor.

Was he alive? If he was, he had to get back to help the soldiers.

Or do I? If he had died, his undead were already untethered. Perhaps none of it mattered any longer. Ennui told him to sit down and let the sands cover him. Be free from the torment of the Inquisitor. Free from the threat of the gnolls.

What was there to go back to? An endless sea of unfulfilled desires. Things left undone, tasks left unfinished, words left unsaid, mistakes uncorrected.

The delicate threads of his life had become a tangled mess. He had pulled on a string, and it had unraveled into a series of tiny but endless disappointments. He'd become a fugitive on the run from the Vesenian Inquisition, for a murder he didn't commit. For being a necromancer.

The real crime was that he wasn't even very skilled at it.

Malfus had no idea where he was going. The black orb had disappeared behind sheets of sand. He almost gave up and stopped right there, but the stinging sand wouldn't stop blowing for his sake.

Then, from somewhere far away, ethereal singing filled the air.

Otherworldly, soft as silk, but sharp as the cutting sands. It sounded like an instrument as much as a voice—inhuman, but undeniably feminine. The hairs on his neck raised in response.

He followed the sound . It was his only landmark in the storm. Its haunting melody evoked the joy of something fondly remembered, but with the pain of knowing he'd never hold it again. It triggered a deep sense of longing—for Kiara, for everything else he'd never have. He didn't understand its words, but they sounded familiar. He wasn't sure if the siren song promised shelter from the storm, or would lead him into a yawning abyss.

Malfus clenched his teeth, pushing through the endless sand. When he thought he could go no further, the sands cleared so abruptly that he stumbled to his knees. Looking back, there was no sign of any storm at all. Just endless red dunes running into the distance. The singing had vanished with the howling wind. Both had been replaced by a venerable silence, like the inside of a temple, or at the mouth of a dragon's lair.

Obsidian tiles cut a path through the crimson sand before him, leading to a raised dais. Atop sat a chaise lounge merged with a throne, brocaded with red silk and velvet. Beside it, a tiered fountain cascaded with blood.

All of it paled in significance when compared to the figure reclining on the lounge.

She was a goddess with ebony skin, tinged with the slightest blue, like a moonless midnight sky. She reclined, but remained regal, like a statue, resting as if she hadn't moved for an eternity. Her feminine silhouette ate the light surrounding it, darker than the obsidian tile underfoot.

As Malfus approached, she propped herself up, resting a hand under her chin as she watched him. She was human, but her beauty rivaled even elven standards. Her face was full and heart-shaped, with high cheekbones. Her glistening, full lips expressed the hint of a smile, as if expecting a joke. Her cleanshaven head shone as lustrous as polished onyx, and her arched eyebrows added a shadow to her angled eyes, which were red as rubies.

As Malfus ascended the steps, she arose. She was tall for a woman—no First Sergeant Goren, but the same height as Malfus, perhaps taller. It was impossible to tell from this angle, as he craned his neck to look up at her.

She wore a sapphire gossamer gown. The sheer fabric, skintight, left little to the imagination. It was embroidered with tiny gems that shone like stars. As she walked toward him, new patterns emerged on the jeweled dress, and Malfus realized—the gems *were* stars. The fabric was a curtain of the cosmos itself, showing another dimension through its folds.

She moved with the calculated grace of a spider, and the strength and confidence of a hunting cat. Each step had a hidden power behind it; she looked ready to pounce forward and devour him.

"You took your time getting here," she said. "Have a lot on your mind?"

Her voice was husky, like smoke from a skoah pipe in the back of a seedy inn, promising the same excitement and danger. The accent was strange, reminding Malfus of the exotic accents he'd heard at Akkadia's harbor—almost like Ornaellian perfume and oil merchants, or Kendreatic tea merchants—with perhaps a hint of the spice traders from the Vitrian Isles. It was like all of those, and yet something else entirely.

"Who are you?" His mouth fumbled, clumsy as a drunk.

"*Who* am I?" The woman laughed, then took a step toward Malfus. Close enough that he felt his skin tingle. Close enough that his breath quickened.

She leaned her head back. "I am Rammani-Thuul, Eternal Empress of the Sand Sea."

Malfus took a step back. "You? The tyrant of the Shal-Umbra Empire? The one that... created the Scar?"

"One and the same." She put her hands on her hips. "Don't believe me?"

"The books said..." He paused, searching for the right words. "History remembers you as... I always thought you were a man."

"Most men do."

"But if you were him—er, her... That means..." Malfus balked. "The Shal-Umbra Empire has been dust for over five-hundred years." Shock made his breath come in quick gasps. "Is this the afterlife? Are we dead? Where are we?"

The Empress smiled. "Slow down, darling. One question at a time. I don't want to *spoil* you prematurely." She chuckled. "No, this isn't the afterlife. I am dead, but you are not. At least, not yet. As for where we are—don't you already know? You *are* a necromancer, aren't you? Haven't you figured it out yet with that *mind* of yours?"

"The rod," he whispered, and the pieces came together. "You're a lich. It wasn't just a magic artifact. It was your *phylactery*."

She clapped. "I knew you would figure it out! Well, it's not the rod—it's the ruby." Her eyes glittered.

The realization sank in. "I've been carrying *you* with me the entire time. Ever since I found your rod? That was you?"

"Perhaps that sponge inside your skull will be of some use to us after all."

Malfus crossed his arms. "If you really are her, what should I call you? Eternal Empress of the Sand Sea? The Scorpion of Vespertine? The Butcher of the Blood Coast? You have taken many names over the years."

Her eyes narrowed. She lunged forward like a dragon, stopping inches away from Malfus's face. Then she smiled. Her ivory teeth shone between her full, black lips. It felt like a viper showing off its fangs to a rodent—a before-dinner smile.

"You may call me Ramma," she said, "but only because you still remain in my good graces." She gave a threatening grin, but behind her eyes, Malfus saw a touch of sorrow. "Let me ask you, necromancer: do you know what *thuul* means?"

Malfus shrugged his shoulders.

Ramma continued. "*Thuul* means slave in Umbranese. I was a slave. Born into it. Simply because my mother was born a slave herself. As was her mother before her. Shal-Umbra was always a dark place. Long before my reign began."

"Why are you telling me this?"

"You know my names. But do not presume to judge my past without knowing its entirety." Her voice was as sharp as the sand. "You of all people should know that."

The truth of her words stung him, and he changed the subject. "Why am I here?"

"You were a stray kitten that showed up on my doorstep. What should I do—let you die there? My phylactery has more than enough space to house such a *tiny* soul as yourself. So I took you in."

He narrowed his eyes. "Why? What are you going to do with me?"

Ramma *tsk*ed, shaking her head. "One of those straight-to-business types. Don't be such a bore. Every woman enjoys foreplay. It's never fun if you rush in and end things too quickly." She circled him, just out of reach. Graceful as a cat, but eyeing him like a circling vulture.

Malfus shuddered. "If you are the Empress, I doubt I'm here on your good graces. I wouldn't be here if you didn't need me for something—unless you like playing with your food."

"You are indeed a tasty little morsel." She sauntered toward him, placing a hand on his cheek. Her fingers were cold as marble. "But as flattering as it is to keep talking about me, why don't we talk about you—and what *you* want."

Ramma looked at him like a concerned mother, as if she knew him better than he knew himself.

"I've seen you struggling, Malfus. You aren't a *failure*. You're too hard on yourself."

Malfus swallowed and tried to glance away, but her ruby gaze seared into him.

"Who can blame you?" she continued. "You haven't had a proper instructor in necromancy. No one has taught you these *dark arts*. It isn't your fault the simpleminded are so afraid of it." She laughed—a terrifying noise. "Imagine it. An academy of wizards afraid to touch an entire school of magic. Wizards, afraid of their own shadows. No wonder they are all kept under lock and key by the church. *Her* church," she said, looking away. "What has this world come to since I left? I can offer you true power, Malfus. Knowledge. Instruction."

He paused. He had to think about it.

Necromancy was the one thing he had an ounce of aptitude for. He wasn't a prodigy, but if he had a mentor—particularly, the most infamous necromancer in history—there was no telling what he would be capable of. He could even bring Kiara back.

But first, he had to know for sure. He had to ask.

"When they called you the Eternal Emperor—er, Empress."

"Yes?" Her eyes narrowed.

"They claim that you ruled for over three centuries by bathing in the blood of the conquered. But can necromancy be used to extend natural life without undeath? Can it call someone's soul back from the plane of death?"

She sighed impatiently, then looked away as if bored. "Oh yes. Your little *finger* girl. Who is she to you? The first girl you ever managed to get your fingers wet in—then you killed her, and took *her* finger as a trophy." She tittered. "That's a weird kink if I've ever seen one, and I've been around for quite some time."

Malfus's face flushed as red as the sand. "No! Not like that. I just want to fix a mistake."

She sighed, then looked him up and down. Measuring him as if he were a cow and she a butcher at market.

"It can be done," said Ramma. "But necromancy is so much more than that. Your first lesson will also be your last lesson, once you fully understand it. And once you understand it, there are no other lessons for me to teach you."

She grabbed his hand, taking it in the both of hers, then traced a line across his palm. "All schools of magic are paths up the same mountain. Just as a high priest can kill with divine energy, a *vile* necromancer can use entropic energy to enslave the forces of life."

Malfus said nothing.

"Energy is energy. You will see. I will show you what I know—if you let me." She released his hand, spinning away from him. Her starred gown swirled like the cosmos.

Malfus crossed his arms, looking pointedly away from her hips. "Only a fool thinks anything is free. What do you want in return?"

"The same thing as you," said Ramma. "Freedom. Oh, and getting a new body." She spun slowly, out of his reach. "Sadly, this beautiful vessel you see is a memory. A great tragedy for all the men of the world—*and* for countless women. This body has long since aged into dust. But there's no point in living forever if you can't change your wardrobe. I'll need a new one if I'm ever going to step out of this cage again."

Before Malfus could consider the implications, she continued.

"Speaking of bodies." She walked over to the fountain of blood. "I believe you need a little help with *yours*."

Malfus swallowed as he followed her to the fountain. She waved a hand over the blood, and it stopped flowing. After its ripples subsided, an image slowly appeared on its surface—his broken body. Covered in blood, its limbs splayed at strange angles.

"You are a bit worse for wear," said Ramma, "but I can still heal you. You'll need to decide quickly, though."

He looked away from his broken form. "Will I be undead? A lich like you?"

She put her hand to her mouth. "Nothing quite so fancy—*not yet*—at least, not if we hurry. There *is* a price. When necromancy heals the body, it borrows your life force from the opposite end of your life. Shortening your candle's wick, as it were, but I'm sure you have plenty to spare." She sized him up again, then winked. "Do we still have a deal?"

Malfus swallowed. "If I agree…"

"Then I return you to your body, *fix* it, solve your little giant problem, get rid of the gnoll infestation, and then—you just need to find me one tiny, little, insignificant body. In exchange, I will save your life. I'll even teach you some necromancy along the way. What do you say to that, my little pupil? All for the price of a single corpse."

"Why haven't you just stolen mine?"

She tutted. "You think I would do such a thing?"

Malfus nodded.

She smiled. "It's not so simple. There is a ritual involved that I can't do on my own. And besides, as handsome as you are…" Her icy hand caressed his jaw. "I prefer to remain a woman. So you'll need to find me one of those." She looked at Malfus's pensive face, drawn with indecision. "I'll need your word, though. Don't take too long thinking." She gestured at the image of his body. "If you don't decide soon, we'll have to consider other *methods* for bringing you back. This is one of those—what are they called?—*limited-time offers.*"

Malfus hesitated. Would he have to kill someone to get her a new body? For that matter, what would happen if he released an ancient evil that literally scarred the world?

Then he looked down at his own body, lying broken. Helpless. He skimmed past his own selfish desire to live, and considered the other soldiers' lives at stake.

What choice do I have?

He sighed. "All right. I'll do it."

"Excellent! I knew you would see reason." Ramma gave a hungry smile again, leaning closer. "Just as a warning though, before we begin. If you even *think* about betraying me—do not doubt my vengeance. I have drunk the blood of thousands whose names I've forgotten, and from countless more whose names I never bothered to learn. For those that have truly vexed me... My immortality affords artistic freedoms for torture that the Inquisition could only dream of. And I've dreamt for *centuries.*"

She pursed her lips. "Even with all of that to draw from, I still can't imagine what I would do to someone who betrayed me after I aided them." She paused. "And I don't *aid* others often. Consider yourself *very* lucky."

Malfus swallowed again, unsure what anyone could say to that.

"Oh. One more thing," said Ramma. "When you return, I can't promise there won't be any suffering."

He swallowed. "What do you mean?"

"You said you wanted to live, didn't you? Suffering is part of the package. Besides, pleasure is always sweetened with a little *pain.*"

She approached ever closer. The predatorial hunger in her eyes spread to her lips. A wordless yearning smoldered in his chest as she drew near.

"Just as I've made room for you here," Ramma whispered, "You will make room for me inside your mortal vessel when you return. There will be a little bit of me *inside of you.*" She grabbed his hips, pulling him against her.

The chill of her dead body pressed against his. She grabbed Malfus by the hair and pulled him to her, kissing him with wet lips—a ravenous kiss that left his passions yearning for more.

But then she slapped Malfus across the cheek. He reeled back, face stinging, and stared up at her in shock.

Ramma smirked. "Don't keep me waiting, lover boy. And don't let go of my rod."

Before Malfus could reply, the red sands at his feet swallowed him whole.

MALFUS - The Eternal Empress — Art by Dejan Delic

Chapter 24
Giant Problem Solver

"The strongest seeds spring from the darkest ash." — Elven saying

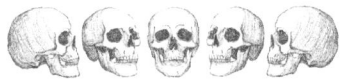

Malfus awoke into hell.

His throbbing head was attached to an agonized body, with his consciousness trapped inside it. Like a fly stuck in a web. A bloated meat prison, wracked with pain.

Malfus looked down and saw the dagger sticking from his chest, next to his heart. It rose and fell with the frantic tempo of his breathing. Blood foamed around the silvery blade. It didn't even look real—more like a first-year illusionist's feeble cantrip. But its pain was real.

He coughed. Agony lanced through his insides; he spat out a mouthful of warm blood with his broken jaw. His tongue was a salted sponge, taking up his entire mouth.

What had he done? What had he agreed to? Why wasn't anything happening yet? He tried to call to Ramma for help.

He managed to bleat like an animal from his split lips. He sounded like a goat being dragged to market.

The stars above, just smears of white, began to dim. Then everything went black again.

A splinter shrieked in his mind.

Oh no, you don't! You aren't backing out of our agreement that easily. Grab the rod.

Malfus opened his eyes, barely conscious. He lolled his head to the side and saw a hazy red light in his peripheral vision. The rod was much farther than he liked.

Wheezing, he stretched his hand as far as he could, but that light was too far away. He pushed himself up with his other arm.

"Gahh!" A broken bone slid through the skin of his forearm.

The pain was unlike anything he'd felt. Malfus wanted to throw up. His breath came out in a hiss. He waited for the pain to subside before trying again. His legs weren't any help. Pain shot down one leg whenever he tried to move it, and the other dragged beside it. He was reduced to wriggling on the ground like a worm. Every inch felt like a mile of effort. Each movement brought the dagger a fraction closer to his heart.

The ruby was getting brighter. His salvation was just a handsbreadth away. He stretched his fingers out again, reaching for it—but he was stuck.

The sleeve of his broken arm was caught on something.

Dammit! I need to get to the rod—no matter what it takes.

He clenched his eyes shut, trying not to think about what came next. Then, in a burst of movement, he forced himself up again with his broken arm. He shrieked in pain, freeing his broken arm, and flopped closer to the rod. He reached out. The tips of his fingers brushed against the cool metal—

And pushed it away.

No!

The rod rolled a few inches, then rolled back toward him. His hand wrapped around it like an octopus. Its metal grew warmer in his palm. The ruby grew radiant.

Ramma's voice sounded in his mind.

NOW THE REAL PAIN BEGINS. YOU HAD BETTER HOLD ON TIGHT.

Malfus let out a blubbering wheeze.

The rod began pulsing in time with his fleeting heartbeat. He felt weightless, like a leaf floating on a gentle stream. For a few seconds, he even forgot about the pain.

THINK OF NOTHING ELSE BUT HOLDING ONTO THE ROD. LET'S NOT FIND OUT WHAT HAPPENS IF YOU LET GO IN THE MIDDLE OF THIS.

He glanced down. He floated in the air, nearly six feet above the giant's empty eye socket. His grip on the rod tightened until his knuckles turned white.

The rod let out a blinding flash, leaving red afterimages in his retinas.

A force snatched at his limbs, stretching them outward like a marionette on a string. Pain seared through his body like white fire. His broken arm twisted, stretching all the way out until the jagged bone disappeared under the skin. His leg jerked around in its socket, setting itself straight. He heard his shattered bones cracking as they ground against bloody meat. He watched in wide-eyed horror as the dagger was pushed from of his chest. It fell, clattering below him.

The pain was worse than anything he could have imagined. He opened his mouth to scream, but before he could, an invisible hand wrenched his jaw. There was a wet crunch as it slid back into its proper place, followed by a sputtering mewl.

He wanted to pass out. His grip on the rod loosened.

NO! STAY WITH THE PAIN.

Grimacing, he grasped the rod as tightly as he could with the last of his strength.

Invisible hands clawed inside him, rearranging his organs, popping his broken ribs back into place, twisting his spine. He felt the urge to vomit and defecate all at once.

The torture paused. Malfus kept his grip on the rod, his breath coming in ragged gasps.

Streaks of crackling violet-black energy scattered across his skin. His heart pounded so fiercely he thought his skull would explode. Harder it came, and harder, until he could feel the blood in his eyes, hear it rushing through his ears. His skin drew tighter, melting around its edges like wax, knitting itself together before his eyes. He could *feel* his broken bones fusing together. Entropic energy overflowed his wards and ran rampant through his body, like icy water coursing through his veins.

For a brief moment, the plane of death flickered in his mind, filling it with nightmarish horrors that tore at his sanity. Gnashing teeth, grasping hands, and faces—so many faces. They leered at him, reminding him of their inevitability. Then the vision faded away, taking the pain with it, leaving a chilling numbness behind.

He held onto the rod, exhausted. He lowered back down through the air. Both of his feet reached the giant's skull and stood firmly atop it, miraculously unbroken. He spread out his fingers, the bone no longer sticking from his arm, then touched his chest. All that remained of his near-fatal injury was a small, puckered scar.

In his mind, Ramma purred. *THERE, NOW. THAT WASN'T SO BAD, WAS IT?*

Before Malfus could voice his frustration, roiling nausea hit him. He retched, spewing oily vomit an impressive distance. It was putrid and black.

"Ugh. What was that?" Malfus wiped his mouth, clicking his jaw back into place.

OH... ABOUT THREE TO FIVE YEARS OF YOUR LIFE, GIVE OR TAKE.

Malfus checked his reflection in the ruby. It was a poor mirror, but it showed a thick lock of bone-white emerging from his black hair. His face looked more gaunt than normal—which was to be expected, all things considered—but he spotted more lines around the corners of his eyes than he remembered.

DON'T WORRY. IT'S A GOOD LOOK ON YOU. THOSE YEARS ONLY MATTER IF YOU END UP DYING FROM NATURAL CAUSES, WHICH IS RARELY THE CASE FOR NECROMANCERS. BESIDES, WE CAN ALWAYS GET THEM BACK. I'LL SHOW YOU HOW AFTER THIS IS ALL OVER.

Malfus swallowed. He'd read enough stories about the Eternal Empress to have a pretty lurid idea about what that involved.

One more thing.

Malfus winced, expecting more pain.

That was just your bargain with Big Daddy Death. Now... it's my turn.

The rod flickered and flashed, a ruby light dancing within the gem.

Malfus felt darkness seep into the fissures of his mind. Words in an ancient language echoed down a long corridor—the roar of a hundred whispered secrets.

His eyes fluttered behind closed eyelids. His mind flooded with subtle corrections—misunderstandings, mispronunciations, and misemphases of spells, as well as a few bad habits he'd picked up. He realized an obvious method for redirecting void energy through his tattoos, allowing them to absorb more energy before overflowing. He made a mental note of a few items to fix in his spellbook; so much came, so fast, that it was like clutching at sand in the wind.

Into his mind's eye flowed someone else's memory: a vast, sandy library, its shelves brimming with scrolls and tomes with covers as large as a man. The vision wasn't his own, but he could feel the heat of the sun on his skin, the dry winds on his chapped lips, and the sharp scent of incense—his favorite smell in all the world, though he'd never smelled it before. He looked at the words on a nearby page, but everything was murky, as if peering through a pool of water.

Don't you have any manners? Hasn't anyone taught you not to watch a woman while she's getting ready? Go. Regain control over your undead. You weren't gone long enough for your commands to wear off, or for any to break free... yet.

Malfus remembered the battle, the soldiers, and the zombies. Taking a deep breath, he dug into the quiet, black earth of his mind.

Deep in his mind lied the nexus of threads binding his undead. It was still intact, but unraveling. He reached into his mind and grabbed it, refreshing each connection, one by one, before they dissolved. There were fewer to connect to; half of his strands had been severed. He shifted his attention to one that remained.

The zombie was surrounded by a tide of pressing bodies, soldiers, and other zombies fighting the gnolls. The invaders surged into the fort. The giant stood astride the gap, cleaving another wedge of stone from the wall with its dragon skull shield. The chunk of mortared bricks flew over the wall, sailing over the gnolls, growing larger in the zombie's vision. It crashed into his zombie and several nearby soldiers. Everything went black. He shuddered as his awareness snapped back to his body.

I have to hurry.

He slid from the dead giant's hairless head and dropped to the ground. The stone around it glistened black with dried blood.

The corpse was as tall as a felled tree. It lay on its back, its arms across its chest as if resting peacefully. A sleeping god, waiting to be awoken.

Malfus felt a reassuring surge of power from the rod. Ramma's voice buzzed in head. WELL? WHAT ARE YOU WAITING FOR? LET'S GET THIS PARTY STARTED.

He flipped through the bloodied pages of his spellbook until he found his reanimation spell.

WHAT ARE YOU DOING? DON'T WASTE YOUR TIME WITH THAT. ALLOW ME.

Following her instruction, he held the rod toward the giant. Negative energy surged through him. The words flowed from his mouth, unbidden, as if an afterthought. A cord connected him to the giant, reaching through the plane of death, like hefting a bucket of water from a deep well. Black lightning arced from his fingertips to the corpse. A cloud of green sparks glimmered, floating in the darkness like sickly fireflies, before extinguishing in smudges of smoke.

Nothing happened at first. Then a few muscles in its massive arm twitched and spasmed. The arm jerked suddenly, the hand planting itself on the ground in front of Malfus. Its palm was as wide as he was tall.

Like a massive tree exploding from the ground, the giant pushed itself up, its broken bones grinding. It towered over him with the awkward grace of a toddler learning to walk. His first instinct was to raise his hand, as if the swaying giant might fall on him.

A bone stuck out from its left forearm, thick as a tree trunk. Patches of skin had been flayed from its body as it fell against the stone, exposing raw muscle. But aside from that, and its missing eye, and its broken arm—it was still in pretty good shape. Other than it being dead.

Malfus looked up at the giant as it stood at its full height. He reached halfway up its shinbone. It loomed over him by at least forty feet, perhaps more.

He visualized a mental command for the giant. It knelt, reaching down to him. A massive gray hand approached Malfus as if to squash a bug. The hand pressed into the ground, palm up. Its head lolled as it stared down at him. One of its black eyes wept pus. The other—ruined by the ballista—was an empty socket.

It must have smashed its face against the cliff, because the lips and cheek on one side were missing, twisting them into a rictus grin. Malfus looked at the platform of dead flesh.

"My chariot awaits," he said. Taking a breath, he stepped onto the hand, clutching the rod and crouching to steady himself.

The hand trembled. His coat fluttered as the giant raised him through the air. Wrapping his arms around its thumb, Malfus held on for dear life as the ground shrank below. The giant rested its hand on its shoulder, waiting patiently for Malfus to dismount.

He eyed the gap between the giant's hand and its shoulder. The fall probably wouldn't kill him, but he wasn't looking forward to bargaining with Ramma again. He swallowed and stepped gingerly onto the giant's shoulder.

It took Malfus a moment to navigate the strange geography of the giant's shoulder, but there was enough room for him to stand. He looked at the giant's head. He only came up to its earhole, where dried black blood ran down its neck.

The head turned slightly toward Malfus, awaiting its next command. The hollow eye socket was expressionless, but its torn grin made it look like it wanted Malfus to lean over and whisper a joke. Each yellow tooth was as large as his skull. He swallowed, imagining how easily they could grind his bones to dust.

He looked up the cliff, picturing the giant's next task. Then he grabbed hold of exposed tendons on the side of its neck. The giant strode toward the rocky cliff and began to climb with its massive, treelike arms.

Malfus clenched his teeth and crouched, holding tighter to its neck, and hoped for the best. He'd never been a fan of heights; he now found himself on top of something very tall, while it climbed something even taller.

It took its handholds at a steady but unrelenting pace, more than halfway up now. Malfus gripped the rod tighter as he saw the lip of the cliff. Was the Inquisitor waiting for him?

Deza was Kiara's father. Malfus didn't know what that relationship had been like. She'd never once mentioned her parents—but then, who at the academy did? Except for those that hailed from the exceedingly wealthy or exceedingly powerful. He doubted anyone would want their peers to know that their father was a member of the Vesenian Inquisition.

The giant neared the top. Only a few more handholds. His heart beat faster, his stomach tying itself in knots as he gripped the rod. He could hear the distant shouts from soldiers and gnolls fighting.

The giant's arm crested the top of the cliff, pulling itself up. Malfus gritted his teeth, mentally rehearsing the words for a spell. His eyes darted around, searching for Deza, readying for a dagger to fly at his face.

He's not here.

Malfus sighed in relief. The giant pulled itself atop the cliff, and he held tight. He feared that it might totter back over the edge—but it pushed itself the rest of the way, standing tall.

He no longer had his crow, but from this vantage, he could see the fighting from across the fort. The soldiers couldn't hold out for much longer. He urged the giant forward. It marched toward the fight with stiff movements, like a small child playing at being a soldier.

He gripped the giant's neck tighter as it strode toward the battle. Borrowing power from an ancient necromantic tyrant felt great, but riding the shoulder of a giant and towering over a battlefield did wonders for his self-esteem.

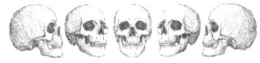

"Whoa, whoa there. Easy does it, fella."

The horses nickered and reared as Peshka approached. The closest one snorted—a grulla mustang. Its nostrils flared as he stepped closer, its large chestnut eyes darting back and forth.

"Trust me, I know. It will be all right. Just calm down for old Papa Peshka." He spoke softly, approaching with raised hands.

The six horses in the stable shifted, pulling at their tethers. The mustang began to calm. It stared at Peshka with a large brown eye.

Then the ground started shaking. Peshka stumbled forward, and the mustang panicked, rearing and kicking, almost knocking Peshka to the ground.

"What the bloody devil?"

He turned and looked over his shoulder. To the west, by the fallen tower, a colossal shape stood over the rubble.

Peshka ignored the protests of the horses. He smiled.

"Well. The bastard managed to do something useful, after all."

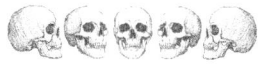

As Malfus neared the battle, a flicker of movement caught his eye. A black-cloaked shadow darted between the buildings, sticking close to the shadows along the wall. The Inquisitor. Malfus tracked Deza as his giant moved, but then the shadow disappeared between two buildings. He'd lost it.

"Dammit," he spat.

He thought of turning the giant to pursue the Inquisitor, but he was so close to the battle now. Soldiers screamed. Every second counted, and it would take time to corner that slippery bastard.

WHAT ARE YOU DOING? JUST CRUSH THAT LITTLE CHURCH MOUSE.

"No. There won't be any survivors by the time I catch him."

WHO CARES? REVENGE IS SO MUCH SWEETER.

Malfus urged his giant toward the battle.

SUIT YOURSELF. LET'S HAVE SOME FUN, THEN.

He focused. For this to work, he'd have to hurry. He couldn't be stuck on top of the giant when the two monsters began to fight.

He was almost in spellcasting range. He'd have to make every moment count. Each step vibrated as he rode his undead siege engine. He held the giant's neck as he raised the rod. Pulling from the entropic energy of the battle, Malfus began casting his spell, savoring the power that flowed through him with each syllable. His eyes darted, looking for the right spot.

There.

As he uttered the final words of the spell, he found the perfect location, near the center of the battle: numerous gnolls and a few undead, and no living soldiers.

A ray of black lightning, thick as his arm, arced through the air. A moment later, it exploded into the ground, creating a black sphere that engulfed at least a dozen gnolls. Their howls and screams died out as quickly as they began. All that remained were the shriveled husks of gnoll corpses. The zombies caught in the blast were unaffected by the void energies; they ran off, looking for their next targets.

Panic spread as the gnolls noticed the undead giant lumbering toward them.

A bloodcurdling roar pierced the din of battle. The living giant stepped through the gap in the wall, smashing several fleeing gnolls underfoot. The giant roared again at its undead kin, then said something in its unknown tongue, its deep voice heavy with grief.

I have to hurry!

Malfus urged his giant into a run, trampling through the ranks of gnolls. He held on tight as his mount reached down and scooped up a handful of fleeing gnolls. They squirmed in its closed fist. The giant raised them overhead, then slammed them against the wall, ending their protests. Then the undead giant braced itself against the wall, freezing in place.

The other giant roared again, then charged. Malfus scurried across the giant's outstretched arm like a rat down the rope of a docked ship. Everything shook as the living giant charged. But the undead giant held fast for him. *Run, run!* He jumped the few remaining feet, right as the living giant collided, thundering like an angry god. His undead giant fell backward, clutching at the wall.

Malfus landed hard amid the flattened gnoll corpses, the wall top knocking the wind from his lungs. The living giant snarled, raising its dragon skull shield against the undead giant, which fumbled against the wall.

He couldn't lose the undead giant so quickly. It was their only chance. He raised the rod, chanting words for his spell as fast as he could spit out syllables. They were still fresh in his mind from his last cast.

The giant roared as it brought its skull down.

A bolt of lightning, darker than the night sky, erupted from his fingertips. It lanced through the void between them, striking the living giant and arcing spiderwebs across its cheek. It lowered its shield, grabbing at its face. It howled as its cheek shriveled and withered away, its skin turning leathery and gray like mummified flesh. The eye on that side of its face became an opaque, calcified orb. *Look—now you're twins!*

The living giant roared in anger, then glared downed at him with its one good eye. It raised its arm to crush him, the shadow from its hand looming overhead. In a futile gesture, Malfus raised his hands over his head.

A bony fist smashed into the living giant's face like a battering ram. Bones crunched and teeth cracked as the undead giant made impact. The living giant reeled backward, howling as the undead giant lunged after it, going for the throat. They grappled with each other, smashing and rolling along the wall. The dragon skull shield was a hindrance now. The two titans fought with the fury of dragons, oblivious to the gnolls smashed underfoot.

Gnolls yelped, scrambling to get away. More gnolls pushed to escape the fort than come in, while the gnolls trapped inside were cut off by the giants fighting, splitting their forces in half. Malfus heard the gnoll chieftain's horn sound somewhere outside the wall.

Nicely done. But be careful taking risks. My pretty little neck is in your hands now.

Malfus got to his feet, then brushed himself off. *I've got it covered.*

He turned to the three flattened gnoll corpses beside him and chanted. He quickly wove their threads to the plane of death.

No risks, this time.

Bones cracked and popped back into place as the zombie gnolls rose from the ground. They grabbed their weapons and stood at attention.

Nice to have some company up here.

The giants collided with the wall again, not far from where he stood. He grabbed the balustrade to steady himself. They needed to get those giants out of the fortress before they trampled the survivors—but first, he had one more thing to do.

Malfus closed his eyes, shutting out the titanic confrontation. He focused. Empowered by Rammani-Thuul, his death-sense stretched far.

Scores of dead littered the ground below. Their bodies had been hacked apart beneath the forces still fighting. Sparks of void energy released into the air with each new death. He stood atop the wall, looking down into the fighting. Chanting, his black robes fluttering in the wind, Malfus raised his arms high, like a preacher before his congregation.

But his audience was the dead.

With Ramma's borrowed knowledge, it was a simple matter of tethering himself to so many corpses at once.

So, chanting his spell, he began to raise them all.

Chapter 25

Siege Breaker

"Justice begins at mercy's end." — Motto of the Inquisition

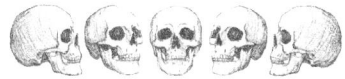

Shouts and the shriek of steel echoed in a frenzied cadence. The living and the dead threw themselves at each other as giants towered overhead, the ground shaking with their every step. Every blow from the giants, strong enough to crack stone, reverberated like a whipcrack. The titans crashed into the wall again, raining chunks of stone down on the hapless combatants. Gnolls yelped and howled as they ran for cover.

Though the gnolls outnumbered both the humans and the undead, they were starting to break. Some fought to push further into the courtyard, while others fled back toward the breach, risking being crushed by the giants as the titans grappled against the wall. Neither option was good. The grand melee regressed into bloody pockets of fighting, where only the most bloodthirsty or desperate gnolls stood their ground.

First Sergeant Goren recognized this and pressed her advantage. She bellowed with authority, managing to be heard over the din of combat, shouting for her soldiers to close ranks. A line of spearmen formed up, but the undead surged forward, disregarding her orders. She'd counted on that. Her spearmen trailed behind the zombies, stabbing over them, pushing the fleeing gnolls back further.

"That's it! Push them back, under the giants!" She led from the front, sending the gnolls fleeing with each swing of her massive sword.

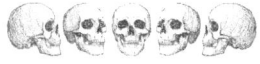

As the humans and gnolls fought for survival, another world hid far below the chaos. A cathedral lurked beneath the pitched battle—a shrine to the dead and the dying. A forest of legs stood astride a morass of corpses, each still and silent as a stone.

The silence of this lowest level was disturbed only by the cries of the mortally wounded before they, too, joined the dead. The denizens here, both the dead and the dying, were no longer as invested in the outcome of the battle as those who fought above, making bloody offerings in their name.

On the wall, far above, Malfus chanted occult words of the Shal-Umbran language, his arms raised high, his dark hair and coat flowing in an unfelt wind. The rod glowed in his hand, its gem bright enough to be seen by the soldiers below. The words of his dark sermon rolled from his lips, calling the dead back from their silence. He pried their eternal slumber away from their cold, dead hands.

Malfus closed his eyes, reaching out with his mind, connecting to the carpet of corpses beneath the fighting. With his expanded death-sense, he could feel each body. The body of a gnoll, with its arm hacked off above the wrist; a young woman, still warm, but unbreathing, blood gushing from a severed artery on her arm; another soldier, an older man, lying in the red mud, one of his legs hacked off at the knee, another hanging on by tendons.

Eighty-seven corpses. He could feel them all. Enough to turn the tide.

Like a spider, his mind skittered from corpse to corpse, weaving a strand to each one, then back to himself. He wove these new threads into the hollowed remains of his current web, replacing all that had fallen in combat. Connected to the corpses, he uttered the final words of his spell in a reverent whisper, sealing them to him. Entropic energy flowed into the corpses like a dark, coursing river.

Yes, the start of our army. Can you feel it? Can you feel the power?

Army. Malfus liked the sound of that. As long as *he* was the one in control. He could feel the zombies. They began to rise—a foul crop, sprouting like seeds from the soil.

The undead were an extension of him. They were a gauntlet, slipped over his hand, giving voice to his rage. They fought where he could not, lending their power of violence to the fury that had pent up inside him, like a silent storm.

He had a new, fractured awareness of all his undead. Like dozens of shards of a shattered mirror, Malfus perceived the senses of each undead at the same time. The zombies arose; through their eyes, he saw ghastly horror in the eyes of the living—humans and gnolls alike—reflected in each broken fragment of his mirror's surface.

The song of battle—shouts, and the clash of steel—silenced for a few moments. Then the next verse began: shrieks of pain, the tearing of flesh, and the snapping of bone. The chattering cries of gnolls were cut off, one by one, in wet yelps. The human soldiers faltered, shocked from the carnage unleashed by the zombies. Panicked gnolls turned to flee, but they didn't get far before being dragged down by the claws of the dead.

Malfus's mind flooded with gushing blood and torn throats in a roil of carnage, fear, and death. It was disorienting, hearing the sounds twice: echoing from below, and in his mind.

An ecstasy of void energy flowed with each new death at the hands of his undead. Malfus laughed—a maniacal sound that echoed below. There were enough fresh dead to cast a second spell, raising even more.

But before he could begin, footsteps scraped behind him.

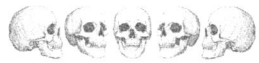

The horse whinnied, pulling at its reins. Peshka shushed it, then reached for the scout door. It opened to a dense patch of shrubbery outside the wall, hiding the exit. The door was wide enough for Peshka to coax the stubborn mustang through, but only after dismounting.

"Shhh. Come on. It'll be all right."

Peshka led the horse down a narrow path that wound through the thick bushes. Crickets were louder than the battle this far from the fighting. It was quiet enough to consider riding in the opposite direction, instead of doing something this foolish. A cricket chirped. He took that as a sign of agreement.

He paused for a few seconds, staring at the reins. Then he grunted and strode forward, ignoring his worries. What was there to think about? Other than wishing, for the hundredth time, that he'd gotten one more drink.

Peshka mounted. The horse grunted at its heavier rider, but bore him without further complaint. He clutched its reins in one hand and began riding along the wall, guiding the horse with his knees.

One final charge. His name might not make it into the history books, but he wasn't going to end his military career crushed beneath a rock, or waiting to die; at the rate things were going, he wouldn't die of old age, either. One last act of daring, then; one more chance for bravery while he could still climb atop a horse, before his belly outgrew his breastplate. He nodded resolutely, but his stomach growled in protest.

He patted his stomach, chuckling. "Doing it bloody sober, to boot."

That was more than he could say for the Siege of DeGaullis. He'd been drunk as a sailor when he made his career-beginning charge. Drinking reminded him of that night of courage. He needed the drink to be brave at all, now. But he could only remember how afraid he'd been on that night. Alcohol had been a poor panacea for his fear, but ever since, it had stuck, becoming part of him. His hands had shaken with fear when he led that charge. Now they shook all the time, unless he had a drink.

If he had a bottle in his hand, he'd still down the entire thing in one swig—but, with all his cards on the table like this, perhaps a clear head and open eyes weren't so bad a thing either.

The battle was getting louder now. He had nearly rounded the wall to the breach, the ground shaking from the fighting giants. Their heads jutted over the wall as they fought each other. Peshka drew his saber and rode.

There it was. The gap in the wall, and the gnolls fleeing from it. "Looks like that necromancer wasn't a complete idiot after all."

His mount pulled at its reigns, veering away from the approaching chaos, but Peshka held firm. "Easy does it, partner. It'll be all right," he lied, patting its flank. Then he surveyed the unfolding scene, scanning the field, searching through the fleeing gnolls for his prize.

"There it is."

The white gnoll stood in the distance on a mound of earth, shouting at the gnolls fleeing past him. Ghostface brandished a wicked sword, as large as Goren's. It blew into its war horn again, but the other gnolls ignored their chieftain, continuing to flee.

Peshka charged. The horse's hooves thundered like hailstones hitting a metal roof, spraying turf in the air. He clenched his teeth, gripping his saber at his last chance for glory.

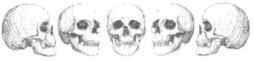

Inquisitor Deza strode toward Malfus, his sword in one hand, arcanull manacles dangling from the other.

Malfus waved a hand. "Deza! I was wondering when you'd show up again. Hope you don't mind that I brought a few friends this time."

His three zombie gnolls stood between him and the Inquisitor, a furred wall of flesh. They raised their weapons as he approached, their eyes as silent and cold as their steel. They leaned forward, eager, waiting for Malfus to command them to attack.

The Inquisitor stopped a sword's lunge away, paying the zombies no mind. He frowned. "I see you aren't dead."

"Tried it for a bit. Got bored."

The towering giants pummeled each other, smashing against the wall a dozen feet behind Malfus. He ignored them.

Deza gripped his sword. "Necromancers. Easy enough to kill—but you have the most dreadful time staying in your graves."

Malfus made a curt bow. "Glad to disappoint. Now, shall we get our little show started? We have an audience to entertain." Malfus spread his arms high over the battlements.

"Won't be needing these." The Inquisitor dropped the manacles with a dull clatter, then kicked them away. "I'll make sure your death *sticks* this time." Deza widened his stance, holding his sword in front of him. Not his Castillean rapier, but a standard-issue longsword.

Malfus shook his head. "You're too late. Don't you see? I've raised an entire army!" He motioned to the battle below. Cries from fleeing gnolls echoed up from the courtyard, while the giants fought in the foreground, a stone's throw away.

"A small matter. Separate the head, and the snake will writhe in death."

"You're insane! Every living soul here is doomed without me—without my power!"

"Not my concern. I heed only my goddess, and my revenge."

"You dumb fuck—"

His voice caught as the giants crashed into the wall, shaking it so hard it made his teeth rattle. He caught the balustrade, balancing, then glanced up to see Deza charging forward, his face grim as a gravedigger.

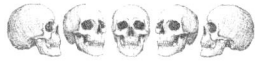

Peshka wove through gnolls like threading a needle, guiding the horse with his knees. He'd shown off for young ladies, riding like this, long before he stepped into a military uniform.

"Still got it." He smiled; it came back so easily. The wind rushed through his hair—rather, through his mustache. But the sensation filled him with the bravado of his youth.

The gnolls he rode past were too busy saving their own hides to attack him. The few that got close enough to strike glanced up at him, their eyes widening. Peshka ignored them. They were beneath him. He held his blade steady, eyes on his prize.

Only a dozen strides left. Ghostface turned to face the charging rider that erupted from the chaos. It made to raise its sword—to raise its horn, to shout, to flee—but it only flailed, stuck in indecision. This much horse flesh bearing down you tended to have that effect.

Peshka raised his saber high. His breath whistled between his clenched teeth, and the weight of his sword steadied his hand. His ass ached from his saddle for the first time in far too many years. Time slowed with each hoofbeat. He was one with his steed. Everything else was far away—the battle was him, the horse, and Ghostface. The bravery of his youth surged within him.

He became weightless.

It took him a moment to realize his steed had tripped on the uneven ground, throwing him into the air. Peshka flew over its mane, his saddle sailing with him. Moonlight and reins flailed around him, and the dark earth hurtled toward him.

A flash of moonlight. He hit the ground. The world flashed again, this time with an explosion of pain.

His ears rang and his vision blurred. For a few seconds, Peshka forgot why he was there. Why couldn't he breathe? Had he passed out from drinking again?

No. This was much worse.

He rolled over, squinting and catching his breath. His hands searched in the dark, feeling for his sword and his shattered courage. He managed to find his sword, at least.

Hefting himself to his feet, Peshka gasped in pain from his injured side. So he gave up and sprawled in the dirt. His horse rolled on the ground at his side. It whinnied, its nostrils flaring as its front leg dangled, broken. It looked at Peshka helplessly as its eyes accused him.

I tried to warn you, you fat bastard, they said. *Look what you've done.*

Ghostface strode forward, gutting the horse with one swipe of its sword. The mustang squealed like a pig. Steaming entrails burst from its belly, spraying the white gnoll with a crimson gout.

The gnoll licked its lips, fixing Peshka with its albino eyes—pink saucers, filled with hatred. It spoke in a guttural growl.

"You've taken a giant, but you will not take my victory, *klom'cha*. I want my prize. I want my fort."

Peshka looked up in surprise. Ghostface could speak the common tongue? He gripped his sword so tight his fingers hurt, coughing as breath entered his lungs like fire.

"Get up, *klom'cha*. Stand and fight," Ghostface growled, raising its sword.

Other gnolls circled them in the bushes and trees, watching the fight unfold. None dared intervene. Retreating gnolls gave them a wide berth.

Peshka wheezed as he pushed himself off the ground.

"Nice trick, doggy," he said. "Who taught you to speak? What other tricks can you do? Roll over? How about play dead? I can teach you that one."

"These will be your last words, *klom'cha*. Do not disgrace us with them." Ghostface strode forward, its bloody sword raised in a two-handed grip.

Peshka spat blood, cursing. He wished he were a couple decades younger. Even one decade would do.

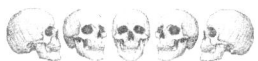

Malfus snarled at his undead gnolls. "Attack!" The zombie gnolls rushed forward, weapons raised, jaws open in silent screams of rage.

The Inquisitor spun backward like a dancer, reaching inside his cloak. He pulled out a vial of clear liquid and threw it at the closest gnoll. The glass shattered, drenching the zombie. The gnoll paused, as if annoyed. Then it collapsed.

Malfus felt its connection to him sever, sending a jolt through his mind like jagged glass.

Arcanull-laced holy water?

No time to figure it out. He began chanting, the ruby flickering with his words.

Deza reached into his cloak again, pulled out his spiked chain, and thrust to his side. Its links chimed like bells as they bounced against the stone.

The zombie gnolls charged, splitting left and right. Deza whipped out his chain. It whistled through the air, wrapping down one gnoll's shoulder and arm, binding to its torso. The zombie stumbled forward.

The other gnoll swung in, hefting its heavy axe in an overhead arc. Deza parried, the metal squealing. The Inquisitor deflected the blow, but its force threw him into the parapet.

Malfus spoke the final word of his spell. A bolt of black energy cracked from his fingertips, arcing through the air faster than an arrow.

Deza kicked off the wall. The bolt missed him, arcing into the moonlit sky.

Malfus cursed, but now the Inquisitor was off balance. The chained gnoll lashed out, clawing at Deza's shoulder, ripping through his flesh.

The Inquisitor grunted, releasing his chain. The zombie shrugged it off, throwing it over the edge of the wall. The weapon writhed in the air like an eel before falling on a hapless gnoll below. The zombie gnoll lumbered forward, its claws outstretched.

Deza spun backward, putting a few steps between himself and the zombies. Malfus didn't mind. Distance was a good thing for spellcasting.

The Inquisitor clutched his holy medallion, wiping it with his blood. He held it out. "Cower in the shame of what you are! Abominations to the cycle of life and death!" The holy symbol glowed, covering Deza in an aura of amber light.

The zombies stopped, dropping their weapons. They fell to their knees, raising their claws to shield themselves from the light.

"What are you doing?" cried Malfus. "Attack him! Must I do everything myself?"

But the zombies refused to attack further.

He was midway through another spell. But even with his new technique for redirecting void energy, he was reaching his limits. He only had stamina for a few more spells before he'd need to rest—or risk rotting his body from the inside out. *Have to make them count.* The frayed edges of his jacket fluttered as he pulled in void energy, concentrating it in the palm of his hand.

The Inquisitor thrust his sword, spearing one of the cowering zombies through the chest. Pulling back, Deza hewed in an upward arc, hooking the zombie under the arm in a fluid motion. It knocked the zombie sideways against the wall. A sharp kick sent it reeling over the edge.

Deza, amulet still glowing, turned to the final zombie and raised his sword.

Malfus spat the last words of his spell. Another black bolt arced outward. This one struck the Inquisitor. Golden sparks sprayed as the black lightning broke apart, skittering across the surface of Deza's golden aura. But the golden shield of light held strong.

Sweat beaded on Malfus's forehead. He could feel the void energy building up dangerously, overflowing from his tattoos. He gripped the rod tighter; its ruby burned bright. A wave of dark forces flowed through his black lightning.

There was a sound of a mirror shattering. Then the lightning surged, overpowering the shield and striking Deza in the chest. The golden light died, and the bolt threw the Inquisitor against the stone parapet.

Deza reached down, clutching at his chest. His amulet rusted, then crumbled to dust in his gloved hand. "Vesenia…" he whispered.

"Your goddess can't protect you." A grin spread across Malfus's face.

Deza started to say something, then wheezed instead. He tried to get up.

His remaining gnoll grabbed Deza from behind, wrapping its claws around him.

Let's see him dodge this.

Malfus pulled on the thickest cord in his web of undead, tearing his giant away from its fight. The undead giant pushed its opponent away, then backed a few steps toward Malfus. The wall quaked as it drew closer. The Inquisitor struggled in the gnoll's grasp, freeing a hand, but the zombie held tight. The undead giant raised a massive fist, then brought it crashing down on the gnoll holding the zealot.

The wall shook. Malfus stumbled, struggling to keep his balance. A cloud of dust bloomed, and a spiderweb of cracks radiated from where the giant's fist had struck the wall.

The living giant rushed forward, taking advantage. It crashed into its undead opponent, slamming the undead giant against the wall. The wall rattled, dropping Malfus to his knees and splintering the stonework. The undead giant punched back, pushing itself off the wall.

Malfus got up, looking around. A figure limped forward from the dust, sword in hand.

Fuck. Why won't he die?

He was running out of space—every wizard's worst fear. The gap in the wall was right behind him, with a forty-foot drop. Deza was less than a dozen paces away.

Malfus reached back with his mind, grasping the pool of void energy. He whipped his hand forward, fingers extended. Four thin tendrils whipped out like black snakes.

Deza leaped to the side, dodging two, but the others hit him in the arm. The black lines burned through the Inquisitor's sleeves, leaving bloody holes in his arm.

He howled in pain, dropping his sword. His bloodied arm hung limp at his side. Clenching his teeth, Deza grabbed the sword with his other arm, moving forward. Only paces away now.

Malfus began casting another spell, but retched. Black bile spewed from his mouth. The void energy roiled inside him, overpowering his wards and running through his body.

Dammit...

He stumbled backward. The sheer drop was only a few paces away. He couldn't cast anything. His wards were already overflowing.

Wait!

He'd nearly forgotten.

Perhaps there was another way—a simpler spell. He fumbled in his belt pouch.

Ghostface rushed in, fast as lightning in a summer storm.

It swung its massive sword in a horizontal arc. Peshka raised his saber to parry, but his blade was comically small compared to the gnoll's. But he surprised everyone there—himself included—as he hopped back like a jackrabbit, avoiding the same treatment his horse got.

Before he could celebrate, the sword whipped back in the other direction. The dull edge of the blade caught Peshka in his side, tossing him like a bale of hay. His world spun, but not before the tip caught his breastplate, gouging the polished metal.

It spun Peshka like a top. He landed hard, shooting pain through his aching body.

Ghostface lifted its head back, letting out a peal of laughter.

"You are their leader, *klom'cha*? Pathetic." The gnoll growled. "Get up so we can end this."

"Just finish me, monster." Peshka spat a mouthful of blood.

"Monster?" Ghostface laughed. "A funny word, *klom'cha*. You call us monsters, when your kind pushed us from livable lands. Pushed us into the *Rak'cha*—the Scar—after your kind made it. And now you use dead to fight your battles. Too blind to learn from your ancestors."

Peshka ignored the gnoll. His fingers closed around a handful of dirt as he grunted, getting to his feet. He turned, but Ghostface was already on him, giving no quarter as it rushed in, swinging. The sword scythed in arcs, as if harvesting grain. Peshka dodged backward, keeping out of reach, but he was getting slower. The gnoll showed no signs of tiring, while Peshka sweated like a pig.

The gnoll's arcing swings slowed as they reversed direction. It wasn't much of an opening, but it was there. That could be his only chance.

Peshka jumped forward after Ghostface's next swing. He threw the handful of dirt in its face, making the gnoll gag and cough. Then he kicked Ghostface as hard as he could in the balls. The tall monster buckled, shouting and slashing its sword in blind anger. The blade hit something so hard it rattled, all the way up its arm, nearly making Ghostface drop its sword.

Ghostface yelped, reeling back. Blood stained its white fur, running down his face, and one ear flopped, hanging on by a thin strand of flesh. It let out a low growl, then ripped its dangling ear the rest of the way off and threw it on the ground.

Barking, Ghostface swung its sword, giving Peshka no chance to dodge. He parried across his body, but his stance had no weight to it. The blade bit hard into Peshka's side, below his breastplate. He felt something crunch. Then he fell to the ground like a broken wine bottle.

Peshka lay on the ground, staring up at the stars. His hip was a throbbing mess. It hurt so bad—his leg must have been cleaved off. Peshka reached below his breastplate to feel his hip. There was blood, but also something metal and sharp. Pulling it to his eyes, he found his metal flask, cloven almost all the way through. It had saved his leg. But that seemed insignificant, now that Ghostface stood over him, leering down with a satisfied grin. A line of blood ran down the gnoll's face from its mangled ear.

Peshka turned his face to the side, expecting the killing blow.

But something else rushed from the wall behind the retreating gnolls.

Goren appeared, her massive sword raised high. A line of zombies and soldiers followed her.

Ghostface saw them, too. A dark tide of death surging toward them.

The gnoll returned its attention to Peshka, only to find a sword pointing at its nethers. Peshka thrust the weapon upward, stabbing Ghostface in the groin, then continued a jagged cut through the beast's gut. He rolled his girth into the gnoll's leg, knocking Ghostface over in a howl of pain.

Peshka got up, hobbling to his feet while clutching his injured hip. Then he turned to the gnoll as it writhed on the ground, whimpering as it wrapped its arms around his open stomach. Peshka would've kicked the gnoll, if he could do so without falling over. Instead, he opted to spit on the brute. Not as painful, perhaps—but just as heartfelt.

"That's for killing my horse!" he yelled. Then he took a few hobbling steps back.

Ghostface screamed as the zombies closed in, finishing the job.

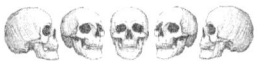

Deza's sword tip shrieked against the stone, leaving a trail of sparks where Malfus's face had been a second before.

Malfus stumbled back. His boots caught on a loose brick, and he fell, striking his head against the stone.

The Inquisitor thrust forward, stabbing Malfus in the shoulder, all the way through. Malfus screamed as his arm seared with fire. Warm, wet blood ran down its length. He'd only been stabbed twice in his life—both on the same night. His eyes watered from the pain, but he managed to cling to his prize, pulling it from his pouch.

Deza strode forward, his sword raised. His grim face showed no sign of emotion.

Malfus whipped out the straw effigy he'd made, dabbed with the Inquisitor's blood. Hopefully the blood was fresh enough to work. The weak incantation would only give Malfus a handful of seconds, at best. He raised the effigy in front of him, then muttered arcane words.

Deza froze, his sword raised as if he were posing for a sculptor. Malfus moved the effigy's arm. Deza strained, veins in his neck bulging. Then his arm twisted around, throwing his sword over the wall.

Malfus stood up, keeping a wary eye on the Inquisitor as he held the effigy in front of him. His shoulder throbbed with pain, his heart pounding in his throat.

Deza gasped. His entire body convulsed as he stood in the awkward stance, his one arm still twisted to the side. Malfus bent the straw doll again, forcing the Inquisitor to his knees.

Malfus approached, glowering at Deza. His anger boiled. He'd been imprisoned, dragged away from what little life he'd managed to scrape together, then stuck in a damn siege—all for this bastard's religion. He wanted to end Deza, to compress his weeks of torture into a single agonizing moment.

But when he looked at Deza's face, all he could see was Kiara's. It reminded Malfus of long ago, before he'd fled, before he'd become a fugitive.

Kiara's face haunted him every night. Memories of her tormented him, like red-hot pokers, searing into his heart. Her eyes stared back at him, her life fragile as a baby bird in his hands. Her head lying in his lap, her neck bent at a strange angle, soft breaths coming from her bloody lips until they stopped.

It was an accident. Both of them were at fault for arguing by the stairs. They should have been somewhere else—anywhere else. He'd never meant to push her, only to grab her, to stop her from telling anyone.

But after the accident, he'd had no choice but to flee. He only had time to grab a grimoire on necromancy and her finger, hoping he could find some way to bring her back. To fix his mistake.

That was the bare truth. He had loved her, and he had killed her. All to protect his little secret. And no matter how many layers of excuses and lies he wrapped it in, the truth—and that face—waited for him whenever he closed his eyes.

He'd carried her finger and the weight of his mistakes ever since he'd fled the academy, Akkadia, and his home. He'd never bothered to look back. That was how he'd ended up in this mess.

Enough indecision!

A ruby ray shot from the rod. The Inquisitor screamed. Still frozen, unable to move.

"What are you doing?" said Malfus.

The energy traveled up the Inquisitor's arm, blistering the flesh and turning it gray. Deza let out an inhuman shriek.

I will make him a revenant. Our undead champion. We will kill him, finish killing the gnolls, then kill every living thing here, to build an even larger army.

"What? No!"

Yes. Don't worry. I won't kill you, my sweet.

The Inquisitor screamed again. The ray crawled further up his arm.

Yes, said Ramma. *Drain his soul. Extinguish the flame. Raise him as our own, and then kill everything. This will be the seat of my—of* our*—new kingdom.*

Malfus wrested the rod away, but ruby energy jolted through him, seizing his heart and wracking him with pain. He smelled his hair burning. His arm was frozen in place. Ramma's voice shrieked so loudly in his head, it was tearing him apart from the inside.

Death to all that lives! Destruction to all that takes breath! Annihilation of all that has life!

Her voice cackled, drowning out the Inquisitor's screams. Malfus reached into his pouch with his other hand. His fingers wrapped around a glass vial. He smashed it into the rod, splashing its clear liquid all over the rod and himself.

Ramma's laughter turned to a shriek as the holy water boiled off the ruby. The arcanull filaments within it glinted in the moonlight. Malfus flung the rod to the ground. His breathing returned to normal. The feeling in his arm returned as well, though his hand still shook.

He looked over at Deza.

The Inquisitor lay on the ground, motionless, but still smoking. Perhaps Malfus had intervened too late. He didn't feel too bad about that.

There was a thunderous crack. A flash of movement caught his attention. The living giant raised its skull shield over the undead giant, as it stumbled backward, off balance and defenseless; it raised its broken arm, too slowly to block the coming blow.

Malfus raised his arm, wincing as the living giant smashed with its shield. It broke the undead giant's hand clean off, exposing the bones of the undead giant's forearm. The living giant followed through, crashing into the undead giant's shoulder, forcing it against the wall beside Malfus.

Malfus flew backward as the wall shook. Fissures splintered all around him. He looked up helplessly as the living giant towered over its zombie counterpart, raising its dragon skull shield for the killing blow.

No!

He had to cast a spell to stop the living giant from killing his own titan—even if it was too much for his wards to handle. He had to do something.

He tried to harness the void energy, but it fizzled, and pain flooded his body. Of course. Arcanull from the holy water glittered in the moonlight, running down his soaked sleeves and jacket. He couldn't do anything with spells. He looked back at his giant.

It raised its arm, shielding itself. Moonlight reflected from its shafts of exposed bone.

There!

He thrust his fingers forward, sending a mental command to the giant.

The undead giant lunged its handless arm forward like a spear. The bones, wide as tree trunks, pierced upward, plunging under the living giant's jaw and out the back of its head. Blood spurted with a horrible squelching noise. The living giant hung there, transfixed, and dropped its dragon skull shield.

"What have you done to me?" said Deza.

Malfus turned around. The Inquisitor shambled toward him, one arm outstretched. Gray skin drooped on one half of his face. He howled like a madman—scared, confused, and enraged.

Malfus tried to cast a spell, but it fizzled again.

Dammit!

The Inquisitor was getting closer. "What have you done? I can't feel her light anymore! Why is everything so dark?" His voice sounded distorted. One arm hung limp at his side. The other reached toward Malfus, sword outstretched.

Malfus backpedaled as he stalled for time.

There was a groaning noise. A darkening shadow appeared overhead. Malfus looked up to see the dying giant tottering like a felled tree, leaning in their direction. He raised his hands over his head as the giant hung there, suspended for a sickeningly long second, before crashing against the wall.

An explosion of bricks threw him back. The wall trembled, buckling from the giant's weight. There was a cracking sound, like a tree snapping in two. The wall leaned precariously.

Malfus looked back and saw Deza staring back, wide-eyed, as the wall began to sway.

The Inquisitor lunged at him.

Malfus opened his mouth to scream, but it filled with dust. There was a thundering crash as the wall finally collapsed around them.

He felt weightless—like when he'd fallen from the cliff. This time, he knew the rod wouldn't save him.

The world turned black.

Something closed around him. He was no longer falling—but rising.

Massive fingers cradled him as stone bricks crumbled. The undead giant lifted him, returning him to its shoulder.

It took several seconds for Malfus to control his panicked breathing. His empty hands frantically searched for the rod. Then he remembered their exchange.

He looked at the wall. The other giant sprawled in the wreckage like a massive drunkard after a night too deep in the bottle. Half the wall had crumbled around it, creating a makeshift bed of bricks.

Malfus urged his giant closer to the wall as his eyes searched. The Inquisitor was nowhere to be seen. Malfus looked at the ruins of the wall from his perch. It was a long drop to the ground, but he could make out shadows running everywhere along the base of the wall.

He hissed. More invaders?

But then he heard an unexpected noise.

They were *cheering*.

He looked down again. The soldiers and zombies inside the fort hacked apart the few remaining gnolls. Outside the wall, soldiers assembled, with Goren standing at their front, brandishing her sword high in the air.

The gnoll forces were in full retreat.

Exhausted, Malfus collapsed against his giant's shoulder. The soldiers continued to celebrate, cheering for him. *At least, they should be.*

In the distance, the dawning sun shimmered, turning the sky blood red.

MALFUS - PESHKA'S CHARGE　　　ART BY DEJAN DELIC

MALFUS - The Final Fight — Art by Dejan Delic

MALFUS - THE FINAL FIGHT   ART BY DEJAN DELIC

Chapter 26

The Next Day

"The deepest scars, no one sees. Even divine healing can do nothing for those. Prayer or meditation may offer a cure, but we must conduct more trials first. By Vesenia's grace, I won't stop until I've found a way to help these poor soldiers." — Journal entry of Sister Bequeth Saratosha, Vesenian Priestess of the Church of Eternal Sun, Gardenia

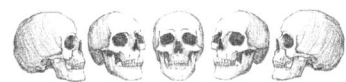

Clouds stretched in the azure sky, like cats basking in sunlight. Curtains of mist retreated into the trees, clinging to them for protection from the rising sun.

A plume of smoke scarred the sky, bringing with it a sweet, acrid smell. Outside the wall, close to where Peshka had made his stand, the offending smoke rose from a growing pyre.

Chirruping crickets had given way to the chirps of songbirds, not needing a reason to celebrate the dawn of another day. But their songs were drowned out by crows, cackling like goblins as they picked over the host of corpses. Finally, the scavengers got free meals that didn't get up and run away.

Pikes, spears, and other long weapons lined the wall, each adorned with a gnoll head—a cathartic redecoration. An albino gnoll head hung higher than the others, its mouth open, tongue lolling out, flies crawling on its face.

By the end of the battle, two dozen gnolls had surrendered, thinking that throwing down their weapons gave them a better chance for survival. Perhaps they were too wounded to retreat with their kin. But after a month of constant raids, and seeing so many comrades fall in battle, the fort was in too foul a mood for taking prisoners.

The surrendering gnolls hung from ropes along the wall at regular intervals, swaying in the breeze. Few of the survivors knew how to tie a proper noose, so they'd tied a variety of basic knots and strung the gnolls up by their necks. They found that death wasn't too picky about which knots they chose. Only one rope had come undone as they threw the gnolls from the wall, but it plummeted to its death all the same, so the soldiers chalked it up as a success.

More crows perched on the dangling cadavers, cawing with laughter at their misfortune, right before pecking out their eyes and other juicy bits.

Below them, a line of zombies shambled through the gap in the wall, dragging the decapitated gnoll corpses to the pyre, before heading back to grab more. They worked like ants, moving in single file.

Inside the fort, the survivors emerged forever changed. Even those who'd managed to come out untouched by blade or arrow had new, unseen scars. The marks were perfectly visible to those who knew what to look for.

Some of the soldiers stared at the walls and sky, and others at their feet; some had a far-off look, blank as zombies. Pale and bloodied as they were, it was often difficult to tell the living from the undead. Some cried in relief together, while others sobbed by themselves. A select few—free from wounds—laughed and joked, slapping each other on the back with the mirth that came only from walking into death's jaws and escaping alive. Some soldiers even sang; some for the dead, others of victory as they lopped heads off gnolls and stuck them on pikes. But most kept silent and busy with their tasks, as if it were any other day.

There was a faint but constant moaning from the wounded, but their suffering was confined to the infirmary. This was more for the good of the others. Most wounds were too severe to survive infection, or to recover without magical healing, which cost far too much to be wasted on common soldiers. Unfortunately, most of the soldiers with non-magical medical knowledge either lay with the wounded, or in their graves.

Even if the medics hadn't survived, the pervasive smell of bacon proved the cook had, at least. Sizzling pig flesh wafted through the air, creating an interesting duality as it mingled with the stench of corpses on the pyre.

In the courtyard, other zombies sorted human bodies from dead gnolls. They laid the soldiers in rows for identification and burial, while they threw the gnolls in a heap for decapitation.

The remaining zombies worked at the collapsed wall, where Malfus and Deza had fought. They dug through the rubble, setting bricks in neat piles as they searched.

Malfus held up a hand, covering his eyes from the glaring sun. Its brightness was starting to give him a throbbing migraine; he was so tired, he felt sick. He'd lost track of the sleep he hadn't gotten. He wished he could draw blood from a corpse to revitalize, but that was no longer an option.

He was covered in scrapes, bruises, and cuts, and had a busted bottom lip—but the most serious injury was the deep cut that thrust straight through the meat of his shoulder. He was reminded of it, painfully, every time he moved his arm, so he'd tied a makeshift sling around it. He hadn't had time to get stitches; he managed to clean his shoulder with sour wine that had been passed around in celebration. It would need proper attention before rot took his arm.

His body felt different, after the bargain he'd made with death. It was an inexplicable strangeness—something he couldn't quite put his finger on—but somehow, he felt one step closer to the grave.

Ramma had said that some of his lifespan would be drained away. Malfus didn't necessarily feel older, but something *had* been taken from him—like part of him had been consumed. He wondered if any of his memories had been erased. He laughed. Was there any way of knowing? If his memories were gone, how could he know which ones had vanished?

He shook the disturbing thought from his mind, turning his attention back to his task.

Zombies dug through the rubble. He inspected their work over their shoulder, like the foreman of a mine, though he was mentally aware of each menial task his undead performed.

He still wanted to be there when they found the body.

He closed his eyes, checking his death-sense impatiently. The closest bodies he could sense were the gnolls swaying from ropes along the wall. More distantly, he could sense the rows of soldier corpses, and the pile of decapitated gnolls—but nothing else. Nothing in the rubble or along the wall, where he'd fought with Deza.

There must be a body. If it's there, I should be able to sense it.

It was hard to feel any relief from winning that battle or surviving the night, knowing the bastard could still be out there. A Vesenian Inquisitor was a dreadful enough prospect; Deza seeking revenge for the death of his daughter was another matter entirely. And the nearby magical artifact, housing an ancient necromancer who wasn't particularly happy with him, did little to reassure him.

The ground rumbled beneath his feet, taking his mind off the Inquisitor.

Malfus looked up as the undead giant lumbered back toward him. The others soldiers froze, staring up at the giant and giving it a wide berth whenever it approached. It was returning from the cliffs after disposing of the second half of the other giant's corpse.

It had been a pity. If they'd been closer to Akkadia, some of the giant's organs would have fetched a princely sum from the alchemists and wizards, but that was a long way from here.

Its corpse took too much energy to raise. As such, it was simply another obstacle to be dealt with. It was too large for even his undead giant to move, so it had to be disposed of in parts. After cutting it in half, the undead giant dragged sections of it away, lugging them over the cliff. That put it far enough away that the smell of its rot would be unpleasant, instead of unbearable.

Now that the giant's carcass was removed, the vicinity could be properly searched, brick by brick.

Though he'd been unable to detect any corpses in the rubble, he could still sense the strong presence of magic underneath the stone. He held a hand out, feeling pinpricks in his palm. He stood over the location where it was strongest.

There.

He motioned with his good arm to the rubble, sending a mental command to his zombies. They dug through the pile. Something metallic clinked under the stone. One of the zombies moved a rock, then pulled out a piece of metal that glinted in the sun.

Not the rod, but the Inquisitor's arcanull chain.

Malfus grimaced. "Be careful with those."

But it was too late. A few seconds after raising the chain aloft, the zombie collapsed to the ground in a limp pile.

Malfus sighed, then grabbed a shovel. He picked up the arcanull chain and set it aside, away from the other zombies.

Two zombies bent over, collected their unanimated companion, and hauled it to the rows of other dead soldiers awaiting burial.

Malfus held his hand back out, concentrating on the needles in his palm again. The presence here was stronger, with the arcanull no longer dampening it. The zombies started digging again.

"Carefully now. If any of you damage it, I'll have the giant rip you in half."

Two zombies picked up a large stone, moving it out of the way. A faint ruby light spilled out from the shadows. The zombies stepped away, revealing the rod, plain as day.

The slender rod had been serendipitously insulated in a pocket of stone, protecting it from the fall. Its spherical star ruby was still unscratched. The mottled black and silver metal of the rod had some brick dust on it, but didn't appear damaged in the least.

Malfus swallowed. There was a growing pit in his stomach, and a voice in the back of his head told him to have the giant pick up the rod and hurl it from the cliff. He ignored his fears and approached the rod. Without it—without Rammani-Thuul, and her power—there'd be no chance to bring Kiara back. Ever.

He grabbed it.

The metal felt as cold as a corpse's flesh. He felt slight relief at not being instantly annihilated, but then he felt something worse—her presence slithered back into his mind, like water trickling through cracks in a rock.

You... Her voice was distant and fragile, but still as sharp as cracked glass. *That was a dirty trick. Holy water from a necromancer? You are a disgrace to necromancers everywhere.*

"I've been called worse."

I thought we had a deal. You betrayed me...

"That was before you threatened to restart your empire here. Before you threatened to kill literally everything. It doesn't take a genius to know I'd be completely expendable after you got your body. You would pop me like a pimple. I'd either become a servant, or another skull for your throne."

Ahhh, lover boy. That isn't true. You give me so little credit. I like you. You're fun to watch. Unique. I would keep you around. Eternity is a long time—I'll need some entertainment.

"I don't think so. After your outburst, I'm rethinking the terms of our deal."

Be careful, fleshling. Your cuteness is a fickle thing. If you betray me again, your soul will spend eternity in a cycle of dismemberment and reanimation.

Malfus yawned. He wasn't sharp enough to trade barbs with an ancient evil. No, this was a puzzle to solve later. After he'd had some rest. He set the rod down.

Don't worry. I know you'll come around eventually. I am nothing if not patient. I'll be here waiting. Watching.

Malfus winced as he picked up the arcanull chain, feeling its leeching cold as it sapped at his energy.

What are you—ugh. So cold. It's so very...

Her voice trailed off as he wound the chain around the rod. The ruby light inside dimmed, but a tiny ember remained, flickering furiously. He ripped off a strip from his jacket and tied it to the chain, securing it around the rod.

He turned his attention back to the pile of stone and focused his corpse-sense. But before he could sense any bodies, he noticed something underneath a brick.

"There. What's that?"

He watched anxiously as they dug. The zombies pulled away the surrounding bricks and rubble, then Malfus pushed them aside.

It was a flattened circle of black cloth. But no body. Not even a trace of blood on the surrounding stone.

"Dammit," Malfus hissed.

He picked up the flattened hat, straightening it. It flopped sideways, but retained much of its original shape.

"Better tell Peshka the good news..."

Malfus left his zombies to continue sorting through bricks for rebuilding—and in case there was a body yet to be found. He carefully wrapped the chain and rod inside the black hat and walked to the command hall.

He passed the row of graves he'd seen when he'd first been escorted through the camp in chains. Only two nights ago. One of the graves had been freshly dug. Malfus looked down and saw a face he recognized—Morten.

The young soldier lied in an open grave on top of another dead soldier. Thin lines of blood ran down his face from his slit throat. Thrown in here like nothing. No dignity. But dignity wasn't worth much to the living, and even less to the dead.

From the surgical precision of the cut, it hadn't been a gnoll's work. No, Malfus knew whose handiwork it had been. He sighed, looking into Morten's glassy eyes, feeling pity. He hadn't gotten to know him very well, but he was the only real friend he'd made out here.

More than that. Morten was the closest thing to a friend he'd ever had.

He knelt down next to the corpse. Morten's pale white skin resembled an alabaster statue, staring up at the sky, his face frozen in anger, confusion, and maybe a hint of disappointment. So very young—too young to throw his short life away for the Tithe. Forgotten by some nobleman living in comfort. He wondered if Morten's parents would get notified of his death.

Malfus stood over the body a while longer, weighed with guilt. He'd tried to save Morten by having him look for bodies, instead of returning to the front lines. But now, he couldn't help but feel the boy's death was his fault. Another face to add to Kiara's, keeping him awake at night.

"Sorry, Morten." Malfus brushed his fingers over the soldier's face, closing its eyelids. "And thank you. For being a friend."

He got up to head back toward the command hall. But then he turned back, giving Morten one last look.

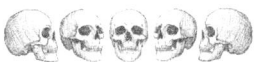

Malfus pushed Peshka's door open with his good arm. A large hole in the center of the roof let sunlight in. A massive chunk of bricks had fallen in the middle of the room, crushing the wooden table, its map, and the troop markers into splinters.

Colonel Peshka stood beneath the hole in his roof, pointing up at it with a wooden cane. First Sergeant Goren stood behind him, arms crossed, silent as an iron golem.

Peshka turned. "Ah, Malfry. Come in."

"It's *Malfus*," he said.

Peshka made no sign that he'd heard him. He walked over to Malfus, wincing as he leaned on his cane, heavily favoring one leg.

"Cane in one hand. I'm surprised there's no drink in the other." Malfus motioned at the Colonel's empty hand. "I figured our unlikely survival would be cause for celebration."

"I'm taking a break from the bottle, I think. Hard to hold a drink and a cane at the same time, anyway." Peshka glanced at his injured hip. "And that pyrrhic victory was hardly cause for celebration. Have you seen how many soldiers are left? I've got more soldiers to bury than can stand guard."

"True. The fact that any of us survived is nothing short of a miracle." Malfus paused. "Though, not the kind Vesenia would condone."

"Can't argue with you there. Speaking of—any sign of our mutual friend?"

Malfus looked away. "Unfortunately, no."

"I see." Peshka pulled at his mustache. "Tell me again what happened up there. Did he die, or not?"

"I can't be certain. He fell. The bricks crumbled around us, but without a body…"

"And you're sure it isn't buried under the wall, or squashed beneath your giant's foot somewhere?"

"No. If there were a body, I would've been able to detect it. I've told you."

"So, he could still be out there." Peshka leaned conspiratorially closer. "What if he says something?"

Malfus considered for a moment. "If he's alive, I think he'll be too busy chasing me to waste time bringing the Inquisition down on your head. But he is nothing if not thorough. If the Inquisition shows up at your door, you'll know why."

Peshka's hand gripped his stomach. Malfus thought he heard it growl.

Goren's voice rumbled from across the room. Malfus had forgotten she was there.

"He'll be too busy chasing you—unless, of course, we arrest you, and turn you over to the Inquisition ourselves."

Malfus looked at Goren, then strode over to her. "You can certainly try, but it won't go well for you. And even if you manage it, the penalty for aiding a necromancer is pretty stiff, if I recall." He glared up at Goren as the tall woman looked imposingly down at him. "And I don't even know what the charges are for knocking out an Inquisitor."

Goren snorted like an angry bull, then turned to Peshka. "I'll check on the soldiers. Make sure they're keeping their heads on a swivel. We're still very exposed. The gnolls could come back at any moment."

Peshka nodded. "And give everyone another share of bacon. Make sure there's enough food to go around."

Goren nodded, and then clattered out the door like an angry drawer of silverware, slamming it behind her.

Peshka chuckled. "Don't mind her. That's how she says thank you."

"With threats?"

"To be honest, using you as a bargaining chip to save my own hide has crossed my mind. But what can I do? As I said, I've got more soldiers to bury than to fight with—and I've seen what your undead can do." He threw his free hand in the air. "What do I care, anyway? You and the Inquisitor have business. As long as I'm left out of it, I could care less what it's about."

"Good." Malfus looked Peshka in the eye. "Now that that's out of the way, we can talk about the price of my services."

Peshka's eyes snapped wide. If he'd had a drink, he probably would've spat it out.

Malfus continued, unabated. "Don't worry—it isn't much. I'll just need two horses and a couple weeks of supplies for the road. And a promise. If the Inquisition does come, you don't mention me. That last part is for our mutual benefit."

Peshka grunted, but nodded in agreement. "Fine. But one of them is the Inquisitor's horse. The beast tried to bite me last night." He looked back at Malfus. "Why do you need two, anyway?"

Malfus looked away. "I'll need one for supplies."

Peshka raised an eyebrow, but didn't inquire further. "Where will you go?"

"Away. Away from here, from the Inquisition's reach. I've got more research to do. I won't tell you specifics, so the Inquisition can't torture them out of you." Malfus had meant that as a joke, but his delivery must have been lacking; Peshka looked like someone on the gallows.

"Anyway. I'll be leaving soon—within the next few hours."

"And what about this mess of zombies on my doorstep?"

"I've released all the human zombies, so they can be buried. The zombie gnolls will stay and guard the camp after I leave. That spell will expire in two days. Once the spell wears off, they'll collapse to the ground—dead. You'll only need to pile them up and burn them."

"Why not do it now?"

"They'll protect you against the gnolls, in case they show up between now and then. Or if the Inquisitor decides to show up again, looking for me. They'll attack him on sight." *Or they'll attack you, if you decide to follow after me.*

"All right. Can't argue with that," Peshka grumbled.

"And if I were you, Colonel, I would get word to that damn duke. Drag him here in chains if you have to. Have him fix this fort, or tie him to the gate yourself."

Peshka grunted in agreement.

"One more thing. It would be wise to ensure none of your soldiers mention anything about the undead or the Inquisition. You should probably agree on a story about what happened, or it's rope necklaces all around."

Malfus turned to leave.

"Wait. Malfus."

He turned around, and Peshka winced as he hobbled over.

"I know it isn't much—but thank you, for what it's worth. Never thought I'd be saying this, but the soldiers owe their lives to a necromancer. Oddly enough." The Colonel leaned forward and pinned a medal to Malfus's jacket. "I know we aren't standing on ceremony, but you deserve this. It was my medal for victory at the Siege of DeGaullis. It's only fitting you should get it."

"Thanks." Malfus looked down at it. The medal was blue and gold, but stained with a bit of mud, blood, or both. He wasn't sure how to take the gesture, because he'd never gotten thanks for being a necromancer before.

Malfus turned to leave again, then paused. "Remember. I was never here."

Then he shut the door behind him.

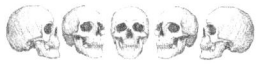

Malfus continued down the road, riding his new steed. He licked his salty fingertips, already wishing he'd taken more bacon with him.

Amber rays from the sun streamed low in the late afternoon sky. Malfus shook out the Inquisitor's hat and put it back on his head. A bit worse for wear, after being crushed by a ton of bricks; it didn't stand up straight anymore, or look nearly as imposing, sitting at such a crooked angle—but it kept the sun out of his eyes, at least.

He gripped the reins nervously as his chestnut horse reached an incline. It snorted and shook its head as Malfus fumbled with the leather. He'd never been properly trained for riding, and was never a fan of horses in the first place. But he'd was even less a fan of walking across the countryside and blistering his feet, so he tried to relax and stomach his fears.

"Steady does it. Not too fast. Remember, I can ride an undead horse as easily as a living one."

The horse didn't pay his threats any mind as it plodded up the path.

Malfus looked over his shoulder. "You doing all right back there?"

Morten rode atop the Inquisitor's black steed, just now starting up the incline. Perhaps saying that the zombie *rode* the horse was a bit of a stretch, since his legs and torso were tied to the saddle, keeping him from falling off. A horse was a necessity for a zombie traveling companion; they were far too slow stumbling around on foot, with Malfus riding. The other horse also held his saddlebags, with the limited supplies he'd been able to pry from Peshka's fingers.

Sneaking Morten out of the camp had been simple. With so much to do, so many dead, and so many zombies already working, no one noticed one more zombie sneaking off into the woods or waiting for him by the road.

The Inquisitor's horse seemed to glare at Malfus every time he looked back. The black charger looked none-too-pleased about carrying a zombie on its back, or being demoted to a packhorse. Not long ago, he'd been tied to the back of its saddle, but now it was tied to his.

Morten's head bobbed as he rode. The zombie seemed oblivious about his ride on horseback; then again, Malfus wondered how many other zombies had been in so privileged a position, or treated so graciously by their master.

Malfus faced forward. A faint smile crossed his face as he remembered his last few moments at the fort.

Most of the soldiers had gathered by the gap in the wall to see him off. Some shook his good hand in rough grips as they thanked him for saving their lives. Others just fixed him with a serious look and said nothing at all. And there had been plenty—that big tin can Goren included—that stood in the distance, glaring at him with a healthy amount of distrust and spite.

As Malfus looked back at his life, he found that it had been devoid of much appreciation, much less for his necromancy. He was hard-pressed to remember the last time someone had thanked him or shaken his hand—for anything.

He wiped bacon grease from his fingers on his jacket, until his hands were as clean as he could get them. Then he reached into his belt pouch and pulled out a small object, wrapped in black silk.

He unwrapped the tiny cloth parcel in the palm of his hand, revealing Kiara's severed finger. He inspected it closely, looking for any signs of rot or decay, but was relieved to find none on her pale white flesh. It looked almost alive, except that it felt as cold as a stone.

Malfus uttered the arcane words needed for the spell of preservation. It was still the only thing he could do for her. He sighed as he squeezed some fleeting warmth into the cold finger.

He'd found his freedom. But he was no closer to bringing her back. At least, not yet.

Rammani-Thuul held the key—and, like her, he was patient. He'd find a way to solve this puzzle and obtain her knowledge, with or without her compliance. If there was a way to bring Kiara back, he'd do it, whatever it took.

Malfus glanced at his saddlebags, wondering if the lich could hear his thoughts. From one of the loose flaps, he could see a trickle of hungry red light, glowing in the shadows of the bag.

He turned back to Kiara's finger and whispered to it. "Don't worry. I'll find a way. I just need more time."

Even though he had died—or come as close to it as possible, without fully crossing over—he was still plagued with unanswered questions. How had he been able to communicate with Ramma inside her phylactery? And with his body lying elsewhere. He hoped that meant there was still some chance that Kiara's soul was intact, somewhere on the other side.

Even if he found a way to bring her back and atone for his sins, nothing would bring his old life back, or give him another chance at the academy. He would be branded as a necromancer for the rest of his life. But he could at least give Kiara *her* choices back, even if he could never undo his own.

Life was such a fragile thing. A delicate blessing? Or a tenuous curse? He wasn't sure. Either way, everything dangled precariously over a yawning abyss. A momentary balance of body, mind, and soul. The living depended on the perfect balance of all three. A single slip—a tiny accident—had cost Kiara her life, severing all three threads. Remove a single piece of the puzzle and life is no more.

He looked over at Morten and wondered. *Do zombies suffer without a mind and just a fragment of their soul? Do wraiths or ghosts long for their bodies in their cursed existence?*

No. Only the living are cursed to know how fragile this temporal balance is—to know we must do anything to preserve it, at all costs, for fear of what awaits us afterward.

Malfus held Kiara's finger in his palm. She was the only one here who had truly crossed over to the other side and stayed there. Morten had taken a brief journey into death, of course. But he had precious little to say about the matter.

He wondered if Kiara's soul longed for its old life, or if it had already ripped to shreds in the plane of death. Perhaps she had been reborn into a higher plane, living an altogether better afterlife.

Malfus certainly didn't know the answer. He wondered how much even the greatest of necromancers, like Rammani-Thuul, actually knew about death. She seemed to be doing everything in her power to escape its clutches. Even the proverbial experts thought death should be avoided at all costs. Ramma was far from the only lich to make unspeakable sacrifices, all to extend their life to an unnatural length, escaping the jaws of death a little longer.

But no one is free. The grave is unescapable.

Our time, as living beings, is so brief, and filled with necessary terror—because at some deep level, even animals understand our delicate balance, and how easily it can be destroyed.

But our mortal duty is to embrace our fears. To do the most with our finite time.

Malfus kissed the finger, then put it back in his pouch. Time to pick back up where he'd left off. The Inquisitor be damned. If Deza was still out there, if he came for Malfus again, he'd be ready. It was still a long way back to Monrovia. But, on the sunnier side of things, a month of walking in chains wasn't half so long in the saddle.

Chapter 27

Epilogue

"The sword may slay mortal men, but the quill can make them live forever. Now, which has the greater power?" — Salvatore Cromarbie, philosopher, poet, and playwright of Ashára, three days before his execution

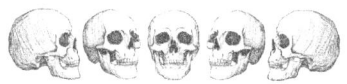

"Sir, are you sure about this?"

"Of course I'm sure! Never been more certain about anything in my life." Peshka stood on tiptoe; Goren had to bend over for him to wrap the sash of command around her shoulder.

Peshka grunted. "Well—we'll have to get a larger one, I suppose." The sash was a tight fit around the larger woman in her breastplate.

Her eyes moistened. It was perhaps the softest he'd seen her stoic face.

"Colonel, I—"

"It's just Peshka now."

"Peshka. I've never been much for words. I've always wanted this, but how do I know if I'm ready?"

"You're never bloody ready," he said, sighing. "Doesn't matter. You're the perfect soldier, Goren. Always have been. You've already been doing my job. If you can serve as a woman, you can damn well be a commander. Balls or breasts be damned." He cleared his throat. "We'll do this again in front of the troops, but the paperwork is approved. It's official—*Commander* Goren."

She blushed and adjusted the sash. "And for you. You're sure this is it?"

"Yes," he said. "My march is over. I can barely ride a horse with this damn hip."

Peshka hobbled over to a mirror hanging on the wall. "I'm going to advocate for soldiers. Make sure these forts are properly supplied. That the wounded are taken care of when they return home. That dead soldiers are—well, that their families know, at least. Someone has to. None of the rich in their castles give a flying fuck about us."

He glanced at his reflection, grunting in frustration. Much of his belly had been hidden by his breastplate. But now that he wasn't wearing it... "I was too rough to be in the court of the leper—that is, the king." He inspected his face. "If being a soldier has taught me anything, it's that with enough polishing, the dullest brass can shine like gold."

He turned back to Goren. "I'll stay long enough to deal with the paperwork for the repairs. After, I'll head back to DeGaullis. Start the next chapter of my life. *Chapter.* I like that. Maybe I'll be a writer. Like General Murmillo."

"That'll be the day," said Goren, chuckling.

"Don't you have a garrison to command? Leave an old man to his dreams."

Goren smiled, then snapped to attention and saluted. "It's been an honor, sir!"

He saluted her back. "Do right by the soldiers, Goren, like you always have."

She nodded, then left.

Peshka looked out the window, musing. "Gregor Peshka, the author. I like the sound of that. Got war stories to write." His cane tapped against stone as he hobbled back to his mahogany desk and picked up a quill. He sighed. Pity he wouldn't be around to appreciate this new command desk. But he had made the right choice.

He began signing the documents piled on the desk. There were more contracts and orders for builders, resources, supplies, and new soldiers. They had been streaming in all day.

Riding one of their few remaining horses, one of his messengers had been able to make it to Almarada and return alive. The Duke heard Peshka's report, or an abridged version—without mention of the Inquisition or necromancy. After learning that Peshka had protected the fief from two giants and an army of gnolls, he'd commissioned a ransom of gold, in repairs and supplies and plenty of new soldiers. None of the previous letters had gotten through. The gnolls must have cut down every rider Peshka had sent.

Someone knocked.

"Is she back already?" he muttered. He raised his voice. "Come in! You know you don't have to knock!"

The sharp knocking came again.

"Come in, I said!"

Peshka signed another document, but the door didn't open.

"Oh, blast it all. One bloody second!"

He grunted as he stood up, and winced as he hobbled to the door, his cane tapping. At least the cane added an air of refinement, aging him with grace. Becoming of an author.

The pounding came a third time.

"Blast it all! Keep your breastplate on—"

Peshka's voice caught as he opened the door. Two middle-aged men stood before him. One tall and thin, one short and plump, and both wearing the white robes of Vesenian high priests. He couldn't tell their exact age. The tall one wore thin spectacles, and the short one had manicured sideburns that wrapped along his lower jaw.

"Hello, Colonel Peshka," said the short one. Peshka gaped at them, confused that they knew him by name.

"May we come in?" asked the tall one, as he strode past Peshka, gliding across the stone.

"The repairs for your fort are coming along nicely," said the short one as he followed his companion, examining the new ceiling where the hole in the roof had been.

"Yes. Quite nicely," agreed the thin one.

"Yes, quite," said Peshka, uncertain.

He gestured to a couple of chairs. They took them, staring at Peshka like snakes waiting for a mouse to dance.

He shook himself. "Can I help you, gentlemen?"

"Oh, I should hope so," said the thin one. "We are searching for an Inquisitorial agent. One Damian Deza."

"A *former* agent of the Inquisition," chimed the short one. "Precision is one of Vesenia's highest virtues, after all."

"Oh yes, a *former* agent," repeated the thin one, not irritated in the slightest over the correction.

"I see." Peshka tugged at his mustache as his stomach rumbled. He walked to the pewter pitcher on the table and filled a metal mug. Peshka drank the cool water to calm his nerves as he formulated a response.

"I hate to disappoint you men for traveling all the way to the Farlands..." Peshka slowed, realizing how immaculate their robes were. Not a speck of dirt mired them. "But, former agent or otherwise, the fort hasn't had any visitors from the Inquisition for some time. Just a horde of bloody gnolls untouched by Vesenia's grace—unlike you gentlemen." Peshka fumbled with one end of his mustache. "If I recall, our last visit from the Inquisition was for our annual Purity inspection. We are more than six months overdue—and with all of these new recruits..."

"I see," said the short one, stroking his sideburns.

"How disappointing," said the tall one, adjusting his glasses.

Peshka bowed. "I'm sorry I couldn't have been more help to you."

"It is unfortunate."

"*Most* unfortunate."

The two white robed men stood. The tall one plucked at his robes, removing a single orange hair from the white cloth.

"Well, we had better continue our hunt. His trail went cold somewhere around here."

"His trail went cold..." said Peshka. Beads of sweat appeared on his forehead. "Perhaps the gnolls got him?"

"Yes. Perhaps the gnolls..." said the thin one, narrowing his spectacled eyes at Peshka.

"Should you remember anything else..." began the short one.

"We'll be around," the tall one finished.

They left, quiet as dust. The door shut behind them, silent.

When he was sure they'd left, Peshka allowed himself a sigh of relief, wiping sweat from his forehead. He clutched at his stomach. It had taken every ounce of willpower to maintain his composure.

Many things about that encounter had been disturbing, but Peshka found it strangest of all that neither of the priests had asked about the necromancer.

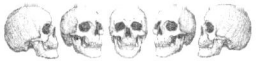

Malfus stood at the splintered wooden counter of the inn.

He held a button that glowed like melted butter in the candlelit tavern. Malfus took a scalpel from his pouch and sliced a small chunk from the button, the size of his pinky nail.

"There. This should be enough." Malfus dropped the gold on the counter.

The leather-faced innkeeper picked it up, held it to the candlelight for a moment, and bit into it with one of her few remaining teeth. Satisfied, she squinted at Malfus with her one eye and nodded. Uneasy, she fixed that same eye on Malfus's traveling companion he lumbered across the room.

"Morrrte," said Morte.

"Shhh," hissed Malfus.

The innkeeper gave both of them a look.

"Oh, don't mind him," said Malfus. "He walks funny from an old war injury. He doesn't say much—he's *simple*." Malfus spoke in short sentences so the old woman could understand him—and loudly enough that the other patrons at the bar could hear him. Hopefully, it would steer away any unwanted conversations.

Morten had started moaning part of his name their second day on the road. So Malfus had begun calling him 'Morte.' He'd never heard of a zombie remembering their name, or anything from their past. It had been exciting for a few hours, until Malfus realized it was all Morte could say, and would say it as often as he pleased—which was *always*.

Still. It was nice to have some conversation on the road. And Morte was a great listener.

He cleaned Morte up a bit, and cast the rejuvenation spell on him to prevent his flesh from decaying. It actually kept the zombie's skin in a fairly healthy pallor, with just a tinge of paleness. Malfus had cleaned up the blood and stitched his neck together as well. Morte wore Deza's wide-brimmed hat to shadow his face. Crooked as it was, the Inquisitor's hat kept people from asking intrusive questions, even in Monrovia.

The innkeeper leered at them, pointed up the stairs across the inn, then resumed polishing dirty glasses with her rag.

Looking upstairs from the counter, Malfus spotted a thin balcony with several different rooms adjoining it. Only a few had doors; most had oiled leather draped over their doorframes.

"Which room?"

The old woman shrugged and kept working.

Malfus turned from the counter and walked through the common room toward the stairs.

A few dwarves huddled in one corner. A hooded man stuck a half-elven ear from his hood to listen in on a neighboring conversation. Everyone seemed content to ignore Malfus and his companion—while eyeing them warily.

They'd just arrived in Monrovia. It was far enough from the Ossory Empire and the Inquisition that more non-humans made an appearance. This swampland was wonderfully diverse—but more importantly, its residents kept to themselves and didn't ask questions.

Besides, a friend here owed him a favor.

He nodded at the dwarves and half-elf as he passed by. They ignored him. Morte lurched behind him, carrying their leather saddlebags as Malfus climbed upstairs.

He stumbled into the first room with a door. Two people were on the bed, mid-coitus. Malfus apologized and shut the door; he doubted they noticed.

The next doored room was empty. Malfus was surprised that its door latch worked. He shut it, then locked it behind them. He lowered the oiled leather shade across the small window, then lit a candle.

When he was sure no one was looking, he removed Morte's hat and cast rejuvenation on him. Then he cast it on Kiara's finger—his nightly ritual. He yawned, looking at the saddlebags.

He'd had a few uneasy conversations with Ramma along the road. He had used the arcanull chain to maintain the upper hand in their current arrangement. But he was too tired to pursue that tonight. He stuck the saddlebag in the corner, checked that the door was locked once more, then blew out the candle, bathing the room in darkness.

He pulled the bedsheets around him. "Good night, Morte."

"Morrrte," moaned the zombie. He remained standing, a silent sentinel in the dark room, illuminated only by a faint blood-red light spilling from the saddlebags.

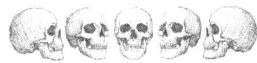

Branches snapped in the dark.

Moonlight trickled through the canopy. Twisted branches overhead tried to capture the moon in their claws.

Deza stumbled through the woods. He pushed through branches until he reached a small clearing. A lake reflected silvery moonlight. He stopped by the water's edge.

When he looked at his reflection, he no longer recognized himself. He looked more like a monster than a man. His clothing was tattered, covered in dirt and leaves. Half of his face had turned gray; the cursed flesh was cracked like leather, and covered his shoulder and arm.

He felt no thirst or hunger; he hadn't needed to eat in weeks. He didn't even need sleep. The sunlight had become glaringly bright. It made him uncomfortable, so he had begun traveling at night. Perhaps this was death, and he was in hell.

"What has that bastard done to me?"

Deza smashed his fist into the lake, scattering his reflection. He reached into the ground and picked up a rock to throw, but instead screamed into the night. He squeezed the rock as he howled, and it shattered into dust in his cold dead grip.

"Everything is darkness. Why can't I hear my goddess? Why has she forsaken me?"

He heard a voice behind him.

You poor, pitiful thing.

He looked behind him. No one was there.

I can show you where he is.

No, not behind him. *Inside.* The voice was in his mind.

"You can tell me where who is?"

You know who.

"He has taken everything from me. My daughter. My life. My goddess."

Then come with me. I can show you where he is.

"Who are you?"

I am your goddess now.

TO BE CONTINUED...

Malfus's misadventures *will* continue.

GREEDY AS A GHOUL - FREE PREQUEL SHORT STORY

Thanks for reading!

Hey good job, you made it to the end! Thanks for reading, I really appreciate it. You've taken the time from your life to read my book and now I'm asking you to take a little more to please, please, please leave me an honest review. I'm a self-published author, and I want to keep writing more books for you to read. The more reviews my books get, the more people will read them, the more people that read my books, the more books I can write! As payment, I left a picture of my co-author August below.

You can follow my progress for Malfus's next novel on my website at www.caseysuttonwrites.com

You can listen to a podcast interview about Malfus: Necromancer Unchained with Oaky Tyree at Tell Me About Your Book!

About Author

My name is Casey Sutton. I am a huge nerd and have been carrying books around with me since I was old enough to walk and carry things. I grew up immersed in fantasy worlds in books, video games, and playing Dungeons and Dragons with my friends. I was usually stuck being the Dungeon Master and creating imaginary worlds and characters for my friends. I used to be in the army and spent my time overseas reading fantasy books and dreaming about being a writer one day, but didn't get the push to follow my dreams until a near-death experience in South Africa in 2018. I decided to quit waiting around to write and started finally writing my book that night—in the hospital bed.

A bit more about me, I love cats and have four. I am also a self-taught mycologist and forage for wild mushrooms, and have grown my own! I still love video games and Dungeons and Dragons too!

You can find out more about me and my next writing projects on my website www.caseysuttonwrites.com.

Acknowledgments

There are too many people to thank. The irony of the word *self*-publishing is that it truly takes a village to write a book. You wouldn't be reading this without the support of my friends, family, and everyone I've met along the way.

I'd like to thank my partner Viktoria for always supporting me and my many late writing nights.

My friends and family for believing in me and helping me proofread.

My cats, especially August, who has put as many hours behind the keyboard as me.

Dejan Delic, an amazing artist, who has helped bring my world to life!

Alejandro Colucci, a fantastic cover artist that I was lucky enough to work with.

My developmental editor Jon Oliver.

Spencer Merrell, the line-editor I didn't know I needed.

Chey Brigham, for a final proofing.

And last, but not least, JD Caron, for "showing me the ropes" of self-publishing.

Social Links

Casey Sutton
- www.caseysuttonwrites.com
- www.facebook.com/caseysuttonwrites
- www.instagram.com/caseysuttonwrites
- www.tiktok.com/@caseysuttonwrites

Dejan Delic
- www.deviantart.com/dejan-delic

Alejandro Colucci
- www.alejandrocolucci.com

Spencer Merrell
- www.spencermerrell.com

Chey Brigham
- www.helluvaeditingco.com

JD Caron
- www.weekendpublisher.com

Made in the USA
Monee, IL
22 July 2023